LINDSAY McKENNA

THE
DEFENDER

D0011050

HARLEQUIN®
entertain, enrich, inspire™

Recycling programs
for this product may
not exist in your area.

ISBN-13: 978-0-373-77710-5

THE DEFENDER

www.Harlequin.com

Printed in U.S.A.

Praise for

LINDSAY McKENNA

"McKenna skillfully shows that it's all about the romance and not only the sex. After all, hard work, honesty and trust is what western romance is all about."
—*RT Book Reviews* on *The Wrangler*

"McKenna's latest is an intriguing tale...a unique twist on the romance novel, and one that's sure to please."
—*RT Book Reviews* on *Dangerous Prey*

"Riveting."
—*RT Book Reviews* on *The Quest*

"An absorbing debut for the Nocturne line."
—*RT Book Reviews* on *Unforgiven*

"Gunfire, emotions, suspense, tension and sexuality abound in this fast-paced, absorbing novel."
—*Affaire de Coeur* on *Wild Woman*

"Another masterpiece."
—*Affaire de Coeur* on *Enemy Mine*

"Emotionally charged...riveting and deeply touching."
—*RT Book Reviews* on *Firstborn*

"Ms. McKenna brings readers along for a fabulous odyssey in which complex characters experience the danger, passion and beauty of the mystical jungle."
—*RT Book Reviews* on *Man of Passion*

"Talented Lindsay McKenna delivers excitement and romance in equal measure."
—*RT Book Reviews* on *Protecting His Own*

"Lindsay McKenna will have you flying with the daring and deadly women pilots who risk their lives.... Buckle in for the ride of your life."
—*Writers Unlimited* on *Heart of Stone*

To Donna Hayes, Publisher and CEO, Harlequin, for her passion in helping save the endangered Peregrine Falcons of Canada. Quest and Kendal could never have a better auntie than you! These raptors have a real champion and the world is a better place for people such as yourself who support our threatened wildlife. Thank you. For the whole story of how Donna got involved with these Peregrine Falcons, just go to http://harlequinblog.com/topics/company-news.

To professional wildlife photographer Ann Brokelman, who not only helps the world see Peregrines, a species at risk in Canada, but freely gives of her time and passion to the Canadian Peregrine Foundation. And who also takes time to help amateur photogs like me get better at photographing wildlife. To appreciate Ann's incredible photography, please visit her blog: www.naturephotosbyann.blogspot.ca.

To the Canadian Peregrine Foundation, who has worked with heart and soul to rescue the beautiful Peregrine Falcon from the edge of extinction in their country. It is all volunteer work and volunteer contributions. They serve as wonderful role models of what we can do in our country to halt the death of so many raptors from pesticides used by agriculture. Visit their website: www.peregrine-foundation.ca.

Dear Reader,

The Defender is a story within a story. Yes, it is part of the
Wyoming series and continues my tradition of danger,
romance and suspense. Here is the "other" story:
over a year ago, I received an email from Harlequin
corporate headquarters. Donna Hayes, Publisher and
Chief Executive Officer of Harlequin, had spotted a
pair of Peregrine Falcons who were about to nest on a
building across the street. Amazed, I read the missive.
The Peregrine has been driven to the edge of extinction
by DDT and other harmful pesticides used by farmers in
Canada and the United States.

As I read the email, I wanted to let Donna know that I, too,
was involved in supporting and donating to High Country
Raptors, Flagstaff, Arizona, USA. I sent her a YouTube
link. My good friend Monica Amarillis had taken her cell
phone and recorded me with Luna, a European eagle owl.
You can see the videos on YouTube; search for "Eileen and
Luna" and "The owl Luna catches a mouse." The raptors
you will see are birds cared for by Susan Hamilton,
falconer, of High Country Raptors, who also holds an
eagle license.

After Donna saw the videos, she sent me an email
telling me I had to connect with Ann Brokelman, a
professional wildlife photographer. I did, and the rest
is history! Because we all support not only with time,
but donations to the volunteers who care for raptors, we
have a wonderful, ongoing triangular connection in this
incredibly magical realm of birds. Raptors do change your
life. I know that for a fact. And always for the better!

For those readers who are avidly waiting for my next book in the Wyoming series, I wanted to get more deeply into another passion of mine: romantic suspense! If you enjoy action, adventure, threat, hot romance coupled with danger, you'll enjoy *The Defender*. Katie Bergstrom is a twenty-six-year-old raptor rehabilitator who tries to help wounded and injured raptors back to health in Jackson Hole, Wyoming. She was abandoned at birth by her mother. Rebelling, lost and always trying to find her mother, Katie goes through many foster homes and gets into teen trouble. She eventually winds up in Jackson Hole, where her luck changes and she's given a new lease on life. Raptors, with their own unique magic, focus her life and give her reason to thrive, despite her dark, unhappy past.

Joe Gannon, born in Jackson Hole, is a Marine Corps captain who was wounded in Afghanistan. He comes back stateside only to find out he can never fight for his country again. The FBI offers him a job. He has been specially chosen to return home to try to get close to Katie. Her birth mother, Janet Bergstrom, is suspected of criminal activity. Can he lie to Katie? Is Katie really a part of her mother's illegal activities? Most of all, Joe finds himself caught in an impossible situation because he must fight his attraction to Katie and remain undercover to discover the truth. Where do lies and truth begin and end? Can their growing love survive?

Enjoy!

Lindsay McKenna

CHAPTER ONE

SUNLIGHT BATHED the golden eagle's half-opened wings, making them appear to be liquid bronze. Katie Bergstrom steadied the sixteen-pound bird on her leather gauntlet, facing him into the cool mid-morning breeze. She stood on the grassy floor of a wide valley, the magnificent Teton Range nearby. The sky was a fierce cobalt blue, the sun glaring at the snowy slopes.

Katie felt Sam's eagerness to fly, his round yellow eyes transfixed on the sky above. He loved getting out of his mew, or cage, and flying the familiar territory near the main highway leading out of Jackson Hole, Wyoming. Giving him a smile, Katie said in a conspiratorial whisper, "Just one more moment, Sam…" and spotted Donna, her foster mother, standing a quarter mile away. Her mother held up her hand, a signal for Katie to go ahead and release the raptor.

Every morning, except on days when it was raining or snowing, her educational raptor was flown. These were raptors with a medical condition that did not allow them to be set free in the wild. Golden eagles were large, and Katie could feel the weight of the bird. Her arm started to ache. His curved talons gripped the thick leather of her glove. Sam's black pupils became pinpricks in the field of gold. He flapped his wings, opening them fully, ready to launch off her arm.

Katie didn't know who looked forward to these

flights more: her or Sam. "Okay," she said in a quiet tone, "off you go…." and she heaved her arm and shoulder upward and forward in order to successfully launch the raptor.

Sam knew her body's signal. He quickly unfurled his massive seven-foot wingspan. With a snap of his wings, he lifted away from her glove, piercing eyes focused on the sky above.

Katie felt instant relief from his weight. Gusts of wind created by Sam's massive wings swirled around her head. Her shoulder-length black hair, tied into a ponytail, lifted momentarily away from her back. The wind buffeted her and her heart swelled with joy as Sam climbed into the sky. The five-year-old golden eagle made powerful sweeping motions with his wings. The sun glinted off his dark brown feathers. Remembering her love of Greek mythology, Katie saw Sam as a modern-day Icarus heading straight into the sun. Unlike the Greek youth, whose waxy wings were unable to withstand the heat of the sun, Sam's feathers wouldn't melt. And the eagle wouldn't fall to earth and die, as Icarus had.

Looking across the grassy, rolling field, she saw Donna witnessing Sam's power-climb into the near-freezing morning air. Like herself, Donna had an eagle license, a very rare certificate given to raptor rehabilitators across the U.S.A. Only falconers who had this valued license could actually fly any type of eagle found in the country. Katie waved joyfully to the forty-nine-year-old redhead who stood downrange. Donna waved back.

A thrill went through Katie. She felt the weight on her shoulders lift as Sam climbed higher and higher. Eagles were known to fly over ten thousand feet high in the wild. Sam wouldn't do that because he knew

Donna had a juicy meat morsel waiting for him on the top of her gauntlet.

A gentle sigh issued from Katie's lips. This was her favorite morning routine: flying her raptors. Not all of them could fly, of course, because they'd been injured in one way or another. But those that could, she flew daily unless the weather hampered her efforts. Squinting against the sun, she saw Sam level off at about five thousand feet. He began to glide as he discovered invisible columns of heat rising from the green earth. Early June could bring sudden snow squalls to this part of Wyoming. The Grand Tetons made their own weather and raptors would not fly in rain or snow. They had no eyelid to close in order to protect their eyes from the harsh elements. Instead, until the weather cleared enough for them to hunt, they were earthbound.

The radio on her belt sputtered to life. It was a necessary form of communication between falconers who were often a mile or more apart when flying a raptor.

"Sam's flying high today," Donna said with a laugh.

Grinning, Katie pulled the radio from her belt. "Isn't he, though? I think three days of rain and snow has left him feeling a little frustrated in his mew."

Donna chuckled. "Oh, I agree. He might be hungry, but right now, he's sailing and just enjoying being out in the embrace of his real mother—the sky."

"He's got excess testosterone to burn off, too. Grounded for three days because of rain has made him antsy to get back into the air."

"Isn't that the truth!" Donna said, humor in her tone. "Let me know when to put the food out on my glove."

"I will. Out." Katie fixed the radio back onto her belt. Sam now flew around in a huge circle at least a mile in circumference above her. His path took him across the main highway leading south into Jackson Hole and north toward Grand Teton National Park. Several cars were now parked along the major road between the town and the two national parks—Grand Teton and Yellowstone—to watch the eagle fly. A number of raptor-loving locals knew she and Donna flew the raptors inside the elk enclosure between June and August. The enclosure was fairly flat and safe. As people drove up the hill and spotted a magnificent eagle or hawk flying, they would pull over and watch them through binoculars. Right now, Katie saw three cars parked on the berm, the people standing near the ten-foot-high wire elk fence, simply watching and appreciating the raptor.

She understood their joy. Sam was the largest eagle in the United States. When he unfolded and stretched those bronze wings, all seven feet of them, it was an awe-inspiring sight. A good feeling moved through Katie. She was glad the people of Jackson Hole loved raptors, supported them through donations and came to watch them be flown.

Up above, Sam continued to fly in a one-mile circle. He wore a radio antenna placed on the quill shaft of one of his tail feathers. Should Sam get lost or not come in to be fed, Katie could use the radio to locate his whereabouts. At this distance, Katie couldn't see the short kangaroo-leather jesses wrapped around his thick yellow legs. One never flew a raptor with long jesses trailing because they could get entangled in a tree branch and trap the raptor. Short jesses insured Sam could safely land and take off from a tree branch without breaking his leg or wing in the effort.

Glancing toward the highway, Katie noticed a dark green car pulling off and park behind the other three cars. Usually, she recognized the people who stopped because they had come to her educational seminars about raptors in town. Over time, she'd gotten to know her raptors' supporters. But the man emerging from the green car, although half a mile away, didn't look like someone she knew. He walked over to the fence near the other spectators. Like them, he had a pair of binoculars in hand. That wasn't unusual at all. People who loved raptors always had a pair. It was the only way to appreciate the birds up close.

Katie looked up. Sam was wheeling above them, his circles growing a bit smaller.

"Looks like he's got most of his steam burned off," Donna called over the radio.

Pulling the radio to her lips, Katie said, "I think so, too. Now, he's decided he's hungry. When Sam starts making these smaller circles, he's ready to come in and get fed."

"Roger. Maybe another ten minutes?"

"Probably." Katie watched the eagle slide upward on an updraft, his wings spread. Beneath each wing were two white patches known as stars. They looked like Xs to the observer on the ground. The Native Americans referred to the golden eagles as spotted eagles and said the white stars symbolized the Milky Way from whence they had originally come. Katie loved the myths and legends about the golden eagle. The Native Americans revered the eagle and it was often at the center of their sacred medicine ceremonies. A golden eagle was seen as the symbol of the east. In the old days, eagle feathers were believed to bring a person closer to the Great Spirit. Because it flew the highest of all birds, feathers from an eagle were closest to the Great Spirit. The feathers carried the messages back to the human who wore them.

"Okay, I'm going to get Sam's food ready."

"Roger that." Katie tucked the radio into her belt, her gaze following the eagle. He was now flying lower and was purposely swinging over the highway where the people were watching him with rapt attention.

Something bothered Katie. It was a prickle of warning, the raising of hair on the back of her neck. What was she sensing? She turned toward the fence, feeling as if someone were watching *her* and not the eagle. All four people had binoculars. Three of them were lifted toward the sky. But the stranger who had arrived in the dark green car had his binoculars trained on *her*.

Katie knew people were curious about falconers, too. Perhaps it was their rather odd costume. Katie had a thick leather gauntlet fitted up to her elbow. When an eagle landed, he would dig his long, curved talons deeply into the material to halt his forward motion. The double-thick leather took the power of his grip without puncturing the falconer's lower arm. A tan canvas satchel hung diagonally across her upper body, the pouch hanging near her right hip. In it was raw rabbit meat to reward Sam for flying back to her. Taking off her black baseball cap, Katie smoothed some strands of her hair away from her eyes. As she settled the cap back on her head, she couldn't shake the feeling of being watched. It made no sense, so she ignored it, focusing instead on Sam's flight.

FBI AGENT JOE GANNON STUDIED Katie Bergstrom through his binoculars. He was glad there were three other people at the elk fence beside him. They were murmuring excitedly between themselves as the golden eagle swooped overhead. Joe was much more interested in the woman. Something odd happened to him as he continued to study Katie Bergstrom's profile: his heart expanded in his chest. What an unexpected sensation.

Removing the binoculars, Joe wondered what the hell was going on. He touched his brown leather bomber jacket, feeling a strange emotion: happiness. *How odd.* Since Zoe had divorced him while he was on his second tour as a Marine Corps captain in Afghanistan, women had left a very bad taste in his mouth. Oh, he liked to look at them. And right now, Katie Bergstrom was certainly worth his attention, but that wasn't why he'd been sent here by his boss in Washington, D.C. Rubbing his chest, Joe tried to will away the unfamiliar joy in his heart.

He hadn't felt this lightness since well before he and Zoe had had their problems. Then his ex-wife's lawyer had sent the divorce papers to him at his unit in Helmand Province in Afghanistan. Joe still remembered that traumatic morning mail call. Zoe hadn't said a word about divorce in their Skype calls to one another. The topic had never been brought up for discussion. Her ending the marriage had been a total shock. He didn't dare go through that again.

Scowling, Joe tried to shove away his divorce memories. He had a job to do here in Jackson Hole. He lifted the binoculars to his eyes and concentrated on Katie. She was definitely attractive. Standing five feet six inches tall, she was slender and all grace. Her black hair was drawn back in a ponytail, giving Joe a chance to see her clean profile. Her brow was broad, her nose reminded him of a statue of a Greek goddess. And those full lips would haunt him. Oh, he had photos of Katie, for sure, but seeing her in person made a different and far more powerful impression upon him.

Joe was stymied by his surprising emotional reaction

to her. When his boss gave him her file, he'd stressed that Katie was likely part of a large drug-and-gun ring just starting to set up in this part of Wyoming. At the time, Joe had felt nothing. Seeing her in person, however, he discovered he was very much affected. Why now? Why *her*?

Mouth lifting, Joe figured it was because he'd sworn off women since the divorce. Zoe had married him just before he'd left for his first tour in Afghanistan, and he'd been gone a year. He'd missed her terribly. Zoe had had a tough time adjusting to becoming a military wife. There had been little Joe could do about it except listen during their conversations and tell Zoe he loved her. It hadn't been enough.

A shout from the man standing next to him jolted Joe out of his reverie. He watched the golden eagle flying in smaller, ever-tightening circles. The two women falconers stood at least a quarter of a mile apart. Joe knew from his own ongoing falconry training in Washington, D.C., that the raptor was getting ready to come in and land. He didn't care about the eagle landing as much as the opportunity to check out Katie. Training his gaze on her, Joe saw her smiling and talking into the radio to the woman who was likely her foster mother.

Then a warm sheet of heat moved through his heart. When Katie smiled, her whole face lit up with an incredible joy. For a moment, she turned toward him as the eagle flew low over her. His breath hitched. My God, how pretty she was! Her blue eyes, large and wide-set, shone with excitement. He understood to a degree her pure pleasure in watching the magnificent eagle fly. He'd felt the same way when Eddie, a falconer, had trained him back in D.C. There was a palpable bond between falconer and raptor. It was a living, vibrant connection and he saw it in Katie's eyes.

His gaze dropped to her curved lips. Joe felt his heart expanding in his chest, just a quiet goodness rippling through him. Right now, he had to ignore its significance. But how to ignore Katie Bergstrom's beautiful lips? Her face was oval and she wore no makeup. She didn't have to, Joe thought. At twenty-six, she was clearly in athletic shape. The flash of her smile momentarily stole his breath. Joe had never witnessed such a glow of happiness on anyone's face. "Raptor magic," as it was called by falconers, could bring almost saint-like elation to a person's face. Joe knew that firsthand from his own falconry training. And he was seeing it in spades on Katie's upturned face.

Something niggled at Joe. He couldn't forget the facts in this case. For years, the FBI had been following Janet Bergstrom, Katie's estranged mother who had given her up at birth. Janet was working with a new Guatemalan drug-and-gun cartel trying to establish a base here in Jackson Hole. Shortly after she had abandoned her child at birth, Janet had fled to Guatemala to connect with Xavier Lobos, the cartel leader. For many years, the FBI had focused on her as a mule running drugs across the Mexican border into the U.S. Another FBI agent had finally nabbed Janet. She'd been caught with a hundred thousand dollars' worth of cocaine in her car at a border crossing. She was convicted and spent seven years in a federal prison.

How was her daughter connected with all this? Joe wondered. He shifted his focus to the golden eagle now flying in even tighter and tighter circles above Donna Pierce's head. Joe had done his homework before coming out here on the mission. He knew all about Katie,

what she did for a living and that she'd recently moved
her raptor facility onto the Elk Horn Ranch, a dude ranch
owned by Iris Mason. Katie always had trouble finding
people to help her at the expanded raptor-rehabilitation
center. Taking care of raptors was a full-time job and
Katie didn't get paid by the state to do it. She did it out
of her love for these birds of prey. While that was ad-
mirable, the FBI felt that, out of necessity, Katie was a
part of Los Lobos. But they weren't sure.

According to the latest reports, Janet Bergstrom had
driven out twice to the gate leading to the Elk Horn
Ranch. Satellite flyovers hadn't found actual proof she'd
met with her daughter. Now it was Joe's job to prove
Katie and her mother had met. His boss at the FBI felt
Katie had gotten mixed up in her mother's drug-running
operation.

Joe found their suspicions difficult to believe. Katie
had the face of an innocent. His boss had warned him
many times that just because a woman had a pretty face
didn't mean she wasn't capable of skullduggery. Still…
Joe would follow his instincts and keep an open mind.
His heart was another matter.

KATIE WATCHED SAM set up for a landing. Donna lifted
her arm high. The golden eagle knew that when a falconer raised her glove, it was a signal for him to land
and eat. Sam performed a swift ninety-degree turn,
one wing pointed at the ground, the other above his
head, his eyes on the prize of rabbit meat sitting on the
glove. As he wheeled, he straightened out, flapping his
huge wings in urgent backward motions to slow his descending speed. Legs outstretched, his talons open, he
landed on Donna's glove. Sam's curved talons bit into
the thick leather and he dipped his head. He scooped up

his breakfast of rabbit with his scimitar-shaped beak. His wings continued to beat as he steadied and balanced himself on the falconer's glove. Finally, Sam folded his wings, gobbling down more rabbit.

Katie grinned as she saw Sam land on Donna's glove. Her foster mother had taught her everything she knew about falconry. Not only that, Donna had helped her get the rare and vaunted eagle license so she could care for wounded or injured eagles found in the Jackson Hole area. Some sheep-ranchers shot them because during lambing season, the golden eagles would steal newborn lambs. It was against the law to shoot raptors in Wyoming, but it didn't stop a sheep-rancher from killing one of these magnificent and badly needed eagles. A sudden sadness moved through her as she remembered that Sam had been one of those eagles nearly killed by a shotgun-wielding sheepherder.

Katie walked toward Donna, recalling a year ago when Sam had been brought into her center. At the time, she'd had her mews behind her rented apartment. She'd just received her eagle license. Sam had managed to fly with fifteen shotgun pellets embedded in his left wing. A kind driver on the road had seen him wobble and land unceremoniously on the muddy berm next to the busy highway. He'd picked up the injured, bleeding eagle and taken it to a vet in town. Later, Katie had received a call from that vet. Could she take the eagle after surgery and nurse it back to health? Sam was her first eagle. And because of the cracks in the bones of his wing, he could never be released back to the wild. If he was released, the knitted bones would never stand the shocking force of striking prey. The bones would shatter and the eagle would eventually die of starvation. So Sam had become an educational bird, teaching children and adults the benefits of raptors in the environment. Katie would care for Sam for the rest of his life.

There was another reason to be sad. Her foster mother and falconry teacher would be moving away in another two weeks to take care of her own ailing mother in Idaho Falls, Idaho. Katie was losing a great friend, too. Soon, Katie would be all by herself again.

Donna had placed the long jesses around Sam's thick yellow legs and wrapped the ends through the fingers of her glove. That way, if the eagle suddenly bolted, Donna could keep the eagle in hand.

"Hey, he made a great landing today, didn't he?" Donna said, grazing Sam's dark brown feathers across his wide chest.

"No kidding," Katie said. "Better than the last time we flew him, huh?" Sometimes Sam would misjudge the speed of his descent to the falconer's glove. Four days ago, Donna had released him and, after flying for a while, he was to land on Katie's glove for his morning breakfast of rabbit. Sam, in his exuberance, had overshot her outstretched glove. He'd grabbed at the glove with his huge talons, lost his balance and flapped into Katie's face. To be struck by a huge wing in forward motion could cause instant pain, not to mention injury. It was like being slapped in the face. Hard. Katie had closed her eyes, fortunately, and had turned her head away to protect her sight.

She'd stood firm and quiet, which allowed Sam to flap his wings around her face in order to regain his equilibrium. He was no worse for wear, but Katie still bore a shallow cut across her temple from the incident. She'd gone into the emergency room afterward and Dr. Jordana McPherson had put in three stitches. Jordana had assured her there would be no lasting scar. It wasn't

unusual to have scars on one's face or upper arms from
an eagle. It was just part of the business of caring for
these magnificent animals. Katie was more than willing to take the risk because they gave her a sense of
freedom she never felt otherwise. A cut every now and
then was a price worth paying.

"You can't even see where the doctor sewed you up,"
Donna said, giving Sam a look of pride. "I think after
being cooped up for three days, he had extra energy to
burn off."

Chuckling, Katie walked with Donna toward her
black truck. "Yeah, he's full of himself for sure."

Donna held out her right arm covered with a bright
red cotton sleeve. "I've shown you my battle scars."

"And I hope I never get the kind you have."

Donna had, at one time, worked with a golden eagle
who was eventually returned to the wild. One day, another falconer had accidentally left the cage door unlocked and the eagle had escaped his mew after being
startled by a nearby truck backfiring. He'd launched
off his perch and flown out the door, frightened and
disoriented. Seeing Donna, who had nursed him for
three months and who represented safety to him, he'd
immediately flown over to her. Only, she'd had no protective gauntlet on her lower arm to save her from the
puncture wounds the eagle inflicted. To this day, when
Donna rolled up her sleeves, Katie could see the puncture indentations left by the eagle's talons.

Donna balanced Sam easily on her left glove. The
eagle was sated, looking around with his piercing yellow gaze. She touched his breast. "Crop's full. He's a
happy raptor."

Katie could see the slight bulge where Sam's crop lay

beneath the shining bronze feathers of his wide upper breast. "Yep, if he could smile, he would."

They both chuckled.

Once they reached the pickup, Katie unlocked the rear and opened up the cab. She had a special perch built on a swing arm for the eagle. The wood was thick and sturdy, covered with plastic outdoor carpeting. The material enabled the raptor to hold securely to the perch so he would not slip off. Katie locked the perch in place and moved to the side of the truck bed.

Donna placed her glove near the perch and tapped her fingers on it. Sam quickly hopped from her glove to the perch. Releasing the jesses so that they were no longer wrapped around her glove, Donna murmured, "Okay, I think he's ready to go home."

Katie gently closed the door to the cab. Eagles were so large they couldn't fit inside a bird box to travel. Special considerations had to be made for these raptors due to their size and weight. The women removed their food pouches and placed them behind the seats. Katie climbed in, shut the door and slid the key into the ignition.

Donna closed her door and pulled on her seat belt. "That was a great flight this morning! Sam really flew high and wide. I really think despite some of his wing bones being fractured, he's getting stronger with age and maturity."

"I think so too, but you have more experience with eagles than I do." Katie slowly moved the truck to a flat, smooth dirt road that would lead them out of the elk enclosure. Soon, they would be on the highway, heading north toward the Elk Horn Ranch.

"You have two years of experience under your belt," Donna said with a smile. "I'm really going to miss working with you, Katie. I know this area is in good hands when I leave. You'll do fine."

"I know, Donna, but I'll miss you on so many levels. I finally put an ad in the newspaper for a full-time falconer. I can't rely on volunteers to come and help me fly the raptors every morning." Katie glanced over at the tall, attractive woman who had been the best of the many foster mothers she'd had. "But I know your mom needs you now."

The older woman patted Katie's shoulder. "Hey, I'm only a phone call or email away. We'll stay in close touch, I promise." Her mouth curved gently and her voice lowered. "Katie, you've matured into a lovely young woman. I don't want to leave either, but parental duties hit all of us sooner or later. You're now the falconer for this area. And if you run into something you don't know, call me?"

Halting the truck at the stop sign, Katie looked both ways. The highway was clear of cars. "I know, but you not only rescued me from screwing up the rest of my life, you taught me how to become a raptor rehabilitator, Donna. I feel in some ways, you're the mother I never had."

Donna's smile dissolved. She kept her hand on Katie's shoulder for a moment. "Well, let me tell you this, Katie girl. Your mother gave you up at birth and I know you've never met her. I know you want to and I hope, for your sake, you do find her. In the end, you have me, and I love you very much. I won't abandon you, Katie. That's a promise."

Donna's lowered voice moved through Katie. She dearly loved her raptor mentor. And in so many ways, over the last ten years, Donna had, indeed, saved her life. "You're my mother incognito," she teased, her voice hoarse. Fighting back sudden and unexpected tears, Katie kept her eyes on the road. "And I don't care what you say, you've been more of a mother to me than my biological mother ever was."

Gently, Donna rubbed her shoulder, trying to ease the pain she heard in Katie's voice. "I know. I remember when the state social worker called me in desperation. You were acting out, you were rebellious. She begged me to be your foster mom. She thought working with the raptors might help stabilize you." Donna removed her hand, her voice wispy. "I remember the first morning you showed up. You were always skipping out of school, always in trouble with your teachers and the principal. You had dyed your hair red and yellow. You came into my raptor facility with a chip on your shoulder. All I had to do was ask you to put on the glove and a miracle happened."

After giving Donna a warm glance, Katie concentrated on driving up the long hill. "I was snotty to you at first. You ignored my antics and brought out Fred, your red-tailed hawk, and put him on my glove." Fred had died several years later, but he'd been a wonderful training raptor for Katie.

"Yes, and your attitude melted away."

Shaking her head, Katie said in a softened tone, "You saved my life, Donna. When Fred perched on my glove and looked at me, I felt my heart blow open like an explosion. I *felt* Fred. Feeling his energy changed me forever."

"Raptors are miraculous," Donna agreed. "That's why I was happy you bonded with Fred. In days, you turned from a rebellious teen into a beautiful young woman. All thanks to the birds."

"And to you. Without your love and you training me

to work with raptors, I don't know how I might have ended up, Donna. I got a high-school diploma. Every other foster family I'd been in thought I'd always be a dropout."

"Raptors are angels in disguise." Donna smiled fondly. "They are earthly angels come to improve our lives and make us better human beings."

Katie drove alertly, remaining within the speed limit. As they broached the hill, she saw the Teton Range rising out of the plain on her left. The mountains shone in the morning sunlight. Snow remained on their rugged blue-granite flanks. Her heart stayed centered on Donna. "We'll never be out of touch," Katie promised her. "Now, I have to hope a falconer will answer my ad to help me out full time."

"I'm sure someone will answer it. We have a number of folks licensed around here. We'll have to hope one of them wants a full-time job working with you. It's lovely of Iris Mason not only to donate enough money to keep your raptors fed, but also to pay you to be a full-time employee of her ranch. She's just the greatest."

"Iris promised to build me a raptor facility if I would move out to her ranch. Now I have the room, the land and the money. Not many rehabilitators have a guardian angel like Iris in their life. I'm so grateful for all she does for us."

"Iris is another angel," Donna said. "Don't worry, someone will apply for the job. I have a good feeling about it."

CHAPTER TWO

JOE SAT ON A STOOL at the counter of Mo's Ice Cream Parlor. It was his first day in town since arriving from Washington, D.C. His cover was solid. His parents owned a small ranch south of the town. With permission from his FBI boss, Joe was allowed to tell his parents the real reason for his return and they had been sworn to secrecy. Anyone noticing him in Jackson Hole would believe he was coming from the hospital after being released from the Marine Corps. Most folks around here would expect him to work with his father. No one would suspect him of being an undercover agent.

After watching the suspect, Katie Bergstrom, fly the golden eagle, he'd decided to grab breakfast at Mo's. A newspaper, the *Jackson Hole Gazette,* had been on the counter and he'd picked it up. It was the easiest way to find out what was going on.

Mo's was crammed with breakfast customers, the noise level sounding like bees buzzing. He'd accidentally turned to the classified ads and his gaze fell on the Help Wanted section. One ad shouted out to him. Was he reading it right? Joe blinked and reread the ad: "Falconer wanted for a full-time position. Apply by calling Katie Bergstrom." Joe studied the ad. Was this kismet, one of those lucky breaks an FBI agent prays for, but never gets? There it was: a job opening with his suspect.

Folding up the newspaper, Joe took a drink of his black coffee, and reviewed the details of the case.

His boss, Roger Hager, had gone over his mission objectives in Jackson Hole. Thanks to information from a local cowboy, Griff McPherson, the FBI was now focused on a man named Curt Downing. There was a possible break in this evolving drug-and-gunrunning case. McPherson and his brother Slade had been born here and owned the Tetons Ranch. Griff also worked at the Bar H and had married the owner, Valerie Hunter. Griff had met Janet Bergstrom by chance at the Horse Emporium in January. She was there to buy a dog collar for her husky, Karl. They'd talked and Janet had said she was on a visit to Jackson Hole to look at the possibility of creating a second courier business in the town. *That* was interesting news insofar as Roger was concerned. Janet already had a courier service established in Cheyenne, Wyoming.

A smiling blonde, blue-eyed waitress brought over a huge oval platter of pigs in blankets. Joe thanked her as she then handed him a pitcher of maple syrup. Cutting into the pancake-wrapped sausage, Joe continued to think his way through the developments in his assignment. When Janet got out of prison, she'd gone to Guatemala for two years. After coming home, she'd started a small business known as Mercury Courier and it became quite successful. However, the FBI agent in Guatemala suspected Bergstrom received seed money from the Los Lobos cartel. Furthermore, an agent had followed her on the flight to Guatemala and taken photos of her with cartel leader Xavier Lobos. The FBI had a growing amount of information on this aggressive man who focused on running drugs and guns. He was buying weapons and selling cocaine to Canada and the U.S.A.

Chewing his food, Joe watched the parlor's clientele come and go. Mo's was always a busy place. Some of the old-timers gave him a long look, as if trying to place his face. Joe had purposely been chosen for this mission because he'd been born in Jackson Hole. His parents, Connor and Lorna Gannon, ran a ranch and a landscape company. They'd given him the small house near the main ranch house for his stay. Roger felt it was perfect cover for Joe. He'd be a local boy come home and completely unsuspected by any cartel members who were trying to establish themselves in the area. Locals would never guess he was an agent. Rather, they'd see him as the wounded son returning home to heal and work with his parents.

"Hey…Joe Gannon? Is that you?"

Turning to his right, he looked into the eyes of Iris Mason, owner of the Elk Horn Ranch. Joe instantly recognized the matriarch. She wore a white blouse, Levi's and scuffed boots, and her elk-skin purse hung from her left shoulder. Iris had silver hair that resembled a disturbed hen's nest. She wore a jaunty straw hat over it. Grinning, Joe slid off the stool.

"Miss Iris! It's good to see you!" Joe embraced the elder.

"You look good," Iris said, stepping back and smiling up at him. "My, how you've grown, Joe! The last I heard, you were injured and at Bethesda Medical Center back East with a head injury." Iris reached out and patted his arm. "Are you okay?"

"Sit down," Joe invited, gesturing to the stool next to his. "Can I buy you a cup of coffee?" She was one of the most knowledgeable people in the valley and Joe felt luck was once more on his side. He could chat with Iris and learn a lot in a little time. Plus, Katie Bergstrom had her raptor facility at Iris's ranch. Kismet had struck again.

"Thanks, Joe, I will." Iris ordered a cup of coffee and a cheese omelet from the waitress. She turned and smiled over at him. "So, how are you?"

"Better than I was," Joe said, lifting the cup to his lips. "I'm sure my mom and dad told you I was injured in Helmand Province in Afghanistan?"

"Yes. You know, Gwen Garner, who owns the quilting store, knows all." She smiled. "Your mom is quite a quilter and she kept Gwen updated on your Marine Corps life."

"After the second tour and getting a traumatic brain injury from an IED, I landed in Bethesda for six months, Miss Iris." Joe touched the left side of his head. "I was riding in the rear of a Humvee when we drove over the damned thing." His voice lowered with pain. "I was the only one to survive."

"That's so sad. Lorna called me right after she found out. They were heading out the door to Germany where you were taken for treatment."

Joe knew his mother and Iris were good friends. Lorna Gannon had always looked to Iris as an extra grandmother in her life. Iris befriended everyone and she was one of the most-loved people in the valley. "I'm sure she was stressed out by the news," he said.

"Yes, they were. I went over to see if I could help them pack." Iris sighed and said in a softer voice, "We all prayed for you, Joe. It's hard losing a child at any age. And thank goodness, our prayers were answered."

"I was kind of happy about it, too." He shared a warm smile with her.

Iris drank her coffee. "So, are you coming home?

Griff McPherson came home after Wall Street crashed. Are you in the same predicament?"

"Sort of," Joe hedged. He hated lying to Iris, but he had to in order to keep his cover. "I just got out of rehab in D.C. and was released from the Marine Corps because of my injury. I came home to help my father and learn his landscaping business. He'd always wanted me to take the ranch over someday and now seems like a good time." Iris looked happy, her mouth drawing upward.

"Oh, good, good. I love when family can come together and be one. Nowadays, sisters and brothers and parents are thrown to the wind. No one lives at home or in the same town anymore. I know I'm from an older generation where that was the norm, but for the life of me, I truly feel a family should stick together." She patted his broad shoulder. "I'm so happy you're home, Joe."

"I'm pretty happy about it too."

The waitress delivered the food and Iris eagerly dug into her breakfast. Between bites, she asked, "So you're going from being an officer in the Marine Corps to turning your talents to ranching? Your dad is very respected around here. I hired him a year ago to come in with his dozer and grader to smooth off a piece of land for me. I wanted Katie Bergstrom's facility built on our ranch. She was struggling something awful. Raptor rehabilitators don't get reimbursed for all the money, time and care they put into saving birds. I saw her give a talk to an assisted-living center a year ago. I was so impressed with Katie and her love of the raptors. She enthralled everyone in the room with her passion for them."

Joe's heart leaped as Iris brought up the woman who kept haunting his thoughts, his suspect. "My father told me you not only donated the land but you had a facility built for her raptors?"

"Yep, I sure did." Iris twisted the lid off a jar of blueberry jam and slathered it thickly across whole-wheat toast. "I'm always on the lookout for a good business move to enhance Elk Horn's reputation as a dude ranch. I saw Katie's talk and was absolutely taken with her passion, her sincerity and love of her raptors. As you know, I pioneered environmental and green ways of living in this valley."

"Yes," Joe said, "you were the first to go green, Miss Iris. And actually, because of your decision, my father was able to launch his landscaping business." His voice lowered with feeling. "We owe you a lot. I hope you always know we're grateful to you."

Smiling, Iris sipped her coffee. "I can remember many of the ranchers were up in arms when Trevor and I decided to go green. Now—" Iris looked around the busy café "—there isn't a rancher around here who hasn't switched."

"You're an inspiration, Miss Iris. You always have been."

"When Trevor was alive, he turned our manure into compost. He built it into a successful business. To this day, we compost all our cow and buffalo manure and sell it to landscaping businesses in four surrounding states. Your dad was one of the first to come and buy from us. Connor always saw our vision for an environmentally friendly valley even when others didn't."

"I recall it all happening when I was growing up," Joe said. He finished off his breakfast and pushed the plate aside. "My father said there was a condominium boom when I left for college. His landscaping business won a number of bids and he brought environmental ways to work with the land and not against it."

"Connor was one of a handful of businessmen in the valley who sided with us," Iris said. She reached out and patted Joe's hand. "It's so good to know you're home! Have you recovered fully from your head injury?"

"For the most part," Joe said. "I get headaches about once a month or when I'm under stress, and when I do, it's like a migraine. All I can do is go to my dark room, close the door, keep quiet and let it pass."

Frowning, Iris blotted her lips with a paper napkin. "I've had a few headaches in my life. And I've hated every one of 'em. I can't even begin to understand how you tolerate such pain."

"They pass," Joe said, seeing the concern in the elder's features. "The doctors say it's just one of the symptoms of my brain healing from the trauma." He watched Iris put her empty plate aside. "Hey, what can you tell me about Katie Bergstrom's ad in the newspaper? Before you walked in I was reading that she's looking for a full-time employee."

"Yes, since she has a much larger facility out at our ranch, she needs full-time help. Katie has a number of volunteers, but, you know, people are so busy nowadays. And Katie has a full schedule of speaking engagements around the county. She just can't do it all alone anymore." Iris tapped the ad with her index finger. "I told her to put in the ad. I'm bankrolling her because what she's doing is good for the environment, Joe. Plus, our dude ranch guests enjoy a raptor show once a week. Katie brings out her raptors, educates the folks and then flies some of them. Our guests take photos of the raptors and are thrilled to death. Katie needs a full-time assistant. She just can't handle the business by herself."

"I see," Joe said, considering the knowledge. He saw the glow in Iris's eyes as she talked enthusiastically about Katie. Did Iris realize her protégé might be affiliated with Los Lobos? Inwardly, Joe hurt for the elder. Iris was unusually good at evaluating people, yet drug and gun dealers were chameleons. Every so often, a local person might be dealing and other locals would never suspect. It would come as a surprise when the person was indicted on drug charges.

"Our ranch guests are in *love* with Katie!" Iris rubbed her hands. "I felt paying Katie a yearly sum, plus footing all the expenses she incurred because of her raptors, was a fine business decision. Since Katie has been there, the Elk Horn Ranch has gotten national press attention. We had reporters from all the major news networks come out, and they did a story on her when Sam, the golden eagle, was transferred to her care. On the internet we've created a weekly blog on Katie and her raptors. Every week we highlight one of the birds, talk about its past and how it got injured. We tell folks how Katie and one of her vets brought the bird back from death. When she's able to release a bird, I get Kam, my granddaughter, to go along and videotape the release, then, we put it in the blog. People from around the world just love being a part of Katie's raptor world!"

Swept up by Iris's excitement, Joe decided to address the ad. "Iris, I know you probably didn't know this, but I'm working toward a falconer's license." He saw her surprised expression.

"Really? Why? I mean, my goodness, I didn't know that! Tell me more, Joe."

"While I was recuperating at Bethesda Medical Center, my doctor suggested I work with Eddie Barton, a well-known falconer, who also has an eagle license, in the Washington, D.C., area. He said working with the birds would help me not only physically but also emotionally. I'd always loved the hawks and eagles here in the valley, so I gave it a try. I spent my recovery going over to Eddie's place and helping him for six months. Eventually, I applied for my falconer's license. It takes two years to get one and I need to find a mentor around here like Katie, who can continue to teach me so I can apply for it."

"My goodness! Why, Joe, I'm just speechless. Are you thinking of applying for the position to help my Katie?"

He could see Iris had a deep emotional attachment to Katie. It broke Joe's heart to lie to this woman who had always been such a positive person and had helped so many people over the length of her life, but swallowing hard, he said, "Yes, I was thinking of calling her up and asking for an appointment. I was hoping she would agree to continue to train me while I help her."

"But what about your dad? You said he was training you to take over his ranching and landscaping business? Could you do both?"

"Not to worry, Miss Iris. My dad is going to retire in ten years. What I'd like to do, if Katie will hire me, is work with my dad on weekends and slowly learn the businesses. I figure in ten years I'll know enough to take over when he retires."

"And how old are you now?"

"Twenty-seven, Miss Iris."

"Oh," she crowed with a laugh, "you're just a *baby* in comparison to me!"

Laughing with her, Joe felt like a traitor. "That's true. Well, if you think it's a good idea, I'll call Katie."

"Absolutely," Iris gushed, her hands clasped in excitement. "I'm going over to the Horse Emporium but I'll be home later. I'm *sure* Katie will hire you! She was very worried no one would apply. Falconers don't grow on trees and she desperately needs someone like you. You sound perfect." Iris gripped his arm and said in a conspiratorial whisper, "Joe, you're just the salt of the earth and I've always admired you. If you take the job, I will guarantee a very good wage for you. Plus, medical insurance is included."

He grinned. "Miss Iris, you're such a saleswoman. But I have to see if Katie thinks I'm right for the job first."

"Oh, of course, of course." Coloring, Iris touched her flushed cheek. "My, this is so fortuitous meeting you here at Mo's. This is our lucky day!"

"It's kismet," Joe agreed. "Let me buy you breakfast, Miss Iris. It's the least I can do," he said, digging into the pocket of his Levi's.

Iris slid off the stool. "Why, that's very kind of you, Joe. You don't have to do it."

"But I *want* to, Miss Iris."

She leaned over and kissed his cheek. "Oh, all right. Welcome home, Joe Gannon. I know Katie will love you as much as I do. Bye-bye…"

Joe paid the bills, feeling pretty good himself. Dizzied by the synchronicity of events, he walked out the door and into the late-morning sunshine. Why hadn't this happened earlier in his life? His divorce from Zoe had devastated him. Now he had some sudden good fortune…and a woman who interested him. It was time to call Katie Bergstrom. Would she *want* to hire him? Joe really didn't know. This was his chance to at least prove one way or another whether she was working with her mother, Janet.

KATIE HAD JUST PUT SAM into his mew after cleaning it out when her cell phone rang. Hurrying up the long concrete walkway between the fifteen mews, she picked it off her small oak desk near the front door.

"Hello, this is Katie. Can I help you?" Her voice sounded breathless.

"Hi, this is Joe Gannon. I saw your ad in the paper this morning for a falconer."

Katie sucked in a breath of air. "Oh!" And then she released the air. "Are you calling about the position?" Iris had persuaded her to try the ad, but Katie had doubted anyone would apply. Her fingers tightened around her phone as she prayed for a miracle.

"Yes, I am. I'm working toward my falconer's license with Eddie Barton, back in Washington, D.C. Perhaps you've heard of Eddie?" Joe knew the man was a very famous falconer who had written a number of books on how to handle eagles. There wasn't a falconer in the world who didn't know about this respected man.

"Why…yes, of course I've heard of Mr. Barton. You *studied* with him."

"Yes, I did. I've just moved back home to Jackson Hole. Is it possible to meet with you and apply for the position in person?"

Katie felt joy thrum though her, as if her heart would explode with joy. She closed her eyes, took a breath and tried to slow down her speech; when she got excited, she talked at the speed of light, or so her friends told her. "Of course I'd be interested. You said you've just come home? Did you live in Jackson Hole before this?"

"I was born here, Miss Bergstrom. It's a long story and I'd be glad to answer all your questions if I can come over."

"Absolutely. I'd love to talk with you. Anyone trained

by Eddie Barton…why…you *must* be good. There's a waiting line of falconers who are dying to train with him."

"I guess I got lucky, then," Joe said. "I just had breakfast with Miss Iris. I know where the Elk Horn Ranch is, may I come over now? Or is there a better time?"

"That would be terrific. Miss Iris loves my raptors. I'm sure she told you she moved my raptor facility to her ranch."

"Yes, she did. I'll be showing up in a dark green Ford Focus."

Katie blinked. She recalled a similar-colored car at the elk fence this morning. Had that been Joe Gannon? Her intuition told her it had. "Great, come on over."

"See you in about twenty minutes," he promised.

Katie moved from one foot to the other. Rubbing her hands in excitement, she danced a little dance around the office area. She heard Hank, her red-tailed hawk, whistling softly. Moon, the barn owl who had the mew next to her office desk, was sleeping the day away in her wooden nest box. Sam, the golden eagle whistled, his piercing call echoing throughout the facility. Laughing, Katie called out, "It's okay, Sam. I'm dancing for joy. There's a falconer coming for the job! Yippee!"

JOE EASED OUT of his car and admired the huge metal-and-glass building with louvered windows. He could see the many mews through the clean glass. The entire roof was draped in dark netting, shielding the inner area from an excessive build-up of heat. Raptors don't do well in high heat. He spotted a propane tank at the other end of the building to warm it during the winter. Huge fans positioned on both ends of the building were turned on to push fresh Wyoming air through the state-of-the-art facility. Iris had said she had spared no expense on this modern raptor facility and she was right.

As Joe shut the car door, he saw the glass entrance door slide open. Katie Bergstrom appeared. He wasn't prepared for her natural beauty as she waved enthusiastically and hurried toward him. Her black hair was loose, shining like a raven's wing in the sunlight, blue highlights dancing here and there. But it was her eyes that mesmerized him as he walked around the front of his car to greet her. They were a turquoise blue, the kind of color he'd found in Belize where he had scuba-dived. Her oval face was wide, her eyes incredibly alluring and yet, as his swift gaze dropped to her mouth, Joe felt himself go suddenly hot. How to keep his face carefully arranged?

"Hi, I'm Katie. You must be Joe Gannon?" She gripped his hand and felt his monitored strength. Indeed, her heart pounded, but not because she was excited about his possibly working with her raptors. No, Joe was ruggedly handsome and he made her pulse race. Katie drowned beneath his very male smile, those forest-green eyes alert as an eagle's. His black pupils were large, the surrounding color reminding her of the Douglas firs on the slopes of the Tetons. What was there not to like about this gorgeous man? Nothing! Breathless with building hope, Katie released his hand.

"Yes, I'm Joe Gannon. Nice to meet you, Miss Bergstrom."

"Call me Katie. I don't stand much on formality. Come on in. Let me show you around."

Joe admired her willowlike form and those legs fired his imagination. Joe tried to tamp down his unexpected reaction toward her. Katie was far more attractive than any photo in the FBI files. Her eyes danced with life, like gold sunlight dappling across a blue lake's surface. She moved ahead of him to the door and turned, a wide smile on her lips. She wore no makeup, and he thought Katie looked more like a wood nymph from the Greek myths than a real woman. He sharply reminded himself that she was suspected of working for the Los Lobos cartel, yet, she had a trusting face.

Inside the facility, Joe stopped to admire it. Katie stood off to his right, cheeks flushed. Why was she blushing? Because he was applying for the job? He secretly wished it was her reaction to him but that was idiocy. "Wow," he uttered, admiration in his tone, "this place rocks. I thought Eddie had a modern facility, but yours puts his to shame."

"Thank you. I owe it all to Iris. I showed her blueprints of other state-of-the-art raptor facilities and she wanted the whole package. I feel *very* lucky to have her underwriting my business." Katie wished she'd stop blushing like a teenager, but the timbre of Joe's voice, the admiration gleaming in his eyes as he absorbed the facility, excited her. If he liked what he saw enough, he might want to work for her. Katie had never thought a man would apply for the job; every falconer she'd ever worked with had been a woman. Could a man be as gentle and intuitive as was needed in order to work with her super-psychic raptors? Katie would test Joe on this very point to find out. If her raptors didn't respond well to Joe, she wouldn't hire him. Her birds would evaluate him.

"Well, this is something else," Joe said in a low murmur. He heard the chirping calls of the hawks on the right side of the concrete aisle. On the left, halfway down, he spotted Sam, the golden eagle. He had a mew twice the size of the hawks or owls. Turning, he held

Katie's warm gaze. Why did she have to look so damned innocent? Why couldn't she be much less attractive? Joe wanted to find some way to dislike her. Katie reminded him of an excited girl who couldn't stand still for two seconds. He could clearly see her interest in him, but how to read it?

"Let me show you around." Katie gestured toward the small office on the right. "You can see we have a cabinet and lockers on the other side of the desk along the wall." She walked over and opened up one of the lockers. "All the kangaroo leather and tools you need to make jesses, hoods for the falcons or anything else are located in here. You can use the desk to work on."

Joe saw the tools of their trade neatly placed in individual drawers. The kangaroo leather was in different colors. "Are your raptors color-coded?" he asked.

"Yes. In fact," Katie said, "I picked up that idea a long time ago from Eddie Barton's books on eagles. You can see there's a name of a raptor on each color of leather. That way, you can identify them." And then she laughed. "Not that you wouldn't be able to recognize each raptor. But you know what I mean." She looked up at him. Joe was pure eye candy. Without thinking, she glanced down at his left hand. Was he wearing a wedding ring? *No.* But that meant nothing nowadays. She didn't dare ask if he had a partner. More than likely, with his rugged looks and fabulously athletic body, Joe had a woman in his life. Maybe more than one. A bit of her found that a disappointing possibility. She closed the locker doors and gestured across the aisleway.

"This is the whiteboard where I write up the list for the coming day. The hours of the job are 8:00 a.m. to 5:00 p.m., Monday through Friday. When you come in each morning, this is the first place you'll come. I have a lot of speaking engagements and I put the info up along with the names of the raptors I take with me."

Joe studied the huge whiteboard. Clearly, Katie was in demand as a speaker. He saw ten engagements in the next two weeks. "You *are* busy," he agreed, his hands coming to rest on his hips. "No wonder you need help." He shared a slight grin with her. Her cheeks reddened even more.

"My passion in life," Katie said, "is educating the public about how important our raptors are to the overall environment. I made a promise to myself to talk wherever I could. The more people who know not to shoot raptors or think of them as vermin, the more I feel I am accomplishing my mission."

"It's a good mission to have," Joe agreed. And it was a perfect cover being part of a cartel, too. Katie could travel wherever she wanted and not be suspected. "I trained with Eddie two to three times a week. He has the same belief as you and he does a lot of speaking engagements around the Washington, D.C., area. One time, he took his bald eagle, Jefferson, into the Senate. The senators had invited him to come and speak to all of them about our country's national bird. Jefferson wowed them by flying from the lectern down on the floor up to where I was standing in the balcony. That got their attention."

"You've got some eagle training, too?" Katie desperately needed a falconer with some knowledge of how to handle an eagle. They were very different from working with a hawk, falcon or owl.

"Yes, I do," Joe said, "but I'm not licensed to work with eagles."

"Right, I understand," she said, not hiding the excitement in her voice. "But working with Eddie, you worked with his eagles?"

"Yes, every day. He has two bald eagles, a golden eagle, a harpy eagle from South America and a Black eagle from South Africa, among others."

Katie said in a wistful voice, "Joe, you are an answer to my prayers. You know that getting an eagle license is rare? Most falconers have *no* knowledge of how to handle an eagle. I told Iris I was praying someone who had training with them would answer my ad." She gazed up into his green eyes. "Truly, you are an angel."

Joe felt his conscience bite him. Was Katie for real? She seemed like a rainbow shimmering in the sky after a destructive storm. And rainbows magically dissolved back into the sky. Yes, *magical* was the word for this woman who held such hope in her eyes. Joe searched her innocent features for the woman who worked for the cartel. Her resemblance to Janet, her mother, was obvious, but unlike her drug-addicted mother, Katie was engaged with her life's passion, the raptors. They were a different kind of addiction: one that grabbed a person's heart and spirit and never let them go.

Joe mentally compared the two. Janet had a deeply lined face with pockmarks caused by a meth habit. Her blue eyes were wild-looking, as if she teetered on the edge of insanity. Joe wondered if mother and daughter were in touch with one another. Evidence indicated they probably were, but it was up to him to prove it. He pulled himself out of his reverie and offered her a slight smile. "Eddie's license allowed me to work with all his eagles. I'm sure you could allow me to work with that golden eagle down there?" He pointed toward Sam's mew.

"Absolutely, I do have an eagle license," Katie said. "Come on, let me show you my raptors."

She was part child, part woman, and as she walked down the clean concrete aisle between the mews, Joe couldn't harden his heart against her. Somehow, he'd have to remain immune to Katie's charisma. Most importantly, he had to pass the tests he knew she'd put him through. Raptors knew people far better than any human did, and sooner or later, Katie would invite him to hold and handle some of the raptors. Birds could pick up on the dark side of a human, and they would never relax on their gauntlet as a result. Instead, they'd move around or, worse, try to fly off their gauntlet to get away from the person. Joe silently prayed he could remain low-key, calm and able to fool even the raptors. If he couldn't, Katie wouldn't hire him.

CHAPTER THREE

"THIS IS OUR STAR, Sam, the golden eagle," Katie said proudly.

Halting in front of the huge mew, Joe admired the curious eagle. "Eddie had two of them when I was training with him." Sam cocked his head, his piercing yellow eyes on him. Joe wondered if Katie would ask him to handle the eagle, but he hoped not. Eagles were heavy, large and given to wanting things their own way. Who could blame them? They were the apex predator of the sky.

"That's great to hear," Katie said, smiling up at him. She liked the way Joe was studying Sam. There were earmark traits all falconers shared. They were laid-back and easygoing. Someone who was hyper or had a type A personality couldn't work around these supersensitive raptors. A tense, stressed human affected the raptor adversely and it would refuse to sit quietly on the gauntlet. Frequently, the raptor would open its wings or try to fly away from upsetting energy. Joe had that quiet, calm demeanor Katie was looking for.

Joe looked across the aisle. "Is this a peregrine falcon?"

Katie walked over to the smaller mew. "Yes, this is Quest. She's an endangered tundra peregrine falcon." Pointing to the cage next to Quest, Katie added, "And this is a male tundra peregrine from the Arctic Circle area in Canada. We call him Harlequin. They're both on loan to me as part of a broader Canadian breeding program to bring the tundra species back to that country."

Joe nodded. Falconers often were part of global breeding programs from other countries, programs that would rescue a raptor species from near extinction. "Looks like those two are lovebirds." He smiled a little.

"Actually, I'm going to be putting them together next week. It's breeding season. As you know, peregrines mate for life. If I'm lucky, they'll mate. Once the eyasses, or babies, are hatched and grown, a member of the Canadian Peregrine Foundation will fly down here and pick them up. Canada has lost most of its peregrines to the insecticide DDT."

"It's a worthy project," Joe agreed, watching the pair who sat as close to one another as they could, the mew wire wall separating them. Clearly, they liked one another and that boded well for a successful pairing. In a stoop or dive, peregrine falcons had been clocked at two hundred and twenty miles an hour. They stunned their prey by striking it with speed. On the ground, the hapless bird's spinal cord would be severed by the hawk's sharp beak. Peregrines mainly hunted other birds such as ducks, pheasants and pigeons.

Joe glanced down at Katie. She was smiling, her eyes soft as she studied the pair of falcons. There was no question she loved her birds. "Do you have any other breeding-program raptors here?"

Rousing herself, Katie nodded. "Yes, let's go down to the end on the left. "I have an African auger buzzard from South Africa."

"Mmm, a red-tailed hawk in disguise?" Joe said teasingly. Although the name was different and the hawk was from Africa, it was from the red-tailed family. Each continent had similar species but their markings were different. As they walked over to the mew, Joe saw the hawk study him.

"This is Nar. He's a male auger buzzard. The falcon society of Cape Town is sending over a female shortly. I've signed up for their breeding program and hope that we'll be producing eyasses for them."

The auger was a magnificent hawk, and Joe had never seen one of his kind before. "Do you use Nar in your shows?"

"Yes, but he's a handful," Katie warned. "He's got a temperament more like a falcon."

"Really?" Joe said, lifting his brows. "I handled a red-tailed at Eddie's and he was a laid-back dude. What makes this auger different?"

Shrugging, Katie said, "I don't know. When he first arrived and I started handling him, he was constantly flapping and trying to escape. I had to put him on a crèche line for a couple of months for fear he'd fly off and never come back. My mentor, Donna Pierce, said that in her experience, overseas raptors have a very different temperament from their American cousins."

"Is Donna your teacher?"

Katie turned and studied his serious features. In some respects, Gannon reminded her of an intent eagle focused on his prey. "Yes, she's actually my foster mother. She's been a falconer all her life and she has an eagle license." The words had slipped out and Katie bit her lower lip. She hadn't meant to say anything about her past.

Joe noticed the sudden darkness cloud her gaze. He took the opportunity, having nothing to lose by asking the question. "Does your mother live here with you? Is she a friend of Iris Mason?"

Katie frowned. "Well…truth be known, I was given up at birth. I don't know who my real mother is. I've been trying for years to get the state to open up the sealed records and tell me." Pushing strands of hair off her brow, she said, "I grew up in a series of foster homes in Wyoming. And when I met Donna at sixteen, she saved my life. I wasn't a stellar human being. I was pretty angry all the time. I got thrown into her falconry program as a last chance. Donna took me under her wing, figuratively speaking, and she taught me all she knows. We really bonded and Donna agreed to legally become my foster mother. It was the best thing that ever happened to me." Lifting her hand, she gestured to the mews. "Donna does know Iris Mason and had approached her about helping me expand my facility. Iris agreed to build this facility for me and my raptors. She's been a godsend."

"I heard that Mrs. Mason donated this land to you."

"Yes, she's very ecologically oriented and wanted to help me expand the breeding programs."

Joe smiled. "You were very fortunate to have a donor. Most falconers struggle all their lives to feed their raptors. The state and federal government don't pay them a thing for all the good they do." He saw Katie's brow wrinkle, as if she were in pain of some kind. Could he really believe she didn't know who her mother was? She sounded genuine, but who knew? And he wanted to ignore the pain he saw in her eyes. Pain over what? That she was lying to him? That she really knew that Janet Bergstrom was her mother? Joe couldn't tell one way or another and it made him uncomfortable.

Katie walked quickly up toward the office area. "I'm *very* lucky. Iris has been a guardian angel to my raptors." She wanted to forget she'd blurted out her sordid past. After all, Joe was a stranger applying for a job—why had she told him about her unknown mother? Mentally kicking herself, Katie knew why. Finding her mother had been her sole focus since she'd turned twelve years old. Why had the woman abandoned her? Did her mother not love her? Was she such an ugly baby her own mother had wanted nothing to do with her? Was she an inconvenient pregnancy, born into her mother's life at the wrong time? Was that why she'd been given up for adoption? Biting her lower lip, Katie forced all of her dark past deep down inside herself. She halted at the desk. As Joe sauntered up the aisle, stopping every now and again to appraise the raptors, she took several deep breaths to calm herself.

"I imagine it must be hard not to know who your mother is," Joe said in an understanding tone. "That's a heavy burden for anyone to carry."

"Yes, it is." Katie wanted to change topics. "So why don't we move on to a happier topic? Do you have a résumé I can look at?"

Joe nodded and drew a folded paper from his back pocket and handed it to her. When their fingers met and touched, hers felt cold. "Here it is…."

Katie's hands trembled as she unfolded it and forced herself to read. Some of her stress melted away. "You were in the Marine Corps?" Glancing up, she gave Joe a sympathetic look. "First, thank you for your service. I'm so sorry you got injured. Are you okay now?"

Touched by her apparently genuine concern, Joe said, "Yes. I'm fine now. It was while I was recovering at Bethesda Medical Center that I was sent to Eddie as part of my rehabilitation. He was in the Army during the Vietnam War era and offered his services to the neurology department at the hospital. I got lucky enough to be assigned to him and began to learn falconry."

Katie looked up at this man who seemed supremely confident. She couldn't see the wounds of war on him. "But you had a head injury." Brows drawing down, she asked, "No other symptoms from it?"

"Just one." Joe touched the left side of his head. "I'll get a migraine maybe once a month. They're brought on by stress."

"Ugh, migraines." Katie wrinkled her nose. "I *hate* migraines! I get them myself from time to time." She tilted her head and searched his face. "Does your migraine lay you low? When I get one, I need a quiet, dark room, and then, I can sleep it off."

"Mine are the same. Noise just amps up my pain."

"I feel for you," Katie said. "Any other injuries? Anything that would stop you from doing the work needed around here?"

"No, I'm fine."

Studying the résumé, Katie gasped. "Why didn't I see this before?" She looked up, satisfaction in her expression. "It's nice to have a hometown person for this job," she murmured.

Joe grinned. "Yes, I am. Does that hurt my chances?" He'd said it with a teasing tone and saw her suddenly smile. Her lips were full and soft. And when Katie's mouth widened, his heart skipped a couple of beats. She couldn't hide any emotion. There was no veneer, no mask in place on Katie that he could discern. It would make his job easier provided she hired him.

"No, no, that's *great*. And your parents must live here, too?"

Joe told her about his mother and father. "On weekends, I'm working with my dad to learn his ranching and landscaping business."

"I see. And your address? Are you at their home?"

He was impressed how quickly she put things together. But then, in Joe's experience with falconers, they were highly intelligent and, like the raptors they saved, had extraordinary observation and alertness skills. "Yes, there's a smaller home near the ranch house and I'm living there."

Katie sighed. "You're so *lucky* to have a mom and dad…."

As he heard the yearning in her whisper, Joe felt his heart suddenly wrench in his chest. He drilled her with a look, trying to ferret out whether she was telling the truth. But he was flummoxed. "We get along well with one another" was all he said. Yes, there was real pain in her eyes. For a second, he thought he saw tears building but Katie dipped her head.

Clearing her throat, Katie studied his résumé some more. "So you want a full-time job, five days a week with me, and you're working with your dad on weekends?"

"That's right."

Katie asked in a concerned tone, "How long before you move into ranching as a full-time job?"

Joe knew she worried that if she hired him, he'd leave. "Not for ten years," and he added a half smile to his answer. Instantly, he saw relief in her face. The stress fled the corners of her delicious mouth. If Katie was this easy to read, he'd have no problem figuring out the connection between her and Janet Bergstrom. "My father isn't ready to retire. My coming home rather unexpectedly because of the wound I received in Afghanistan got him thinking about offering me the ranch." Joe opened his hands. "I can't go back into the military. This IED concussion ended my career. I hadn't really figured out what I was going to do after the hospital released me and I got my walking papers from the Marine Corps. When I was sent to Eddie for rehab, I fell in love with falconry. My dad called me and asked me to come home and offered to teach me the business, and I accepted."

"I know about your dad's landscaping business because Iris hired him to come out here with his construction equipment to level the land where the facility would be built. I remember him. He was a very nice person."

"My dad is an easygoing type and he's built up an eco-friendly landscaping business here in the valley over the years."

"Did you *want* to become a rancher?"

"I loved the military. I was an officer and I was a good leader. I wanted to put in my twenty years and retire." Shrugging, Joe said, "You know how life can twist and turn? I knew my two tours in Afghanistan would be dangerous. I lost some of my people to IEDs. And then my turn came." Joe told her the truth. He purposely left out that during his recovery the FBI had asked him to work for them. He'd spent a year in training after the six months of rehab. The FBI had wanted to put him as an undercover operative in Katie's life. They wanted actual proof the daughter was working with the Los Lobos cartel.

"I think it's great your dad has offered you a new career." Katie smiled a little. "This way, you can be home to enjoy your parents and this beautiful area."

The wistfulness in her tone told Joe she was wishing she had the same life as he did. After all, being abandoned at birth would be a huge emotional hole in anyone's life. Gently, he said, "Yes, I count myself lucky."

The glass doors slid open. Iris Mason stepped in wearing her gardening gloves, a bunch of weeds dangling from her left hand. "Hey, am I disturbing you, Katie? Hi, Joe, nice to see you again."

Katie lifted her hand. "Hi, Iris. I see you're weeding again." In the morning, Iris could usually be found out in her flower beds. "Do you know Joe Gannon?"

"Yes, I do. Glad you could make it out." Iris dropped the weeds in a nearby barrel and pulled off her muddy gloves.

Joe nodded deferentially to Iris. "Good to see you again, Miss Iris. Looks like the weeds are losing."

"Oh, they are. Amazing how weeds spring up overnight." The woman smiled up at him before turning her attention to Katie. "What do you think? Is Joe a good choice to work with you out here?"

Katie handed her the résumé. "What do you think? You're the one paying his salary."

Chuckling, Iris took the résumé and quickly perused it. "Well, darling girl, if you like his abilities and you think he's the ticket, I'm all for it." She handed the paper back to Katie. Her eyes sparkled as she met Joe's gaze.

Joe flicked a glance toward Katie. He saw the love mirrored in her face for the silver-haired elder in the floppy straw hat. Something told him Katie was like a long-lost daughter to Iris. The woman's family had recently expanded. Kamaria Trayhern, the daughter of Rudd Mason, her own adopted son, had returned to the Elk Horn Ranch a few years ago. Kam had proven that she was Rudd's daughter through a DNA test. Iris had been beside herself with joy. Now, Kam was married to Wes, a wrangler who worked on the ranch. Joe knew from his study of Iris and her family that Kam was expecting a baby girl shortly. Iris was well-known for finding strays, embracing and helping them. It was her nature to help underdogs and she had helped many in the valley.

Iris removed her straw hat and ran her fingers through her mussed hair. "Joe is a known factor," she told Katie. "You've met his father already. As you know, not much isn't known about those who live in this valley." She chuckled and settled the hat back on her head. "If you want to hire him, I'm all for it."

Katie nodded. She looked up at Joe. "I'd like to test you with a few of the raptors. I want to see how you handle them."

Iris smiled. "Good. Well, I just wanted to drop in and say hello." She picked up her muddy gloves. "Katie, you put him through his paces. Nice seeing you, Joe." She waved to them and disappeared through the glass doors.

Internally, Joe went on guard. Would the raptors give him away? God, he hoped not. Would Katie ask him to work with Sam? Eagles were more persnickety than the hot-blooded falcons.

"Your choice. Would you like to work with Harlequin?"

"Sure," Joe lied. *Great, a falcon.* They were well-known to be flighty, nervous and to pick up quickly on a person's energy.

"Do you have your own falconry equipment with you?"

"Yes, it's in my car. I'll bring it in…."

Katie watched him leave. There was nothing to dislike about Joe Gannon. He was respectful. He seemed to listen. His handling of a raptor would tell her a lot more than any résumé. He soon returned with a black canvas bag across his shoulder. He took the bag over to the desk and opened it. Curious, Katie watched him draw out a

dark brown gauntlet. She saw all the scratches across
the well-used kangaroo-leather glove. It was a good sign
he had been working regularly with Eddie.

"Why don't you go down and get Harlequin? I'll
stand to one side and just watch. If you need anything,
I'll be there to coach you."

Joe pulled on the glove. "Do you want me to feed
Harlequin?"

"Actually," Katie said, "he needs to be weighed.
Every morning each raptor is weighed on those scales
over there." She pointed to a long desk on the other
side of the aisle. There were two scales on the table.
One was for the eagle and the smaller one was for the
rest of her raptors.

"Okay," he said, heading down the aisle. His heart
was pounding. He *had* to get this job. It didn't matter
what Iris Mason wanted and Joe knew that. It would all
come down to this: how he handled a raptor. Swallowing
hard, Joe forced himself to take a deep, calming breath.
As he approached the mew and unlocked it, Harlequin
warily eyed him from his perch. Joe knew better than
to look any raptor in the eye as this was a sign of threat.
Averting his eyes, he focused on quietly entering the
clean cage and closing the door behind him. One never
left a door open. Ever.

Katie stood back, attentive. She watched Harlequin,
who was a red-hot pistol to deal with. If Joe could handle
this testy tundra peregrine, he could handle any raptor
under her care. She liked the way Joe moved. He slowly
brought his glove up to the perch. Harlequin looked at it
and then at Joe. A slight smile pulled at Katie's mouth.
Harlequin was all male. And she knew he was sizing
up this male stranger in his mew. Raptors remembered
faces and they literally memorized everything they saw.

Would Harlequin suddenly fly away from Joe because this was the first time he'd ever seen him?

Joe tapped the glove with his index finger. It was an unspoken command every raptor in captivity understood. The falcon looked disdainfully at the index finger on the glove. And then he looked away, toward the other mew where Quest was perched. "I think Harlequin's focus is elsewhere," he joked to her in a quiet tone.

Chuckling softly, Katie said, "Gotcha. Yes, he's wanting to be in her mew. It's time they mated. Keep tapping your glove. He'll eventually climb on it."

Liking her quiet direction, Joe did as he was told.

Harlequin really didn't want to leave his mew or his mate-to-be. He flapped his wings but remained where he was, ignoring the signal.

"This guy has attitude," Joe said.

"Yeah, he does. Keep at it. You have to be more stubborn and persistent than he is."

Smiling a little, Joe again tapped his glove.

Harlequin hopped onto it.

With quiet, smooth motions, Joe attached the jesses to the soft kangaroo leggings around each of Harlequin's yellow legs. So far, so good. After placing the jesses between the thick fingers of his glove, he slowly lifted the falcon up and headed for the door. If Harlequin tried to bolt and fly back to his perch near the lady falcon, Joe would now have control over him.

Katie nodded her approval. Harlequin seemed all right being on the man's glove, but he kept looking back with concern toward Quest. "I think once you get done weighing and feeding Harlequin, we'll transfer him over to the other mew after we weigh and feed Quest."

Joe walked the falcon up the aisle. Harlequin was looking around, suddenly caught up in viewing all the other raptors on either side of him. "Do I need to put a hood on him? He looks like he's getting ready to fly."

"No, he'll be okay." Katie knew that most falcons, when brought out of a mew, were always hooded. That kept them from being overstimulated by the changing environment, making them stressed and flighty. "Harlequin is pretty laid-back for a boy falcon," she said with a laugh. "The only time I'll hood him is when I take him out for flying time."

Joe caught her gaze. Her smile melted his heart. She was happy. And so was he, despite the worry the falcon might take flight. Walking to the counter, he placed his glove next to the perch wrapped with outdoor carpeting and securely taped to the top of the scale. Joe tapped the perch with his index finger. Harlequin quickly leaped from his glove, fluffed his feathers, preened a bit on the perch and looked around as lord of all he surveyed.

Katie walked up and picked up a nearby clipboard. "Every morning you'll weigh each raptor. Depending upon his or her weight, you'll feed them a certain amount of meat." She flipped the pages to Harlequin's file and read the scale numbers. "What amount should he be fed based upon this weight?"

Joe knew the test and glanced at the numbers. Every raptor had a normal weight for their age and size. "I think he'd like about two ounces of meat."

"Good call. I agree. Hold on…" Katie crouched down to a small refrigerator beneath the counter. Opening it, she drew out a plastic bag bearing Harlequin's name. "You can do the feeding."

Joe withdrew the quail meat. He placed it on his glove between the thumb and forefinger. Harlequin instantly gobbled it down and appeared satisfied. Joe smiled and handed the bag back to Katie, who then placed it back in the fridge. "He was a little hungry, wouldn't you say?"

"Yes, I flew him yesterday."

"Makes sense," Joe replied. "Back to the mew for now?"

"Yep," Katie said, stepping away.

Harlequin was a good boy this time and with one tap on his glove, he hopped from perch to the fist. Wrapping the jesses around his fingers, Joe walked him back to his mew.

Once Harlequin was on his perch and free of the jesses, Katie said, "Every morning after weighing and feeding, you'll need to clean all the mews." She pointed to several small feathers on the gravel beneath Harlequin's perch. "You can pick up feathers, scat, give them clean water in their bowl. The bath bowl is changed daily."

Joe nodded and shut the mew and locked it. "That's what I did at Eddie's place."

"Cleanliness keeps them safe. Mites and other insects won't be around to give them problems," Katie said. She walked with Joe up to the front once again. He took off his glove and placed it carefully back into the canvas bag, then Katie said, "You handled Harlequin really well. Now, I want you to take out Hank, the redtailed hawk. We're going to fly him outside the building. He's already been weighed and I purposely didn't feed him because I knew you were coming."

Surprised, Joe pulled his glove back out of the bag. He'd thought the test was over. Judging from the serious look on Katie's face, it wasn't. "Great. I love the flying. It's the fun part." He cracked a grin as he pulled on the gauntlet.

Katie smiled back. "I know, but work before play.

Go get Hank. He's a sweetie and won't give you any problems."

The cool morning air was warming as the sun's rays slanted across the lush green valley. Joe felt happy carrying the red-tailed hawk on his fist. Katie led them to a flight oval located on the southern side of the building. A flight oval was usually a quarter of a mile long with four stout metal perches placed around it. He saw that each perch, all large enough for Sam the eagle to land on comfortably, was covered with outdoor carpeting, so that the raptors could grip it and not slide off.

"Go over to the north perch," Katie instructed. "I'm going to place a dead mouse on the south perch. When I tell you to release Hank, do so."

"Right," Joe called, carrying the dark brown hawk with a rust-red tail to the north perch. His heart rate picked up. He liked flying raptors. They were incredible in motion. He saw the hawk eyeballing Katie as she walked toward the southern perch. He could see her placing a white mouse on top of it. The jesses on Hank were very short. Katie waved her hand as a signal to release him. He'd barely lifted his glove upward when Hank exploded off it and flapped quickly into the air. Within five wing beats, he pounced upon the south perch with glee. As he landed, he simultaneously grabbed the mouse in his curved yellow beak. Folding his large wings against his body, Hank gulped down his meal.

Katie had given him a canvas bag filled with raw meat. Joe pulled out the morsel of quail meat and placed it on the perch. Instantly, Hank lifted off and flew to where he stood. In seconds, the raptor had landed and gulped down the meat. Grinning, Joe watched as Katie walked to the west perch where she placed more food. Hank instantly took to the air, heading in her direction.

Joe never grew bored flying a raptor. They were supreme hunters of the air. He observed how naturally Katie called to Hank after he landed and ate his food. She was smiling. But it was her eyes shining with undisguised love that mesmerized Joe. Her full attention was on the hawk. What would it be like to have Katie look at him with that wonderful, glowing expression?

Shaken by his thoughts, Joe scowled. For a moment, he was shocked. There was no way he could get personally involved with this woman. Oh, it was true, Katie was attractive, and so trusting of strangers like himself. Who would have thought she'd be this innocent after being handed off from one foster family to another? He'd read her records. She'd had ten foster families by the age of sixteen. Katie had been in trouble, rebellious and skipping school. She'd had a tough life, there was no doubt. So how could she be so damned open and good-natured now? Was it all really just an act, as his boss Roger Hager wanted him to believe? Rubbing his jaw, Joe wasn't so sure. There was something pure about Katie that defied logic and Hager's dire warning.

"Here he comes!" Katie called.

Damn! Joe had forgotten to place the meat on the perch. The bird landed with a flap of his wings, his yellow eyes focused on him.

"Yeah, I screwed up," he muttered to the hawk. After digging into his pouch, he found the meat. He placed it on the thumb of his glove and lifted it. Instantly, Hank leaned forward and grasped it in his beak.

"You gotta stay awake," Katie called and laughed as she walked to the east perch.

"I know," Joe called out. "Sorry…"

"Not to worry." Katie placed meat on the perch. She watched Hank fly swiftly to where she stood. Smiling, she saw Joe place meat on the perch next to him, and the bird took off like a rocket, wings causing air turbulence around her, lifting strands of her black hair from around her face. Katie liked Joe's work ethic. Clearly, Eddie had taught him well. Joe didn't get flustered or tense and the raptors liked him.

Walking toward Joe, she said, "Go ahead and put Hank on your gauntlet. He's had his breakfast and we'll put him back into the mew. The next bird out will be Quest. I want to fly her in the oval and she can have her breakfast out here."

"Okay," he called and Hank hopped onto his glove. Wrapping the jesses between his fingers, Joe brought the red-tailed hawk down to a comfortable height so he could hold him steady. Hank was ruffling his feathers and shaking them.

"That's a good sign," Katie said as she walked up to Joe. "A bird that trusts you will always ruffle its feathers. It shows it's relaxed and happy."

Inner relief flowed through Joe as he walked with Katie back to the facility. "Hank is a nice hawk. He's easy to handle."

Katie entered the building and stood aside as Joe walked in with Hank. "Well, now you're going to get to handle Quest. She's a piece of work." Katie walked with him down the aisle to Hank's mew. Joe entered and closed the door behind him. "Quest was shot in Canada and a hiker found her limping around on the ground. He cast her in his T-shirt and hand-carried her to a vet. She doesn't trust men at all. I don't know if it's from being wrapped in the T-shirt or she hated the man who shot her. Or both..."

Joe nodded and came out of the mew with Quest. Turning, he locked the door. "A lot of raptors hate being cast. It makes them feel out of control and trapped."

"Casting a falcon is really hard on its psyche. They're more easily stressed. More so than a hawk or eagle." Katie stood near the cage. She met his gaze. "I like the way you work with my raptors. I'd like to offer you the job, Joe. What do you say?"

CHAPTER FOUR

SHOULD SHE TRY to get in touch with her daughter...or not? Janet Bergstrom sat in the office of Mercury Courier, rubbing her aching head. She had the window open so her cigarette smoke would drift outside. With her fingers drumming on the chipped walnut desk she'd picked up at Goodwill years ago, Janet pursed her mouth. What to do? She glanced out the window and saw storm clouds gathering across the city of Cheyenne. It was summer and they could use the water.

The door to her office was closed but she had exquisite hearing. Janet could hear the bells tinkle as the door opened and another customer arrived. Her help, one of the Los Lobos drug soldiers, Pablo, would take care of the package to be sent by courier. Turning in her squeaky wooden chair, Janet finished off her cigarette and stubbed it out in a green glass ashtray on the corner of her desk.

She stood, realizing she needed to move around. She could never sit still for too long. Running her polished red fingernails through her dyed blond hair, she started to pace. On her desk was a photo taken by a nurse of the baby she'd given up twenty-six years earlier. It was the only photo Janet had of her baby girl. *What to do? What to do?* She rubbed her damp hands down the sides of her dark green polyester slacks. Janet struggled to think.

Earlier, she'd slipped out the back door and into

the alley and smoked part of a joint. A little weed was the only thing that could calm her raw, jittery nerves. But she couldn't keep a thought in her head. Her mind swung back to her daughter she'd given away so long ago. Should she try to contact Katie Bergstrom in person? On a whim, Janet had driven from Cheyenne to the Elk Horn Ranch where her daughter was living. For years she'd followed her daughter's career via the Jackson Hole newspaper. She enjoyed the articles on Katie and the raptors. Twice, Janet had chickened out at the front gate of the ranch, parked off the road, trying to build up courage to meet Katie.

"Damn fear," she said in a gravelly tone, turning on her heel. *To hell with it.* Janet jerked open the back door. She was desperate for some fresh air. If Pablo needed her, he knew where to find her. Stepping into the alley, Dumpsters on either side of her, three-story redbrick buildings rising around her, Janet wished she was out in nature. She hated cities, even Cheyenne. She preferred the quiet of a rural town.

Fingers trembling, she pulled out the rest of her joint from her pocket. The lighter was always in the other pocket. Placing the joint between her red lips, she lit it and inhaled deeply. She dropped the lighter back into her pocket and began her ambling walk down the empty alley, puffing and holding the smoke in her lungs. The small road was closed off at one end and open at the other. Her car, a gray Subaru that had seen better days, was parked near the rear entrance to her business. Peering out of the alley, Janet watched the traffic zooming back and forth on the four-lane street. The noise and hustle of Cheyenne was diminished by the alley. This was a place where Janet felt somewhat safe.

As she walked, her mind shorted out as it always

did and she forced herself to think about contacting her daughter again. What was driving her to do it? Maybe, at age forty-two, her hormones were changing and she was going into menopause? Or maybe age was maturing her a little? Most likely, it was the daily guilt that continued to gnaw at her. Yes, that was it. Guilt. Damned guilt! There wasn't a day gone by that Janet hadn't thought of her daughter.

Pushing her fingers through her short hair, Janet exhaled a small gust of smoke, finding calm gradually descending over her edgy nerves. She had just gotten her hair cut and shaped yesterday. As she moved her fingers across her oval face, she could feel wrinkles forming here and there. Janet had thought the new hairstyle would make her look younger. Xavier Lobos, her lover from Guatemala, would be visiting her later today. She critically studied her carefully pressed slacks. God knew, she dieted all the time.

Xavier... Janet halted in the middle of the alley, yearning filling her. How long had it been since they'd made love? Six months? *Way too long!* Janet felt threads of happiness winding through her chest. She loved the cartel leader with a desperation that drove her crazy. If it wasn't guilt over giving up Katie, it was missing Xavier's arms around her.

Her addled brain focused on her daughter. Somehow, Janet wanted to contact Katie. What would she do? Say? Would she be angry? Pissed off, tell her to take a hike? Janet felt anxiety zigzagging through her, erasing her excitement over Xavier's arrival. Angry that she was allowing fear to run her, Janet finished off the last of the joint. Turning, she walked back to her office.

Pablo, who was twenty-one, entered her office just as she sat down.

"What is it?"

He closed the door and spoke in Spanish. "Señorita Janet, Don Xavier just contacted me. He said to tell you he'll be here in one hour."

Nodding, Janet sat down. "Good. Thanks, Pablo."

"Si, señorita."

Alone once more, Janet got to her feet. She moved to the bathroom and turned on the light. Xavier was a sinfully handsome dude. She critically studied herself in the dirty mirror over the sink. Liking the short cut, Janet had dyed her black hair a blond shade yesterday. Xavier liked blondes. Oh, she knew he had a lovely young wife in Guatemala who shared his bed, but when he came for a visit, she became his bedmate. Janet lived for these meetings. Staring at her oval face, she picked up her pancake makeup and added a bit more. Her cheeks looked pale so she added blusher. Janet added blue eye shadow. Lastly, mascara to make her short, thin lashes look fuller. Now, as she studied herself in the mirror, Janet felt beautiful. Once again, her lover would arrive and sweep her into his arms. Xavier knew how to treat her right. He would reserve a room at the most expensive hotel in Cheyenne, wine and dine her. They would make desperate, torrid love two or three times a night. Janet felt her breasts and lower body contracting with need of his masterful touch once again.

XAVIER LOBOS WALKED through the rear door of Mercury Courier. He knew Cheyenne well. Since she was eighteen Janet Bergstrom had fronted his drugs and arms efforts in order to establish a base of operations in the States. Quietly closing the door, he found Janet standing, her face filled with happiness as he stepped like a shadow into her office.

"Xavier!" Janet cried, throwing her arms around his lean shoulders.

He smiled slightly and took her full weight. Janet was five feet six inches tall and he was two inches taller than she. As he pulled her into his arms, he thought she looked old and tired. "It's good to see you again," he whispered in Spanish near her ear. He could smell the dye in the strands of her hair. She always wore heavy perfume and he hated the odor. Wrinkling his nose, Xavier forced himself to hold the embrace for a proper amount of time. Janet used to be beautiful, curves in all the right places. Now, she was overweight, breasts beginning to hang, her skin sagging everywhere. Xavier knew drugs could turn youth into old age in a matter of years. And Janet, the addict she had always been, never gave up her drug habit no matter how many times he'd pleaded with her to get clean. He kissed her, trying to put passion into the meeting of their lips, telling himself this was necessary because she was his anchor in Wyoming. He needed to keep her happy. Xavier visited his people in the States every year. It was wise to keep tabs on them and make sure they remained loyal to his cartel.

"Oh, Xavier!" Janet said brokenly, tears in her eyes, "I've missed you so much!" She stared up into his dark brown eyes framed with thick, long lashes. Xavier always wore his black hair over his ears. His thick, black mustache only made him look more dashing—and dangerous. She slid her lacquered nails across his shaven cheek. "You look so good." And then her voice dropped to a whine. "I'm so lonely...."

"Hush, sweet one," he said, kissing her wrinkled brow. He saw the pancake makeup sitting in lines across her forehead. "I've come to rescue you, take you on a magical carpet ride for tonight." He forced a big smile and held her at arm's length. "Come, I have the hotel prepared. Only the best for you, Janet."

All her depression melted beneath his hooded stare. Her gaze settled on his full mouth. What a wonderful lover Xavier was! Her body literally ached to feel his hands playing her like a beloved instrument. "Oh, yes, I'm ready!"

"Good, then come. First, we will have dinner in the room, talk business, and then—" his mouth pulled slowly into a feral grin "—our bodies will whisper lovingly to one another all night." Xavier knew he had to keep Janet satisfied. She was the hub of his business in Wyoming, and he was wisely making plans to move his work elsewhere. Janet would never know of his plans, of course. He was going to manipulate her into creating a second courier business based in Jackson Hole, where he would establish a second hub for the state and beyond.

"It sounds wonderful!" Janet sighed, picking up her purse. "Let's go!"

"WELL, DID YOU HIRE JOE?" Iris asked as she came into Katie's office area.

Turning in her chair, Katie smiled. "I did. He's perfect, Iris."

"And your raptors behaved?" Iris stood in the entrance leading to the mews, smiling down at her.

Laughing, Katie nodded. She touched the résumé Joe had left with her. "He's a really nice person."

"What's good about Joe is that he's a local," Iris said, lifting the straw hat off her head.

"And I like the idea of hiring a military veteran," Katie said. "So many of them are having trouble finding a job after returning home."

"Yes, Rudd and I like your choice for all those reasons." She studied Katie for a moment. "I need to sit for a spell and talk to you about something important. Do you have a moment?"

"Sure, sit down." Katie moved a chair to the side of the desk for Iris. "Are you feeling all right?"

Iris said, "I'm fine. Don't worry, I may look old but I'm not going anywhere soon." She grinned and set her straw hat on the desk. "I need to let you know I've been up to something that involves you."

"Oh?" Katie noticed how serious Iris had become. It unnerved her. She was always worried her world would take another unexpected turn. Katie never got used to the ups and downs, twists and turns her life took. Moving to the Elk Horn Ranch had given her a modicum of stability she'd never had before and she found herself liking it. Maybe too much? She held her breath as Iris became pensive. Fear entered her heart. Something was wrong. What was it?

Reaching out, Iris must have seen the anxiety come to Katie's eyes. Gently, she said, "I hired a woman investigator to look for your mother, Katie."

Eyes widening, Katie gasped. "You did?"

"Yes, because I know you've spent your entire life looking for her and coming up empty-handed." Her fingers tightened over Katie's hand.

Heart starting a slow pound, Katie looked into Iris's narrowed eyes. The words whispered out of her mouth were loaded with anguish. "Did she find her?"

"Yes, my investigator found Janet Bergstrom. I know the state is never going to open up its sealed records and give you want you want. You didn't realize it, but your mother allowed you to have her surname. I know this is an anchor around your neck, Katie. After getting to know you over the past year, I felt you deserved some help. I know your dream is to make a connection with your mother."

Automatically, Katie's fingers brushed against her pounding heart. "You found her? Where? Does she live in Wyoming? Or somewhere else?" Katie had never thought to look for a Bergstrom because the state never told her one way or another if that was her real mother's name. She felt as if she was going to suffocate.

Patting her hand, Iris released it. "I'm going to invite my PI, Norah Merton, to come in and share the information she's discovered. Would you like to hear what she found?"

"I would." She stood up and slipped her arms around the older woman. She kissed Iris on the cheek. "You don't know how *much* this means to me."

Chuckling, Iris hugged her back and said, "Let's get Norah in here, then."

Katie was reeling in shock. By the time she had brought another chair over to her desk, a tall woman in her fifties had entered the facility.

"Katie, meet Norah Merton," Iris said. "Norah, this is the young woman you're working for."

"Hi, Ms. Merton. It's nice to meet you." Katie winced as she heard her voice crack with emotion. The tall, slender woman wore a cream-colored linen pantsuit with a white silk blouse beneath it. She seemed elegant, her dark brown hair coiffed and shoulder-length. The sparkle in her hazel eyes made Katie feel a little less tense.

"Hi, Katie. Nice to meet you, finally. Mind if we all sit down and I'll give you my report?"

"Please," Katie said, gesturing to her chair. Iris sat down and so did she. Clasping her hands in her lap, Katie tried to sit still. She chewed on her lower lip as the woman pulled out a file from a black calfskin brief-case she carried.

"I've got a lot of information for you, Katie," Norah said. "And some of it is very upsetting." Her voice lowered and she went on. "Janet Bergstrom gave you up for adoption when she was sixteen years old. You were born in Cheyenne, Wyoming. Your birth mother gave you her last name. And that made it a lot easier for me to track her down."

"She was sixteen?" Katie said, thinking about herself at that age.

"It's very young to become pregnant," Iris consoled her.

Norah nodded. "Normally, when a teen becomes pregnant, her family steps in. That wasn't the case. Candy Bergstrom, Janet's mother, was a drug addict herself. Janet was born with cocaine in her system. Candy gave Janet up for adoption right after birth. It was the start of a pattern. When Janet gave birth to you, she gave you her name, Bergstrom, and gave you up at birth. But she lied about who your father was. She put down Lawrence Kincaid, but there is no proof he ever existed. Janet probably lied to protect the real father for whatever reason. That means I wasn't able to trace your grandparents, either. I'm sorry."

She felt as if someone had struck her in the chest with a hammer. Katie touched her heart. "At least I know," she managed in a strained voice. "What else?"

"Candy Bergstrom died at age forty of hepatitis B. She got the disease through a dirty needle. She died of liver failure."

"Did…my mother know her mother?"

Shaking her head, Norah said, "No. I don't know if your mother tried to find out or not."

Norah handed Katie several black and white photos. "I found these photos of Candy Bergstrom at the Cheyenne Police Department. She was up on drug charges at least ten times in her life."

Katie stared down at the mug shots. There were some full-face and two profiles of her grandmother. "I can see the shape of my face in her face," she said in a low voice. But that was all. Lifting her head, she asked, "Do you have photos of my mother?"

Norah nodded and handed her three photos. "These are mug shots too, Katie. You need to prepare yourself. Your mother, Janet Bergstrom, was in federal prison for five years."

Katie's hand shook as she took the photos from Norah. "Prison?" Her voice cracked.

"Yes. Your mother grew up in ten different foster homes. I can only surmise she was rebellious but I can't prove it. At sixteen, she was impregnated by someone, but we don't know who it was. Your mother gave you up after birth and got tangled up with a drug-cartel boss named Xavier Lobos. When your mother was thirty years old, the FBI caught her running guns to Montana. She never gave up Xavier Lobos in court and went to prison for five years because she refused to cooperate with the FBI. They offered her a plea deal if she'd turn in the evidence, but Janet refused."

"My mother's a drug dealer?" Hot tears jammed her eyes. Valiantly, Katie tried to handle the shocking news. She felt Iris grip her hand to comfort her. The older woman was also moved to tears. "This…this is awful.… I had dreamed my parents were great people, important…successful.… God, I was so wrong…"

"I know, honey," Iris whispered. "I know you thought

your mother was someone special, that she had a good life and was happy."

Norah added in a sad tone, "So often, abandoned children grow up with an incredible dream that their parents are accomplished, successful and happy." Opening her hands, the investigator said, "Unfortunately, it's usually the opposite, Katie. A young teen mother has no home support, so she gives up her baby. And sometimes, she spirals down after that instead of trying to mature and remake her life into something positive."

Katie wiped her eyes with trembling fingers. She sniffed. "You're right, Norah. I had these crazy dreams my mother was a pilot, a ballet dancer or maybe a famous artist...."

Iris said, "Honey, as you know, Rudd was adopted by Trevor and me. We know how painful it is for someone like yourself to discover her roots. And often, it's not what you might have imagined. You're looking pale. Do you want to take a break? Maybe get some coffee at the ranch house? Or would you prefer Norah come back another time? I know this is a lot to absorb."

Katie squeezed the older woman's work-worn hand. "No, I'm so thankful you hired Norah. At least now I know the truth. I can stop worrying and wondering who my mother was...."

Iris nodded to the private investigator. "Go on, Norah. Katie might look young and innocent, but she's tough on the inside."

"Okay," Norah said with a slight smile. She turned and focused on Katie. "After being released from prison, your mother went to Guatemala. She remained there for a year. I can't get any information on her there except that the police had proof she was living with Xavier Lobos. And then she moved back to Cheyenne. At that

point, she built Mercury Courier service. It's a state-
wide courier service delivering packages and other
communications around the state. I'm assuming Xavier
Lobos underwrote her business. She didn't have any
income that I could detect. In other words, the police
and FBI suspect but can't prove she's being bankrolled
by Lobos."

Dragging in a ragged breath, Katie couldn't take her
gaze off the black-and-white mug shots of her mother.
Her hands turned damp and cool as she touched the
photos. "She's still a drug dealer, then?"

"Most likely," Norah said, "but again, understand
the authorities can't prove it. If she is, she's very good
at it. Janet's been out of prison seven years and hasn't
been caught. Maybe she's not aligned with the Lobos
cartel. I think you should assume she's innocent until
proven otherwise. Many times, prison will change a
person for the better."

"She's really beautiful, isn't she?" Katie said, still
mesmerized by her mother's photo.

Iris heard the wistfulness in Katie's voice. "Yes, Janet
is very attractive, but so are you."

"We—look a lot alike, don't we?" She lifted her gaze
to Iris, whose face had gone tender with sympathy.

"Very much," Iris agreed. "Listen, Katie, no one in
this life is perfect. We all make awful mistakes. I hope,
like Norah, that your mother straightened out after leaving prison. And that she's gone on to become a successful businesswoman."

"Norah, do you have a phone number for her?" Katie
asked.

"I do." She handed Katie the information sheet. "Everything you want to know is here."

Feeling dizzy as the file with the information slipped

between her fingers, Katie stared down at it, unable to speak. Finally, after twenty-six years, she knew where her mother lived, what she did for a living and her phone number. God, how many times had she dreamed of this moment? Closing her eyes, Katie pressed the file to her breast. The only sounds she heard were her breath and her pounding heart. *My mother.* And all it would take was one phone call. One. Opening her eyes, Katie stared over at Norah, who had a very compassionate expression on her face. This was probably not the first time Norah had been hired to hunt down a missing parent.

"Thank you, Norah. This means the world to me. Truly, it does." Katie reached over and squeezed the woman's hand.

"I wish I had happier news for you, Katie. I never know where the leads will go or what will be revealed. It's always a journey."

Raising her brows, Katie placed the file on the desk. "That's it, isn't it? We're all on a journey?"

"It's lifelong," Iris agreed. "Would you like to ask Norah any more questions? She'll leave her full report with you."

"No…not right now." Katie managed a tight smile. "I need time just to take all of this in. It's…shocking."

"You can call me at any time, Katie," Norah said. She handed her a business card. "Iris has paid for my services. All the information I've shared with you is private. No one else will ever have it unless you decide to divulge it."

"That's good to know," Katie replied. "I don't think many of my friends would think as highly of me if they knew my mother had been in prison." Her voice fell and she rubbed her head. "I mean…"

"We know what you mean," Iris said. "Okay, we're

leaving. If you need me, you know where I am. If you want to talk, I'm here for you, Katie." She gave the young woman a warm look. "You're like another grand-daughter to me, Katie. You're beautiful, you have a good heart and you treat people right. That's why I wanted you here on the Elk Horn. You do good things for people and animals. And now, let me be here if you need someone to listen."

Katie stood when Iris rose from her chair and gently hugged her. "Thank you, Iris. I've always seen you as my fairy godmother who cares." Katie released her and held the woman's tear-filled gaze. She realized Iris was crying for her.

"You're not alone in this, Katie," was all Iris could choke out. After giving her a swift peck on the cheek, Iris walked to the sliding-glass door.

"Norah, thank you for all you've done," Katie said, her voice wobbly. "You've given me back my life, whether you realize it or not."

Warmly shaking Katie's hand, the investigator nodded. "Call me if you have questions, okay?"

"Okay." Katie watched the two women leave. Behind her, Sam shrieked. She knew from long experience that raptors could easily pick up on a human's emotions. And right now, she felt as if a tank had run its treads over her heart and torn it apart in her chest.

Sam chut-chut-chutted. He flapped his long wings from his perch.

"It's okay, Sam," she called. "I'm okay. Really, I am…"

The eagle tilted his head, his yellow eyes piercing as he studied Katie in the aisleway. His whistle carried loudly throughout the facility.

Tears formed in Katie's eyes as she walked back to her desk. Sam knew she wasn't all right. Staring at the pictures and the report, Katie released a ragged breath. Tears spilled silently down her drawn cheeks. Suddenly, the make-believe world she had lived in for twenty-six years had been forever shattered.

CHAPTER FIVE

SOME OF JOE'S HAPPINESS eroded as he entered the raptor facility the next morning. Katie was sitting at the desk, poring over a file. She quickly shut it, as if embarrassed to be caught looking into it. Her eyes were reddened. Had she been crying? Joe didn't expect the punch to his chest at seeing her so sad. Secretly, he was glad to see her again. "Good morning," Joe said, stepping through the glass doors. He pulled the canvas bag containing his equipment off his shoulder. "Where would you like me to stow this?"

His smiling face changed to one of worry. His gaze probed hers, as if silently asking her what was wrong. The file Norah had given her yesterday was beneath her hand. Nervously, Katie stood, leaving the file on her desk, and pointed to two nearby green metal lockers. "You can use the second locker next to my desk and put your equipment in there." Katie walked across the aisle to the weighing station where she pulled plastic bags of meat out of the refrigerator.

"Okay," Joe said. Later, when Katie wasn't around, he would try to see what was contained in the file. He heard the chirps of welcome from the raptors. Sam's chutting was a lot louder. Glancing down the aisle, he asked, "How are the birds this morning?"

"Fine, fine." Katie's hands shook as she finished putting either mouse meat or rabbit meat into the smaller bags. Her gut churned and she felt nauseous. She'd completely forgotten Joe was coming in for his first day of work at 8:00 a.m. She wasn't emotionally prepared. She'd slept poorly because of nightmares in which Janet Bergstrom screamed at her to go away, not even to try to make contact. Katie had awakened at 3:00 a.m., sobbing into her pillow. She hadn't been able to get back to sleep after that.

She hoped Joe wouldn't see she'd been crying. Every time she recalled yesterday's conversation with Norah, tears would form. Girding herself, Katie forced down her feelings. She had to train Joe today. She heard the locker door open and close and turned as Joe pulled on his gauntlet. His handsome face had darkened with concern. Of course he could see she'd been crying. *Great.* Not exactly the foot she wanted to get off on with this trainee.

"Everything okay?" Joe asked, keeping his voice even. Katie appeared disheveled this morning. Her black hair was mussed, as if she hadn't combed it. Her face was pale, redness rimming her blue eyes. An acute desire to reach out and touch her shoulder took him by surprise.

"Yes, yes, everything is fine," Katie managed. Her voice sounded off-key even to her. Moving to the aisle, she said, "Joe, will you start on the left and go to the first mew? I'm a little out of sorts and the birds will feel it. Bring them up here one at a time. You weigh them, I'll write down the numbers and then I'll feed them. Afterward, you can return them to their mews. Okay?" She searched his pensive features. His green eyes were speculative and focused on her. A lump stubbornly remained in her throat. Grazing the area with her fingers, Katie added a limp smile to go along with her request.

"Sure, no problem." Joe turned and walked down to the first mew on the left. The name *Moon* was on the cage door. Below it: *Barn Owl*. He opened the mew. Moon was not to be seen and Joe knew she would be found in her wooden nest box since owls slept during the day. He peeked in and kept his voice soft.

"Moon? You ready to be weighed?" Joe saw her heart-shaped white face lift. The barn owl had been sitting on the floor of the nest box, fast asleep. She revealed her round black eyes and opened her beak, as if to yawn. Joe forced himself to focus on the owl. He wanted to know why Katie was so upset. It had something to do with that file. His mind whirled with possibilities as he gently tapped the front of Moon's box. A trained raptor knew the tapping meant they were to sit on the glove of the falconer. Moon stared sleepily at him.

"I know, you haven't had your coffee yet, Moon, but you gotta come to my glove," he told her with a grin.

Katie heard Joe talking to Moon. She looked around the corner. Joe was peering into the nest box, his glove even with the opening. She heard laughter in his tone as he spoke quietly to the owl. Her heart suddenly opened. Instead of pain, she felt a sense of calm. She studied Joe for a moment, really appraised his features and manners. He was dressed in a long-sleeved white cotton cowboy shirt and Levi's. His dark brown hair was short and had been recently washed. She found herself liking his quiet demeanor and he certainly knew what he was doing with the raptors. Moon peered drowsily out of her nest box. Then she looked up at Joe, studying him. This was the first time Moon had seen him. He kept his glove on the lip of the box so she would climb onto it when she was ready.

"Have you handled many owls?" Katie called.

"No," he said, glancing over his shoulder. Katie was standing in the aisle, a bag of food in her hand. It upset him to see how wan she looked. "Anything I should know about Moon?"

"Owls are the opposite of hawks, falcons and eagles. They're slower. Owls think a lot about something before they do it, unlike other raptors. Moon is memorizing your face right now. All birds memorize. Keep talking softly to her, gain her trust and eventually she'll climb onto your glove."

Nodding, Joe kept up his quiet banter with the sleepy barn owl. Moon's white breast feathers were dotted with caramel and black spots. "Listen, Moon, we got a bunch of hungry hawks, falcons and eagles in here. Are you going to hold up the breakfast line for all of them?" He grinned as Moon tilted her head, peering intently up at him. Then, unexpectedly, she hopped firmly on his glove. Her claws dug in, she fluffed her feathers and seemed content. Joe slowly eased her away from the nest box. Once out of the mew, he shut the door and walked Moon to the weighing station.

Moon hopped on the perch to be weighed. Her attention was on Katie, who stood next to Joe. Moon's focus was on her opening the bag that contained some delicious dead white mice; the barn owl keenly eyed her breakfast.

Joe read off the numbers and Katie wrote them down on Moon's file. The barn owl opened her beak and began a begging cry to Katie.

"How old is Moon?" Joe asked, watching Katie pull out a dead mouse by its tail.

"She's three years old." Katie lifted the mouse up and Moon gobbled it down in three gulps.

"How did you acquire her?"

"Moon was discovered in a rancher's barn. She'd fallen out of her nest as a baby. The fall broke her right leg. The rancher discovered her on the floor, picked her up and called me. I drove over and got her." Katie smiled softly as she fed Moon a second mouse. "She was nothing but a ball of fuzz and fluff. So ugly but so cute…"

Smiling, Joe enjoyed the huskiness of Katie's voice. It calmed him, yet excited him at the same time. She worked quietly and without any swift movements around Moon. "And she became an educational bird because of her broken leg?"

"Yes, the break was an open fracture." She glanced over at him. "Moon's fracture was so bad the vet said she could never be released into the wild. If Moon pounced on prey, it would break her leg again." Katie closed the bag and gently ran her index finger down the soft feathers of Moon's breast. The barn owl gave her a begging look for another mouse. "No more, Moon. Your eyes are bigger than your stomach. Go ahead, Joe. Take her back to her nest box."

Joe placed his glove next to the perch for Moon to step upon. The owl continued to gaze adoringly over at Katie.

With a slight chuckle, Katie said, "No, Moon, I'm not taking you back to your box. Joe is." She tapped the thumb area of Joe's proffered gauntlet. "Come on, you have to get used to having him take you back to your home."

The owl hopped on Joe's glove.

"Does Moon understand English?" he asked teasingly as he slowly lifted the gauntlet with Moon on board.

Shaking her head, Katie managed a half smile. "No, but these birds are so psychic they pick up on what we want. As soon as you put Moon in her nest box, she'll go back to sleep."

"Right." Joe saw that Katie looked a bit more perky than before. He knew raptors had a phenomenal ability to change a person's mood. It was bird magic, he decided. Once in the mew, the barn owl leaped from his glove back into her nest box, trundled around, sat down and promptly closed her eyes.

Joe moved to the next mew, which contained two Harris's hawks from Arizona. "Who's first?" he called.

Katie looked around the corner. "Take Maggie first. She always wears the red jesses on her legs. Her mate, Mac, wears blue ones."

"Got it," Joe said, opening the mew. He knew the black-and-reddish-colored hawks from the southwestern desert of Arizona were among the few social hawks in the world. Many generations in the same family lived together. Maggie flew to a cottonwood branch, which acted as her perch. She was more than ready to hop on Joe's glove. The hawk's eyes were twinkling and he liked the ebullient energy around the Harris hawk. In the meantime, Mac sat on the back perch, shrieking and flapping his wings because he was going to be left behind.

After shutting the mew, Joe brought up Maggie to the weight table. The hawk, unlike the owl, was fast. Before he even got his glove to the scale, Maggie flew to the perch. If hawks could smile, Joe thought she was smiling. "She's hungry?"

Katie laughed softly. "Not really. Maggie, you'll find, has a mind of her own."

"I guess," Joe said with a smile as he leaned down to read the hawk's weight. "I like women with minds of their own."

Katie jotted down the numbers. Joe made her want to talk, to be closer. She liked the warmth that exuded from him like sunlight. While she felt great around him, there was also this black hole. She got the feeling she would never escape the depression hounding her. And yet, with Joe nearby, she felt a niggle of hope. How could he lift her spirits when she felt so despondent? After Katie fed the hawk, Joe took Maggie back to the mew and brought up Mac.

As they worked seamlessly, Joe felt driven to try to establish a more personal connection with Katie. He knew he had to do it for professional reasons. Last night, after talking to his boss in Washington, D.C., Joe had hung up the phone not feeling good about it. The FBI was convinced Katie was a criminal. His gut told him she wasn't, but he couldn't convince Roger. At least, not yet. And every time Joe looked at Katie, his heart lurched in his chest. The reaction continued to surprise him. Joe had no idea what it was all about.

Next came Sam the eagle. Katie asked, "Do you have an eagle gauntlet?"

"No, I don't." Joe grimaced. "Do you have an extra glove? Maybe a little bigger one?"

Katie walked over to the first green metal locker and opened it. The locker was seven feet high and she stretched up on tiptoes to grab a dark-colored leather gauntlet sitting on the top shelf. "Yes, here's a man's-size eagle gauntlet."

"Good," Joe said with relief. Their fingers touched. Instantly, he felt a mild electric shock travel through his hand. Joe hid his reaction and took the glove. He pulled his off and placed it on the desk next to the file. "Thanks. I'm going to have to order my own eagle glove."

"Yes, you will," Katie said. "Now, Sam will be eager to get out, so expect his testosterone, okay?"

Joe tugged on the glove. It fitted right up to his elbow, longer than the regular gauntlet. "I wonder if he'll be as aggressive as that harpy eagle Eddie has?"

Katie shrugged. "I don't know. I've never handled a harpy. They have a fierce reputation and Sam, although he's a boy eagle, isn't aggressive. He's just confident, is all." She met Joe's warm green gaze and her pulse quickened. Miraculously, the pain she'd been feeling in her heart dissolved. What kind of magic did Joe Gannon possess? The birds, thus far, had responded wonderfully to his quiet demeanor. Was she also responding to him? Confused, Katie didn't have time to figure it all out. The report on her mother hung like a lead cape over her. It was impossible for Katie to sort through all the emotions.

"Well, I guess I'll find out," Joe joked. Some of the darkness in her blue eyes lessened. And when the corners of her soft, beautiful mouth lifted, Joe felt happiness. Tearing his gaze from hers, he forced himself down the aisle toward the chut-chut-chutting Sam.

Katie watched Joe handle the excited golden eagle. No one like being fed more than Sam. Joe guided the eagle onto the glove. When Sam unfurled his wings, the seven-foot wingspan was enough to rattle any falconer. Yet, as Sam spread his wings, Joe stood quietly and continued to wrap the jesses between his fingers. This was one raptor that he couldn't trust to stay on his glove to be weighed. Eagles were at the top of the food chain, which explained Sam's bold and confident nature. A trickle of relief moved through her as Joe successfully brought Sam out of his mew.

"Nice going," she praised Joe.

"He's a cupcake compared to the harpy."

"Sam's still a handful, though." Katie met Joe's gaze and melted beneath his widening smile. Man and eagle looked comfortable with one another. "You're a good fit for Sam. He likes you," Katie said, turning to the weight table and bringing the large scale forward for Sam to perch upon.

"I like him. He's a beauty and really, very well-behaved."

"Mmm," Katie said, standing aside. The weight area was ten feet wide and when Sam spread his wings, the air rushed by her head and lifted strands of her hair. Joe guided him expertly onto the perch. Sam ruffled his bronze feathers and chirped pleadingly toward Katie.

"Weight first, big boy," she told the eagle, "then food. You know the drill…."

Chuckling, Joe remained close, the jesses strung between the fingers of his glove. One never allowed an eagle loose in a facility. If he did get loose, he'd destroy his wing feathers because of the cramped quarters. Eagles had to be kept in a controlled state while indoors. Joe read the weight.

"Great," Katie said, picking up the large plastic bag that contained half a dead rabbit.

Sam chutted excitedly, watching her open the bag.

"Joe, get Sam on your glove. I don't feed him on the perch."

Nodding, he tapped his glove. Sam leaped onto it, his talons curving around Joe's wrist. Lifting and turning him so he faced Katie, Joe held his arm still for the feeding. A sixteen-pound eagle put a lot of stress on anyone's arm. Sam gobbled the rabbit as if starved. Joe's lower arm muscles began to burn from the weight of the raptor. He was glad when feeding was complete.

And he was relieved when Sam was back in his mew. As he shook his arm, he noticed Katie watching him.

"He's heavy."

"Yeah."

"You okay?"

"Sure. Who's next?"

"We have the tundra peregrines, Quest and Harlequin, on the other side of the aisle to feed now."

Joe liked that she used *we* instead of *I*. "I'll go get the first one."

For the next half hour, they worked with one another to weigh and feed all the raptors. But during this time, his mind kept going back to the file folder on Katie's desk. It was unmarked and obviously important. What was in it? He saw an edge of a black-and-white photo sticking out of it. Maybe he could ease into it, try to establish a more personal rapport. "I told my mom and dad I got the job yesterday."

"Oh?" Katie wrote down the numbers on Harlequin. "Were they happy for you?"

"Yes, they were." He grinned. "I have a true story to tell you." He wanted to lift her mood. "My mom loves birds and she has a green parakeet named Skippy."

"Is that an earned name? As in skipping out of town? Escaping his cage?" Katie asked, hearing the warmth in Joe's low voice. She fed Harlequin and kept glancing over at Joe. She was amazed at their teamwork. Truly, he was good with the birds and that lifted a lot of worry off her shoulders.

Joe laughed a little. "Yes. Skippy likes to escape out of the house any time he sees a door open. He's been doing this for five years, now. The last time he escaped, Mom had to go next door to a neighbor rancher who had a male parakeet called Zeus. Skippy would fly over

there and sit outside the window where Zeus's cage
was and chirp for hours. I think she was in love with
him. They set Skippy's cage outside the window and
she eventually flew into it because she was hungry or
thirsty. Then my mom shut the cage door quickly and
Skippy's wanderings were over until the next time."

Katie laughed over the picture Joe painted. She finished feeding Harlequin, who was looking for more
handouts. "Skippy is a bold little girl! Either that or she
was helplessly in love with Zeus."

"The plot thickens, though. There's a local red-tailed
hawk in the area and he usually sits in a cottonwood
tree near the front door of my parents' home waiting
and watching. He's aware Skippy escapes and is just
waiting for the right day and moment to snatch her."

"Not good for Skippy," Katie agreed. She felt more
of her gloom lift. Joe was lucky to have parents. Did he
know that? Katie smiled up at him as he lifted Harlequin off the perch. When he smiled back, she felt as if
light were lancing through her inner darkness.

Joe brought Quest up to be weighed and fed. As they
worked, he asked, "My mother has always loved para-
keets. I was raised with one around the house. Did you
ever have a parakeet when you were a kid?"

A shaft of pain struck. Swallowing, Katie found
herself blurting out the truth. "My growing up years
weren't exactly great. I never had a pet of any kind."
She compressed her lips to stop the flow of words. What
on earth had she just said? Katie was normally very secretive about her childhood. She looked over quickly
at Joe, dismayed at his perplexed gaze. Who wanted to
hear her sad story? She was sorry she'd said anything.
"Most kids don't have great childhoods."

A flush raced across Katie's pale skin. Joe saw her

gulp and quickly avoid his eyes as she fed Quest. He'd touched a nerve. He knew from her record that her childhood had been a massive, ongoing car wreck. How she'd survived amazed him because she seemed so damn fragile and otherworldly. His job was to get her to talk and trust him. Joe searched his memory for something that wasn't as prickly a subject that she might respond to.

"Life can be hard."

His voice was low with understanding. Katie's anxiety shifted and dissolved. He stood with the peregrine on his glove. She felt a powerful sense of protection emanating from the man. The knot in her stomach lessened. "Your life as a Marine Corps officer was very dangerous."

Joe knew she wanted to avoid talking about her childhood. Okay, he'd go where she wanted. "I liked what I did in the Marines, Katie." There, he'd used her name. Joe had seen an instant response as her name rolled off his lips in a husky whisper. Katie's expression changed instantly and more of the darkness left her exquisite dark blue eyes. Katie was deeply touched by the simplest things, he realized. "I liked being a leader. And I had good men working under my command. We shared a common bond and brotherhood."

"Yes, but you nearly died in Afghanistan."

"Came close," Joe agreed, one corner of his mouth tucking inward. "I'll be back." He went to put Quest away.

Katie waited until Joe brought up Hank, the redtailed hawk. The raptor was eyeing Joe, as if deciding whether he liked him. Then she smiled as Hank ruffled his plumage. Yep, Joe had won him over. After weighing the hawk, she said, "I'm sure your parents were worried when you were wounded. I can't think of a more awful place to be as a parent."

He liked her sensitivity. Katie could feel for other people and realize the pressures and stresses upon them. Originally, he'd thought she might be completely self-centered, as drug addicts and children of drug addicts sometimes were. He was wrong and the discovery made him happy for no accountable reason. "Yes, my poor mother was stripping gears to find out about my medical condition. Eventually, they flew to Landstuhl Medical Center in Germany to be with me."

"Wow," Katie said, feeding Hank, "that must have cost them a lot of money."

"It did. But you do anything for the ones you love. They cashed in their retirement savings. I was one happy guy when they showed up. I'd just come out of surgery, and to wake up and see my mom and dad at my bedside was a huge plus for me."

"I can imagine. I can remember so many times when I wished my parents had been there for me."

Katie was sorry she'd said anything.

Gently, he said, "What do you mean?" It was an opening. Would she go there? Fear and anxiety suddenly came over her expression. His gut tightened. Could someone fake such a visceral reaction? Joe didn't know. Katie looked genuinely stressed over her admission.

Katie looked away. "Don't mind me, Joe. I'm emotionally off today. I'm just not myself. Go ahead and take Hank back to his mew."

So close and yet, so far away... Joe nodded and carried Hank to his mew. For a split second, he'd thought Katie would divulge something about her past to him. And then she'd closed up like a safe.

In the last mew was a female great horned owl with

the name of Athena. This owl was the largest of its
kind in the United States. She was multicolored with
black, white, gray and brown feathers. Athena's sharply
pointed feather ears made her appear alert. She was
snoozing on a large perch at the back of the mew when
Joe disturbed her. Opening her huge round eyes, Athena
stared unblinkingly at him.

"Is Athena a cranky sort when you wake her up?"
he called to Katie

Katie walked to the entrance. "No, why?"

"She's giving me a funny look."

"Oh, Athena is a really slow awakener. If you think
Moon was slow, Athena's ten times worse."

Glancing toward her, Joe grinned and said, "Hey, I
relate to that. When I was a teenager, my mother used
to pound on my door forever to wake me up. I was always a deep, late sleeper."

"And you were probably late more than once to catch
the school bus?" Katie guessed, feeling warmth drench
her as he gave her that very male smile. Hungrily, she
absorbed the care banked in Joe's eyes. His mouth was
beautifully shaped and she found herself staring at it.
Inwardly, Katie felt her heart beat a little faster as he
shared that intimate smile with her. It made her feel
desired. Those unexpected sensations flummoxed her.
Katie didn't know what to do. Joe made her feel special
when she knew she was not.

"Yep, you guessed it. My mother about pulled all the
hair out of her head during my teen years. I was a late
sleeper. Even two alarm clocks wouldn't wake me up."
He chuckled fondly over those memories. Athena finally
walked up to where he had his gauntlet placed against
the branch. She fluffed her feathers repeatedly and then
climbed, one foot at a time, onto Joe's proffered glove.

"Are you still like that?" Katie wondered as Joe walked to the mew door.

"No. I got the stuffing kicked out of me in college. After graduation and joining the Marine Corps, I was one of the lightest sleepers in the world."

"And when you came home to visit your parents, I wonder if your mom wasn't surprised?" Katie laughed.

Joe allowed Athena to hop onto the perch to be weighed. The owl began whistling softly at Katie, who was holding a leg of a rabbit for her. Joe read the numbers and she jotted them down. She held up the rabbit leg. Athena opened her mouth and promptly grabbed it. Katie was always amazed how a long foreleg of a rabbit could disappear into the owl's throat so quickly, but it did. Once the meat and bone were gobbled down, Athena fluffed and then her eyelids half closed.

"Oh, she's a very satisfied owl," Katie assured Joe with a grin. "When her eyes go to half-mast like that it means she's not only filled up, but very happy."

Joe watched the owl. "I don't have much experience with owls and I'm glad you're sharing all of these behavior patterns with me."

"I love owls. They're slow, conservative, but they miss nothing. Athena is particularly good with teens. Moon is just the opposite. She loves the kindergarteners and younger children."

"They're just like people, aren't they?"

"That's the truth," Katie said, putting the leftover bags into the refrigerator.

Joe was about to settle his gauntlet against the perch when Athena suddenly flapped and flew up into the air. Surprised, he jerked back as the owl's wing barely grazed his cheek as she sailed past him. He heard Katie sigh, but his focus was on the huge owl. Athena flew around the office area, her wings stirring up gusts of wind. As she wheeled and dipped toward the desk, the file folder flew open, papers and photos tumbling into the air. Joe's eyes instantly narrowed. One of the black-and-white photos flipped and turned right side up as it landed on the concrete floor in front of the desk. A mug shot? He barely got to see it as Athena flew past him and headed down the aisle.

Katie gasped as the file flew into the air. The last thing she wanted was for Joe to see what was in the folder! Her gut tightened as one of the mug shots of her mother landed on the floor. "Joe, get Athena," she ordered.

Joe hurried down the aisle, his glove lifted above his head so Athena could land on it. Katie scrambled and gathered all the strewn photos and papers. Jamming them inside the folder, she quickly shoved it into the top desk drawer. Her heart pounded, and she looked upward. Had Joe seen the photo of her mother? If he had, he would know it was a prison picture. Maybe she was overthinking. She craned her neck and looked down the aisle. Joe had coaxed Athena back onto his glove and had taken her to the mew.

Pushing strands of hair off her brow, Katie stood by her desk and tried to shake off her anxiety. She didn't want Joe to know her mother had been in prison. She quickly smoothed down her hair and walked over to the weight station. Breathing erratically, she tried to calm down.

By the time Joe reached the office area, he glanced to his left. The file was gone. So was the picture from the floor. Looking to the right, he saw Katie cleaning up the weight and feeding station. Her fingers were trembling. She seemed out of breath and he could feel her tension.

After taking off the glove, he placed it back into his locker. Right now, he sensed Katie needed some space. Where had she put the file? The top drawer wasn't completely closed. Had Katie put it in there? Joe would have to be patient and wait. His boss was behaving as if struck by a bolt of lightning. She worked swiftly, shifting from one foot to another. "Would you like me to start cleaning out the mews?" he asked in a quiet tone.

Katie barely turned her head. "Yes. The cleaning supplies and tools are at the other end in that gray metal locker, Joe."

He couldn't see much of her face, but he noticed she was paler than before, if that was possible. What the hell was in that folder? Curiosity ate at him but he knew better than to pry right now. Katie would have to go to lunch and when she did, he'd make an excuse to stay behind, rifle through the desk and locate the mysterious file. Joe moved down the aisle, giving her the space she needed.

As he opened the cleaning locker, Joe wondered if the file was an order from Los Lobos cartel. Had her mother sent her photos of someone she was to meet? Maybe to swap guns or drugs with them? Clearly, the file wasn't meant for eyes other than hers. He unwound the green garden hose because he'd be giving each raptor fresh bath and drinking water. Stringing the hose down the aisle, he decided to start near the office entrance and work his way toward the rear. That way, he could rewind the hose as he went and it wouldn't become a tripping hazard.

From time to time as Joe cleaned the first mew, he'd glance toward the entrance. Katie was walking back and forth, clearly agitated. He really began to feel sorry for her. The more he saw of her, the less he believed she was the drug-dealer type. A field agent knew how to shove down all his emotions, control his body language and keep his face carefully arranged so no one could read his intentions. Not so with Katie. In many ways, she had a falcon's temperament. Falcons were supersensitive to everything and would overreact. That was why they were hooded until they were flown. The outside world impinged upon them too much and they became flighty, restless and agitated. Just like Katie.

He'd bide his time. Lunch would come in three hours. Then he'd find out what was in the file.

CHAPTER SIX

"I HOPE YOU HAVE something to report," Roger Hager said.

Joe moved uncomfortably at his kitchen table. "I do." He told his boss about this morning's incident with the file on Katie's desk.

"You said you saw a mug shot on the floor?"

Mouth twisting in frustration, Joe said, "Shortly after it happened, Katie sent me outside to put the feathers and scat into the compost pile at the other end of the building. When I came back, she was nowhere to be found. I made a quick search in the desk for the file, but it was gone. When she came back, she seemed calmer. I suspect she walked the file over to her suite at the ranch house."

"Obviously."

"Yes, but I'm not familiar enough with her routine to know where I might look. I can't just waltz into the Mason ranch house and search for it."

"It's good to confirm Katie's living at the Elk Horn Ranch. We have her foster mother's address as hers."

"Yes, Iris Mason has given her a suite at the main ranch. I think she got Allison Mason's old suite. Allison is Rudd Mason's ex-wife and she's in prison for twenty-five years."

"And unless you get invited into Iris Mason's home, you can't snoop around."

Joe heard the disappointment in Hager's gravelly tone. "That's right. But why would she have a mug shot? That's what confuses me. Law-enforcement agencies might give one to reporters for transmission on a news story, but they don't give them to people off the street."

"Perhaps Janet Bergstrom gave it to her daughter."

"Maybe," Joe said, worried. "I know that's the right logic, but I'm having a helluva time convincing myself, much less you, that Katie is in cahoots with her mother and the cartel." Frustration deepened in his tone. "She's just so... I don't know the words to use, Roger. Katie appears innocent and almost otherworldly. Her world revolves around her raptors. She's very trusting. I don't see drug-addict behavior. She drinks only coffee and she doesn't smoke. I'd almost use the word *teetotaler* to describe her."

"It's early in this investigation, Joe. And you know a sweet, pretty face hooked up with innocence doesn't mean anything one way or another." Roger sighed. "The good news is you're in. You're going to have to do the dog work and just wait and watch. That mug shot is provocative."

"It is." Yet, Joe's heart was screaming at him that Katie was not involved. He felt torn over continuing his undercover work with her.

"It sounds to me as if trust is a big issue with her. You need to be there for her, become sympathetic, be someone she wants to talk with when she's feeling bad."

"I know, I know. It didn't go well this morning, though. When I started to ask her questions, Katie retreated."

"It's your first day," Roger said. "In this kind of work, things don't unfold neatly or on time. Be a good falconer, give her the help she requires and let time yield whatever is there."

"I will," Joe promised. "I'll call you in a week unless something important comes up." Pressing the end button on his phone, Joe pushed the chair back from the table. Getting up, he ran his fingers through his hair, aggravated by the mug shot he'd seen. Why did Katie have it? How did she get it? And what else was in that file folder? Joe had seen a number of pages with single-line sentences upon them. Moving to the counter, he noticed night had fallen in Jackson Hole. The sky was a dark red ribbon along the western horizon.

It was time to eat, but he wasn't hungry. His gut churned over whether Katie was truly as innocent as she seemed. Joe opened the refrigerator and drew out some sliced turkey. He wasn't the world's best cook. In fact, the Marine Corps had fed him for so many years he honestly didn't know how to make much except sandwiches. After slapping some turkey onto whole wheat bread, he added hot mustard and iceberg lettuce and placed it on a plate to take into the living room to watch TV. He wondered what Katie was doing at that very moment.

KATIE SAT IN HER SUITE, the file on her mother across her knees. It was nearly 9:00 p.m. and she was anything but tired.

After Allison Mason had been imprisoned for trying to kill Iris and Kam, Iris had had the suite completely redecorated. Allison had been all about gaudiness and bling: Katie wanted soothing cream and light blue to remind her of the sky her raptors loved to fly in. Iris had given all the furniture to charity and now simple Scandinavian birch chairs, table and a couch graced the open and airy suite instead. Katie loved nature and had a special love for wood products. The suite gave her a sense of safety and the quiet she always needed.

Memories of her many foster families shadowed her as she carried the file into the kitchen. Often, she had been one of many foster kids in a family. She'd never had a room of her own, generally having to share with another teen girl who'd insisted on loud, blaring music. The sound always drove Katie out of the house and she wandered the streets in search of a little quiet. Silence always soothed her raw nerves. Loud or constant noises made her feel raw and vulnerable.

Katie poured herself a glass of water and sat down at the table. She opened the file and stared at the two mug shots. Why was her mother a drug addict? What had driven her into that kind of life? Her mother's hair was messy, as if it was rarely combed or cared for. Her mouth was turned down at the corners. The early lines around her mouth that told Katie she'd had a hard life. Katie's heart pulled one way and then another. This woman had carried her for nine months. She was her mother. And yet, Katie automatically felt disgust and shame over her mother's sordid life. Why did her mother live in such violence? What drove her in that direction?

Sipping the water, Katie frowned. Was she like her birth mother? Her stomach twisted in fear. Did she have it in her to be an addict or a trouble-seeker? Had her mother been on drugs while she'd carried Katie? It all scared her.

She looked around the quiet kitchen, which was painted a soft yellow color. Night had fallen and all she saw out the kitchen window was darkness. It worried her that she had her mother's genes and that her unknown father was more than likely a drug addict, too. There might be no escape at all for her.

Katie desperately needed to talk to someone about all this. She thought her way through the few friends she had. Oh, she had plenty of acquaintances, but really, other than Iris and Donna, whom she trusted with her life, Katie couldn't name one other person she could openly confide in. Closing her eyes, she relaxed against the birch chair. Joe Gannon's face slowly materialized behind her lids. A sigh slipped from between her lips. He was so good with the raptors. And he'd been gentle and sensitive toward her. She'd never met a man quite like him. Katie opened her eyes and sat up.

What was it about Joe that she automatically trusted? Was it his low, measured voice? His easy smile that came often? The crinkles appearing at the corners of his eyes when he smiled? His eyes drew her the most. They were an unusual green color and Katie felt as though she could see into his soul. He was a kind person; more than once, he'd gently brushed one of the raptor's feathered breasts and she'd seen the hawks and falcons respond.

Tired yet wired, Katie sipped the water. Could she trust Joe enough to confide in him? He was, after all, an employee, not a friend or confidant. Yet, Katie wanted him to be all of that. Confused, she closed the file. Tomorrow would come soon enough.

There was a lot of work to do in preparation for the raptor show at the ranch the next afternoon. Joe would have to learn the rhythm and demands of their show days. The edginess within subsided a bit. She realized that when Joe was around, her anxiety was nonexistent. How could that be? Katie couldn't begin to understand. She finished off the glass of water and stood up. It was time for a long, hot bath and then off to bed.

JOE SAW KATIE looking much better when he walked into the facility the next morning. She was opening Sam's mew.

"Good morning," he called, lifting his hand in greeting.

She looked hot in her T-shirt that outlined her upper body to perfection. She was lean and her breasts were small. Joe appreciated the way her jeans outlined her shapely lower body and long legs. Her black hair was pulled into a ponytail and she was wearing a black baseball cap.

"Hi, Joe. Come on down." Katie liked the way Gannon walked. It reminded her of a cougar moving silently through the woods on the prowl. Today, he wore a white cotton long-sleeved shirt with pearl buttons. His hips were narrow, legs powerful beneath his jeans. His gaze met hers and she managed a slight smile of welcome.

"You've already got everyone fed and weighed?" he wondered as he halted nearby, hands on his hips.

"Yes."

"What time did you get here?"

"Six o'clock."

Brows raising, Joe whistled. Sam chirped from his perch, head tilted, giving Joe an interested look. "Uh-oh, I shouldn't whistle, should I?"

Katie smiled. "It can cause quite a stir." She motioned behind her as both peregrine falcons answered his whistle, too.

"I'll try not to do that," Joe promised. He searched Katie's features. Today, her eyes were not red-rimmed. In fact, she seemed calm and at peace. He still wanted to ask her about the photo, but it would break any trust he was trying to build with her. He stuffed down the need and sternly told himself to remain patient. As his gaze fell on Katie's full mouth, the corners lifted, and he felt his lower body go suddenly hot with yearning. He didn't dare be drawn to this woman. She was his mission, not a potential lover.

"This morning we're going to prepare for the show we put on at the dude ranch once a week. Iris said if I could entertain the guests with a weekly show, she'd consider her money well-spent on this facility."

"What a deal," Joe said, impressed. "Do you have a vet on staff, too?"

Katie kept her hand on Sam's door. She'd opened it, but she didn't want to leave any distance between it and the mew. Sam might try to fly out of it. "We have two vets who offer their services free to us."

"Yeah, but they have clients who help offset their time when they tend to an injured raptor. You don't."

Nodding, Katie felt herself being pulled into the warmth in Joe's green eyes. He had thick, short black lashes that made the iris seem a richer color, if that was possible. His pupils were huge and black. He didn't miss much. "Vets are key for all raptor rehabilitators here in the U.S. Without their goodwill, none of these birds would survive. I'm lucky to have the two vets here in Jackson Hole who assist me."

Joe felt a frisson of excitement because this morning Katie was talking easily with him, unlike yesterday morning when she had clearly been stressed and upset. "You do have luck."

Shrugging, Katie replied, "I had no luck until I came to the raptor facility a decade ago."

Joe watched Sam unfurl his wings and flap them several times. The golden eagle clearly wanted to get out and fly. He took a risk and gave Katie a warm, concerned look. "Are you feeling better?"

Her fingers tightened momentarily on the mew door, but his caring eased her nerves. Her heart expanded. She fought the desire to speak openly about yesterday. She licked her lips, somehow managing to speak. "Yes, I'm better. Thanks for asking."

"Sure?" Cocking his head, Joe purposely held her shy blue gaze. Katie was clearly an introvert. He gave her a slow smile and her eyes widened in response. There was an inexplicable magical connection between them. His heart beat harder for a moment.

Katie was so tired of hiding from everyone. She'd done it all her life. What little of herself hadn't been gobbled up by her abandonment, she'd selfishly guarded against the harshness of the world around her. Joe's green gaze was warm and inviting. She could see his sincerity. Rubbing her chin, she said in a choked voice, "I—I was just having a bad day, Joe. There are times when it really tears me up that my mother abandoned me at birth and yesterday was one of those days."

Joe kept his face carefully arranged. The change in Katie's expression brought a completely unexpected reaction out of him. He wanted to sweep Katie into his arms. The desire stunned him. As he studied her expression, he saw her raw vulnerability. He realized she had opened up to him. Though he wanted at least to reach out and touch her sagging shoulder, Joe fiercely told himself no. He couldn't touch Katie. It might be interpreted as invasive. "That's a really tough road to walk," he sympathized.

Katie felt the wings of her heart opening wider to his compassionate response. "I guess I never expected anyone to know what it's like to be without a mother and father, but I feel you do."

"I can't walk in your shoes, Katie. I can only try to

understand how alone you probably feel most of the time." Joe peered deeply into her blue gaze. He'd never thought he'd have such a powerful, instinctive need to protect a woman. Katie stood before him with every emotion clearly written across her face. Feeling guilty, Joe tried to tell himself he had to play this part with her, even though the real person within him wanted to protect and care for her. He saw the devastation of loss in her gaze and it affected him in ways he never expected.

"You're only the third person to try and understand what I've gone through. Iris and Donna are the others. Iris adopted Rudd, her son, so she knows through experience what a child who has been given up feels like." Connecting with his green gaze, she asked, "How do you know? You have a mother and father who love you."

It was Joe's turn to shrug. One corner of his mouth lifted. "I had several Marines in my company over in Afghanistan who grew up as foster children. They were always getting in trouble one way or another. I made it my business to find out why they were so angry and acted out all the time. I sat down with each of them and asked about his background. Every one of them saw himself as having been abandoned by his birth parents. I realized that not knowing where you came from can have a permanent, scarring effect on a person."

Touched by his story, Katie asked, "Were you able to help them?"

"I think so," Joe replied. "In each case, these men felt left out. After talking with a psychiatrist at headquarters in Kabul, I got a better understanding of what was driving them. I worked with the sergeants of their squads to get them personally invested in different ways so they felt part of something greater. The military is a family of sorts."

He seemed like such a caring man. Katie stopped herself from walking those few feet into Joe's arms. She knew on some instinctive level that if she did he'd open his arms and allow her to lean against him. But she just couldn't. She swallowed against a lump forming in her throat. "You were like a father figure to them. You must have played such a positive role in their lives."

"If the Marine psychiatrist at headquarters hadn't guided me, I wouldn't understand one tenth of what I do." He held up his hands and added, "Not that I know everything. I don't."

"You're a humble man."

Joe grinned a little. "I might have been a captain in charge of running a company of a hundred and forty men, but I'm not a psychiatrist. I feel I'm pretty good at assessing a person, abilities and all, but the abandonment issues my men had on my first tour threw me. I had to get help because I honestly didn't understand what it meant to be abandoned by a parent."

"It's a stain. You never get rid of it. You can't pretend it's not there, either. Every time I see children with their parents, my heart tears in pain." Katie touched her chest. She lowered her gaze because Joe's eyes suddenly sharpened. "I find myself jealous of kids who have parents. I feel this anger and rage toward my mother and father who threw me away. I have a lot of anger. And I sure wasn't a peach to those foster parents who tried to make me feel like a part of their families."

"I had one private who had a similar story to yours, Katie. He was always getting in trouble with his foster families. In fact, he had quite a few run-ins with the law. A police captain gave him a choice. He told the kid at eighteen either to join the Marine Corps or get thrown into federal prison for a year."

"The police captain helped him, Joe. Tough love. I wish…I wish I'd had that kind of intervention…."

Hearing the bereft tone in her voice, Joe forced himself to keep his hands at his sides. For a moment, Katie looked utterly lost. And then she changed. She straightened, lifted her head and shook off the deep, wounding emotions that lived within her. "From what I understand," he said carefully, "Iris Mason was the captain who helped you change your life. Didn't she help you find yourself with the raptors?"

Katie liked Gannon's perceptiveness. "Actually, my lifesaver was Donna Pierce, my last foster parent. I was wandering around the state fair when I was sixteen, angry and resentful. Donna was a falconer and held an eagle license. She and her volunteers were putting on a raptor program at the fair to educate people as to why they shouldn't shoot these birds. I remember standing at the edge of the huge crowd, in awe. I'd never seen a falcon or a hawk fly. I started to cry and I didn't know why. Donna saw me, but she was busy putting on the show. I ran away from the crowd, found a place to hide. I cried for so long my throat ached. I rarely cried, Joe, but seeing those birds fly just triggered something so visceral within me, it was all I could do."

Joe frowned, noticing the bewilderment in her eyes. "Maybe the birds represented a freedom you never had?"

She dragged in a deep breath. "Yes…exactly. Donna found me after the show. She was like the mother I never had…. In fact, she was the mother I'd always dreamed of finding someday. She invited me to come to her home to look at the raptors. When I found out she trained people to get their falconer's licenses, I felt like the world had suddenly opened up to me. Donna saved my life.

I'd been running away from so many foster homes that the police knew me on sight. I never did anything legally wrong, I was just running away."

"Or maybe trying to run toward finding your real mother?" Tears were winding down Katie's drawn cheeks. God help him, he wanted to sweep her into his arms and hold her safe from a world that had gone so terribly wrong for her since the moment she was born.

Katie shrugged. "Maybe. Donna officially became my foster mother after that. I lived with her for two years and she helped me on so many levels. I received my falconer's license thanks to her. Working with the raptors calmed me. It still does." Katie touched her stomach. "I can't explain it, but I've always had this anxiety. The only time it goes away is when I'm with the birds. It's as if they understand me. They accept me for the way I am and they give me so much in return." Katie saw Joe nod, his mouth tight, as if holding back an unknown emotion. Feeling the connection with him strengthen, she added, "Very soon, Donna is moving away to take care of her aging mother in Idaho. She contacted Iris Mason and asked her to help me out, and she did."

Her story tore at his heart. Joe felt sympathy for Katie, and something else so unexpected he couldn't articulate it, even in his own mind. Gently, he reached out and touched Katie's shoulder. "Iris is a guardian angel and Donna's truly a mother to you, Katie. At least you got to know what a real mother would have been like."

"I'm grateful to Donna for saving my life." Her tone turned anguished. "And yet, to this very minute, I want to know my biological mother." Katie's throat closed with tears. She couldn't get out the words to tell Joe her biological mother was a convict. The shame was just too great and she didn't want the man to think ill of her.

Still, as she lifted her head and drowned in his softened expression, she knew Joe would keep her safe from the insane world. He would protect her. And no man in her life had ever made her feel secure. Not until now...

CHAPTER SEVEN

XAVIER LOBOS SAT smoking with Janet Bergstrom in the office of Mercury Courier. She was behaving like a giddy schoolgirl after they'd had sex all night. He was tired, but he had to think clearly. Sneaking into the U.S.A. in disguise twice a year was damned dangerous. If border officials recognized him, he'd be arrested and his ass would be tossed in federal prison for a long time. Janet looked insanely happy. Xavier suspected she had no other man in her life but him. He hated to think about having sex only twice a year. That was insane to him. His wife was eager to please him several times a week.

"I'm going to leave you a hundred thousand U.S. dollars," he told her, sipping his coffee.

"Me?" Janet's brows flew upward. "For what?" Xavier always brought money for her business. But never that much.

"I'm expanding your business, *mi corazón,* my heart. I want you to drive over to Jackson Hole, lease building space and create a second courier business there."

"Jackson Hole?" Janet rubbed her nose and looked through the haze of smoke at her lover. "Why there?"

"Because my cartel needs to expand. A Mexican cartel is moving into the town. I need to establish a foothold."

"That's dangerous, Xavier."

He laughed. "When isn't it?" He reached over and

squeezed her hand. "I've brought Eduardo Vargas with me. He's one of my best lieutenants and speaks fluent English. You will hire him to run your business in Jackson Hole."

"Do I have to be there?"

Shrugging, he said, "You'll be driving back and forth, of course. And at first, you need to be there full-time in order to get it up and running." He set the black cowhide briefcase filled with money on the desk and opened it.

Janet gasped. "My God, that's a pile of money, Xavier," she said, her voice hoarse. She stood and stared into the briefcase. Her heart started to race with excitement.

Picking out the wrapped bills, Xavier stacked them into three different piles across her desk. Pointing to the first one, he said, "This first one is for the yearly lease and redecoration. You will make it look exactly like your business here in Cheyenne." He pointed to the second stack. "This is to rent an apartment in Jackson Hole. You're going to need a place to live."

"You do know Jackson Hole is like Palm Springs, California? It's expensive as hell, Xavier."

He slid her a sly smile. "I'm assuming one hundred thousand dollars a year will keep you well cared for?"

Stubbing out her cigarette, Janet grinned. "Yeah, I think it will. Thank you."

"The third stack is for daily operating expenses." He stared hard at her. "As usual, you never put any of this money in the bank."

"I understand. Anyone putting over ten thousand bucks into a bank gets an automatic red flag with the FBI. Don't worry, it will be stashed under my mattress." She grinned.

"Just keep cooking the accounting books, Janet," he warned her. "That way, your IRS will see this as a natural outgrowth of the money you're making here in Cheyenne. I do not want to raise their curiosity." He stared into her murky, blue, red-rimmed eyes. She'd done a lot of coke last night and was still coming down.

Janet walked around the desk and threw her arms around him. Kissing him on the mouth, she said, "I'm yours, Xavier. I always have been. Thank you for taking such good care of me. You are my knight in shining armor."

Tolerating her sloppy kiss and the red lipstick haphazardly smeared across her lips, he returned her embrace. But not with equal passion. He gripped her shoulders. "I have much to do today. And so do you. Make the calls to a real-estate agent over in Jackson Hole. I'll be back tonight and you can tell me of the progress you have made."

Happiness filtered through Janet as she regarded the stacks of bills before her. "Only one more night with you," she said in a whining tone. "I hate seeing you only twice a year, Xavier. I wish…I wish you could visit more often."

"So do I, *mi corazón.*" He pressed a kiss to her temple. "I'm off. I have to drive to Casper and check on things over there. I'll be back tonight and we'll talk more about your second courier business when I return. Adios…"

SHOULD SHE CALL Janet Bergstrom or not? Katie's hand hovered over the phone in her suite at the Elk Horn Ranch. The clock on the wall read 7:00 a.m. Yesterday, she'd had an emotional meltdown and blathered part of her past to Joe. Though she was ashamed of herself,

Katie shored up her strength. Sleeping poorly, torn between denying Janet was her mother and wanting desperately to meet her, Katie had gotten up at 5:00 a.m. She'd made coffee, read Norah's report once more and stared at the mug shots of her mother on the kitchen table.

It didn't matter. Katie felt her heart tearing open in her chest. This situation was driving her mad. She *had* to know. She had to make this call. Would Janet answer? Oh, God, she was scared of her mother's reaction. Wiping her wrinkled brow, Katie took a deep breath. She had to try…

THE PHONE RANG. Janet scowled. Xavier had just left and she was getting her office in order for the day's business. Hell, it was only 7:00 a.m. Mercury didn't open up until 8:00 a.m. Probably some jerk wanting a package sent overnight and desperate to find someone to do it. Hesitating, Janet waffled about whether to answer it. Maybe it was Xavier. No, he never used land-line phones for fear of being tracked by the FBI and ATF.

"Damn," Janet muttered, jerking up the phone. "Mercury Courier, can I help you?"

There was silence at the other end of the phone.

Janet grew agitated. "Hello?" Her voice was hard and gruff.

"Hi…"

A soft, feminine voice came over the phone. Janet scowled. "I can't hardly hear you. Can I help you?"

"Uhhh…yes, I'm calling for Janet Bergstrom. I— Is she there?"

What a ditz, Janet thought. Whoever it was sounded frightened. Just her luck to get someone like this when she was busy. "This is she. Who am I talking to?"

"I... Janet, you don't know me and I'm sorry to bother you at this time of the morning, but I had to call. I'm Katie Bergstrom. A private investigator found out that you're my biological mother. And I was hoping to make contact with you."

Shock rooted Janet to the spot. Her eyes widened enormously. *My God!* Her mouth dropped open. Fingers tightening around the black phone, Janet croaked, "Daughter? What are you talking about?" Her mind whirled with confusion. A private investigator had found her? Part of her had wanted to contact her long-lost daughter. And now...of all things, was this *really* her? Licking her lips, Janet said, "How do I know you're tellin' the truth?"

"I'm your daughter, Janet." Katie reeled off the name of the hospital and the date when she was given up.

Sitting down, Janet felt fear race through her. Heart pounding, she tried to think through the haze of the drugs left in her system. Resting her elbow on the desk, hand pressed to her brow, she stammered, "Where are you calling from?" How had a private investigator found her? Rattled, Janet heard the younger woman's voice fill with tension.

"I'm calling from Jackson Hole, Wyoming, Janet. I was wondering...could we meet sometime? I'd really like to talk with you."

Janet's fear ratcheted up. Her stomach, which had always been her weak point, twisted into a painful knot. The tears in Katie's voice were real. "I don't know," she said in a harsh tone to cover her fear. "I need to think about this. Those records were sealed with the state. You aren't supposed to know who or where I am."

"I know, I've wondered how you are and I've always

wanted to meet you. I don't expect anything of you. I just would like to see you…just once. Please?"

"Dammit, give me your phone number. I'm busy right now." Janet heard Katie's gasp over the phone. Wincing because she was scared and didn't know what to say, she scribbled down Katie's phone number. "I gotta go—"

"Wait! Can—can you tell me when you'll return my call?"

"I don't know!" Janet growled. She slammed the phone down, breathing hard. Rubbing her face, she tried to think straight. Dammit, of all things! What was she going to do? Hand shaking, she grabbed for another cigarette from the pack on the desk. The lighter shook as she lit it. As she dragged in puff after puff, Janet tried to ignore the yearning deep in her heart. Her daughter had just called! Janet realized her mistake. When she'd given up her newly born daughter, the nurse had asked what last name would she give the baby. Janet hated the drug addict who had gotten her pregnant. She'd have been damned if she'd given this kid his name and so had given her the name Bergstrom, instead. *What a stupid move.* Janet sat there wondering why she hadn't given the kid a name like Smith. That was how the investigator had found her. It was too late now. *Damn*…

Finishing off the cigarette, Janet pulled open a drawer where she had some rolled joints stashed. Right now she needed one. Her heart was pounding with dread. Guilt washed through her, making her feel edgy and rattled. What was she going to do about the phone call? Hadn't she wanted to meet Katie? *Yes.* That's why she'd sat at the Elk Horn Ranch gate twice, gotten cold feet and couldn't face the girl. She'd driven back to Cheyenne feeling like crud.

Getting to her feet, Janet shoved the chair back

against the wall of her small office. She shakily lit the joint and inhaled. She closed her eyes and willed the calm that always came from getting stoned. She desperately needed fresh air. Opening the back door, Janet walked into the alley. After six or seven puffs, she finally calmed down. At one end of the alley she watched cars moving back and forth, people on their way to work. What the hell was she going to do about Katie's unexpected phone call?

Emotions Janet had buried years ago roared back to life. She closed her eyes. Memories came with those emotions, too. She saw herself on the delivery table, grunting and groaning. She was swearing like a trooper at the nurses and doctor. She swore at the man who'd nailed her with this unwanted kid. Yet, when her daughter was born, wiped off, wrapped in a soft pink blanket and placed upon her chest, Janet had stopped cursing. The baby weighed five pounds and was wrinkled. And when she opened her huge blue eyes for the first time and looked directly into Janet's eyes, something beautiful happened. Janet felt her heart open like a flower and she began to cry as she hesitantly touched her daughter's thin black hair.

As much as Janet wanted to forget that miraculous moment when she'd felt clean and happy, she couldn't. And she'd never forgotten the innocent babe in her arms. *Not ever.* As much as Janet wanted those memories and feelings to leave her alone, they never did. Now… Katie…Katie Bergstrom had called her out of the blue. Rubbing her face, Janet felt tears jam into her eyes. Her daughter had more courage than she did. Oh, God, she couldn't cry! She hadn't ever cried about giving up her daughter. *Not now!* Hardening herself against those tender emotions, Janet willed them away.

Desperate, she felt she needed to talk to Xavier. She relied heavily upon him. He knew she'd given up her daughter. It wasn't a secret, but it was shaming to her. Xavier had never seemed to care about her choice one way or another. He made sure when they had sex that she would never have a child by him. He was married and already had a family, and he wasn't about to spawn a brat from her, he'd told her once.

Mouth pinched, Janet slowly trudged toward the door of her business. Yes, Xavier would have the answers she sought. He'd just given her a huge raise, a ton of money, and more than anything, she wanted to please him. He'd know what to do. And whatever he decided, Janet would blindly follow his decision.

JOE ENTERED THE raptor facility at 8:00 a.m. just as Katie was feeding the birds. He hadn't slept well at all last night. Dreams of Katie—of her as a human being, not as a suspect—haunted him. He slid the glass door shut and called out, "Good morning…"

In Sam's mew, Katie straightened up when she heard Joe's voice. The golden eagle was sitting on his perch, sated from his meal. "Good morning, Joe." She forced a smile she didn't feel. Joe looked exhausted. In fact, he had dark circles beneath his eyes as he sauntered down the aisle toward her. His brown hair gleamed from a recent shower. Sensing more than seeing Joe's protectiveness toward her, Katie didn't trust herself around him right now. She was too upset from speaking to Janet this morning.

"You must have come in early. You're halfway through the cleaning," he observed, looking at the mews on the other side of the aisle. All the raptors had clean water and their mews were spotless. He saw how pale

Katie looked, her eyes sad. Joe struggled to stop caring about her, but it was impossible. Right now, she seemed utterly defeated and alone.

"Yes, I am," Katie said. She cringed beneath Joe's perusal. His mouth was tight with concern. God, how she wished she could hide her feelings. She was an open book, with every emotion written across her face. Today she didn't have the strength to hide them. Joe cocked his head, studying her in the building silence.

"Are you okay?"

Katie moved in a jerky motion to pick up some white fluff Sam had preened out of his breast earlier. "I'm fine."

"Doesn't sound like it."

Katie moved around the mew. She felt trapped. How desperately she needed to talk to someone about the phone call she'd made to her mother. Iris was away on a business trip to Montana. And her foster mother, Donna, was now on her way with a moving van to take up residence in Idaho Falls, Idaho. Katie felt the two women she trusted with her heart had been taken away from her when she needed them most. She could tell these women the truth and they wouldn't judge her. Katie had relied heavily upon them, especially at times like this.

Turning, her hand filled with feathers, Katie hesitantly met Joe's gaze. "I lied to you. It's been a very upsetting morning." She opened the mew, stepped out and locked it. Joe moved aside and she saw his worried look turn to genuine concern.

"Do you want to talk about it, Katie?"

She closed her eyes for a brief moment, as if to find the words. "I feel like I'm using you, Joe. Yesterday was bad enough. You had to listen to me…"

To hell with it. Joe reached out and briefly touched

her shoulder. "I don't consider any personal conversations a yoke around my neck, Katie. I care for you." There, the words were out, never to be taken back. Katie's eyes widened. All Joe wanted to do was protect her. He removed his hand from her shoulder. "Why don't you stop for a break? I see coffee's made. We can take five and chat."

Idle chat wasn't what it would be, Katie realized. Her skin tingled pleasantly where his fingers had grazed her shoulder. Joe's touch had calmed her; it had been exactly what she'd needed. "Yes, that sounds good."

"Great, come on." Joe led the way.

Katie placed the feathers in a cardboard container in her desk as Joe came over with two cups of coffee. He handed one mug to her and sat down on the chair beside her desk. Almost reluctantly, Katie sat down. She wondered what Joe would think once she'd spilled the whole story about her mother. Most people didn't have a convict in their family tree. Katie wrapped her hands around the mug. "Joe, I feel like you're getting the short end of the stick when it comes to us. Yesterday I dumped on you. Today, I will, too. You weren't hired to be my therapist."

"Katie, I think you're an exceptional person. I see the way the raptors respond to you. They love you. I'm already learning so much from you about them. I don't consider our talk yesterday as 'dumping' on me. We all have problems. And it's nice to find a friend who is willing to listen, don't you think?"

Sipping her coffee, Katie burned her tongue. Frowning, she absorbed Joe's reasonable explanation. "You're right, we're all in a battle called life. And friends are indispensable."

"And you're looking pretty embattled right now. The

least I can do is listen, Katie. Now—" and Joe gave her a slight smile "—I can't guarantee I'll have any answers for you on how to fix it, but I have a broad set of shoulders and a pair of good ears. And I'd like to be your friend, Katie."

His voice, deep and low with sincerity, made all of Katie's arguments go away. It was Joe's eyes, burning with tenderness, that gave her the courage to speak. Taking a deep breath, she launched into the whole story, from beginning to end. Her hands were damp and she hugged the mug because it was warm in comparison to the cold, desolate feeling inside her. After hearing the story, Katie was sure Joe would quit. Who would want to work with someone who had so much baggage?

Joe listened without interruption. When Katie finished, she took a gulp of coffee, as if to fortify herself. Reading her gaze, he could see she was frightened and unsure of how he was going to react. His mouth was dry, his heart pounding because his biggest question had been answered. Keeping his tone nonjudgmental, he asked, "This is the first time you knew where your mother lived?"

Katie nodded. "Yes. I didn't know Iris had hired Norah to try and find her." Voice softening, Katie added, "Iris loves me. She always has. And in some ways, I guess I'm like a granddaughter to her. Iris knew how important it was for me to find my mother. And she knew the state wasn't going to give me the information." Katie rubbed her brow. "I think because her adopted son, Rudd, had gone through the same terrible questions not knowing answers about his own background, she was able to understand what I was going through on a daily basis."

"It must be hard," Joe said, "always to wonder who

your mom and dad were." There were tears in her eyes. Sitting a little straighter, Katie gave him a slight nod. Her hands were moving the mug around and around in a circle.

"The questions are always there," Katie said. "You wonder why they abandoned you. Was I not wanted?" She gave him a flustered look. "Joe, I often thought I must have been such an ugly baby that Janet gave me up."

"I hope that kind of thinking changed when the PI's report was given to you." Now he knew what the file on her desk had been all about. And why Katie had taken it with her after the picture had fallen out yesterday morning. It was Norah's report on Janet Bergstrom.

"Sort of," Katie hedged. "I hope Janet will return my call. Oh, God." She looked up to the top of the ceiling, her voice wobbly, "I pray she calls me back, Joe."

Reaching out, he stilled her restless hands for a moment. "Listen to me, Katie. You're a beautiful young woman with a heart of gold. There isn't anyone who isn't touched by your kindness and care. Look at the raptors and how they respond to you." His fingers tightened momentarily on her damp hand. "Iris and Donna love you." He almost said, *And I care so damn much for you my heart aches,* but he didn't dare. Katie was too focused on finding Janet. She had enough to deal with.

Joe's hand was dry and warm across hers. Her heart beat wildly in her chest. Katie melted over his deep voice. But she was unsure of what was going on between them. All she could do was stare at him. "You're right. My head knows that, Joe, but my heart doesn't. All my life I've tried to be ruled by my head." Pressing her fingers against her heart, she said, "But in the end,

Joe, my feelings run me. I could never stop thinking about who my mom was."

Joe forced himself to release her hand. "And I'm sure it stunned you to hear she'd been in prison."

Her voice dropped to a whisper. "I was so ashamed, Joe. I felt so horrible knowing my mother was a drug addict and a gunrunner. And I don't know who my father was." She gulped. "I—I had other ideas about who she was."

"That's understandable," Joe soothed. He ached to pull Katie into his arms. Right now, she was stripped bare, grappling with some devastating news. But the woman had steel in her spine. Katie's shoulders were not stooped and she wasn't hanging her head. Instead, she sat straight, her chin slightly jutted out, as if finding some hidden strength deep within her to survive this experience.

"I hardly slept last night, Joe. I knew I had to call her. And I was never so scared as this morning when I did."

"At least she didn't hang up on you."

"I know…I'm trying to see the positive side of our conversation."

"Do you think Janet will call back?"

Shrugging, Katie said in an anguished tone, "I don't know, Joe. I hope with every cell in my body, she does. But then, I wonder what's next? Will she meet me? Or will she tell me she wants nothing to do with me?"

Joe set his cup on the desk. He rose and held out his hand to her. "Come here, Katie. I need to hold you for just a moment. You can't go through this alone. I'm here for you.…"

Without thinking, Katie stood and stepped into his arms. She was exhausted by events, craving the support Joe was offering her. She didn't see hungry desire in his eyes as he made the offer. No, he was sympathetic, caring, and her heart had screamed at her to take him up on his offer. In his embrace, her head nestling against his jaw and shoulder, his arms encircling her, a tremulous sigh broke from her parted lips. She could smell the scent of fresh pine lingering on his dark blue cotton shirt. Instinctively, Katie inhaled his male scent and felt her nerves calm. His arms were strong and she could hear the slow, thudding beat of his heart beneath her ear. And most of all, Katie felt all the fear and anxiety dissolve as he held her against him. Whether Joe knew it or not, Katie realized that for the first time in her life she felt safe.

CHAPTER EIGHT

JANET DRUMMED HER FINGERS on the office desk. "I don't know what to do, Xavier." He'd just arrived a half hour earlier from Casper. It was dark, nearly 9:00 p.m., and he looked weary. Janet didn't hold back anything about the unexpected phone call from her daughter. She searched his darkening features as he sat down in front of her desk and tugged at his black mustache, a sign he was in thought.

"I'm sure it was a surprise," Xavier agreed. He slouched in the chair. "You said you drove over to the Elk Horn Ranch to see her twice before this? That she's working and living on the ranch in Jackson Hole?"

"Yes, I managed to track her down through the state agency. It wasn't really hard to do since I'd given her my last name." Janet inhaled the smoke from the cigarette. Xavier didn't do drugs and refused to allow her to smoke marijuana in his presence. Her nerves were jangled and her fingers shook as she tapped the ashes into the green ashtray.

Shrugging, he tiredly wiped his watering eyes. "That's how she got to you." He thought it had been stupid of Janet to give her daughter her last name. But this might be a good thing. Hand dropping from his eyes, he stared across the desk at Janet. Her dyed-blond hair was piled up on her head. When she wasn't drugged up to her eyeballs, she actually looked quite the American businesswoman. She wore a dark blue pantsuit and a tasteful white silk T-shirt along with some gold earrings and a slender gold necklace he'd gifted her with a long time ago. One thing about Janet: she was loyal to him. She was someone he could count on when others in his organization were always suspect. He smiled a little. "This could be a windfall, *mi corazón*."

"How?" Janet frowned. She puffed on the cigarette, wishing it was a joint. She'd been high on weed all day until Xavier had arrived at her office. Now, her raw nerves were screaming and a cigarette certainly did not do the trick.

Sitting up, Xavier smiled. "You're going to set up a new business in that town. Wouldn't it be fortuitous to reacquaint yourself with your daughter? Did she say how long she'd lived in Jackson Hole?"

"No, and I didn't ask, either."

Nodding, Xavier said, "If your daughter is a well-liked and known quantity in Jackson Hole, this could work well for you, Janet."

Janet quirked her eyebrows. "I don't see how." And yet, deep down, she wanted to see Katie. How had life shaped her daughter without her being around to screw it up? Was Katie into drugs, too? After all, she had druggie parents, although Janet felt she kept her addiction under tight control.

"If your estranged daughter is well thought of by the local people, especially the police department, then she can provide good cover for you. Once you find the right building space to lease, we'll be moving drugs and guns through it. And if you connect with her, become her mother once more, the police are going to be a lot less likely to suspect you."

"Hmm, hadn't looked at it from that angle," Janet

grudgingly admitted. She sat back in her chair and felt relief. Xavier always knew what to do. "She could provide cover if she's not in trouble with the law."

"You need to find out if she has a criminal record. Just go to one of the many sites on the internet, pay your money and get an illegal activities report on her."

"I'd done some research on her, Xavier. From what I can tell, Katie's a raptor rehabilitator who lives with the Mason family. You aren't aware of them, but they have the largest, richest and most successful ranch in that valley. Iris Mason is a well-respected woman in Jackson Hole. I don't think Katie would be invited to live on her ranch, much less live in the main family house, if she had a prison record."

"True," Xavier said. "I like the way this is shaping up. Katie could be vital cover for you. If Iris is held in high esteem, Katie likely will be, too. You are known by the friends you travel with." He grinned a little. Janet seemed pensive and he knew she was feeling her way through the process. "I like the idea of you returning her call. Meet with your daughter as soon as I leave. You have to go over to Jackson Hole anyway to lease space for your next courier service."

"I'm worried about the Mexican cartel that's trying to move into the town, Xavier. I don't want any gunfights to break out. You know if they do, the cops will be down on me in a heartbeat. I can't erase my prison record or the fact I work for you."

"The FBI and ATF can't prove you've worked for me since you got out of prison. I've taken great precautions not to be identified when I am in this country. Don't you think if they suspected anything, they'd have busted you by now?"

"Yeah, I know you're right." Janet stubbed out the

butt in the ashtray. She wanted a hit of grass so badly her hands shook. "The Mexican cartel has me worried. There's an unwritten rule among cartels that if one lays claim to an area, the rest of them respect it and move on."

Shrugging, Xavier smiled. "I'm from Guatemala. I think differently." He saw the worry in her blue eyes. "That's why you're going to have a legitimate store-front. No one will suspect what is going on. We'll use the packages to transport drugs and guns just like we do here. You've been in business a long time here in Cheyenne and law enforcement has left you alone. What we're doing here and how we're doing it is working, Janet. We'll employ the same tools the same way over in Jackson Hole. You'll keep a low profile. It will be another layer of protection because you'll have your daughter working for you."

Janet said, "I hadn't thought about her working for me, but it's a good idea."

"How do you feel about meeting her?"

Janet lit another cigarette, the white smoke encircling her head. "I guess I've been wanting to meet her for a while, Xavier."

Standing, Xavier reached across the desk and patted her hand. "It's understandable. Return the call to Katie after I leave."

Janet nodded and squeezed his hand. Xavier's nails were manicured. So handsome, he always wore impeccable business suits that probably costs thousands of dollars. She released his hand and asked, "What if she doesn't like me, Xavier? What else can I do?"

"I don't know of any child who doesn't want to re-connect with its mother, do you?"

"I wouldn't know." She managed a pained half smile.

Janet felt extreme anxiety over calling Katie. Yet, her stupid, foolish heart had wanted this meeting.

"It's time," Xavier said softly. "Things will go fine, *mi corazón.*"

"Maybe it's menopause," Janet mused. "I feel driven to meet her. Before this, I never cared. Now, the last year, it's all changed. I feel like a prisoner to my hormones."

Laughing, he held out his hand. "Come, let's drive to my hotel and have dinner, shall we? It's our last night together before I leave for Idaho and Montana."

"WHAT MAKES YOU THINK Katie Bergstrom isn't a viable part of the Los Lobos?" Roger Hager demanded.

Joe paced the living room. It was early on Saturday morning and he was checking in with his FBI boss. Today, he didn't have to go to work, although he wanted to. Being around Katie always lifted his spirit. "It's a gut call," he said. "Nothing more than that at this point. I'm going to visit a woman here in town who is the go-to person for the town. Gwen Garner is the mother of sheriff's deputy Cade Garner. She's considered a reliable person who knows the town's gossip. I'm hoping she can give me a different angle on Katie."

"Good."

Joe halted in front of the window which looked eastward. He'd drawn up the venetian blinds and saw that the lawn was green and trim. The bushes were low so the valley surrounding them could be seen and appreciated. "Okay, I'll call if I hear anything new from Gwen." Joe ended the call and slipped the cell phone into his pocket. The sun was barely touching the horizon. Inhaling, he could smell coffee drifting down the hall from the kitchen.

He grabbed his socks and boots, sat down on the bed and pulled them on. Moving to the closet, Joe chose a blue chambray shirt. Today, he'd be working with his dad and learning the landscaping business. His afternoon, however, was free and he'd visit Gwen Garner at that time.

After combing his short brown hair, Joe looked at himself in the bathroom mirror. He couldn't shake the guilt he felt over remaining incognito to Katie. He had learned in Afghanistan to trust his gut. When he'd followed it without question, it had always kept him safe. When he'd ignored it, he had gotten into trouble. The morning his Humvee had hit an IED on the side of a dirt road leading into a village, his gut had warned him to take another route. He hadn't. Mouth thinning over those memories, Joe placed the comb on the black granite countertop. His gut was telling him Katie was innocent.

Opening the door, he walked down the long hall toward the kitchen. The coffee smelled great. And he was happy to be near his parents, even though once this mission ended he'd be sent elsewhere. Joe had learned to appreciate the small everyday things of life. A chance to be with his parents at this stage of his life was a gift.

"JOE, NICE TO SEE YOU," Gwen Garner called as she saw him walk to the counter of her quilting store. "How are you?"

Gwen was at one of the large cutting tables. She had just folded up fabric for a waiting customer. "Hi, Mrs. Garner."

Gwen handed the material to the woman and thanked her. She moved around the counter and went to greet Joe, who was standing at the counter. "Now, you know better, Joe. Just call me Gwen. What brings you here? Does your mother want something?"

Smiling a little, Joe looked down at the gray-haired woman who was always spunky and warm. Gwen reminded him of a nurturing mother. He felt her care radiating toward him. "Actually, no. But do you have a minute? I have something I need to talk with you about."

"Sure." Gwen slipped her hand around his arm and led him to a quiet corner in the busy store. "Come this way…"

Once in the corner, Gwen released his arm. Automatically, she made sure each bolt of fabric sat correctly on the shelves, straight and neat-looking. "Who do you want to know about?" She looked up at him and smiled.

Joe pushed his hands into the pockets of his slacks. "How did you know?"

"Oh," Gwen said with a chuckle as she moved down the row of colorful batik fabrics, "men don't usually come in here wanting quilt material." And then she raised her gray brows. "But we do have some gentlemen who are wonderful quilters." Her voice dropped to a conspiratorial whisper. "Somehow, I don't think you're one of them, are you? As a kid, you were into football, Joe. I remember."

Joe dipped his head, a sheepish grin spreading across his mouth. "You're right, Gwen. I was into football, not sewing." He saw her bend over, her fingers flying across the different bolts of fabric, straightening them here and there.

"I want to know about Katie Bergstrom." He saw Gwen straighten and a twinkle come to her eyes. What was her reaction all about?

"Ahhh… I hear you're enjoying your new job at her raptor facility?"

Uncomfortable, Joe gave her a limp smile. "You knew I work there?"

"Well, it's no secret. Iris Mason was in here yesterday. She was praising you to the rafters." Gwen smiled. "Are you happy out there, Joe?"

Suddenly, the tables were turned on him, he realized. Gwen Garner was very good at pulling information out of everyone, including him. She should have been an interviewer for the FBI. Moving a bit nervously, Joe said, "Yes, I like falconry."

"Well, you know, if someone had asked me what Joe Gannon would do in life, falconry wouldn't have come up. Oh, with your athletic background, the Marine Corps was the perfect career for you." Gwen's eyes narrowed as she held his gaze. "But falconry? You're not a hunter like your dad. And you weren't much of a hiker growing up. Though I know you enjoyed skiing and were very good at it."

Twisting inwardly from Gwen's appraisal, Joe felt trapped. He told her the truth about how he'd stumbled into falconry after being wounded in Afghanistan. Gwen was easy to talk with, and she was sincerely interested in every word.

"And so you've discovered—by accident—that falconry appeals to you?"

"Yes, I have," he said. His heart was beating a little more quickly because he could see Gwen weighing and measuring his sincerity against what she remembered of him as a kid in town.

"I always find it fascinating how life sometimes picks us up from one place and plops us down in a completely different position. You're a case in point, don't you think?"

"I do," Joe agreed. He felt guilt over not telling Gwen

the rest of the story. He wondered if she suspected his reason for being in Jackson Hole.

"This is a nice way to leave the Marine Corps and come home. You have a new skill and you're already employed. You're very lucky, Joe."

"I am and I'm grateful."

"You know, Katie's life up until Donna became her foster mother was chaotic and messy. I find it interesting that you're falling into falconry after being knocked about by life, too."

Joe knew he couldn't press Gwen too much about Katie. She was smart enough to see straight through him. And Joe couldn't afford for that to happen. "Falconry is a way of life," he agreed. "And I really enjoy it." And he did.

Nodding, Gwen moved to another section of fabric bolts against the wall. "You didn't know Katie in high school, did you?"

"No. When did she come to Jackson Hole?"

"When she was sixteen. Before that, she was over in Casper going through a gazillion foster homes. Poor girl was angry and rebellious. But who could blame her? Good thing Donna met her that day at the state fair. They just clicked, you know? And when Donna found out Katie was on the run, that she'd hitchhiked from Casper to here, well she realized the girl was in dire straits."

"What did Donna do?"

"She called the Casper police and let them know she was safe in Jackson Hole. And to make a long story short, Donna applied for and received permission to foster Katie. Katie bloomed under Donna's direction and care. Any kid who is abandoned by birth parents has extra mountains to climb, and it was very hard on

Katie, as you might suspect." Gwen leaned over and picked up some thread she'd spotted on the floor next to the fabric bolts.

"I can't even begin to imagine," Joe said. "She did speak to me the other day about being in a number of foster homes."

"Ah, well, that bodes well for you, then."

"Pardon?"

"Katie's life was saved by Donna and her raptors. She completed the last two years of high school and graduated with honors. She also stayed out of trouble. But Katie is a strange one, in some ways. I rarely hear her talk about her past. She's ashamed of it."

"Why?"

"I don't know if she shared this with you or not, Joe, but her mother, Janet Bergstrom, was in prison for five years because she ran guns and drugs."

Feigning ignorance, Joe said in a quiet voice, "I didn't know…" He wondered how Gwen had gotten hold of the information. Norah, the PI, had just given Katie the report less than a week ago. He studied Gwen. How did she know? Had Norah come in here and told her?

"I just found out from a close friend of mine. Katie knew nothing of her druggie mother who lives over in Cheyenne. And I must swear you to secrecy on this, Joe. I know you and you're a trustworthy individual."

"Actually," Joe said, "Katie told me about the private investigator's report yesterday."

"Oh. She did?"

Gwen appeared surprised. Joe said, "She called her mother Janet yesterday."

"Really?" Gwen crept closer to him, her voice barely above a whisper. "What happened? Can you tell me?"

Uncomfortable, Joe hedged, "I'd rather not say. All

I'm doing is double-checking what you know up to this point. I feel if Katie wants to talk to you, it should come from her, not me."

"Wisely said," Gwen agreed. "I'm so proud of Katie for making that phone call! I know she's been yearning all her life to find out who her mother is. When Iris came in yesterday and shared the information, I was elated. I was also bummed Janet was a convict."

Joe realized after he left yesterday, Katie spoke by phone to Iris. At least the information wasn't handed over by the private eye. To have done that was against the law. "I see."

"I don't know much more about Janet Bergstrom," Gwen said, worried. "I wonder if she's going to call Katie back. If she hasn't cleaned up her act, how will it impact on Katie? I fear for her. I've seen how hard it is for folks to get off drugs. And they don't, unless they really want to."

"I'm concerned, too." At least that wasn't a lie. "Janet lives over in Cheyenne. That's clear across the state. Will Katie move over there, I wonder?"

"You're worried about your job?"

"Sort of," Joe admitted. "I think everything's up in the air until and if she calls Katie. I was hoping you might have a feel for this."

Giving a chuckle, Gwen placed her hands on her thick hips. "How I wish! I'm not a fortune-teller, Joe. Oh, I can surmise sometimes and I'm usually pretty good at it. But not always."

Joe had been giving deep thought about Janet calling. Would she ask Katie to move to Cheyenne? He'd go with her if he could. But would Katie want him to tag along? It would certainly get him a lot closer to

Janet Bergstrom and that was a decided plus. He tried
to ignore his personal worry for Katie. But he couldn't.

"You like Katie, don't you?"

The question caught Joe off guard. "Me? Well…yes,
she's a very nice person."

Gwen snorted. "Not from what I see in your face,
Joe Gannon. You wouldn't be hedging a bet with me,
would you?"

Joe squirmed, took his hands out of his pockets—
they had suddenly grown damp. Wiping them down the
sides of his slacks, he managed a twisted smile. "Caught
red-handed. You're too good, Gwen."

"Your voice gives you away. When you say Katie's
name, your tone goes soft. I see a special look come to
your eyes. I know you divorced Zoe."

"Zoe…yes, we got divorced." Old pain rose up in Joe.
"It was a tough time," he admitted.

"But you're over her. And now you're looking for a
special woman to share your life? At your age, I sure
would be. People aren't meant to live alone, Joe."

"Well, uh, yes, I guess I'm over the divorce. And I
agree no one likes being alone." He certainly didn't.

Gwen's expression sharpened and she refused to let
him off the hook. "I've known Katie since she was sixteen. That's a good ten years. I've seen her grow up.
She's a beautiful person, Joe. And she has a good heart
and soul. Katie's found her niche in life with the raptors and she's good at what she does."

"I was wondering," Joe said, clearing his throat, "if
Katie had someone special in her life."

Gwen chuckled. "Well, now we get down to the nuts
and bolts of why you're here, don't we?"

Joe felt heat flood his face. Was he blushing? He

hadn't done that since he was a teenager. "You caught me dead to rights, Gwen."

Patting him on the shoulder, she said, "Now, wouldn't it have been less painful just to come straight out and ask?"

It was his turn to grin. "Gwen, has your deputy-sheriff son ever told you that you'd be one hell of a law-enforcement investigator?"

Laughing with him, Gwen nodded. "Yes, my son takes cues from me. I taught him early on to look at people, study their expressions, their body language, and listen to the tone of their voice. It tells a lot if you know how to translate it."

"You also have insight into people few ever will," Joe said. He saw her preen beneath his sincere compliment. "Now, back to why I was here. Is Katie seeing someone?"

Gwen sighed. "In the ten years Katie's been in Jackson Hole, she's had three serious relationships. And each time, she broke it off. Right now, there's no one in her life." Her lips twitched. "Except you."

The heat wouldn't leave his face. Joe wondered if it was beet-red because it sure felt like it to him. "Katie never married?"

"Came close the third time. But the guy turned out to be a real jerk. He was actually an addict and he kept it from her. Katie hates people who hide things from her. I can't say I blame her. Maybe that's because she's so open and honest. You can read her face like a road map and know exactly what she's thinking and feeling."

"Very true," Joe agreed. "So the last guy was a drug addict?"

"So were the other two, the poor thing. The first two

guys were up-front about it. Katie seems to attract those needy types. Isn't that sad?"

"Does Katie do drugs herself?" Joe knew it was wrong to ask, but he had to. He saw Gwen frown.

"Not to my knowledge. But knowing her one parent, I can see how Katie draws that type of man. It's in her genes. She herself won't even touch alcohol, Joe, and she knows drugs are a poison. She loves her mocha lattes and likes chai tea but that's it. She's clean as a whistle."

Joe trusted Gwen's information and was relieved. Katie did not have a drug addict's personality nor did she behave like one. "Good to know. But what about these three relationships? Does Katie realize she's drawing the wrong kind of guy?"

"Oh, yes," Gwen said, giving Joe a sad look. "Katie and I have had our chats."

"Do you know the name of the last guy? The one that tried to cover up his drug habit from Katie?"

"Oh, yes, I won't forget the sneaky little jerk. His name was Renaldo Garcia."

The name shocked him. He felt as if someone had struck him in the chest with a fist. "What?" he blurted.

"You act like you know him."

"Uh...no, no, I don't."

"Funny, it looks like you did."

Rubbing his jaw, Joe stepped back. "No, I don't know him." But he did. Oh, God, Katie had tangled with the son of the Mexican cartel, Juan Garcia, who was trying to establish a base of operation here in Jackson Hole. "What happened to him?"

"I don't know. After Katie gave him his walking papers, Renaldo disappeared. I never liked him, Joe. He was a sneaky bastard at best. He'd been caught lying to a number of other people here in town. I didn't like his looks. Made me think of a weasel. And he sure didn't treat Katie well. I don't really think she realized at first what kind of man he was. Of course, how could she? She was raised in foster homes where no drugs were allowed. And when she came to Jackson Hole at sixteen, Donna protected her a great deal from kids in high school who were doing drugs. She got Katie immersed in falconry, so she didn't have to hang out with those types." Gwen shook her head. "No, Katie had no way of knowing who this dude was."

"He disappeared?"

"Yep, no one's seen him since."

"That's good to know." His stomach knotted. Joe wanted to make a call to Roger Hager as soon as possible. Did this implicate Katie with the Mexican cartel trying to establish a beachhead here in this town? If Gwen were to be believed, Katie was a pawn. But why did the son of this cartel leader pick her? Did they know Janet Bergstrom? Did they realize Katie was her daughter? Joe rubbed his chest, feeling danger for Katie. She could still be under the scope of this cartel. And he knew Renaldo Garcia was one mean son of a bitch who took no prisoners. Tearing his thoughts back to Gwen, he asked, "Did this guy ever harm Katie?" Renaldo was known to beat up his women.

"No, not that I'm aware. Why?"

"Just asking."

"Hmm."

"Thanks, Gwen, you've been a big help."

"Not so fast, Joe Gannon." She eyed him. "What are *your* intentions toward Katie?"

What a loaded question! Joe worked his mouth and thought carefully about his response. "I like her, Gwen."

"Okay."

"Probably more than I should. I came home to heal up, not to get involved in a relationship." That was true, and Joe hoped Gwen took him at his word.

"Pity," she said. "Because from where I'm standing, you two make the perfect couple."

CHAPTER NINE

THE NEXT MONDAY, Joe arrived at the facility at 8:00 a.m. to find Katie with a cast raptor on her desk. Someone had wrapped a dirty T-shirt around the bird. On the floor next to her was a cardboard traveling box. "Hey, what's up?"

Katie glanced over her shoulder. "Hi, Joe. Come over and help me?" Her breath caught in her chest. She'd forgotten how handsome Joe was. "A guy just found this young red-tailed hawk flopping around on the berm next to the highway. He saw the hawk diving across the road in pursuit of a rabbit and it hit the windshield of an oncoming truck."

Joe came to her side. Katie gently held the struggling raptor in the T-shirt. "He must have just brought it in."

"Yes, he did. Can you carefully hold the hawk? I need to call Randy Johnson, one of our vets, to see if he has an opening to look at the hawk. I think it has a broken wing."

"Sure." Joe carefully placed his hands over Katie's. It was a thrill to touch her. He knew that raptors were often hit by vehicles. His fingers carefully closed over the cloth wrapped around the hawk. It repeatedly tried to peck at his hand. Katie stepped clear and picked up the phone.

Joe studied the young hawk. It had some blood on one side of its yellow beak, otherwise, it looked in good shape and was alert. He listened to the phone conversation. The vet had an opening—good news for the hawk. Raptors could die of shock rapidly. The T-shirt surrounding the bird was smeared with grease here and there. Still, the man, who had been kind enough to bring the bird in for help had done what he could for it. Most people didn't know that it was important to wrap or cast a raptor in a piece of cloth. It prevented the bird from flapping its wings and possibly injuring itself even more.

"We're leaving," Katie said, breathless as she hung up the phone. "The vet can see the hawk right now."

"What do you want me to do?"

"Come with me." Katie hurried to the desk and retrieved her purse and a traveling bird box.

"What about the weighing and feeding?"

"Already done." Katie retrieved a special cloth that had Velcro on two sides of it. "I'm going to put this below the raptor's back. Then, I'm going to use a pair of scissors to carefully cut away the T-shirt and then use this clean cast instead."

Nodding, Joe watched her quick efficiency. It was a brilliant idea. "You've done this once or twice, haven't you?"

She laughed a little as she gently slid the brown velvet cloth beneath the bird. "Just a few times. Great. Now lay the hawk on the table…."

Within moments, Katie had removed the greasy T-shirt and gently but firmly wrapped the hawk's body in the thick brown velvet. The Velcro closed over the hawk's brown-and-white-speckled breast.

"That's a great idea to use Velcro. That way it can be opened and the scissors kept away from a struggling raptor."

"Donna showed me this trick. It was her idea." Once the hawk was completely cast in the brown fabric, only its head showing, it settled down. Bringing over the green cardboard carrier, Katie opened it up. "This is my special carrier for vet-bound birds." She opened it. Inside it was long enough for a big hawk like a red-tailed. Firm foam lined the sides. She picked up the hawk and carefully laid him down in the box. The foam would prevent the bird from being tossed about during the drive. She quietly shut the carrier.

"The hawk will settle down and relax now," she told him, picking up the case by the handle on top. "The darkness soothes them. I hope that by the time we reach the vet in Jackson Hole the hawk will still be alive. I'm sure it's in a lot of pain with a broken wing, but the casting will act like tape to hold it in place."

Joe picked up her purse and followed Katie out into the morning sunlight. "Anything else you need?"

"No, just follow me to my truck."

Once in the vehicle, Joe positioned the carrying case between them on the seat. She drove carefully down the one-mile asphalt road leading to the main highway.

"Did you have a nice weekend?" Katie asked after turning onto the major highway.

"I did."

"Were you working with your dad? Did you learn something new about landscaping?"

Joe smiled a little. "He went over the different types of stones and gravel one uses if the soil is sandy, clay or waste type. Sounds interesting, doesn't it?"

Laughing a little, both hands on the steering wheel, Katie said, "Kinda boring, huh?"

"I like the excitement of being a falconer. You never

know on a given day what is going to walk through your door. Like this morning."

"Usually, Fish and Game calls me about injured raptors. The folks who live around here know I have a license and sometimes they just drop the bird off to me instead of calling the officials first. I already made the call to F and G to close the loop on this raptor."

"Was the guy who brought this hawk in an auto mechanic?"

She grinned and shared a quick look with Joe. "Yes. How did you know?"

"As I was turning in to the ranch, a guy drove out in a tow truck." He met her smile. Katie's blue gaze was clear today. Joe hoped the weekend had helped her sort out her feelings about the call to her estranged mother.

"Still—great deduction, Watson!" Katie teased him. Her laughter riffled through Joe like a fresh breeze filled with the promise of life. "Thanks, Sherlock."

Her laughter was like music and it delighted him. Little did she know how much of a Watson he really was. He took no joy in it and he didn't look forward to the time when she would discover his true identity. Heart squeezing in pain, Joe frowned. He didn't want to hurt Katie. She'd already been hurt enough.

In no time, they were at the south end of Jackson Hole, pulling into a very busy vet practice run by Randy Johnson, DVM. Katie drove around to the rear of the cinder-block building and parked.

"Randy likes me to bring his free patients in the back door." She climbed out of the truck.

Joe brought the bird box and Katie walked to the rear door and opened it. Inside the cool facility, Joe could hear dogs barking and cats mewing. Katie signaled him to follow her into a large room on the left.

"You can set the bird box on the exam table? I'll go get Randy."

Joe placed the box on the spotlessly clean steel table. He could smell various medications and saw above the door a sign that said Operation Room. He heard Katie's laugh as the door in the hall opened. Deep masculine laughter followed and soon a tall, thin African-American man in a white lab coat entered. His gaze settled on Joe.

"I'm Randy," he said, offering his hand. "Katie here said you just joined her facility."

Joe reached out and shook the vet's hand. "Joe Gannon. And, yes, Katie just hired me. Nice to meet you, Dr. Johnson."

Randy released his hand. "Call me Randy," he said, carefully opening the bird box. Katie stood at the other end of the table. "So, you think the hawk's got a broken wing, Katie?"

"Yes, the left one. The tow-truck driver said he struck the windshield of an eighteen-wheeler. The hawk bounced off the glass and tumbled onto the berm."

"That was kind of the guy to pick him up," Randy said, easing the hawk out and cradling him between his long hands. "Hmm, nice youngster, this red-tailed." He peered closely at the hawk, who was staring fearlessly back at him. "Yep, I'd say he connected with the windshield on his left side because there's some blood coming out of his left nostril. Maybe he suffered a concussion, too…" The vet continued his careful, gentle examination of the bird.

At one point, he asked Joe to hold the raptor. Going to a shelf, he prepared a shot. He then slid the needle into the bird's upper left wing.

"This will kill the pain he's in," the vet told Joe. "All animals feel pain. They have nerves and, just like a human, when they break a bone, they're going to feel it. And pain puts them into shock and it can kill them." Randy gave Joe a quick glance. "You worked with vets before?"

"No, I haven't."

"Well," Randy said as he peeled the Velcro apart, "no time like the present to learn. As I remove the fabric, I want you to hold the hawk, but place your hand beneath that left wing so I can examine it."

For the next few minutes, Joe watched the vet work deftly with the hawk.

"Yep, he's got a break. The good news is the bone isn't compound or sticking out of the skin. Otherwise, that would really put him in danger." Turning, the vet walked to the shelf. "Katie, will you help me?"

"You bet."

"Wash your hands, please."

"Of course." Katie walked to the double sinks and scrubbed her hands with surgical soap. When she'd dried them, the doctor gave her a pair of gloves. She pulled them on and stood to the left of Randy. They worked like a good team to save the hawk.

"Okay, the bone is set," Randy said softly, eyes on the partially outstretched wing. "Hand me the tape?"

Joe watched the ballet between them as they worked with careful precision to tape the broken wing. Once it was done, the vet placed a light cotton netting over the bird's head. One side of the netting closed the injured wing next to the hawk's body to stabilize it. The other side allowed the hawk's good wing to be pulled through an opening so it was able to flap it.

"One of my assistants has a cage prepared for him in the room across the hall," Randy said, lifting the hawk in his hands. The bird had stopped struggling.

"Would you like to feed him?" Randy pressed on the hawk's crop. "He's pretty close to starvation. I'm sure he saw a rabbit, dove for it and didn't even realize cars could kill him."

"I think you're right," Katie said. "Do you think he'll make it?"

"He's young," Randy said. "But he's skin and bone. A lot of first-year hawks die of starvation. They never learn to hunt well."

Katie opened the door to the recovery room. It was large and airy. There was a cage at the end with a door open. "Here?" she asked, hurrying toward it.

"Yep. I'm going to put him on a low perch. We've got water in there for him. Usually, after having a bone set, they aren't too interested in eating."

"I have some rabbit meat in the truck. Can we see?"

"Sure," Randy said placing the hawk's yellow feet on the perch. "Why don't you go get it?"

Joe watched the vet work with the hawk, who seemed slightly dazed. "Why is he having problems sitting on the perch?"

"The bird is in shock." Randy patiently curved the hawk's claws around the thick perch wrapped with plastic carpeting. "In a couple of hours he'll snap out of it. He's actually looking pretty good." He removed his hands from around the hawk, and the bird remained steady on the perch. Randy smiled and nodded, pleased with his medical efforts. Already, the red-tailed was looking around his new home.

A few minutes later, Katie arrived with the food. Randy had closed the cage door. She peered in at the hawk. "He looks pretty calm."

Randy nodded. "The painkiller is helping him a lot. Why don't you try to feed him?"

Katie opened the door. From the pouch slung across her body, she drew out a piece of raw rabbit meat. She wiggled it a little in front of the hawk to entice him.

Without needing too much coaxing, he hawk speared the rabbit, gulping it down.

"Well!" Randy said with a deep chuckle. "He's a hungry boy! Go ahead and feed him, Katie. It will help his body work out of the shock and he'll have a chance to recover."

Nodding, Katie knew a starving hawk had little chance of survival even after a vet helped him to mend. In a minute, the young red-tailed had gulped down so much meat that his craw bulged noticeably out of his upper breast. She shut and locked the cage door. "I'll come back tonight, Randy, if you don't mind. I think he'll be ready to eat a little more."

"Sure. You have a key for the back door, so just help yourself."

"Thank you, again," Katie said. She went over and washed her hands and then hugged the veterinarian. "Thank you so much. You're the best, Randy."

"We're a team," he agreed, embracing and then releasing her.

"What's the percentage on this hawk?"

"He's got a sixty percent chance. It just went up because he wasn't too shocky to eat. Starvation overcame the shock and that's a good sign he's going to recover."

"I'll be back at dusk," Katie promised him with a smile.

Joe saw her face light up with hope over the vet's pronouncement. Randy glowed after Katie had hugged him. Who wouldn't? Joe wondered what it would be like to hold Katie in his arms. Really hold her. Kiss her. Groaning inwardly, he tucked the forbidden desire deep down inside himself. There was no way he could ever kiss her.

ON THE WAY HOME, Katie casually asked Joe, "Do you miss being in the Marine Corps?"

He smiled fondly. "I do."

"Why?" Katie saw the pensive look come to his face, and she realized just how curious she was about him. He rarely talked about himself. Maybe it was because he'd been in the military, or maybe it was his personality.

"I like organization. The military is like a big, messy family. I'd been in long enough to understand my own management talents and weaknesses. When I finally made captain and was awarded a company going over to Afghanistan, I felt good about it. My goal was to keep my men safe so they could come home to their families at the end of the tour." His brows fell. "Nine months into the second tour, it was me going home."

Hearing the disappointment in his voice, Katie reached out and gently touched Joe's arm. "I'm sorry. I'm sure your men missed you."

"I had a very capable lieutenant who was my executive officer. When I regained consciousness in Germany at Landstuhl Medical Center, I knew the company would be okay without me." His lower arm tingled lightly over her unexpected touch. Joe *wanted* contact with Katie. He found himself living for the moment. He didn't think an undercover agent should be yearning for his suspect in this way. He tried to distract himself. "Still no word from your mother?"

Instantly, Katie's brows drew downward. Her hands momentarily tightened around the steering wheel as they climbed the hill up and out of Jackson Hole. "No…"

"If I'm being too personal, let me know. I can take it."

She glanced in his direction. "Joe, you're the easiest man to talk to. My past is littered with bad choices of men who were quiet. I couldn't get two words out of them." Managing an embarrassed laugh, Katie added, "You're the first guy I've met who is sensitive and cares."

"I think being a good listener is a skill that's always needed." He saw a sudden light in her blue eyes. Usually, there was a hint of darkness in their depths, but not right now. His heart swelled as he began to realize the invisible connection he had with Katie. He should have been elated for his mission, but he wasn't. He couldn't stop how he was feeling toward her, no matter how hard he tried.

Katie opened and closed her fingers around the steering wheel. They crested the hill and the gorgeous Teton Range came into view on her left. "You're right." She felt happiness threading through her heart. Usually, she only felt emotions for her raptors. They were safe in comparison to humans. Yet, Joe opened her up like a rosebud ready to burst. Her smile widened. "You have to admit, Joe, you are unusual. Most guys have problems with communication. Women find it easy to talk, but men don't. How did you avoid being closed up?"

"Blame it on my mom," he told her. "She wouldn't let me sulk or go to my room without first dealing with the conversation we needed to have."

"That's wonderful." A large raven flapped across the highway. Down on their left was a stand of trees with moose usually among them. "Is your dad a quiet type?"

"I don't think so," Joe said. "He and Mom are always talking and discussing things."

"I wish…I wish I could find a man like that."

Hearing the sudden wistfulness in her voice, Joe

studied her profile. Katie might be gentle and open, but she had a stubborn chin. She had an inner strength and he was glad for her sake. "Maybe you will, some-day. I believe that good things come to good people."

"Really? Then there's hope for me." She laughed.

The teasing in her voice made Joe feel happy. They hadn't worked together very long but Katie trusted him. He knew Janet Bergstrom hadn't called back and sometimes, when Katie didn't seem to realize he was watching, she would become sad. But then, the sadness would dissolve as she worked with one of the raptors—or talked with him.

"What are your dreams, Katie?" Joe tried to pro-tect himself from the way her mouth softened after he'd asked her the personal question. The agent in him wanted to continue to establish trust. The man in him burned with curiosity about what made Katie the way she was.

"Dreams…oh, well, you know the first one. Find-ing my mother."

"Any others?" he pressed gently.

"Others…well." She gave him an embarrassed look before returning her attention to driving, "Finding the right man. I'm twenty-six. I dream of having a family someday."

"Do you like kids?"

"I adore them! I love being invited into a children's classroom to show them my raptors." Her voice became animated. "We have a school appointment tomorrow. You'll see what I mean. I love the children's faces, love to watch their eyes widen in astonishment as Hank flaps his wings. They are so precious. So…innocent in our world."

"Children today live in a very threatening world,

unlike the one I grew up in," Joe said. "I had a home, we didn't move, my dad taught me to fish, hunt and hike. My mom taught me to cook and clean." He smiled fondly. "Growing up here in this town was safe. We don't seem to have the human predators many other places have."

"I know," Katie said. She braked the pickup for a right turn onto the Elk Horn Ranch road. "I grew up in Casper, a big city. My different foster parents were always freaking out when I'd run away. They'd find me on the streets, looking…"

"Looking for?"

"My mother. I just had this driving sense she lived somewhere in Wyoming." Katie made the turn. "I'm a Pisces, a water sign, and I'm very psychic. I've lived my life on intuition. It has kept me from getting harmed. When you're eight years old, crawl out a bedroom window and walk miles into town looking for your mom, a lot of bad things could happen. But they didn't." Katie drove slowly down the two-lane asphalt road toward the ranch, hidden behind a rise of hills.

Shaking his head, Joe said in a strained tone, "I can't imagine your childhood, Katie. And I'm sure your foster parents were beside themselves with worry."

"Oh, they were." Her mouth thinned. "Looking back on those times I ran away to search for my mother, I understand now how much I hurt my foster parents. I'm sorry I did that to them." She shrugged. "Over the past two years I've written each of them a long letter apologizing and trying to explain why I was the way I was. It wasn't their fault and I didn't want any of them to think it was. It was me. I was desperate to find my mother. It was a driving force so large within me, I felt controlled by it." Katie slowed at the top of the rise. Below, the ranch lay before them. She took a side road that led to the raptor facility. "And what's great is that every one of my foster parents replied to my letter of apology."

"Did they forgive you?"

"Yes, they did. I wanted to go over to Casper and see them in person, thank them for putting up with me and give them each a big hug of thanks. I was such a rebellious little kid. I had temper tantrums." She parked the truck next to the door of the facility. Looking over at him, a half smile on her mouth, she added, "I cried all the time. In kindergarten, I threw books at teachers. I wouldn't listen. I'd do just the opposite of what the teacher wanted."

Joe felt his heart squeeze in sympathy for Katie. "You were a child. All you knew is that you'd been abandoned by your mother. That can create a lot of anger, don't you think?"

Katie sighed and relaxed against the seat. "I know that now. After Donna took me in, I think I developed maturity. She's such a wise person, Joe. I miss her terribly."

"I'm sure you do. Now, she has other responsibilities."

"Yes. I know Donna had to leave, but I'm feeling selfish about it." Katie lifted her head. "My emotions are like rubber bands. I've been ruled by them for as long as I can recall. Donna would sit me down and help explain why I was feeling like I did. She has so much common sense…."

Joe heard the need in her voice and forced his hands to remain still. "You'll stay in touch with her, won't you?"

"Oh, yes." Katie smiled a little. "We're close, Joe. I

know she's taking care of her mother who is bedridden, and I'll call her often to see how she's doing."

"Listen," Joe said, his voice deep, "if you want to talk, I'm here, Katie. I know you don't know me that well yet, but I do care." Shocked at the words coming out of his mouth, Joe abruptly stopped. Her eyes went tender as she regarded him. What the hell was happening? Why couldn't he keep his distance from her? Oh, he knew why, all right. Katie touched every yearning chord in his heart.

He wished he could share his personal dream of the perfect woman he'd meet someday. Katie would laugh when she heard it. He'd thought Zoe, his ex-wife, was the one. But she wasn't. And Joe knew two overseas deployments back-to-back had been partly responsible for their divorce. Katie wouldn't be so quick to give up on them. Joe didn't know how he knew it; he just did. She was a dreamer, and clearly, she'd held on to the dream of finding her mother from the time she was born. Joe knew in his gut if Katie were his wife, she'd wait until hell froze over and never leave him, no matter how long he'd been gone overseas. Shaken by this awareness, Joe opened the door and climbed out of the truck.

"Time to go to work?"

Katie nodded. "Yep, it is. We have to prepare for Mrs. Turner's third-grade class at 9:00 a.m. tomorrow morning." As she rounded the front of the truck and met Joe at the door, Katie reached out and touched his broad shoulder. "Thanks, Joe. For everything…"

CHAPTER TEN

ONCE THEY RETURNED from the grade school, Joe brought Hank's traveling case into the facility. He spotted a note on Katie's desk. "You got a message," he called to her over his shoulder, walking down the aisle. The warmth of the afternoon sun would have made the area hot if not for the louvered windows that were open to allow cooler air in to circulate within the facility.

"Okay," Katie called as she walked through the sliding doors. She set Harlequin's traveling case on the desk and picked up the scrawled note. Her mouth widened in a brilliant smile. Setting the note on the desk, she picked up the case and walked to the peregrine's mew.

Joe watched Hank fluff his feathers, preen a little on his perch and relax. The red-tailed was an excellent education bird and the children had loved watching the raptor fly across the room from his glove to Katie's. It was a sight those children would never forget. One piped up excitedly that watching a hawk fly was even better than riding a broom in the Harry Potter books. Joe had to smile over the child's exuberance.

He was ambling up the aisle, casually checking the raptors in their mews to make sure they were all right when Katie called out to him.

"Joe, you're invited to Iris and Rudd's tonight for dinner. Can you come?"

Halting at Harlequin's mew, he watched Katie lift

the peregrine falcon out of the box and place him on his perch. "Was that the note on your desk?" He enjoyed watching her move. Katie was graceful. Of course, working around raptors, one never made sharp, sudden moves.

"Yes." She turned and walked out of the mew, travel case in hand. "Can you make it? Dinner is at 6:00 p.m." She locked the mew and walked up the aisle at his side.

"Why would they want me to come to dinner?"

Katie felt happy. She was sure it was the thrill of educating the third graders about the raptors. Joe had been a stellar partner and their show was a solid hit with the kids. "Iris and Rudd are like that." She placed the travel box next to the lockers. Straightening, she added, "When I first got here, Iris offered me a beautiful suite in her family's ranch home. I didn't have any money because I was spending it on food for the raptors. I took her up on the offer. I eat with the family most nights now."

"That's nice," Joe said. He saw her eyes go soft.

"Iris and Rudd treat me like a granddaughter. I love sitting down with the family. Kam, her granddaughter, and her husband, Wes, are usually with us, too. It's a great family, Joe. You should accept their offer."

As Katie pushed some tendrils away from her brow, Joe felt his lower body tighten. Last night he'd had a torrid dream about undressing her, exploring and loving her. Joe had awakened early in a sweat and hadn't been able to shake the dream all day. "I'll go. Is there anything I need to bring? Flowers? A bottle of wine? What do you think?"

"Oh, no, just bring yourself. It's a warm family environment. I love their dinners because Iris has a woman chef who cooks nothing but organic food. The table talk is fabulous. They've traveled the world and I've learned so much from all of them."

Her excitement was endearing. "Okay, I'll leave at four today and show up here at six?" He'd have to leave an hour early to get home, shower, change clothes and look presentable.

"Great. But don't dress up. We all show up in jeans." She grinned. "It's a ranching family, Joe. Not a social event."

Smiling a little, Joe nodded. Katie had sat down at her desk to do some paperwork when the phone rang. Instantly, he noticed her tense. It had been nearly a week since she had called her mother. His heart twinged as she paled. Every time the phone rang he knew Katie was hoping it was Janet. She had said she would call back, but he had his doubts.

"Katie here."

"It's Janet Bergstrom."

Instantly, Katie's heart slammed into her throat. For a moment, she couldn't respond. The woman's voice was gravelly, like that of a smoker. Fingers gripping the phone more surely, Katie said, "Yes…thank you for calling back. H-how are you?" She closed her eyes, trying to steel herself against what her mother might say.

"Listen, I'm coming over to Jackson Hole next Monday. Can you meet me at Mo's Ice Cream Parlor at 3:00 p.m. for coffee? We need to talk."

The guttural voice tore through Katie. Her fingers instantly turned cold and damp. Hopes soared and she gasped a little. "W-why yes. I can meet you over there."

"Good, I'll see you then."

Katie tensed as the phone connection went dead. Stunned, she slowly placed the phone on the receiver.

"Katie? Are you all right?" Joe approached her after

seeing how ashen she'd become. Without thinking, he reached out and placed his hand on her shoulder.

"I—uh…" Katie felt the steadying warmth of Joe's hand on her shoulder. It grounded her and helped clear away her shock. Turning around, she looked up into his darkened eyes and worried features. "It's okay, Joe." Her voice wobbled. "Janet is going to be here on Monday. I'm going to meet her at Mo's at 3:00 p.m." She pressed her hands to her face, fighting back tears.

Joe removed his hand. "Hey," he said, "that's great news, Katie."

Dragging in a ragged breath, Katie allowed her hands to fall to her sides. Tears remained in her eyes. "I don't know. She sounded so terse and robotic. As if…as if she wasn't looking forward to meeting me at all."

The forlorn sound in her whispering voice cut through him. He crouched down in front of her, his hand resting on her left upper arm. "Listen, Katie, she's probably scared, too. And when people are scared and defensive, they can sound tough and threatening."

Katie reached out and touched his broad shoulder. "Joe, you really know people's ways." Her fingers curved against the material on his shoulder and she felt the muscles beneath leap beneath her grazing touch. Looking deep into his eyes, she said, "You're probably right. I don't have what it takes to see her side of things."

The intimacy, sudden and unexpected, trickled through him. Katie's hand on his shoulder made him feel good. Like a man. Her touch was butterfly-light and he yearned to lean up and kiss her parted lips. He couldn't stand to see a woman or child cry. It always tore him up.

Squeezing her arm, he said, "You're not expected to, Katie. This is good news. I think Janet wants to meet you." He tried logic with her because her blue eyes were confused and dark. Joe could literally feel her terror, her joy. She seemed to waffle between the two emotions. Damn, he wished he could guard her from all of this. The more he discovered about Katie, the more Joe wanted to shield her from the brutal life she'd had. But it wasn't possible.

His boss would be elated to know that Janet was meeting Katie. And it would put to rest any assumptions Katie had known her mother before this moment. They had not previously met. Inwardly, Joe breathed a sigh of relief. It meant Katie was not a part of the Los Lobos ring, at least not yet.

Kate removed her hand from Joe's shoulder and wiped her eyes free of tears. "You're right. I—I guess I can't be objective about this at all. I've dreamed so long of this happening, Joe. All my life…"

Joe stood up, releasing her arm. If he didn't distance himself soon, he was going to kiss Katie. And right now, her mind and heart were focused on meeting Janet, not on him. Taking a couple of steps back, he said, "It's a good day for you. Enjoy it. You'll have a lot to tell Iris and Rudd at dinner tonight…."

"WHY, THAT'S WONDERFUL NEWS!" Iris crowed as the chef brought out the main course of buffalo roast. "This is a dream coming true for you, Katie. You must be walking on air."

Katie thanked the chef as the plate was placed before her. There was braised buffalo with small red potatoes and sliced early tomatoes from Iris's greenhouse. "I don't know if it's air or not," she joked, giving the family a warm look. "Emotionally I feel like a shuttlecock hit back and forth between dizzying joy and abject terror."

Kam sat to the right of Katie. She placed her hand on her shoulder. "Katie, before I discovered Iris and Rudd, I was lost like you. I didn't know Rudd was my father. All I had was my mother who had died in the California earthquake. My adoptive mother, Laura Trayhern, helped me find my family of origin." Beside Kam, her husband, Wes, watched her with adoration. "I was so afraid, I went undercover when I came to the Elk Horn. I was hoping so badly Rudd was my father and yet cringing in terror that he wasn't."

"Or," Wes added in a gentle voice, giving his wife another tender glance, "if he were your father, that he wouldn't accept you as his daughter because you were born out of wedlock."

Kam nodded. "That's right." She looked deep into Katie's fearful eyes. "And that's where you are right now. You've found your mother. The bigger question is whether she'll accept you as her daughter."

Katie whispered, "I'm so glad you understand."

Rudd was cutting his meat and looked across the table at Katie. "Don't forget, Iris took me out of a foster home and adopted me. I was too young to really understand what you and Kam have had to go through." He gave Iris, who sat to his right, a loving look. "Iris seems to pick up strays." He grinned as he teased his silver-haired mother.

"Strays are tough and they're survivors," Iris said pertly. She added a bit of gravy to the red potatoes on her plate. "Rudd, I loved you the instant I saw you." Iris gave Katie a reassuring smile. "I'm sure once your mother sees how beautiful and accomplished you've become, Katie, she will fall in love with you all over again." She patted her adopted son's arm. "Our hearts are much wider and deeper than we can ever know."

Katie ate but she didn't taste the food. It smelled delicious but her stomach was tense and her emotions flip-flopped between fear and joy. "I really appreciate your stories and support. I need to hear them."

After witnessing this show of support, Joe felt like an outsider of sorts. The Mason family was a patchwork quilt of outsiders who had been assimilated and were well-loved. Rudd, who ran the dude ranch, clearly loved Iris as the mother she had become to him. And Kam had found heaven by returning home. Rudd had fully embraced his daughter without hesitation.

Joe wondered darkly if Janet would be as open and loving. He didn't think so. And what would that do to Katie? He forced himself to eat the delicious food but his heart was focused upon Katie. Joe knew her mother was a tough drug addict and a survivor in a world that destroyed people in a heartbeat. He feared for Katie.

"Joe," Iris said, between bites, "your family's been here in the valley how many generations?"

Rousing himself, he said, "Three. I'm the fourth."

"And you've come home," Rudd said, pleased.

He hated lying to these wonderful people. "Yes, I have."

"Think you'll stay?" Wes asked.

Joe looked around Katie to the cowboy, Kam's husband, who was the ranch manager. "I'm intending to," he said.

Kam held Joe's gaze. "I find it interesting that so many who leave this town come back sooner or later. I wonder what kind of magic it has that calls the wanderers back home?"

Joe smiled. "I hadn't thought of it in that way," he admitted, then turned his attention to Iris, who was so regal in her lavender dress, her hair twisted up on her head. "What do you think, Miss Iris? What draws us back?"

"I think it's these mountains," Iris said, pointing in the direction of the Tetons that were visible through the large plate-glass window. The sun was setting, the eastern flanks on the Jackson Hole side of the range becoming darker and shadowed. Iris speared a potato. "When you look at the geology of this area, we're really in a huge caldera of a mega volcano, and the center is located in Yellowstone Park. We're in a pretty powerful place. I think there's a call to come back to such energy if you were born here."

"It's the everyday magic," Kam agreed. She blotted her lips with the dark green linen napkin. "I know when I first arrived here, I'd never seen the Tetons. As I drove in and saw them for the first time, I felt my heart burst open with an incredible joy I couldn't understand."

"It was your blood, your memory," her father said. "You might not have been born here, but the memory of this place is in your genes."

She smiled. "I think you're right, Dad. And what's wonderful is every morning when I wake up and see the Tetons out our bedroom window, my heart flies open all over again. It's the magic of the place. It can't be explained."

Katie sighed. "I was born in Cheyenne, but when I was brought over here and Donna became my foster mother, I fell in love with the Tetons. When I first saw them, I cried. They are so beautiful. Donna took me on many hikes on their slopes in the summer. I just loved it. I think she and those mystical mountain beings gave me my life back."

"Or maybe you were at an age and maturity to appreciate Jackson Hole," Joe wondered. He saw the glimmer in Katie's eyes, a dreamy look mixed with happiness.

"I was sixteen and I agree I was finally growing up," Katie said with a short laugh. "But when I saw those mountains, Joe, something happened to my heart." She touched the purple T-shirt she wore, her hand pressed against it. "I can't put it into words. When I saw them, my breath was stolen. I felt as if…as if I were standing before sacredness."

"All of nature is sacred," Iris intoned. She finished the last of her meal and set the plate aside. "And it can inspire that kind of a reaction in a human being."

"When I was in Afghanistan, the mountain ranges there reminded me a little of the Tetons," Joe said. "They were just as rugged, jagged and beautiful."

"I've heard their mountain ranges are very tall and lovely," Iris agreed. "Do the Tetons hold you in thrall, too?"

"I'm too logical for the magic," Joe said with a slight smile. "Although Katie is certainly showing me it's possible to live in it."

"Katie is part fairy," Iris informed him archly, her silver brows rising to punctuate her statement. "Fairy people exist here on Earth. They are very otherworldly, like our Katie. And we need their dreams to offset the harshness of life down here."

"I've never thought of myself in that way." Katie laughed. She felt heat tunnel into her face. "I always thought I was different because I was born under the sign of Pisces. Is that how you see me, Iris?"

Iris picked up her coffee and sipped it. "Katie, there's just something ethereal about you. I can't put my finger on it, but you remind me of the flowers I pick and make healing essences from. You've got an invisible connection to the Other World. How do you explain your abilities with all those raptors? They are super-sensitive and very psychic. You can't work with them if you aren't like them, can you?" Her eyes sparkled as she held Katie's gaze.

Laughing a little because she was embarrassed, Katie said, "I don't really know."

"Donna is the same way," Iris said with assuredness. "Now, some people think she's strange, but I don't. I've watched her handle raptors of all kinds over decades and Donna has a touch with them most of us earthlings will never have. You have the same touch, Katie."

"I guess I've never realized this about myself."

"You didn't have anyone to reflect it or point it out to you, is all. When Donna took you in, she clearly saw your abilities. She knew what you needed to get your life in order."

Iris's smile softened as the chef came through the door. Dressed in a large white apron over tasteful brown slacks and an orange top, the woman began to collect the empty plates.

"Donna did share with me that those drawn to fal-conry had special gifts."

Chuckling, Iris nodded. "Well, Donna is a nuts-and-bolts kind of gal. I'm the woo-woo specialist here in the valley."

Everyone laughed. Joe felt the warmth at the table like an invisible embrace from the family. Happiness thrummed through him. Katie's face lit up with joy. It was good for her to see how others valued her gifts. In a way, he realized, the Mason family took the place of her missing parents. Maybe cosmic parents like them were better than the parents who had abandoned her.

"Oh, Iris, you aren't woo-woo," Katie said.

The chef returned with chocolate cake drizzled with caramel sauce and raspberries artfully placed on each plate.

"Oh, I like being known as the woo-woo queen of the valley." She chuckled.

"What is woo-woo?" Joe asked, cutting into the dessert.

Iris shrugged. "I talk to my flowers. I ask them permission to take a blossom to make my flower essences. Isn't that woo-woo?"

Shyly, Katie said, "But I thought everyone talked to trees, flowers and rocks."

Iris grinned. "You and I are the same in that respect."

"Iris is teaching me to do it, too," Kam volunteered.

"I think women in general," Rudd said to Joe, "have this sixth sense. We men are a dumb box of rocks when it comes to this more refined stuff."

"I'm with you there, Rudd," Joe said with a grin.

"But Katie's different," Iris said, enjoying her dessert. "And Pisces people are supersensitive, vulnerable and wear their hearts on their sleeves. They have to learn how to protect themselves from the hardness of this world around us."

"Oh." Katie laughed. "I do that by hiding with my raptors in the wonderful facility you've built for them."

"And I was more than happy to do it, Katie. Donna brought up the idea and we thought it was a perfect place for you and the birds."

"Donna always said I was sensitive," Katie agreed, suddenly glum. "I miss her so much but I know she needs to be at home to take care of her mother."

"Yes, she does," Iris agreed. "We all get parent duty sooner or later. It's part of life."

Katie wondered if her mother would want her around

when she was older. Would Janet take one look at her and leave the restaurant? Fear ate into her. She fell silent, unsure of what path her life would take in just a few days. Katie sank into a morass of imagining herself being abandoned once more by her hard-talking mother. What would happen at the meeting?

"THAT WAS A NICE DINNER," Joe told Katie as he walked her to the raptor facility. Before going to bed, Katie always came out to check one last time on her raptors. He walked closely with her. Above them, the night sky was clear, the stars glittering shards of ice strewn across it. The cool temperature made Katie wrap her arms around herself as they walked down the lighted sidewalk between the ranch house and the facility.

"It was very nice," Katie agreed. "I feel lucky to be living in the house with Iris and Rudd. "I feel so sad for Rudd, though. He hasn't recovered from his ex-wife, Allison, trying to kill Iris and Kam. Tonight was one of the few times he seemed really present and happy."

"You have to admit, it's a helluva shock for your wife to go gunning after your mother and daughter."

"I know." Katie sighed. "Allison has been in prison for a year. Her two children, Regan and Zach, live in town. They moved out of the ranch and abandoned Rudd and Iris. Those two had everything, Joe, but they chose their mother over all of this. Iris and Rudd have never done anything but shower them with love and money. They wanted for nothing."

Joe watched a meteorite streak across the sky to the west. He heard the pain in Katie's tone. "What is it about a mother, whether she's a good or a bad person, that the child will always choose her?"

"I don't know. I guess, in some ways, I'm in the same

boat." Katie slowed and turned and looked up into Joe's pensive features. He was incredibly handsome and self-assured. "My mother is a criminal, Joe. She's been in prison. And yet, I find myself absolutely fearful she'll throw me away again. She'll take one look at me and decide I'm ugly, or…" She avoided his sharpening gaze and stared at the concrete at her feet.

"Listen to me," he said in a hushed tone, gripping her arm, "don't go there. *You* are the jewel, Katie. You might have had a rough time growing up, but you were never in prison. And, yes, she's a drug addict. Probably still is, but that's to be determined. You've never taken drugs, Katie. Everyone had wine tonight except you. You stay away from anything that might be addictive."

She felt the warmth of his strong, caring hand on her upper arm. Joe was only a foot away from her, his eyes burning with care. The desire to reach up on her tiptoes and kiss his mouth shimmered though her. For a moment, the fear was erased, and in its place was a dawning realization she liked Joe. Katie could feel the monitored strength of his hand on her arm. Past relationships vanished with Joe right in front of her. He was staunch, confident, funny and sensitive to her needs. Drowning in his burning look, she felt the energy flow through her, wrap gently around her heart and then, like a bolt of lightning, dive into her lower body. Katie inhaled his male scent. It was wonderful and simply increased her desire to kiss him. But she couldn't.

Stepping away, she gave Joe a soft smile. "I think intuitively I know what will keep me healthy and what won't. I'm not sure where the knowing came from. A drug addict created me." She sighed and looked up at the sparkling night sky, feeling a peace descend upon her. "Iris and Donna have said that children come *through* a parent, not *from* them. I'm not like my mother or my unknown father. And—" she frowned for a moment "—I'm glad. Really grateful. But, Joe, do you think Janet will like me?"

He wanted to cry. The words were from a little girl standing and waiting for her mother to come back and take her into her arms to love her. Without thinking, he cupped Katie's cheek. "I don't know. I wish I did for your sake, Katie." With his thumb, he traced the curve of her eyebrow, grazed her cheek and allowed his hand to drop to his side. "This has to be the scariest thing you've ever encountered."

"It is." A delightful tingle remained on her cheek. She looked deep in his eyes. "No matter what happens at the meeting, Joe, I know I have you, Iris, Rudd and her family. They love me. I have to keep that at the fore-front at all times, no matter what Janet says or does. I am loved."

Hearing the grit behind her words, Joe knew she believed every one of them. The words, *I love you, too,* nearly tore out of his mouth. It took everything Joe had to remain silent. Katie had included him among those who loved her. He understood how she meant it, but Joe found himself wishing mightily Katie would love him as a woman does a man.

That could never happen. Not ever. He was living a lie.

"Well, soon enough, you're going to have the answers you've been waiting a lifetime for, Katie. I'll be here, like Rudd and Iris, to support you no matter how it turns out."

CHAPTER ELEVEN

JANET BERGSTROM HAD CHOSEN a corner booth in Mo's Ice Cream Parlor. She was dying for a cigarette, but this was a smoke-free area. *Damn*. Seated on the red leather bench, she tapped her foot beneath the shiny red table and looked at her wristwatch again. She constantly looked toward the door, waiting for a daughter she'd not seen since birth. She had newspaper articles of Katie holding a hawk on her glove; she would recognize her, for sure.

Fearful, Janet touched her stiff, coiffed hair. She'd gone to a beauty parlor yesterday in Cheyenne. After driving over last night, she'd gotten an expensive room at the Wyoming Inn. Thanks to all the money Xavier had generously given to her, she could afford such digs. Normally, she would never stay at a three-hundred-dollar-a-night hotel.

Where was her daughter? Wiping her perspiring brow with her fingers, Janet felt gnawing fear in her belly. Would her daughter hate her on sight? What was she expecting? Janet had tried her best to look presentable. She'd chosen a tasteful dark green pantsuit with a teal silk blouse beneath it.

She tapped her fingers on the table in time with her shoe and watched with anxiety as the door opened and closed. Mo's, on the main plaza in northern Jackson Hole, was a favorite place for locals and tourists. Now it was filling up with lunchtime patrons. Soft classical music played in the background and it irritated Janet. She preferred screamingly loud punk-rock music. That kind of music always made her soar when she was high.

The coffee mug was nearly empty. Janet wanted something a helluva lot stronger, but Mo's didn't have a liquor license. Suddenly, Janet spied her daughter. A skinny young woman with black hair and blue eyes pushed open the door. Janet's eyes widened and her breath caught in her chest. The girl was almost a spitting image of her at that same age! Shocked, Janet could only stare as her daughter hesitated just inside the restaurant. She was wearing a lavender T-shirt with a purple skirt that hung to just below her knees. Her black hair reminded Janet of a raven's wing.

Janet's hands curled in anticipation and nervousness. As Katie's gaze swung in her direction, Janet's fear level shot up. Her daughter's eyes widened enormously as the two women stared at each other.

Janet felt frozen in time. Katie had blue eyes, the same color as her own. Instantly, her heart tumbled with anxiety and excitement. As she lifted her hand to gesture for Katie to come to the table, her heart burst open. For a moment, she thought she was going to cry! Shocked, she ruthlessly shoved the reaction deep down inside herself. No way could she cry. Katie seemed to float toward her. Janet critically searched her pale features. Yes, she could see some of herself in the girl. But other parts of her face were not her own. She sat still, hands on the table, waiting....

"Hi," Katie said, her voice off-key. "Are you Janet Bergstrom?" Standing uncertainly and clutching a small white leather purse, Katie stared down at the blonde woman. Her hair, piled on top of her head, was carefully coiffed, the dyed platinum color not right for her complexion. Unable to tear her gaze from Janet's puffy forty-two-year-old face, Katie saw the makeup and heavily rouged cheeks. The false eyelashes made it look as if two black caterpillars were crawling across her eyes. Katie saw pockmarks, indicators of acne she'd had at a younger age.

"I am. Have a seat, Katie," Janet said, gesturing to the opposite side of the booth. No way was she going to stand up, hug and be motherlike. She fought the need to do just that.

"Thanks," Katie said, giving her a slight, nervous smile. She slid into the red leather booth. Unable to tear her gaze from the woman who had given her up, Katie felt tears leak into her eyes and mingle with her fear. Would Janet tell her to leave? Tell her she was not worth knowing? Hands damp, Katie quickly slid them beneath the table.

A young waitress with brunette hair and dancing brown eyes came over. She handed them menus and asked Katie if she'd like something to drink.

"Ice water," Katie requested. "With lemon?"

Janet sat stunned. She loved ice water with a slice of lemon in it! Gulping, she said nothing, craving a cigarette. When Katie looked across at her, she saw the girl's anxiety clearly written in her features.

"You don't wear any makeup?" Janet demanded.

Katie cringed, a little taken aback by Janet's gruff demeanor. "Uh…no. I never have."

"You look like a ghost. You oughta do something to look more alive." *Damn.* Janet scowled, angry at herself. She saw her words land visibly upon Katie. Waving her hand around, she added, "You look sick, is all."

Katie cleared her throat. "I'm not sick. Just…scared,

is all…" There, the honesty of how she felt was out on the table.

Janet sat back as if struck, but Katie had no way of knowing if her honesty was welcome or not. Janet didn't seem to live by a code of honesty. Her mother's unnatural blond dye job covered what Katie thought was probably darker hair. The woman's lacquered red nails drummed incessantly on the table. She was overweight by at least thirty pounds, the pantsuit tight and pulling at the seams here and there. Her face was puffy and there were bags beneath her eyes. She'd obviously lived a hard life. Her heart breaking, Katie realized the picture she'd had of her mother was shockingly different from the reality.

"Thank you for coming to meet me. I know you didn't have to," Katie finally managed.

"I'm over here on business."

The waitress brought Katie's lemon and water.

"Order something," Janet said, picking up the menu.

"I'll be back in a few minutes," the waitress said with a smile.

Katie stared at the open menu, seeing nothing she wanted to eat. Her heart hurt. There was no love in Janet's eyes for her. She had to remind herself this was probably nerve-racking for her, too. The words *Why did you give me up?* almost leaped out of her mouth. She compressed her lips to hold back the question. With Janet's dictatorial manner, Katie was afraid to say much of anything. Clearly, her mother was the general in charge of this meeting.

"I think I'm going to have the chicken salad," Katie said, trying desperately to establish some kind of neutral tone.

Janet looked over the menu at her, surprise in her voice. "So was I."

Katie smiled hesitantly. They might have been separated all these years but it appeared they had similar tastes. Her heart warmed with hope.

"I suppose you like pickles on the side, too?" Janet demanded.

Lifting her chin, Katie closed the menu and set it aside. "Yes, butter pickles. What about you?"

"Same."

Her mother's hands trembled as she dropped the menu on the table. She was constantly tapping her long, red nails on the table. In fact, she couldn't seem to sit still for more than a few moments. Anxiously searching for another neutral topic, Katie said, "You said you're here on business?"

"Yeah. I own Mercury Courier Service. I built it up from scratch over in Cheyenne years ago." Waving her hand, Janet added, "I'm over here for a couple of days to lease some space in a building. I'm putting up a second store." And then she added with a triumphant smile, "I'm a businesswoman."

How she wanted Katie to admire and respect her, despite her checkered background. She saw the girl's brows move upward and pride shine in her eyes. Something good flowed through Janet. It was an unfamiliar feeling, and yet, it made her feel happy. Her, happy? That was a joke! Janet always felt edgy, nervous and needy. Never happy. Yet, what she felt in her heart now was happiness. Fleetingly, Janet pondered how long it had been since she'd felt this emotion. Reaching up, Janet briefly touched the heavy gold necklace Xavier had given her a long time ago.

"You have a courier service? Like FedEx or UPS?" Katie saw the triumph in her mother's heavily lined eyes.

"Well, I'm not as big as the big boys," she said, feeling Katie's respect, "but I started off Mercury with the reasoning that even a little guy like me could provide a service. And now, I've gotten big enough to start spreading out. I'm going to lease a building here, get it fixed up, hire some good people and start doing courier service between the two cities."

"Why did you name it Mercury?" Katie noticed the waitress coming their way. She was thrilled to see her mother animated and engaged with her. Some of her anxiety lessened. Maybe Janet wasn't going to tell her to get out of her life, after all.

"Mercury, or Hermes, is the Greek god of transportation and flight," Janet told her smugly. "I can tell you don't know much about Greek myths."

"I don't," Katie admitted.

"May I take your order, ladies?" the waitress asked.

"Yeah, we both want the chicken salad with butter pickles on the side."

"Great. Thank you!" The waitress smiled, picked up the menus and left.

"It must have been tough creating a business out of nothing," Katie said. She rested her clammy hands on the table. Folding them together, she reasoned it was better to let her mother talk about something she felt was important.

"Oh, it was, it was." Janet saw the interest in her daughter's face. She was such a pale thing. Didn't the girl ever get any sunlight? Surely, flying raptors outdoors would give her a tan?

"What led you to want to create Mercury Courier?"

Shrugging, Janet looked around. She never stopped assessing people coming and going. In the drug-trafficking and gunrunning trade, one had to be alert. "I like movement. I can't sit still too long. I got to think-ing that in Cheyenne there had to be a demand for local, city-wide courier service. I figured it all out and got some money and built my dream." She left out the fact that Xavier had suggested the company because it would be a good cover for his drugs and guns to move through the state.

"I don't like staying still too long, either," Katie ven-tured shyly. "I like to move around—like you."

Frowning, Janet said nothing. "I have an appoint-ment with Bobby Fortner of Raven Reality in…" and she glanced at her watch "…about fifty minutes. I called him a week ago and told him my needs. He said there are three buildings that might fit my company's needs."

"I see…"

"Well, you have to have so much square space. I have to have a counter and desk area out front to take customers' packages. And then I have to have a much larger area in the rear where all the packages and en-velopes are kept to go out the next day."

"It sounds like there are a lot of details to your busi-ness." Katie stopped the word *Mother* from flying out of her mouth. Clearly, Janet wasn't the warm, fuzzy type. Instead, she was all business, abrupt, wanting to talk only about herself and her needs. Katie swallowed hard and tried not to allow the disappointment to ruin her day. After all, she reminded herself, Janet hadn't sent her packing. They were having the first conversa-tion of their lives and Katie clung to every word. Still, she tried to quell her expectations.

"Oh, there are, there are," Janet said. "I've got two

guys who run the counter over in Cheyenne. I do all the accounting, book work, scheduling and keep the IRS happy." She managed a grimace over the acronym *IRS*. Twice she'd been hauled in because of her tax forms. Janet was sure it was harassment. They knew she'd been a convict and they were paying extra-special attention to her because of her status. There was nothing she could do about it. No one listened to an ex-con griping to the feds about anything.

The waitress brought their food. She refilled Janet's coffee cup and added cold water to Katie's glass.

Janet dug into the platter, starving to death. She noticed her daughter barely picking at the food. "What's the matter with you? Aren't you hungry?"

Fear frissoned through Katie. She looked up and smiled. "I'm not really too hungry." Then, she risked it all and asked in a small voice, "How do you want me to address you?"

Janet held her fork frozen in midair. She couldn't mistake the tremor of emotion in Katie's tone. "Why… er…just call me Janet. That will do." She felt guilty over the disappointment in the girl's eyes. "Look," Janet added harshly, "we really don't know one another."

Katie nodded. "You're right, we don't."

"You think this is any fun for me?" Janet demanded, waving her fork in Katie's direction. She remembered Xavier wanted the girl as part of the cover for the operation she was setting up here. As much as she wanted to get up and walk out and never see her again, Janet was under orders to do the opposite. She hated the hurt look on her daughter's too-readable face. "I'm looking to hire a person. Are you interested?"

Swallowing hard, Katie set the fork down beside her plate. She wrestled with so many emotions, and tried to think clearly through the haze. Finally, she met her mother's angry gaze and said in a quiet voice, "This is hard on both of us." Something inside of her clicked. She was trying to like her mother, despite the shock of her appearance. Janet might be a businesswoman, but she seemed so anxious. "I would like to help you, if you want. Maybe part-time?" She held up her hands. "I'm a great typist, I know the computer and maybe I could be helpful." Katie wanted to please her mother, was desperate to erase the anger in her eyes.

"Oh…well…let me think about it." Janet dug into the food, starved. Between bites she said, "I've already hired one guy, Eduardo. You're too thin and weak-looking to move those heavy boxes that come through my business. I need some muscle."

"I may look thin to you, but I'm pretty strong," Katie said, checking her anger. She didn't care for her mother's opinion of her. "I'm tall, Janet. And certainly not a ninety-pound weakling."

"Yeah? Well, what do you do for a day job? Sit behind a computer all day?" Janet wasn't about to let on that she knew a great deal about her daughter.

Katie compressed her lips. "No, I'm a falconer."

"A *what?*" Janet tilted her head, eyes narrowing. "What the hell is a falconer?" Janet already knew she was but pretended to not know.

Quietly, Katie explained what she did for a living. When she said that Iris Mason had donated a building and acreage on her ranch, Janet shook her head with disbelief.

"Are you the kind of kid that steps in manure and comes out smellin' like a rose?"

"I guess I am," Katie said, her voice firm. She saw her mother's face move into a grin.

"So you're out saving the world? One bird at a time? And then you tell me the state of Wyoming doesn't pay you one red cent for their food, your time or anything else?" She waved her fork in Katie's face, voice condescending. "You'd never make it in the business world, girl."

"My name is Katie."

"Yeah, all right, Katie. You're basically poor. You have no real business that makes you money. I'll bet you don't even own a house."

"Iris gave me a suite in her ranch house."

"See?" Janet shook her head. "You didn't get my business genes, that's for sure." The drug dealer who'd got her pregnant was a total jerk. So where had this love for nature come from? Janet wasn't sure because all she wanted to do was stay high and run away from the pain of living in this hell called earth.

"You're right," Katie conceded. "I rely on the goodness of others who have more money than I do."

"I'm surprised you're not on the state dole for food stamps."

"I've been on it from time to time in the past," Katie admitted, feeling shame. Her mother had no respect for her chosen vocation in life. That hurt. "When Iris gave me the donation, it allowed me to get off food stamps."

"Thank God. Us taxpayers are the ones footing your bill."

Frustrated, Katie added, "Sometimes it's important to do things for the good of all, Janet. I am poor, that's for sure. But I'm happy. I contribute to the ecosystem in this area. I help injured birds and set them free once they heal. I don't think everything in life should be viewed as either making money or not making money."

Janet chewed her food and studied Katie's set face.

"Well, I was wonderin' if you had a backbone or not. I guess you do." She grinned. Her daughter's face turned stubborn, her jaw jutted outward. There was fire in Katie's eyes.

"My backbone is about helping raptors. I know you don't think much of what I do, but for me it's fulfilling." Katie almost blurted, *And are you happy? You sure don't look it.* She swallowed the words and they became a lump in her throat.

"You gotta fight for everything you get out of life."

"That's for sure." Katie watched her finish off the huge plate of chicken salad. She felt nauseous and had no appetite.

"So, getting back to my new business here." Janet pointed to her plate. "You gonna eat that?"

"No."

"Good, I will." Janet reached out and dragged the plate to her side of the table. "Anyway, as I was sayin', my new business here, I might be able to use you part-time. I'll know in a couple of weeks." She peered intently at Katie. The girl was more foggy mist than human. There was something about her Janet couldn't put her finger on. She was like a shadow who appeared and then disappeared. Right now, Katie sat stiffly, hands clamped together and her face more pale than before, if that was possible. "With your bird job—"

"Falconry."

"Okay, whatever. Do you have time on your hands to do some part-time work at my new office once it gets up and runnin'?"

Shrugging, Katie said, "Sure. I wouldn't offer otherwise."

"Do you have any help with your bird duties?"

"Yes, I just hired a full-time employee, Joe Gannon. He's a falconer, too."

"For a donation kind of business, you're doing okay. Maybe this Iris Mason is your fairy godmother? Sprinkling you with cash whenever you need it?"

Hearing the teasing in her mother's roughened tone, Katie said, "Iris is very generous to me. And, yes, she was the one who suggested I hire a full-time employee. She's paying all my bills."

"What the hell do you get out of this?"

"A sense of accomplishment. I'm helping nature stay in balance."

Shaking her head, Janet ate voraciously. "You're a strange one."

Hurt flowed through Katie. Their conversation had turned to sparring and she felt off balance by her mother's judgments. The woman had been a convict, but Katie wouldn't throw darts at her. Her mother would never know what Norah had discovered about her sordid past. There were no words she wanted to fling back at Janet to equal the hurt rolling through her now. Gripping her hands together, Katie felt coldness and dampness between them.

Janet ate without looking up at her daughter. *Strange one.* Yeah, the girl was that for sure. Janet wondered if her life hadn't been about drugs and falling helplessly in love with Xavier down in Guatemala, she would have turned out like Katie instead. Pondering the possibility, she looked up between bites. "Animals are okay."

"Do you own a dog or cat?"

"At one time I had a husky. Life got too busy and I gave him away. I don't like taking care of anything except the important stuff."

Taking a deep, ragged breath, Katie nodded. Her mother kept on eating and sipping her coffee. The tension at the table thickened until Katie wanted to run away. Yet, she was the one who had initiated this meeting. A crushing disappointment flowed through her. It was as if she were a target to be shot at.

"I remember a friendly dog down in Guatemala," Janet said. "He was a small yellow mongrel. Xavier loved him. Animals always want something from you. I could never figure out why anyone would want a cat or dog for long. They're just one more thing to take care of and I'm too busy to do that kind of thing."

"Who is Xavier?" Katie asked.

"Oh, he's my lover." Janet smiled a little and blotted her lips with the napkin. "When I was younger, I followed him back to his country. We were very happy for a number of years."

"Do you like Guatemala?"

"Sure I do. Beautiful tropics. I love the rain, the thunderstorms and being right on the Caribbean. We did a lot of scuba-diving. Nice to hunt for lobster, catch it and then have it for dinner that evening." She smiled fondly over those memories. "Yes, those were very happy times."

Katie was dying to ask if she had any other children. Norah had said she didn't, but one never knew. "Maybe your love of nature expressed itself in those ways? I like the sky and watching birds fly. You love the ocean and swimming in it."

Janet pushed the empty plate away. She blotted her mouth again, wadded up the paper napkin and threw it on the plate. "Maybe you're right. Maybe we do share a little bit, after all. I like birds. Down there in Guatemala, the birds are colorful, like a rainbow."

Relief pushed away her fear. Katie nodded. "It sounds like a nice place to visit. I've never been out of the state of Wyoming."

Janet glanced at her watch. "I gotta go. Time to meet the Realtor." She grabbed her purse and stood up. "Don't worry, I'll pay for this."

Katie started to move but her mother opened her hand and stopped her. Didn't she even want a hug? Just one?

"I'll call you in a week," Janet said. "Nice meeting you, Katie." The woman took off in a hurry for the cash register near the door.

Katie felt crushed. Hot tears jammed into her eyes. She forced them back, gulping several times.

CHAPTER TWELVE

JOE FORCED HIMSELF not to ask Katie questions after she walked glumly through the door of the facility. Judging from the look on her pale face, things hadn't gone well. He was sweeping the front area when she arrived.

"Hi," Katie said, placing her purse in the drawer of her office desk. "How are the raptors?"

"Doing great," Joe said a little more enthusiastically than necessary. He forced himself to keep sweeping and not pay attention to her wounded look. Fighting himself, the desire to shield her, Joe kept his tone light. "Oh, the Idaho Falls, Idaho, television station called. They're doing a piece on falconry in the area and wanted you to call them back." He pointed to a piece of paper he'd placed on her desk.

Katie nodded and picked up the note. "I see Donna suggested the story. That's so sweet of her." Some of her dark cloud lifted. She smiled and held up the note to Joe. "This is important. It's tough to get airtime on raptor rehabilitation. Donna's very proactive in the world of raptors. She figures the more people understand the value of hawks, falcons and eagles, the more people will protect them instead of killing them out of ignorance."

"That's good news," Joe said, resting his hands on the top of the broom. There was some life returning to her blue eyes. "Are you going to call them?"

"Yes, right now. It's an opportunity and I don't want to miss it." She sat down and picked up the phone.

Joe continued sweeping as Katie talked to the producer on the phone. Keeping the raptor area clean was their number-one priority. Fleas, mites and other vermin could invade the area, get into the birds' feathers and cause all kinds of grief. A clean facility was the only way to go. He was finishing up, dumping the last bit of dirt in a large trash can at the rear of the building when he heard Katie hang up the phone.

"Guess what?" she called, walking down the aisle.

Joe straightened up and turned. "Good news?" What a change in Katie's demeanor. Her cheeks were flushed, her eyes bright with excitement. A smile even lingered on her lips.

"Is it ever! Donna has outdone herself on this one, Joe. This is much larger than I thought." Breathless, Katie said, "This is going to be a *national* one-hour television special. PBS will feature it across the U.S.A. Donna was called by the producer and she suggested filming my facility." Clapping her hands, Katie added, "Isn't this wonderful, Joe? A national platform to get the word out on our raptors." Joyous over the news, Katie spontaneously threw her arms around Joe's broad shoulders and hugged him fiercely for a moment. Just as quickly, she stepped back and saw the shock on his face.

"You don't know me very well yet. When I'm happy, I go around hugging people." She laughed, then turned to go back to her desk.

The producer had asked for specific scenes he and his camera person could shoot when they arrived at the facility a week from now. She had to get busy creating some interesting photographic opportunities. The lunch with her mother no longer felt as sharp and hard in her chest. The good news was helping her climb out of the doldrums.

Joe stood in the aisle for a moment absorbing Katie's unexpected hug. In that moment, she looked joyous, a wide smile on her lips. His shoulders still tingled where her arms had rested. For a second, he'd inhaled her feminine scent and it made him nearly dizzy with need of her.

LATE IN THE AFTERNOON, Iris Mason dropped by just as Katie finished with her photographic scenes for the television crew. Katie excitedly told Iris about the opportunity.

Iris took off her straw hat and grinned. "That's wonderful news, Katie. I hope you get the producer to emphasize that rehabbers like you get no financial support from the state to do what you do."

"Oh, I've got that in my notes," Katie agreed, tapping the paper beneath her hand. "Can you look at what I've written? Maybe I've missed something?" She handed it to the older woman. Katie's heart flew open as she watched Iris carefully read her notes. She loved the elder fiercely.

"I like these ideas, Katie," Iris said, handing the paper to her. "I would add that few people in the U.S. are awarded an eagle license. I'd explain the difference between hawks, falcons and eagles. People don't realize eagles are different and it requires someone with a lot of falconry experience to work with one."

"Great. Anything else?" Katie said, writing quickly.

Iris smiled and waved hello to Joe who was cleaning up some feathers in Sam's mew. "Not right off the top of my head. I'm sure you'll fly Sam. He's so gorgeous to watch."

"I will." Katie touched her chin in thought. "I need to work more with Joe and Sam this week. I know he has eagle experience, but I need to get him and Sam working well with one another for the videotaping of the show."

"Good idea," Iris praised, settling her straw hat on her head. She watched Katie with pride. "This is a great opportunity for you, Katie, for your career. Did the TV producer say when this one-hour special was going to be shown on PBS?"

"He said in nine months. It takes a long time to do the editing, the voice-overs and things like that. He said it's already on the PBS schedule, but right now, it's tentative. They'll firm up a date later on and let me know."

"Might be good to let our local newspaper know, too. They could come out and do a nice piece with photographs on you and your facility while the TV crew is here."

"Great idea," Katie enthused, writing it down.

"Frankly," Iris said, "I think the Elk Horn Ranch might send out a press release to all the major TV stations in the state of Wyoming and let them know, too."

"Would you?" Katie's heart pounded, underscoring her excitement. Iris was a queen of public relations and had boosted her ranch to national notoriety. The elder knew how to maximize press releases to lure radio and TV people to film and talk about the huge ranch.

"Sure." Iris smiled and patted Katie's shoulder. "Why not? It's good for you and for us."

"Especially you," Katie said, becoming serious. "If it wasn't for your grant, Iris, I wouldn't even be here."

"It was a grant given with love," Iris said, smiling. "I'll see you at dinner tonight?"

"Yep, I'll be there with bells on. Thanks for all you

do." Katie stood and gently embraced her. "You're my guardian angel, Iris!"

After giving her a kiss, Iris held Katie at arm's length and said, "Katie, I love being your cosmic grandma."

The words touched her deeply and Katie hugged her again. "Iris, you have no idea how badly I needed to hear that today. Thank you…"

Releasing her, Iris said, "Gotta get back to work! I'm cutting the rhizomes on my iris bed and Kam is helping me start a whole new bed on the south end of the ranch house."

"Get to work," Katie teased and waved goodbye. She had a lot of paperwork to fill out for the state on the immature red-tailed hawk they'd taken to the vet yesterday. Her heart was singing, but as happy as she was, today's meeting with Janet continued to plague her.

Joe was getting ready to leave at 5:00 p.m. when Katie asked him to sit down at her desk.

"Do you have a few minutes?" she asked him, looking at her watch. Joe was gathering up his bag of falconry gear from the locker. "Or do you have someplace you need to go?"

Joe set the bag on the corner of Katie's desk. "No, I'm just going home to make my dinner." He noticed the worry in Katie's eyes. He suspected she wanted to talk about her mother. Pulling over a chair, he sat down.

"Thanks, I need to talk." She took a deep breath and dove in. "Joe, how does your mother treat you?"

He absorbed her question. "Depends upon what age you're talking about?" His mouth curved ruefully. "As a teen, I was a handful."

Her nervousness dissolved beneath his smile. She liked the tenderness lingering in his green eyes. There was such instant trust with Joe. "That's a fair question. How does your mother treat you now?"

Joe chose his words carefully and said, "With respect."

"What do you mean by that? Can you give me an example?"

Joe had a feeling things hadn't gone as well as she'd hoped with her mother. "I'm living in their rental house. I know my Mom wants it kept clean and picked up. I can be kind of a slob and leave socks and stuff lying around," he joked. "I respect her and I want to make my mother happy. I pick up my stuff and I keep the house clean so she doesn't have to come over and do it."

"I see…" Katie thought for a moment. "I guess I meant otherwise."

Joe's brows moved down in confusion. "How do you mean?"

"Well…" She took a deep breath and released it. "Does your mom ever hug you?"

"Not all the time," Joe said. "But every once in a while, yeah, she'll hug me. And I'll hug her back."

"Hmm…" She squirmed in the chair, the silence heavy. "Does she kiss you on the cheek sometimes? You know, to let you know she loves you?"

Smiling, Joe nodded. "Yes, she does. Not often, but when I was a little boy growing up, she was always kissing my hair, squeezing me and she always gave me a good-night kiss at bedtime."

Katie stared at him. Joe's expression was serious, his voice low with sincerity. He was able to soothe her fractious state with just his voice, whether he knew it or not. "Do you share certain food likes and dislikes with your parents?"

"Yes. My mother hates okra because it's slimy if

cooked the wrong way. And I don't care for it, either. We both love a lot of salt on our food. My dad doesn't. And I know a lot of salt isn't good for you. My mother is never that thirsty. She might drink one or two glasses of water a day and that's all. I'm the same way. And we both love vinegar. My dad hates it."

"I discovered my mother and I like chicken salad. I ordered it and so did she. That shocked me."

"Why?"

"I don't know. I was thrilled, to tell you the truth, but she seemed surprised, too."

"Mothers always share similar traits with their children. But you grew up in foster homes, so you couldn't know that until now."

Katie sighed. "Did your mom ever make you feel like she didn't want you around?"

Joe drew in a deep breath. "No. Never." He searched Katie's confused gaze. "Why?"

"When I asked Janet how to address her, she got really angry." And then, Katie shared the incident with him. As she did, the expression on his face grew grave. "Did your mom ever do anything like that to you, Joe?"

"No, and no decent parent would ever make their child feel like Janet made you feel." His remark had teeth in it. Joe couldn't keep the emotion out of his tone. If his FBI boss was still convinced Katie was working with Janet, this was clear proof she was not. This innocence could not be an act on Katie's part.

"Janet said I'd never make it in the business world." She told him the rest of the story.

Joe sat quietly listening as Katie struggled with her emotions. He hung on to his building anger, not wanting Katie to know how upset he was. "Iris thinks differently about you. She believes in your ability to run a business, Katie, or she wouldn't have spent over a hundred thousand dollars to build this facility and underwrite your efforts. While your mother may see herself as a good business person, Iris is a proven product. She put her money on you."

"Maybe I shouldn't believe everything Janet said about me."

"Maybe not," Joe agreed in a quiet tone.

She liked how understanding he was. He wanted her to see that her mother might not always be right. She then told him about Janet's reaction to her being a falconer and needing donations in order to survive. "She said I was a strange one." Tilting her head, she asked, "Joe? Am I strange?"

Damn! He knew how much this meeting had meant to Katie, and from the sounds of it, Janet wasn't anywhere near a good parent, much less a loving mother. "You're not strange. Why do you think Janet said that?"

Opening her hands, Katie shrugged. "She likes to make money and yes, I know money is important. We got into kind of a tense argument. She didn't approve of the way I was living my life. Falconry relies on donations. I don't make a dime, really. And she thought I was 'strange' for being okay living that way."

Sitting back in his chair, Joe pushed his fingers through his hair. He had to be careful and quell his anger. "I think most parents want their children to make enough money to be secure. Maybe she was thinking along those lines?"

"Well, she must have been because she's offered me part-time work in the office of the courier service she's going to be bringing to town pretty soon."

"Really? Can you tell me more about it?" Joe's heart took off in excitement mixed with dread. It was a possible clue that Katie had no connection with her mother before this. But if Katie did start working for her mother, it wouldn't be a safe job if Janet was still dealing in guns and drugs. But was she? No one had proof. As he listened to Katie's account of the lunchtime conversation, his mind spun with options and choices.

"And is she going to hire you when the store is completed?" Joe asked.

"She said she'd call me next week."

"That's hopeful, isn't it?"

Katie stood up and gathered the papers into a neat stack. "I guess. I don't know. I got the feeling she wanted a worker bee in the front office. She said I was too skinny and weak to work in the back room hauling boxes and stuff to the truck."

Joe stood. He couldn't stand the hurt in her voice. "Hey," he said in a whisper, grazing her shoulder and turning her toward him. "You're hardly weak." A smile tugged at his mouth as he cupped her shoulders. They were so close. He inhaled her special scent and it was like drinking an aphrodisiac. Hands tightening, he added, "And take it from me as a man, Katie, you are not skinny. You're beautiful in every way…."

Katie drowned in the sincerity of his deep voice and the burning look in his eyes. She hadn't thought of kissing Joe, but right now, it seemed like the most right thing in the world. She had been wounded by Janet and wanted to neutralize those feelings. Lifting her hands, she framed Joe's face, the stubble making her palms tingle. His gaze turned predatory. Breath hitching, Katie closed her eyes and leaned up…up…to feel his mouth settling hotly against her lips.

Whatever pain and uncertainty she'd felt seconds before fled as he tenderly captured her. Katie felt his lips take hers more surely as she sank against his hard, tall body. He was taller than she and easily took her weight. The kiss deepened and her breathing became as ragged as his. The scent of pine encircled her. She felt his hands move from her shoulders and embrace her, bringing her fully against him. Anchoring her whole existence on his mouth plundering hers, she responded with equal fervor. Joe's kiss was dizzyingly wonderful and so different from that of anyone she'd kissed before. His hands ranged slowly down her long spine, sending wild, fiery tingles all across her back. It was as if he were memorizing her, inch by inch, the sensation one of velvet luxury. Every time his fingers moved, her flesh responded wildly. She felt her breasts tightening, her nipples growing hard against his broad chest.

Joe groaned. What was he doing? He tore his mouth from Katie's and held her at arm's length, staring down at her. His whole body was on fire, a throbbing ache making him wildly aware of how quickly the kiss had enflamed him. Katie's eyes opened wide and he saw an unnamable emotion in them. Her mouth was soft, lips parted, beckoning him to kiss her again. No, he couldn't. She blinked several times, as if coming out of a stupor. Joe didn't dare release her because she swayed slightly, her fingertips coming to rest on her lips. There was a look of shock mingled with pleasure in her gaze.

"I'm…sorry," Joe managed in a strangled tone. "Are you all right?"

Shaken and feeling heat racing between her mouth, breasts and lower body, Katie raised her brows and nodded. "Yes…" She stared wonderingly at Joe. His green eyes were narrowed with hunger—for her. His kiss had rocked her world. Her lips tingled as though tiny flames licked across them from the power of his mouth searching hers. As he steadied his hands on her shoulders, heavy desire coursed through her.

"Katie, I didn't mean for this to happen," Joe said in a ragged voice. "It shouldn't have happened…I'm your employee. You're my boss." He lifted his hands from her shoulders.

"You're right," she managed, touching her brow. "I'm the one who should apologize. I kissed you first. I don't know what happened…."

The forlorn look in her eyes gutted Joe. Mouth tightening, he forced himself to step away from Katie or he was going to drag her back into his arms and finish what they'd started. His FBI boss wouldn't be pleased, that was for damned sure. Katie was his target, not his lover. Joe couldn't mix business with pleasure, but damn, she tasted like sweet clover honey straight out of the comb. He never wanted to forget her taste, her texture or that fragrance that was only her. Zoe had never made him feel the way he felt right now. Mind tumbling like an avalanche out of control, Joe reached for his falconry bag.

"Listen, I think we need some time to feel our way through what just happened. We can talk tomorrow?"

"Sure, no problem," Katie heard herself say, her wispy voice sounding as though she was in an echo chamber. Fiery explosions were still occurring deep within her. Trapped in the strength and tenderness of his kiss, Katie lifted her hand in farewell to Joe. He nodded, gave her a strained smile and left the facility. Katie sat down before her knees gave out. What had just happened?

She felt shell-shocked, as if a bomb had exploded between them. Why, oh why had she initiated the kiss? What had driven her to do that? Joe had never made any overt moves toward her. She had always treated him as an employee. Resting her elbows on the desk, Katie closed her eyes, trying to think her way through the unexpected kiss. What had she done? Would Joe quit? Her heart skittered with fear. Suddenly, Katie realized just how much she liked him. Unlike her past partners, Joe was steady and reliable.

Moaning, Katie sat up and rolled her eyes over her assertiveness. Had she just lost the man who fitted into her own and her raptors' lives like a glove on a hand? Miserably, Katie's imagination ran away with her, as it always did when she was under stress.

As the sun moved lower in the sky, Katie glanced at her watch. It was nearly time to eat. Hurrying through the facility, she made one more check on her raptors and then closed up for the night. Her mind and heart lingered on Joe. She walked across the parking lot to the ranch house, realizing she'd all but forgotten about meeting Janet. Such was the power of Joe's kiss upon her lips.

JANET'S FEET ACHED. She hated dressing up but she'd had to look at potential leases for her courier service. Inside her newly rented apartment, she kicked off her shoes, threw her purse on the dark brown sofa. She shut the door, craving a drug fix. Only cocaine would do. Hurrying to the bedroom where she had a suitcase, she opened it and dug into one of the pockets. Locating the coke, she laid out the powder in thin, white lines. She took a small straw from her purse and quickly snuffed the powder into her nostrils. She closed her eyes and stood in her stocking feet on the cool tiles of the kitchen, sighing.

The euphoria started to move through her, making her feel heady and light. How good it felt! Opening her eyes, she made it to the bedroom and flopped down on it. The window in the room was large and western sunlight was shooting across the room to the beige wall opposite. Her eyes were sensitive to light and she closed them. She relaxed onto the bed and sighed. Finally! Relief from this damned hard world.

As she fell into the pleasure of the drug, her mind moved back to lunch today. Her daughter was pretty. She wiped her mouth and smeared the red lipstick. Katie was soft, not hard like her. She even had a soft voice. Her hands were soft. There were no calluses on the palms like there was on hers. Where the hell did she get such softness? Janet wondered. God, she'd thrown her baby to the wolves of the world. Yet, as Janet had looked at her across the table in the booth, the girl had seemed absolutely unscarred by life. How could that be? No one escaped the misery of this hell they called Earth.

Her cell phone rang in her purse. Groaning, Janet sat up, disoriented. Rummaging and fumbling through her huge leather purse, she found it. Blearily, she looked at the caller. It was Xavier! Quickly sitting up, Janet opened the phone.

"Xavier. What a nice surprise," she said.

"I'm back from Idaho Falls. How did things go today? Did you find a place to put the courier service?"

"Yes, yes, I did." Janet scrambled to focus on the conversation. She didn't want to tell him she was high. He disapproved of her doing such a thing when there was work to be done. She didn't want to disappoint him. "I found a nice redbrick two-story building a block off the plaza. The first floor has three thousand square feet available."

"Good, good. And have you signed the lease agreement?"

"Yes, I did. Tomorrow, I'm going to get one of your men over in Cheyenne to drive a truckload of machinery and office equipment over here. The place needs to be painted. I need to find a desk and stuff like that tomorrow."

"And your daughter? Did you see her?"

Wincing, Janet mumbled, "Yeah, I saw her."

"You sound disappointed?"

"She's weak, Xavier. Nothing like me."

Laughing, Xavier said in a seductive tone, "*Mi corazón,* few women have a set of balls between their legs like you do."

Janet chuckled over their private joke. "She's a girly girl."

"Will she work at the office?"

Hearing the edge in Xavier's tone, she said, "I talked to her about it. There's been no firm decision. I told her I'd call her in a week. I figure it's going to take me that amount of time to get this new office up and running. There are electrical and plumbing problems that have to be resolved. I need to make sure the rear room where all the packages come in is made secure."

"Yes, that's most important. Well, get her to say yes, eh?"

Janet scowled. "Listen, Xavier, I may not care much for her being weak and all, but I don't want to put her life in jeopardy, either. I worry about the Mexican drug ring trying to set up shop here in Jackson Hole. You know their way to get rid of any competition is to kill the enemy."

"Tut, tut, Janet. Your weak little daughter is safe and sound."

"I don't know," she grumbled, frowning. "She's the type that would faint at the sight of blood."

Laughing, Xavier said, "She'll come around. She's

your daughter, Janet. Some of your genes must be in her?"

"I didn't see any. The only thing we agreed on was we both liked chicken salad."

Xavier laughed deeply. "Give her and yourself some time to get to know one another, eh? As you *Norte Americanos* say, she's a chip off the ol' block. *Sí?*"

"Sí," Janet agreed, feeling her focus dissolve. The cocaine was deepening inside her and all she wanted to do was stop talking, lie down and float away. "Hey, are you going to come over once I got this place prettified?"

"No, I can't. I don't dare show my face there, you know that."

The censure in his tone scared her. "Okay, no problemo." Janet was always afraid of losing Xavier. Oh, it was true he had a wife and children, but she didn't want to be thrown away for not doing what he wanted done.

"I'll be going incognito shortly and heading south to Guatemala. You have plenty of dollars to get this business up and running. As soon as you do, use a throwaway cell and call me. Then I'll have one of my lieutenants come up and work with you for a week or so until we get the new routing completed."

Her nose was running like a faucet. Janet unsteadily pushed to her feet and grabbed for a bunch of tissues from the box on the chest of drawers. "Yes, that sounds good, Xavier. Be safe crossing the border. I miss you already." She wiped her nose and sniffed.

"Are you crying?"

"Sure I am. You know how much I love you, Xavier. We've been together since I was eighteen. It's a marriage of sorts," she said.

"A long time, *mi corazón.* But I am already married, as you know. What we share is different."

Janet wished otherwise. She'd begged Xavier to marry her when she'd lived with him. His father, who was not into drugs, wanted a Guatemalan woman for his son's wife, and Janet was sure Xavier had bowed to the stern man's wishes. Damn the old bastard. "I just wish," she slurred, "that this kid of mine was your daughter, too." The words slipped out before Janet could stop them. Alarmed, she felt her heart start to pound. There was a long silence on the phone. Gripping it, Janet added hastily, "Forget what I said, Xavier. I'm just wishing in the wind, I know. Have a safe trip south."

"I will. Adios…"

The cell phone went dead. Janet stared at it and cursed softly. When would she learn to keep her mouth shut? Xavier was impatient and dismissive when she brought up his family. He was utterly protective of them. *Dammit.* Throwing the cell against the wall, Janet sank back onto the bed with a frustrated groan.

Her last thought was she had to get her weakling daughter on board. Xavier wouldn't take no for an answer. Yet, as she felt herself floating into euphoria, Janet was worried about the other cartel. From long experience, she knew warring cartels took no prisoners. She might not think much of Katie, but she sure as hell didn't want the kid caught in a crossfire, either.

CHAPTER THIRTEEN

"AT LEAST WE KNOW Katie Bergstrom wasn't working for her mother before this," Hager told Joe.

Joe stood at the picture window in the living room. The sun was still below the eastern horizon. "My gut was telling me as soon as I met her that she wasn't hooked up with Janet."

"You were right. Now, Katie is being drawn into Janet's fold."

Rubbing his brow, Joe felt his heart squeeze in fear for her. "I don't know if she's going to work for her or not. Janet's supposed to call her in a week."

"No other contact with her that you know of?"

Joe shrugged. "Katie's world revolves around her raptors. She feels safe with them."

"Not surprising that she's found an anchor after being tossed around like a billiard ball on a pool table. She went through a lot of foster homes."

"Right," Joe agreed. He stopped pacing and felt his nerves tighten. He shouldn't have kissed Katie. And his boss would never know about it. Above all, Joe had to keep his eye on the prize: connecting Janet Bergstrom to the Los Lobos cartel.

"The Garcia cartel from Mexico is starting to create a beachhead in Jackson Hole," Hagar went on, "and now, we know Los Lobos wants to do the same thing. That's a serious problem because sooner or later, these two cartels are going to have bullets flying at one another. I need you to go over to the sheriff's office and let the commander know what's happening. We need to make them aware of this escalating situation."

Joe glanced at his watch; it was 6:00 a.m. "I'll get over there before I have to go to work."

"There's a deputy sheriff by the name of Cade Garner who is the head of the drug task force for Teton County. He's the one you want to make contact with."

"Okay," Joe said. He saw a raven fly nearby, cawing into the dawn light.

"Tell Garner to contact my office and we'll send him everything we've got. From now on, we coordinate. You'll be the field agent on this, Joe. You're doing a good job."

Joe halted, staring blankly at the rose-colored sunrise. "Mr. Hagar, I wonder if we need to shield Katie Bergstrom in all of this? She's walking into this crossfire and hasn't a clue about what's going on. Don't we morally owe her a warning about her mother and what she's up to?"

Hagar sighed heavily. "Sometimes people get used as pawns. Katie can't help that she was born to this woman. And it's certainly not her fault her mother turned to drugs and gunrunning. I'm sorry, Joe, but you can't say anything to Katie."

Fear rose in him. "At some point, we have to tell her. I mean, I can't let her walk blindly into the situation. She could easily get killed if there's an attack on Los Lobos by Garcia." His hand painfully tight around the cell phone, he waited to hear what Hager would say.

Sighing, Hager said, "Maybe. Maybe not. We're going to have to monitor this one step at a time."

"We're leading a lamb to slaughter."

"I don't see it that way, Joe. I know you're upset and you're worried for Katie, but she's all we've got in this case. We have to get legal goods on Los Lobos. I wish it was different, but no one knew at the outset of this mission that Katie Bergstrom was innocent and had no connection to her mother. We had two satellite intel photos of Janet parked at the entry to the Elk Horn Ranch. Right now, I've got to think the mother was going to introduce herself to her estranged daughter, but got cold feet and backed out."

Joe began pacing the length of the living room. "It's the only logical explanation we have. Janet *never* contacted Katie. I don't think it's right at all to lead Katie on. She could get hurt, or worse, killed."

"You've got two roles to play, Joe. One is to be our eyes and ears on the ground through Katie's daily schedule. The other is, if she takes the job as a clerk in the store, you've got to monitor that situation, too."

"How?" Joe nearly shouted the words. "I can't be at Mercury Courier to watch over Katie and you know that. And we know Garcia has a stronger toehold here in the valley than Los Lobos. I'm really worried that we're setting Katie up. I don't feel good about this."

"I know you're upset, Joe, but right now, just keep doing what you're doing. Maybe we'll get lucky and find Xavier Lobos. He runs back and forth across the border in disguise. We know he visits Janet and his other key people who are setting up the new distribution system for him here in the U.S. There's a lot at stake. Katie is our point person, whether she knows it or not. The mother is willing to trust her. We've tried to get people inside Janet's operation with no success. Katie is the key to this lock, Joe. You have to make peace with what's happening and stay alert. Katie needs your full focus. All right?"

Hating Hager's decision, Joe said in a low, stressed tone, "Boss, I don't like the decision, but I'll abide by it. I understand the larger picture."

"Sometimes, Joe, people get entangled in the investigation. The good news is, you are there. You see Katie five days a week. She has you as a guard whether she knows it or not."

Joe wiped his aching brow; one of his migraine headaches was coming on. "I've got to go. I'll report in tomorrow. Thanks." He clicked off the cell, pulverized by the fear he had for Katie. Walking to the bathroom, Joe grabbed his pills and filled a glass with water. It was time to get dressed, but first, a shower. God knew, he felt dirty in a way he'd never felt before. As he stripped out of his pajama bottoms and left them lying on the floor of the bathroom, Joe wondered if being an FBI agent was the way he wanted to live his life. His parents had raised him to be honest and to have integrity. Joe hated lying to Katie. He turned on the faucets and stepped into the shower.

DEPUTY CADE GARNER SHOOK Joe's hand. The sheriff's deputy led him to a glass-enclosed room where they sat down. To Joe's surprise, the FBI office had already faxed and emailed a large amount of information.

"I haven't had much time to go over this material," Cade said, gesturing to it. "The gist is, from what I can tell, we're dealing with two competing cartels moving into our town."

Joe felt the pain in his head, but, luckily, the medicine was working. Coffee also helped the headache turn down a notch. "That's right."

Shaking his head, Cade muttered unhappily, "Two?"

"I'm afraid so."

Pushing through the papers so far collected, Cade drew out a photo of Xavier Lobos and one of Garcia. "These are two bad dudes. I've been working with the sheriff's departments in Phoenix and Maricopa County. They've given us a lot of useful intel on these two nasty cartels."

"Good, because you're going to have to start pooling every resource from anywhere you can get it," Joe said. He sipped his coffee and watched the deputy's brow wrinkle with worry. "You said earlier you knew of Garcia?"

"Yes, he started landing a float plane on Long Lake, ten miles south of here. He got caught because the owners of the Bar H, who own half the lake, were being awakened twice a week by a low-flying plane over their home. We captured two drug soldiers and a local kid by the name of Zach Mason. We've been hoping to implicate Curt Downing, who is a major rancher and very rich, in the Garcia cartel, but we couldn't. The two drug soldiers turned over evidence on the same man who hired the Mason kid to help unload the marijuana bales off the float plane. One of the owners of the Bar H, Val Hunter, saw the bales in an underground basement at Downing's largest barn, but her camera didn't work. And we didn't have enough legal reason to get a judge to sign a search warrant to go in there."

"Downing..." Joe said, raising his eyes in thought. "I've heard of this man."

"Yeah, he owns Ace Trucking Company here in town. The FBI said they suspected he was using his trucks to distribute the marijuana." He smiled and picked up his mug of coffee. "They said they were sending out an agent. That must be you?"

"I guess so," Joe said. "I wasn't given a lot of info on Downing. My focus is on Katie and Janet Bergstrom. Was Janet on your radar?"

"Not at all," Cade said, picking up a recent photo of her and intently studying it.

"So we know Downing is moving drugs. We just can't prove it legally?"

"Correct. Since the float-plane capture, Downing hasn't been seen much in town. We think he's lying low to let this incident die down. The guy is arrogant, filthy rich and thinks he knows everything."

"Is he doing drugs?" Joe wondered.

"I've never seen Curt high on drugs, nor has anyone else." Cade smiled. "It doesn't mean he's not on them, however. He's just real careful."

Nodding, Joe pushed the chair away from the table. "It looks like you have a bunch of strings but none are connected."

"Not yet," Cade agreed, shuffling all the papers and pictures into a file in front of him. "Give me a day or two to catch up with all this intel? I'm going to call my friend at the Maricopa County Sheriff's Department for an update on those two cartels. Both are very active in the Phoenix, Arizona, area. If I hear anything, I'll give you a call to keep you in the loop. I'll assign another one of my deputies to keep Mr. Hager notified as well."

Rising, Joe shook the man's hand. He liked Cade Garner. He was efficient and knew his business. "Good enough." Glancing at his watch, he said, "I've got twenty minutes to make it out to the Elk Horn Ranch to start my undercover day job."

Grinning, Cade said, "I know Katie Bergstrom. I've

seen Katie put on education shows with her raptors for a lot of the clubs and schools around here. She's well-respected. And I'm glad to hear she's not involved with her drug-running mother. Stay safe out there, okay?"

"I will," Joe said, leaving the room. More than anything, he wanted Katie to remain safe. But how? It ate at his stomach as he left the sheriff's department and walked out to the parking lot. And now, he was going to have to face Katie and the fact they'd kissed one another last night.

JOE FOUND KATIE hard at work at her desk. This morning, she wore a pink T-shirt that matched her pink cheeks. Her slightly curly black hair lay around her shoulders, blue highlights here and there. As usual, she had on jeans and boots. When she heard the sliding door open, she twisted around and looked toward him.

"Hi, Joe. How are you this morning?"

Katie sounded upbeat but Joe saw the look in her eyes. "Okay." He tapped his brow. "Every once in a while, thanks to my injury over in Afghanistan, I get a migraine headache." He stopped at the corner of her desk. "And one came on this morning." He saw her brows move up, a look of sympathy crossing her features. Raising his hand, he added, "I took my medicine and I'm okay. It's just that when they come on, sometimes I'm not myself and you should know that in advance." He added a slight smile to go with the warning.

"I remember you put that information down on your résumé." Katie couldn't help but stare at his curved mouth. A mouth she'd kissed ardently yesterday. "Listen, do you want to go home? You do look a little pale."

"No, I'm fine," Joe said.

"Have a seat," Katie invited, gesturing to the wooden

chair at the end of her desk. "I think we need to talk about yesterday evening."

Surprised, Joe nodded and sat down. Katie, as ethereal as she was, had more strength than he'd thought. He had to stop seeing her as a helpless young woman. "I think we need to talk, too," he agreed. Katie gathered the papers and placed them beneath her clasped hands. He saw maturity in her eyes. And she was somber. Why? It suddenly occurred to Joe she might already be involved in a relationship. If so, why had she initiated the kiss with him? Mystified, he waited for her to speak.

Just then, a woman appeared at the glass door with a box in her hand.

Instantly, Katie was on her feet. "This woman just called me about ten minutes ago, Joe. She's bringing in an injured bird."

Joe stood up as the middle-aged woman entered the facility. She managed a slight, strained smile.

"Hi, I was told you folks take care of injured birds." She held the small cardboard box toward Katie. "I was driving to work this morning and I found this hawk, or whatever it is, flapping on the side of the highway. I pulled over and picked it up." She held up her index finger after Katie took the box. "The thing bit me, too."

Katie peered into the box. "This is a hawk." She gave Joe the box. "Thanks so much for bringing it in. We'll try to save it."

The woman nodded and said, "Great. Well, listen, I've got to go. I have a job to get to and I'll be late. Thanks so much!" She turned and left.

Joe placed the box on the desk. Katie slowly opened the lid of the box.

She studied the frightened hawk. "It's another immature red-tailed and it too looks like it might have a broken wing. We'll take this one to Dr. Shep Baldwin. He's the other vet I work with."

Joe got busy and found a cloth to make the box dark. Raptors felt safer without light. The bird stopped moving around when Joe picked up the box. That was a good sign. Katie grabbed her purse and they headed out to the parking lot to her truck. Joe sat in the passenger seat and held the box.

Once Katie was on the main road leading into Jackson Hole, she was on her cell phone calling Dr. Baldwin. After receiving approval to bring the raptor to his clinic, she gave a sigh of relief. She pressed the cell phone off, and placed it in the center console. "Good news, Shep can take the raptor."

"You alternate between Dr. Randy Johnson and him?"

"Yes, I try to not take advantage of either of them."

"Spread the work out. Good idea." Joe inwardly chafed. He wanted to talk with Katie about their kiss. Maybe later.

Dr. Shep Baldwin met them at the front desk. He smiled warmly at Katie as he took the box from Joe. "Hey, good to see you again, Katie. And you say you have a young red-tailed in there?"

Katie smiled and moved to the side of the desk. Shep had a very busy practice. There were dogs and cats, plus a white cockatoo waiting to be seen. "Shep, this is Joe Gannon. He's my full-time employee out at our facility."

Shep nodded toward Joe. "Nice to meet you. Come on back…" He turned and walked down the green-and-white-tiled hall.

Katie rushed ahead and opened a door on the left. This was where Shep worked on the raptors.

"Thanks, Katie," he said.

Joe shut the door. He watched the doctor carefully place the cardboard box on the stainless-steel examination table in the center of the room. Katie's head was almost touching Shep's as he carefully examined the hawk. Standing there, Joe felt sudden jealousy. Caught off guard, he scowled. What were these feelings? Watching the two talk in low tones, Joe realized with a shock he was actually envious of the vet. Baldwin was tall, deeply tanned, athletic and handsome. Joe saw no ring on the doctor's left hand. He watched Katie's reaction to Shep. Was there something more between these two? It sure looked like it to Joe. He forced himself over to the examination table. Neither seemed to notice his arrival.

"Well," Shep murmured, "it looks like this guy is lucky. He's clipped his right wing, probably on a power line." He carefully examined the hawk's wing. "And no open fracture, which is good."

"Can you save him, Shep?"

Looking up, the veterinarian smiled over at Katie. "I think so. Appears to be a straightforward closed fracture."

"Phew, that's good news," she said in a whisper. The hawk was very still in the box, as if it knew these humans were not going to hurt it, but help it. The raptors were exquisitely tuned into everyone's emotional reactions. And Shep was one of the kindest and most gentle people she knew. He loved what he did and it showed. "Do you want us to stick around to help?"

"No," he said. Turning, he placed a cover over the box so the hawk would remain calm. He looked at his watch. "I'm in surgery at 10:00 a.m. I'll get one of my assistants to prep him and we'll take care of him right away."

"Great, thanks. Just call and let me know when to come and pick him up."

"Sure. You got room for him?"

Nodding, Katie said, "Yes, we do."

"Great." Shep turned and nodded toward Joe. "Nice to meet you. If you'll excuse me, I've got a bunch of four-legged patients waiting for me."

Joe nodded and stepped aside. Shep walked to the door and opened it.

"Katie, how about me buying you a mocha latte at Mo's some Saturday soon? We need to catch up with one another."

"Terrific, Shep. Give me a call."

Smiling, he said, "I will. Later…"

On the way back to the ranch, Katie noticed how quiet Joe had become. Fingers opening and closing around the steering wheel, she said, "Are you all right?"

Joe glanced over at her. "Yes, I'm fine."

"You seemed…" and she searched for the right word "…uncomfortable at Dr. Baldwin's? Or am I wrong?"

Joe was shocked, squirming inwardly at her ability to sense his emotions. She was just like her raptors. "You seem to be good friends with the vet."

"Shep has been a bedrock to Donna and me. He's given so many hours of his time to the birds we bring to him. I really like him, Joe. He's just a salt-of-the-earth kind of guy."

Joe felt envy gnawing away at him. Why the hell was he reacting this way? He shouldn't be. "That's decent of him to give so much of his time."

Frowning, Katie heard an edge on Joe's voice. What was going on? His brows were drawn down, his eyes straight ahead. She could feel him wrestling with something. But what? "So what about you? Do you miss somebody? Are you sure you're okay?"

Katie's questions were softly spoken and Joe didn't

consider them intrusive. "I'm okay. No, I don't miss anyone, but I do miss the idea of marriage. Zoe, my ex-wife, got tired of me being sent overseas a year at a time to Afghanistan. Not that I blame her. She married me because she wanted me around, not gone all the time."

"It had to be hard on both of you. Frankly, I don't see how any military family makes it through two, three or four deployments. I feel it's asking too much of our volunteer military people. It just isn't right." She glanced at him. "And I've been hearing constantly on the news how these long deployments are tearing up families and divorces are high. It sounds like your marriage was a casualty?"

Joe watched the Tetons emerge from the flat plain on the left as the truck breasted the long hill. He was glad he didn't have to lie to Katie about his background. "It was."

"What was Zoe like?"

"Beautiful. Accomplished. She was born here in Jackson Hole, where I met her. Now, she's moved on to Chicago where she works at a law firm."

"You met her here? Was she a high-school sweetheart?"

"Yes, she was. I was the captain of the football team and she was a cheerleader."

"And so you knew her for a long time?"

"We did. We dated in high school. Then we went to different colleges. When I graduated, Zoe was back in town visiting her parents. I heard about it and drove over to see her. She'd just finished four years of learning to become a paralegal in corporate law. We lost touch with one another over the years."

"Something must have happened when you met?"

"For sure," he said, fondly recalling the special time

with Zoe. "It was as if we picked up where we left off. I asked her to marry me before I left for my first tour in Afghanistan. She was getting ready to move to Chicago to take a position at a prestigious law firm. We agreed to marry quickly because I had thirty days before I left for advance officer training at the Marine Corps at Camp Pendleton, California."

"A whirlwind romance?"

"It was. I helped Zoe move to Chicago, find a nice apartment and we spent the rest of our honeymoon in the city. I don't like big cities, but she did." Joe shrugged and recalled the noise and pollution. He preferred the wide-open spaces of Wyoming and a blue sky that arced over them and went on forever.

"You were happy?"

"Very." He rubbed his brow. "But I was worried, too. I didn't know if Zoe really understood the stress of our being separated for a year. Once I graduated from officer training, received my lieutenant bars, we stayed in touch by emails and Skype calls."

"At least you had amazing technology to stay in touch. The soldiers from any other era only had letters."

"You're right."

"But it wasn't enough?"

"No. Zoe really got angry when, after returning home for five months, I had to leave again for another tour. I kind of knew when I left the second time it wasn't going to work out. We'd had a lot of arguments about what a marriage was and wasn't. She was upset, and I don't blame her. But there was nothing I could do about it. I couldn't disobey orders."

"And then, before you got wounded, did she file for a divorce?"

Pain hung in his heart. "Yes, she filed for a divorce six months into my second tour."

"I'm so sorry, Joe." Katie eyed him sadly and saw the disappointment in his face. "It wasn't anyone's fault, really."

"Zoe blamed the war and Congress. She wanted her husband around, not gone all the time." He shook his head. "Military spouses are a special group. They can tough out the times when the man or woman is gone. It takes special strength and one hell of a backbone."

"At least you and Zoe didn't have any children, right?"

"Right. If we had had, it probably would have pulled our marriage apart faster. I'm just glad there were no children involved."

She heard the relief in his deep tone. Slowing down, she turned into the entrance of the Elk Horn Ranch. "Children are so special."

He looked over at her. "Do you want kids?"

"Oh, absolutely!" Katie grinned, excitement entering her voice. "I dream of teaching my children about loving nature."

Joe tried to stop the question from leaving his mouth, but failed. "What about you, Katie? Is there someone special in your life right now?" Probably Shep Baldwin.

Laughing, Katie drove over the sloping hill. Below lay the sprawling Elk Horn Ranch. The raptor facility gleamed in the sunlight; the day was cloudless and a deep blue. "Me? Oh, no. I'm afraid I've got a track record no one would be proud of."

"How so?"

"I was an angry teen, to say the least. I didn't like boys when I was growing up. I don't know why. Probably because I was focused on finding my mother. I was so wrapped up with why she left me, and being unhappy in every foster home, I had no time for them." She gave him a glance. Joe seemed interested and she trusted him. "When I got to Jackson Hole and Donna became my foster mother, I settled down. I learned too late that boys wanted a girl for only one thing. I was really dumb and kept making the same mistakes over and over again."

"Maybe *naive* would be a kinder word to use?"

She shrugged and pulled into the parking lot. Hands resting on the steering wheel, Katie said, "I have a very poor track record in relationships, Joe. I'm twenty-six years old and I've decided I'm lousy at choosing the right guy. My last relationship lasted six months. When I found out he'd lied to me and was a drug addict, I quit. He was hiding the truth from me." Opening her hands, she added, "I know I'm messed up, Joe. At least, emotionally. My whole life has been focused on finding my mother."

"And now you've found her." He saw her brows draw down, the smile dissolving.

"I guess I'm just too much of an idealist. I dreamed my mother to be very different from what she really is. Iris says my Pisces nature is to be a romantic idealist and a daydreamer. It fits. I always have trouble accepting reality versus my dreams of what life should be like."

Joe unsnapped the seat belt. "There's nothing wrong with dreams. You have dreams of having children someday."

Opening the door, Katie said, "Someday I'll find the right guy. I just feel it here, in my heart. Right now, I've just had one dream come true—finding my mother." She closed the door and walked around to join Joe. They walked to the facility.

"So the next dream is what? Finding Mr. Right?"

Walking into the facility as the door slid open, Katie laughed. "I'm not so sure about that, Joe."

"You seem to like Dr. Baldwin."

Turning, she set her purse on her desk. "He's very nice," she agreed.

"Single?"

"Yes, he is."

Joe kept his face carefully arranged. It wasn't what he wanted to hear, but he knew he had no business caring about it one way or another. Yet, kissing Katie had changed his world, whether he wanted it to or not. And he could feel the gnaw of the jealousy as it constantly ate away at his heart. "Then, the kiss we shared yesterday was nothing more than you just needing a little TLC?" He'd said the words softly and left the judgment out of his tone.

Katie looked up at him. "I guess it was, Joe. Thank you for being there for me. I don't know what came over me. I—I was more distraught and upset than I realized."

"You were under a lot of emotional pressure yesterday," Joe said, placing his hands in his pockets. He could see the confusion in Katie's eyes. "People need one another. Especially in times of trouble and trauma. I think you reached out to me because of that."

"You're probably right." Her fingers wrapped around his upper arm. "I wasn't thinking. Thank you for not taking it the wrong way. You're so good at knowing people."

As Katie released his arm, his flesh burned beneath her shy touch. Joe saw embarrassment over the kiss clearly written across her features. "No harm, no foul," he told her a little more gruffly than he'd intended. Why the hell was his heart wishing Katie had wanted to kiss him because she was drawn to him? Joe knew that path led to a different kind of hell. Another part of him was relieved. Still, just thinking of Katie having a relationship with the vet bothered him a lot more than it should.

"Hey, we have to get busy. Weighing and feeding time." She looked at her watch. "We're a half an hour behind schedule." Peering down the aisle she heard the raptors chutting and whistling, and she said, "They know it's past their breakfast time!"

Lifted by her enthusiasm, Joe managed a crooked smile. "Want me to bring them to you for weighing?"

"Sure, why not?"

Joe grabbed his gauntlet and walked down the wide, clean aisle. His heart lifted with joy. Once more he was alone with Katie. He had her full attention and could absorb that wonderful smile of hers. It always sent warm, flowing ribbons through his chest and his heart expanded with silent joy. It shouldn't have, but it did.

CHAPTER FOURTEEN

THE PHONE RANG at the raptor facility. Sitting at her desk Katie answered it.

"This is Janet. I thought you might want to come in and look at the place I just leased for my courier service."

Katie gulped and gripped the phone a little tighter. She wanted to say, *Hi, Mom,* but swallowed her instinct. "Hi, Janet. Sure, I'd love to come in. What time?" Her heart pounded with excitement. Her mother had said she'd call in a week, but only four days had passed since their first meeting. She clung to Janet's every word.

"Now."

"Oh." Katie looked over at Joe who was finishing the cleaning of the mews. "Well, yes, I can make it. Why don't you give me the address?" She quickly jotted the information in her notebook.

Joe looked up and heard the excitement in Katie's tone. He dumped the last of the refuse in the garbage can and walked toward the office area. Katie was flushed, her eyes sparkling as he came up to the office area. "Who was that?"

"My mother!" She gave him a dazzling smile. "Joe, I've got to meet her in town. She's leased space for her courier service." Grabbing her purse out of the drawer and slinging it over her shoulder, she asked, "Can you take care of things while I'm gone?"

"Sure," he said, setting the broom against the wall. "I thought she wasn't going to contact you for a week?"

Shrugging, Katie grabbed her baseball cap and settled it on her head. "Well, I guess she wanted me to see her new office. I'm so excited!" She flashed him another huge smile.

He nodded and managed to return a fraction of her joy. "Okay, just let me know when you're coming back."

She rushed out the sliding door, fumbling to find her truck keys and calling over her shoulder, "I'll be in touch by cell."

Joe watched Katie drive off. Frowning, he rubbed his chin and felt torn about the whole situation. It probably wasn't a great idea for her to see her mother again. But what else could she do? As for his own feelings, he was unable to forget the softness of her mouth against his. Somehow he continued the normal morning routine.

Iris Mason showed up a few minutes later as Joe was putting away the scale.

"Hey, Joe, good morning," she said, entering the facility. "I saw Katie take off like a shot. What's going on?"

"Janet just called and wants Katie to see her space she just leased in town for her business." He tried to keep his voice neutral.

"You know," Iris said, draping her hands on her hips, "I got a bad feeling about this, Joe. Have you met that woman?"

"No, I haven't." Just in his nightmares, was all.

"Well, I did. I ran into her by accident yesterday at Mo's Ice Cream Parlor. She was having lunch by herself when I came in to grab a sandwich. Mo, the owner, took me aside and told me who she was. Of course, I wanted to meet her."

Joe offered Iris a chair and she took it. He leaned against the doorjamb. "You met her?"

Wrinkling her nose, Iris placed her work gloves on Katie's desk. "You get close to her and she smells like marijuana smoke." She pushed a strand of hair from her brow. "I'm worried, Joe. The woman is coarse. She reminds me of a third-string boxer who gets beaten around the head and face. In fact, I hate to say this, but she's a nervous wreck."

"Tell me about it?"

"I went over to introduce myself and said that Katie's facility was on our ranch. I stuck out my hand and she just glared up at me. When I looked into her eyes, they looked blown, as if she were high." Sighing, Iris said more softly, "Zach Mason, my grandson, is a pothead. I recognized the look because he was always smoking when he lived here. I could never get him to quit."

Joe knew it was painful for Iris to talk about Zach. The kid was now in prison for his part in burning down three of the Hunters' fishing cabins and setting up Val Hunter to be kidnapped. Fortunately, that hadn't happened, but Zach had been caught and tried for his criminal acts. "I'm really sorry, Iris."

"I know." She made a sour face. "Anyway, the point I'm making is that Janet Bergstrom has the same look, like she's in outer space. It scared the bejesus out of me, Joe. When I repeated who I was and how I was connected with Katie, she just continued to glare at me. She wouldn't even shake my hand."

"What did you do?"

"I wished her good day and left. I went and ordered my sandwich at the cash register and never looked back."

"Did you tell Katie about your meeting?"

"No. I thought about it, but that girl has spent her life looking for her mother." With a grimace, Iris said, "And I hired Norah to track her down. Now, I'm sorry I did. Janet is a piece of work. God knows what else she's into. And poor Katie is so starry-eyed about finding her mother she can't see the truth." Touching her heart, Iris said, "Katie is such a beautiful soul of kindness and generosity. The complete opposite of her mother. I don't know what to do. Should I try and warn Katie or keep my mouth shut?"

Shrugging, Joe said softly, "It's a tough dilemma, Miss Iris. When Janet called here a while ago, Katie lit up like Christmas-tree lights. She was excited. There was hope in her eyes."

"Do you think Katie realizes her mother is probably a drug addict?"

"I don't know," Joe said. The older woman's wrinkled face grew concerned. "Are you thinking of an intervention?"

"Yes. Was I that obvious?" She managed a twisted grin.

"Not really."

"Have you been around druggies, Joe?"

Joe had to lie. "A few. But I haven't met Janet yet, so I have to rely on your experience."

"I'll tell you," she said forcefully, standing up, "don't ever get mixed up with drugs. Zach is going to spend five years in prison because he can't stop using drugs. He got mixed into the wrong crowd and look where it's got him." Shaking her head, she pulled on her gloves. "Do me a favor? When Katie returns, would you let me know? I need to get closer to her and get involved in her desire to know her mother better. I just have a bad feeling about Janet. I feel like the woman's up to no good...."

Joe made a fresh pot of coffee after Iris left. Unsettled, his stomach knotting, he was worried for Katie. Iris Mason knew from experience with her grandson Zach Mason that drugs destroyed lives. He didn't want Katie destroyed by getting too close to Janet. What the hell was he going to do or say?

KATIE PARKED THE TRUCK on the plaza. Her mother was standing by a two-story redbrick building at the end of a wide wooden porch. She wore a gray pantsuit, silver jewelry and a bright red scarf that went well with her white blouse. As she slipped out of her truck, her heart beating hard, Katie waved and smiled at her mother.

Janet nodded.

Why did she look so stern? Almost disapproving? Katie ignored those feelings and observations. Janet was her mother. She wanted to love her, not judge her. As Katie approached, she noticed the heavy makeup on her mother's broad face. Her hair was coiffed as usual, hairspray sternly holding it all into place. It was her eyes that got Katie's attention. They seemed out of focus.

"Hi, Janet. How are you this morning?" She walked up the steps to the wooden porch.

"I'm fine." Janet struggled to stay on target. She'd had a small bump an hour ago. A call from Xavier had goaded her like a cattle prod to reach out to her daughter. He was insisting Katie be brought into the fold. Janet had argued with him, to no avail. She did a couple of lines, but only to soothe her anger. Her daughter looked beautiful even though she was wearing work clothes. "Don't you ever dress up?" she demanded.

"Excuse me?" Katie was taken aback by the snarl

and censure in her mother's voice. She looked down at her orange T-shirt and jeans.

"Your clothes," Janet snapped. "My God, you look like a waif. Don't you ever wear good clothes?"

Laughing to take the edge off Janet's continuing scowl, Katie said, "I work for a living and raptors don't need fancy clothes." Inwardly, she was hurt by her mother's disapproving appraisal. "Is this the building you're going to lease?" She gestured toward it, hoping to get her mother in a better mood.

"Yeah, it is." Fumbling in her huge white leather purse, Janet finally located a set of keys. She was a little unstable and almost tripped over her own feet as she turned and unlocked the front door. "Come on in."

Katie watched her mother weave as she entered the empty first floor. What was wrong with her? Was she ill? She was sweating, huge beads across her upper lip. Trying to ignore her mother's tight slacks, the seams pulling and puckering, Katie chose instead to look around the empty building.

"Shut the door."

Katie closed it. "This is a really huge building. I like the oak floors. They're beautiful."

Janet anchored her feet apart so she wouldn't weave. She opened her purse and found a piece of paper. "Here, look at this." She tossed it in Katie's direction.

Katie couldn't catch the paper and it drifted to the floor. Why was Janet so gruff with her? Was she like this all the time? Picking it up, Katie unfolded it and walked over to her. "This is a drawing."

"Yeah, I made it last night." Janet poked her index finger at it. "This is how I'm gonna get it laid out. I've hired a carpenter and drywall guy to come in today and start putting up the walls. This front part is the desk and where you'll be. This wall will have a door to it and behind it all the boxes and envelopes will be stored. You'll be out here." She jabbed at the paper several times.

"I see," Katie said. "What about a counter? Have you found one yet?"

"I bought an oak counter yesterday from the Goodwill store." She smiled a wolfish smile. "In business, you find something cheap. You never pay full price if you don't have to."

Katie tried not to wrinkle her nose. The sickeningly sweet smell was strong around her mother. She was behaving as if she were drunk. "I see. Will someone be bringing it over?"

"Hell, yes. I'm not gonna be hefting that stuff around."

"Are you okay, Janet? You look…well…like you don't feel well." Katie gazed into the woman's bleary eyes.

"I'm fine! Just mind your own business, dammit!"

Though wincing inwardly, Katie kept her poker face. "I was worried." Everything about her mother was sloppy today, unlike their first meeting. She was continually sweating and wiping her upper lip with her bejeweled fingers.

Stumbling around the first floor, Janet growled, "It's just menopause. Just wait. All I do is sweat like a damn pig. I hate it!"

Katie followed her mother around, watching her walk the perimeter. Sometimes, her hand would snap out and she'd anchor it against the wall. Fearing for her safety, Katie searched her memory for menopause. She'd never seen a woman drunk and staggering around like Janet. Sweating? Hot flashes? Janet could have been menopausal. Yes, Katie had heard Donna griping about it from time to time. But Donna didn't act drunk like Janet. Fearing she was ill, Katie walked up and touched her mother's elbow as she leaned heavily on the wall for support.

"Janet, let me get you to a doctor, you're—"

Jerking her arm away from Katie, she stood up and yelled, "Dammit, don't touch me! What's the matter with you? I'm fine!"

Katie stepped back. "You're not well. I'm worried."

"Well, I'm not sick, dammit. And stop acting like a damn wimp." Breathing hard, Janet glared up at her tall, willowy daughter. In her heart, she felt the anxiety in her girl's expression. "Look, I'm okay," she said, lowering her voice. "Just menopause is all. Come on, I gotta check out the back. You got a pad and pen?"

"Yes, I do."

"Go get it. I need an office assistant."

Eager to do something that wouldn't upset Janet, Katie retrieved the pad and made notes. By the time they were done, half an hour later, they ended up at the front door of the building.

"I never realized there was so much to setting up a business," Katie said, handing her mother the notes.

"It's a helluva lot of work. You gotta know plumbing, electrical, drywall and a ton of other stuff. It ain't easy," Janet grumbled.

"No," Katie agreed, "it's not." She liked the redbrick walls. The structure had been built in 1900. The oak floors creaked but she liked the sound. "Do you have to hire people to do all of this?" She pointed to the paper in Janet's shaky hand.

"Yeah. I got Eduardo coming in. I'm on a deadline to get this place up and runnin'."

"Is there anything else I can do to help you?" Katie was desperate to prove she was worthy to her business-minded mother.

"You don't know nothin'."

"Do you have a computer? Surely you keep track of all your clients and their packages?"

Janet nodded. She opened the door and stepped out. The coke was starting to wear off and she was thinking a bit more clearly than before. "Yeah, I have a specially written software I use. My computer guy, Kyle, will be bringin' it out in three days. We gotta be on the same page insofar as routing the packages, boxes and envelopes."

"Is that what you want me to train on?"

"Yes, it is." Scratching her head, she said, "I'll give you a call. You can meet Kyle and he can train you."

"Great, I'd love to do that," she said. Janet's eyes didn't look so bleary as before. They were bloodshot and Katie wondered if she had trouble sleeping.

"Okay, I gotta go. I'll talk to you later." She locked the door, wobbled off the porch and headed for her car.

Biting her lower lip, Katie waved goodbye to her. Why couldn't she hug her long-lost daughter? Sure, Janet didn't seem like a touchy-feely type, but Katie wanted so badly to touch her mother, to feel her love and arms around her. She watched Janet drive away. Katie battled her disappointment as she went to her truck. She reminded herself that Janet had asked her to meet her. Maybe it was the only way her mother knew how to deal with people. She had a hundred questions to ask the woman and didn't dare ask even one.

JOE SAW KATIE DRIVE into the facility parking lot. He was sitting at her desk and had just taken a message from

Dr. Shep Baldwin, the vet. Katie's expression was one of concern. She had left earlier full of life and excitement. Now, her face showed disappointment and worry. What had happened? He rose and met her as she walked into the facility.

"Hey, how did it go?" he asked.

Katie rallied when she saw Joe. There was care burning in his eyes—for her. She remembered kissing him, and how he'd returned the spontaneous embrace.

"I'm okay. I'm learning a whole lot about setting up a business." She opened the drawer to her desk and placed her purse inside it. Shutting it, she straightened and forced a smile she didn't feel. "My mother is keen on getting her courier business up and running. I really liked the building she leased. The oak floors are a honey-gold color and I love the redbrick exterior."

Joe poured her a cup of coffee and handed it to her. "So why the look on your face?" Their fingers touched momentarily. His heart lurched. Trying to ignore how she affected him, Joe held her gaze.

"Thanks. Coffee is just what I need, Joe. You're a mind reader on top of being wonderful at falconry." Katie sat down at her desk. "My mother is a corporate tiger." She managed a one-shoulder shrug. "And why wouldn't she be?" She told Joe about the meeting and the building premises.

"Has she hired anyone but you so far?" Joe asked. He placed his hands on his hips and watched her face.

"Yes, she has. Some guy…Eduardo." Katie sipped the coffee, grateful for Joe's care. Her mother could have at least had coffee with her over at Mo's place. It was half a block from the building she'd leased. Katie cautioned herself she was expecting too much too soon from Janet.

"You'll meet him soon?"

"Probably." She told Joe about Kyle, the computer nerd coming from Cheyenne. Joe seemed very interested, his gaze narrowing speculatively upon her. "My mother said she'd call me when he arrived. He's going to train me on the software system."

"I see." Joe pursed his lips as he watched Katie enjoy the hot coffee. Color had come back in her cheeks and the sparkle in her eyes returned, too. He wondered if it was in reaction to him. *Maybe.* "What did you look so worried about when you came back?"

"Oh, that." Katie waved her hand dismissively. "My mom was sweaty and she was having trouble walking a straight line. I asked her if she was okay and she said it was just menopause."

Joe compressed his lips and said nothing. "Iris was over here earlier. She wanted to see you when you had time." He pointed to the message on the desk. "Dr. Baldwin called and said the red-tailed hawk went through surgery fine and he's ready to be picked up and brought here. Do you want me to do it?"

Brightening, Katie said, "That's great! Yes, could you? I'll go find Iris. I need to tell her about my mom's business, anyway. It was kind of exciting. I learned a lot."

Nodding, Joe took the keys to her truck. "I'll get the travel case ready and take off."

Katie stood. "Everyone okay here?" She peered down the aisle at the mews. The raptors were all sitting on their perches and most of them were sleeping after their midmorning feed.

"All's well," Joe assured her, picking up the travel case from below the weigh-in desk.

"I'll be back in a little while, Joe." Katie exited the facility.

Scowling, he retrieved his falconry gear and picked up the carrier. He was bothered by Katie's reactions. She seemed so enthusiastic, so oblivious to her mother's flaws. Janet Bergstrom was probably high when she met with her daughter. It made Joe uncomfortable that Katie would get involved in the woman's business venture. Joe felt edgy as he left the facility.

Once in the truck and driving toward Jackson Hole, Joe called his boss on the phone.

"Hager here."

"Boss, this is Joe. I've got some more info for you." He told the FBI boss about Katie's second meeting with her mother.

"Sounds good," Hager said, congratulating him. "It's vital we get in to look at the computer setup. I'm sure it will prove key in finding those guns and drugs over time."

"I'm worried about Katie. She knows nothing of what's going on. Furthermore, she couldn't even tell her druggie mother was high this morning. She believed Janet when she told her it was menopause."

Laughing heartily, Hager said, "That's a new one for the books! Okay, so the girl is naive. She knows her mother was in prison for running drugs and guns. Don't you think she'd put it together?"

"Not necessarily," Joe said, frustrated. "Katie was raised in foster homes where there were no drugs."

"Can't be helped. Eventually, she'll figure it out. It's not your job to educate her. We *want* her to get close to Janet. We want her to retrieve what's in the computer database. We've had our people trying to hack into her computer system in Cheyenne repeatedly without success. Whoever Kyle is, he damn well knows how to throw up a security wall. This guy is a premier hacker, no question. We desperately need Katie on the inside."

"Do you really think the computer geek is going to show her how to find the real truth of what's hidden in the database?"

"No, but once she's in and Janet trusts her in the position, you can then work with her to find out. I'll be sending out one of our top geeks to train her when the time's right."

"Okay," Joe said. His brow wrinkled. "The guy Janet has hired is named Eduardo. No last name yet. I think he'll be a key player and I hope we'll be able to track him to Los Lobos."

"I agree," Hager said. "Our man inside Xavier's organization has compiled a list of names of everyone he's met or heard of in the cartel. If we get lucky, the dude's name might be on the list."

"I still worry about Katie's safety." Joe tried to keep the force of his concern out of his tone. He knew his boss wasn't one for emotional displays, warranted or not. "Do you have anything on Garcia's cartel?"

"Nothing. It's quiet. Since the float-plane incidents on Long Lake, the cartel's gone underground."

"What about Curt Downing?"

"He's doing his trucking. And he's got that endurance horse ranch where he spends most of his time."

"Maybe that's a good thing," Joe said. "I just don't want Katie caught in a crossfire between the two cartels."

"None of us do, but for now, Joe, maintain. Be her friend and listen to her. You're asking good questions and you're on top of things as they're breaking. It doesn't get any better than that."

Unable to still his aggravation and worry over Katie's potential danger, he said, "All right, I'll call you whenever I find something new. I'll send a report to you tonight."

CHAPTER FIFTEEN

OUTSIDE THE FACILITY, Katie saw Iris's truck approaching. The morning was clouding up, as if rain would arrive by midday.

Spotting Katie near the front entrance, Iris plopped her straw hat on her head and made a beeline toward her. "Good morning, Katie," she called, and the two of them went into the building. Katie busied herself making a second pot of coffee. She wore a dark green T-shirt and jeans. Her shoulder-length hair was gathered up in a ponytail.

Grinning, Iris took off her hat and placed it on a wall hook. "I just dropped over for a few minutes to see how things are going." It wasn't a complete lie, Iris told herself. She walked over to the desk and sat down.

"Things are going great," Katie said over her shoulder. "You look pretty in your bright yellow blouse and purple slacks. Are you all gussied up to go into town and have lunch with one of your friends?" She flipped the switch on the coffeemaker and then opened a cabinet above, removing two white ceramic mugs.

Iris placed her colorful gardening gloves on the edge of the desk. "Where's Joe?"

"He's in town to pick up an injured raptor at Shep's vet clinic."

"And how are the two latest injured raptors doing?" Katie brought the cream and sugar over to the desk.

She knew Iris liked both in her coffee. "Great. We have two wonderful vets who have hearts of gold. If they didn't volunteer their time, these birds would have been put down."

"I've been meaning to donate some money to Randy and Shep," Iris said. "I'll put it on my memory list and get it done. They should be at least paid in part for what they do for free. What goes around, comes around." She watched Katie pour the hot brew into the mugs. Katie was happy this morning. She decided to broach the serious talk with some lighter topics first.

"Here you go," Katie said, handing Iris a mug. She sat down and watched Iris place the cream and sugar into her coffee.

"You know about the summer armory dance coming up?"

Katie nodded and sipped her coffee. "Yes."

"The whole Mason family will be there, and I was hoping you and Joe might come along, too."

Katie smiled wistfully. "That would be wonderful."

"You're so busy taking care of your raptors that I just don't see you getting out too often, Katie." Iris smiled. "It's good to be social."

"I don't have a dress," Katie said, thinking out loud. "Most of my clothes are T-shirts, jeans and one winter jacket."

"Well, I was going into town after lunch to shop for a dress. How about you come along?"

"I don't want you to buy it for me, Iris. You do so much already...."

Holding up her hand, Iris said, "You forget, you get a salary."

"Yes, and I definitely have enough saved to buy me

a dress." Katie brightened. "I'd love to go in with you. It's about time I got something girly, huh?" She laughed.

Iris grinned. "Yes, we ranchers sometime forget we're girls, too." She'd not seen Katie this happy—ever. Did it have to do with meeting her mother? Or Joe? Iris hoped it was Joe. She liked the young man and knew he was a good citizen. Someone who was safe in comparison to Janet.

"What time are you going in?"

"One o'clock? Does that fit with your schedule?"

"Yes, Joe will be back in about an hour. We have to prepare for a talk at the Soroptomist Club in town tomorrow. I'll give an educational speech and we'll bring along three of our raptors for show and tell."

"Keep spreading the word," Iris agreed. Setting her cup down, she said, "Do you remember meeting my grandson, Zach Mason?"

"Sure." Katie saw Iris become serious, her brows drawing down. Reaching out, she whispered, "I'm so sorry he's in prison. I know how hard this is on you and Rudd. It's heartbreaking."

Iris squeezed Katie's hand and released it. "I knew Zach was into marijuana and with him living under our roof from the time he was born, I saw the boy go from a beautiful baby to a drug addict."

"So much has happened in your family since Kam came home," Katie quietly agreed. There was real pain in Iris's eyes.

"Do you recall, when you met Zach, the look he had on his face?"

Thinking, Katie said, "What do you mean?"

"It's pretty easy to spot people on drugs. Their eyes can be unfocused. He sweated a lot. And he couldn't sit still. He was always tapping his foot, drumming his fingers on the table, twitching or twisting around, more than what the average teenager might do. When he'd come to dinner with the family, he'd be irritable, defensive and just plain rude at times—again more than just a rebellious teenager. Also, he suddenly became secretive. He developed this new personality. Over the years, I realized those were more serious symptoms of a drug problem. I tried to stop him. I talked to the sheriff and I got the boy to a good drug counselor." Opening her hands, she said sadly, "All for naught. The drug counselor had warned me beforehand that if Zach didn't want to stop doing drugs, there was no way to force him to stop. And she was right."

"It's so sad," Katie said. She sat thinking about Zach's symptoms. "It's funny you should tell me this, Iris. When I met my mother earlier, she acted a lot like how you've described Zach."

"Is she on drugs?"

Shrugging, Katie rolled her eyes. "Oh, Iris, you know I'm such a dummy when it comes to this stuff. I really don't have that much experience. I've been focused on other things. I should know. All three of my past relationships were with drug addicts. I just shrugged it off as they were having a bad day or didn't feel well. Sometimes I think I subconsciously don't want to see it. I guess it's a flaw in me. I always want to see the best in people."

"Surely you saw drugs in school?"

"Yes, in high school. But I was a loner and I didn't run with a crowd."

"Do you remember seeing some kids in school acting or behaving like Zach?"

"I did, yes." Frowning, Katie brushed some strands

of hair away from her brow. "Iris, I think my mother has a problem."

Gently, Iris reached out and touched Katie's hand. She had wrapped them around the mug as if to anchor herself symbolically against the answer. "It sounds suspicious. Remember Norah said she'd been in prison because of drugs and gunrunning. So many of those people get caught up in drugs."

Katie glanced at the older woman. Fear moved through her. "But…she's a businesswoman, Iris. She's creating a second courier business." Katie gave her a searching look. "Can someone on drugs be in business? I mean, can they run one successfully?"

"Sure they can," Iris said. Seeing the pain flit through Katie's eyes, Iris felt badly for the young woman. "I'm just worried for you, is all. I feel you need to be more aware."

Katie sat back in her chair and felt her heart rip a little. "How do I deal with Janet, then?"

"You need to study her, study the symptoms," Iris counseled in a gentle tone. Katie's mouth drew downward as she considered the advice.

"Did it help you with Zach?"

"Yes," Iris said with some finality. She finished her coffee and folded her hands in her lap. "When I knew Zach was high, I knew the behavior he'd exhibit. You become somewhat of a psychologist, Katie. It doesn't fix the problem, but more importantly, when Zach was acting out at the dinner table, we knew not to take what he said or did personally." She held Katie's worried gaze. "And that's as good as it gets. Not taking their abrupt, angry, irritable behavior toward you personally. They're high on a drug, and they aren't socially responsible. They say a lot of mean things and it can hurt."

Katie rubbed her chin. "Iris, that's what happened. My mother was…well…really cranky. It's as if I couldn't do anything right. She was angry all the time. I couldn't figure it out…until now."

"It's a tough place to be," Iris said. "I have a good friend who is a drug counselor, Pamela Brookings. She helped me enormously through all the years of dealing with Zach and his addiction. Maybe you'd like to talk with her sometime? She's got information you can take home and study."

"Sure, I'd like to meet her." Katie made a face. "This is just so upsetting to me. I had this dream…" Katie shrugged. "Now I know my mother is still using."

Iris patted her hand. "We'll get through this together, Katie. Don't forget, you have us. You know that?"

Nodding, Katie managed a partial smile and squeezed Iris's hand. "I do. With Donna gone now—I miss her terribly—I really rely on you. And I'm so grateful, Iris." She brightened a bit. "You're like the grandmother I wanted. I hope you don't mind me seeing you that way?"

Iris chuckled. "Of course not. You deserve a nice grandma like me."

Some of her depression lifted as Iris gazed at her with pure love. Katie absorbed her warmth, starved for it. "So." She sighed. "This wasn't what I imagined, Iris." Katie tapped her head and gave her a wry look. "I've decided I live in an idealistic world. I'm not so good with reality, I'm discovering. The truth is…well…tough."

"Don't ever lose your idealism or ability to see people's goodness, Katie. That's a gift and I don't ever want you to throw it away, okay? Because, as hard as reality is, and it's harsh, we still have to hold on for hopes and dreams of a better day."

"I understand, Iris. It's just that…well, I'm really

wrestling with who my mother is versus what I fanta-sized her to be."

"It's normal to do that," Iris said. "When Trevor and I adopted Rudd, our adopted son had expectations, too. It took us a good year or two to work through his projec-tions and dreams. You're going to go through the same thing. And we're here to support you, Katie. You don't have to do this alone."

"I'm so relieved to know that. And Joe is becoming a good friend, too. He has such depth. But sometimes, when we talk, he becomes like an iceberg."

"What do you mean?"

"So much about him remains unseen. I see the tip above the water, but I sense so much of him is hidden or cloaked." Shrugging, Katie gave an embarrassed laugh and said, "I get these intuitions about people, like I do with the raptors. And Joe, although he's wonderful and knowledgeable, he's hiding something."

"I think he's a great friend to you, Katie. He's prag-matic and realistic."

"Yes, the opposite of me." She managed a grin.

Iris laughed. "Opposites attract! It's not a bad thing. The other partner often offsets and supports us. I know when Trevor was alive, I really relied on him. He had a different set of eyes and ears on the world. I could go to him with anything and he'd allow me to see things in a new perspective. It always helped me. We made this ranch the richest in the valley because we were differ-ent, we had different perspectives, but we also folded them together to create a dream come true."

"That's so romantic!" Katie sighed. "And you know, Joe is sort of like that with me. He sees the world very differently than I do, yet, we seem to magically overlap here and there. Is that how it was between you and Trevor?"

"Yep. Now, with Timothy in my life, he's not like my Trevor, but he still brings a unique take on the world. I find it not only exciting but helpful and it gives me direction."

"It's wonderful that Timothy came here for a week at your dude ranch and you two fell in love." Katie clasped her hands to her heart. "See, Iris? Idealism, a romantic outlook on life *does* have a place in our world. It doesn't always have to be cold, hard reality. I like a choice!"

Iris rose and smoothed her slacks. "There's room for both, Katie." She looked at her watch. "I'll come and pick you at one and we'll go shopping. You have invited Joe to the dance, haven't you?"

"I haven't, but I will." She felt lifted by Iris's visit. "Thanks for all your help." She hugged Iris. "I couldn't wish for a better grandma than you!"

TWENTY MINUTES LATER, Joe arrived with the injured red-tailed hawk in the travel case. For the next half hour, Katie and he were busy getting the young hawk acclimated to the small mew designed especially for injured birds.

"Hey," Joe said, closing the mew, "I don't know about you, but I'd like a cup of coffee. You must have made a new pot." He walked with Katie toward the office area.

"Yes, I did." Her heart beat a little harder. "Joe, I want to ask you something, but you don't have to say yes if you don't want to."

He nodded as they walked into the offices. "Okay, what's up?"

Katie sat down at her desk and watched Joe pour himself a mug of coffee. "Iris was just over here. There's a summer dance at the armory in town. She wants me and you to go." She held up her hands as he turned around. "Now, you don't have to go if you don't want to. Iris is inviting all her family and us, her cosmic family." She smiled. As he stood with cup in hand, he looked excruciatingly handsome. This morning Joe wore a dark blue long-sleeved shirt, the sleeves rolled up to his elbows, some well-worn jeans and work boots. She enjoyed drowning in his green eyes. Their color reminded her of the dark forest covering the slopes of the Tetons.

"Sure, I'd like to go," he murmured, sipping the coffee and taking a seat on the chair next to her desk. Joe darkly reminded himself she could have invited Shep instead. Maybe Katie wanted him along because he was safe. A friend instead of a lover. He knew she was uncomfortable about starting another relationship, even with Shep, whom she'd known for a long time.

"Really?"

"Why not? I'm assuming you and I will go as friends?" Joe liked the idea of holding Katie as they danced. He shouldn't, but he did. Seeing her cheeks go pink over his question and remembering their kiss made Joe happy.

"I'd love to have you as my dance partner. I loved to dance in high school but since then, I've done very little. I might step on your toes."

Joe laughed. "That makes two of us, Katie. I've been in the Marine Corps, fighting overseas. We didn't have any dance floors over in Afghanistan."

"Good, then we can forgive one another." She nodded with relief. "Iris is going to pick me up at one and we're going shopping for dresses for the dance."

Seeing the joy in her eyes, Joe felt warmth flow through his heart. "Uh-oh…women shopping," he teased.

She liked the way his mouth curved and found herself wanting to kiss Joe again. "Hey," she joked, "I have one skirt in my closet! One! Just goes to show you how often I go out."

"Then, you and Iris should make a day of it, enjoy yourselves and come back with something you can hardly wait to wear for the dance."

"It will be a lot of fun. I'm looking forward to it," Katie said. In the back of her mind, she wondered if Janet would want to go. Her instincts said no, but she wanted to include her mother in the social fabric of Jackson Hole. Did she dare make the call?

JANET HAD JUST GOTTEN BACK to her apartment when her throwaway cell phone rang. The only one who would know her number was Xavier and her drug soldiers who ran her courier business in Cheyenne.

"Janet here," she answered, unlocking the apartment and stepping inside.

"Xavier here."

Brows raising, Janet threw the keys on a small desk near the door and pushed the door closed with her heel. "Xavier! What a nice surprise! Are you checking up on my progress?" She dropped her huge purse on the kitchen counter and kicked off the heels she hated to wear.

"Yes and no. We've gotten word of Garcia moving around the town. He is our enemy, Janet, but you know that."

Scowling, Janet lit a cigarette and sat down on the dark brown couch. "Yes, of course I know. What's happening?"

"We know Garcia was trying to bring in bales of marijuana by float plane. That got axed by the FBI.

I've been waiting for him to make a chessboard move and start up again."

Janet knew Xavier was a chess fanatic. He was one of the best players in Guatemala. And he saw everything he did in his life through chess. Janet hated the game because it was too complicated. "And he has?"

"Yes. My spy in the town saw a lot of activity around Ace Trucking. It's owned by a man named Curt Downing. We've known for some time this gringo was working with Garcia. My man works for a mechanic shop nearby. Downing's manager sends his trucks over to this business for repair. The other day, he saw a new driver for Ace Trucking. The man is Mexican and our guy knew the dialect he was speaking. It looks like Garcia might work directly with Ace Trucking."

Sighing, Janet puffed on the cigarette and flicked the ashes into a nearby ashtray. "Okay, so what?"

"If Garcia is positioning his men as drivers for Ace Trucking, that means Downing has agreed to work with him."

"But you said Downing has been moving drugs for years."

"On his own. Now, it looks as if he's hooking up with Garcia."

"Why don't you fly up here and make him a better deal then?" Janet knew cartels were always manipulating people and businesses to carry their drugs into North America. She certainly was not at the level to speak on behalf of Xavier or his cartel. He'd have to do it himself.

"Because we don't know if we can trust Downing. And here's where you come into play. You're opening a courier service. I want you to take Downing to lunch and see if he's interested in handling some of your more regional packages."

"What? Tell him we're running drugs and guns?"

"No, no."

Janet heard the frustration in Xavier's tone. Sometimes, he treated her like a child and she resented it. "What then?"

"See if he's interested in working with you, business to business. The legit side, not anything illegal. That way, you can get an in to his trucking company. He's not going to know you work for me. You're a white woman born in the U.S.A." He chuckled.

"So, I'm to be an undercover mole?"

"Exactly. We know your business has about twenty-five percent regional packages and you have to go through established national couriers to deliver them. Let's get Downing to agree to handle them instead."

"What if he wants some irrational sum of money to move them, Xavier?"

"You know how to dicker. You're a good horse trader. You can't give Downing everything. But we must get him connected with us. Neither Garcia nor he will know you're my eyes and ears. Get Downing to like you."

"Sleep with him?"

"No. And you can't be on drugs when you take him to lunch. He'll know it, Janet, and we can't afford to have Downing realize you're a drug addict."

"I understand." Janet knew if she didn't follow Xavier's direction, he'd not only cut her off from drugs, but he'd pull out of her business. She'd be destitute. "Be a buddy to him."

"Exactly. And listen, when the regional packages have to be shipped from your business to his truck, *you* are to drive them over. I do not want my man, Eduardo, who is clearly from South America, being spotted at his terminal. If Garcia is planting men at Ace, they'll recognize him and get suspicious. You keep my man in the rear. Let your daughter run the front desk. That way, if Downing comes over, he'll see her and no one from Central America. Got it?"

"Yeah, I got it. Still, Xavier, Eduardo can't hide. The dude has to have a place to live and he'll be seen around town."

"Yes, that's fine. I don't want my man to be seen at your business. Downing could put it together and get suspicious. I want him to think you're a legit business. And your daughter working there only adds to the strength of the story we want him to believe."

Sighing, Janet said, "I don't know about my daughter. Katie's not very…realistic, I guess you'd say."

"So what? She knows computers, right?"

"Sure, every kid is weaned on them."

"And she's going to work for you?"

"Part-time."

"Then you must run the front desk when Katie's not available."

Janet groaned. "Okay, I can do it. When do you want me to set up a lunch date with Downing?"

"As soon as possible. The sooner you can get inside his terminal the sooner you can see how many drivers are from Central America."

"Okay, I'll call him tomorrow," she promised.

"Excellent, Janet. I miss you already. I'm sending some of those Brazil nuts covered with chocolate you love so much. They should arrive by the end of the week. I love you, *mi corazón*."

Brightening, Janet felt her heart expand with joy. "I

love you, too, Xavier. I miss you so much. I wish…I wish we could see one another more than twice a year."

"I know, I know. But we must be grateful for those two times, eh?"

"I guess so, Xavier," Janet muttered.

"Okay, be a good girl, trash this phone. I'll destroy this one."

Glumly, Janet hung up. She dropped the cell phone on the couch and rubbed her face. The makeup was itching and she wanted to wash it off. Getting up, she moved toward the bathroom to have a shower. Xavier sounded worried. The last thing she wanted was to get caught in a war between two cartels. People died when that happened. And in a town this size, only one cartel would win. As she pushed open the bathroom door, her thoughts went back to her daughter. Katie was a huge disappointment to her, but she was still her kid. The last thing Janet wanted was to have her blood spilled in a cartel war.

CHAPTER SIXTEEN

JOE PARKED HIS TRUCK near the armory. Stars sparkled like white sugar sprinkled across the dark heavens. Country music drifted out the open doors of the large building. As he climbed out of his truck he saw that the place was packed with vehicles. A large crowd congregated near the doors. Farther away, in a smoking area, stood those with cigars, pipes and cigarettes.

His heart raced in anticipation. He stopped and smoothed his clothing. This was the West and nobody wore standard business suits. He'd gone to a men's clothing store in town to buy a dark brown Western suit. And of course, he needed a Stetson. His ostrich-hide cowboy boots were polished to perfection.

As he walked slowly toward the door, Joe wondered if Katie and Iris and her family were already inside. He ached to kiss Katie once more. He tried to erase his torrid dream from the night before. It had been so real, he'd awakened near dawn, drenched in sweat. His heart felt as if it would leap out of his chest. Where did FBI agent and man begin and end? The question hung front and center in him as he wove between the parked SUVs and trucks and continued toward the armory.

As he looked around, he noticed a big Dodge Ram truck with enough chrome on it to be called a bling-mobile. Slowing his pace, he realized that the driver must be Curt Downing. The man drove into a no-

parking zone and parked. Joe shook his head. The guy
was arrogant and thought he owned the town because
he was a millionaire. Joe watched Downing climb out
of his truck and settle a gray Stetson on his head. It
matched his light gray suit. He'd come alone. Downing was known to hang out with a number of women,
but none had joined him tonight. Why? Joe had never
met Downing and this would give him an opportunity
to study him a little more closely. Iris Mason had told
him the summer shindig brought out the rich, the famous and the poor alike.

The air was coolish, a slight breeze coming off the
hills above the narrow valley. Joe was glad to step inside. The country music was loud and the dance floor
crowded with couples. Standing off to one side of the
doors, Joe looked around. Someone had decorated the
ceiling with colorful crepe paper, battery-operated lan-
terns hanging among them along with sprigs of silk
flowers. Chatting and laughter mingled with the fast
music. A caller was singing out the changes in a square
dance. Joe saw women in sleek, fashionable dresses that
must have cost plenty. Some women wore plain skirts
and blouses or more conservative pantsuits. The bling of
expensive jewelry, bracelets and rings flashed and glit-
tered with every movement. The men were dressed in
their finest Western duds. Every set of boots gleamed.
Tapping his toe in time with the music, Joe roused himself and gazed at the hundred or so round tables set
along the walls of the armory.

He spotted Downing with a group of what appeared
to be businessmen, although he knew none of them.
Downing was in the center and appeared to be telling a
joke. The men laughed in unison. Such was power and

money, Joe thought, as he skirted them, looking for Iris Mason and her family.

The music stopped and the crowd on the dance floor hooted, yelled and clapped. Joe spotted Iris in a pretty blue skirt and a white blouse with a blue bolero jacket. The color brought out the silver in her hair. Iris was in the arms of Timothy, her new husband, a professor who had retired from Harvard University.

Iris and Timothy cut across the crowded dance floor to the opposite side of the building. Moving among smiling couples, they halted at a large round table set with white linen. A bouquet of summer flowers in a red vase echoed the theme of the dance.

And then, he saw Katie. She was sitting with her back against the wall, smiling as Iris and Timothy approached the table. His heart squeezed. She was beautiful in a white silk chiffon dress with red poppies across it. When she stood up, the dress flowed around her willowy figure. Her black hair hung softly around her shoulders, a counterpoint to the bright colors she wore. She was breathtaking. He forced himself to ignore the yearning, the scalding heat coming to life in his lower body. Joe scowled. His erotic dream hung stubbornly in his memory.

KATIE WATCHED AS Joe Gannon wove through the jovial, partying crowd. He made her breathless. How dangerously sexy he looked in the dark brown Western suit. A Stetson of the same color hung casually in his left hand. He matched the image of the cowboy he truly was. His shoulders were broad and thrown back with a natural pride. Joe walked like the military officer he had been. Inwardly, Katie grieved for him losing his career. The expression in his green eyes was one of leadership, someone in command, someone who had real authority. When his gaze met and locked with hers, she flashed him a smile.

She quickly told the Mason family that Joe had just arrived.

Iris welcomed him to the table and gestured to the empty chair next to where Katie stood. "Glad you could make it, Joe. Sit down and join us."

Thanking Iris, Joe nodded and greeted the family. They had the largest table in the room to accommodate the growing Mason dynasty. He shook hands with the men and nodded to the ladies. His heart, however, was centered on Katie who stood with her hands clasped in front of her sleek dress. When he finally managed to move behind the table to reach Katie, her winsome smile widened. He felt as if he were bathing in pure sunlight.

"Joe!" Katie greeted him. She stepped forward and threw her arms around his broad shoulders. After giving him a quick embrace, she stood back and smiled up into his shadowed features. His eyes narrowed as she withdrew. Breasts tingling where she'd pressed herself against his chest, she felt her heart flutter with need. "Come, sit down. I'm so glad you could make it." She pulled out the chair for him.

Joe grinned sheepishly, then saw how everyone's expression seemed to approve of Katie's unexpected embrace. "Thanks, here, you sit down first." He took her elbow and guided her to the chair. For a moment, he inhaled a faint scent of jasmine floating around Katie's black hair and across her shoulders. After seating Katie, he hung his hat on a peg on the wall behind the chair and sat down.

"We were wondering if you were going to make it or

not," Rudd Mason said, smiling and lifting a wineglass in his direction. "Katie was beside herself."

Joe nodded and slid a glance toward her. "My mom has the flu, so I was making a run to the grocery store to buy her some chicken soup."

"Oh, your parents can't make it?" Katie asked, suddenly disappointed.

"No. Mom is feeling pretty punk and my father is staying home to take care of her. She'll be okay in a day or two."

"Flu is going around," Iris said. "It's starting early this year."

"I was so hoping to meet them," Katie told Joe. "You always speak so highly of them."

Joe nodded. The last thing he wanted was for Katie to meet his parents; she was still officially under investigation. "Maybe another time," he murmured.

The band struck up a slow dance. Katie reached out and grabbed Joe's hand. "Will you dance with me?"

Her fingers were warm and sent wild longing through him. He uncurled his hand and gripped hers. "Sure, come on." He rose and pulled back Katie's chair.

"You two go out there and enjoy yourselves," Iris called.

Joe led her to the crowded dance floor.

Katie sighed as Joe gathered her into his arms. She inhaled the lime scent of his soap. His hand twined around hers, his other hand resting firmly against the small of her back. Looking up, she drowned in his gaze. "Remember? I might accidentally step on your foot." She grinned and watched a slow, heated smile curve his masculine mouth.

"Forewarned," he teased in return. "I've got two left feet, too. We'll make a great couple." He forced himself not to haul Katie solidly against his frame. Her laughter was breathy. She was like lava in his arms as she swayed naturally to the music. "I like your dress."

"Iris helped me pick it out." She released his hand and picked up the filmy material for a moment. "I love flowers. Iris found it and urged me to try it on. I didn't think I'd look very good in it, but she said I did."

Joe nodded and captured her hand once more. "You're beautiful in it. The red poppies look nice with your shining black hair." He watched her cheeks turn almost the same color as the poppies. Joe then realized that without a mother, how would Katie have been taught about dresses, fabrics and clothing in general? He was sure the foster parents must have given her some training, but she seemed awkward and unsure even though she sizzled in the dress.

"Thanks. I feel beautiful tonight." She drowned in his smile. Without thinking, Katie rested her cheek against his shoulder. She closed her eyes and instinctively moved closer. As she felt the heat radiating from his body, Katie was happier than she could ever recall. And when Joe took her hand and pressed it between them, an ache grew within her. She recognized that gnawing sensation. For too long, she'd been without the love of a man.

Joe absorbed Katie's spontaneous nearness. When her body pressed lightly against his, he drew in a deep, ragged breath. Did she know how much she affected him? He could feel her small, rounded breasts beneath the silky material moving against his suit. The scent of jasmine encircled him, strands of her ebony hair tickled his jaw. The softness of her hand was real.

"You remember our kiss?" he asked her, his lips near her ear.

Nodding, Katie lifted her head and drew back just enough to meet his shadowy gaze. "I do."

"I remember saying something like it was a friendly kiss," Joe said in a husky tone. Her eyes shimmered with something resembling desire—for him.

"I know...." One corner of her mouth pulled upward. "It was more than that to me, Joe." Searching his face, she sensed his yearning for her. "Was it for you?" In her dreams, she and Joe were not only friends, but lovers. Katie wondered if she should admit it to him or not. He exuded power and masculinity and excited her as no other man had.

Compressing his mouth, Joe leaned over and whispered, "Yes, the kiss was much more than just being a friend to you, Katie."

Mesmerized by his dark, deep voice, she stood up on tiptoe and whispered into his ear, "Take me home, Joe. I'm a lousy dancer but I'd love to spend some time with you. I know Iris and her family would understand."

His heart pounded violently. Katie was guileless, Joe decided. He felt her hand leave his and her fingers trail slowly up his neck to graze his jaw. The longing in her blue eyes tore at him. Oh, God, he was in trouble. Deep, deep trouble.

"Yes, let's go home...." he said.

"We'll go tell Iris we're going to leave," she whispered. "And we'll tell everyone good-night."

"I DON'T KNOW WHAT IS HAPPENING, Joe. And I don't care," Katie said as he led her into his home. She wrapped her arms around his shoulders as he tossed his Stetson on the couch. The house was small but clean. To Katie, it looked as if a man lived in it. There were no living plants to make it come alive. Right now, her heart was focused

on him. She felt his hands come to rest around her waist.
It was a wonderful feeling to be desired.

Nuzzling her soft hair, the jasmine filling his senses
and making him reel, Joe said unsteadily, "I don't,
either, Katie. All I know is I want you. All of you…"
He eased her away from him just enough to see if she
agreed. The vulnerable smile appearing on her lips told
him everything. "Come on," Joe said as he led her down
the hallway.

It was so easy for Katie to walk into his bedroom. A
tan, brown and dark gold spread was across the king-
size bed. The curtains were gold and closed, making the
room dark except for the night-light in the hallway near
the door. There was something so vital about Joe she
didn't even question her heart. In the past, Katie knew
it had led her wrong, but tonight, nothing had ever felt
so right. She kicked off her shoes as he shrugged out
of the suit coat and boots. Appraising the white cotton
shirt, black tie and brown slacks, she drank all of him
into her heart. She reached up, untied the black tie and
allowed it to fall to a nearby chair against the cream-
colored wall.

"I don't know why I want you so much," she whispered as she kissed his jaw, feeling the sandpaper of his
beard beneath her lips. Her fingers moved slowly across
his chest and she began to unsnap each button of his
shirt, revealing the dark curled hair beneath.

"Not as much as I want you…" Urgency tunneled
through Joe as he felt Katie's warm, searching fingers
move across his exposed chest. She was fearless and
he got caught up in her fervor and openness. Without a
word, Joe shrugged out of the shirt, allowing it to drop
to the waxed cedar floor. He felt powerful as she gazed
admiringly at his naked upper body. And when her fin-

gers slid provocatively around his waist, a flash of heat exploded deep within his lower body. As she searched for and found the belt, opening it and pulling it out of the loops, he admired her boldness.

Katie wanted him. All of him. And she was no game player. She was amazingly honest and the conflicted feelings Joe had dissolved as her fingers eased his slacks open. Heat curled and anchored in him and he groaned. She slid her fingers beneath the elastic band of his boxer shorts. In one slow, sensual movement, she pulled the fabric down across his hips and thighs and allowed it pool around his feet.

Katie stared at his hardened body and then lifted her gaze. The look Joe gave her was hungry and filled with urgency. His hands captured the zipper at the back of her dress. Her spine tingled wildly as he deliberately brushed her skin and touched the small of her back. He slid his roughened hands beneath the shoulders of the fabric and eased the material away. In moments, the silk chiffon fell as if it were a red-and-white waterfall pooling around her bare feet.

She met his smile and sighed as he expertly released the silky white bra and removed it. His hands moved in slow adoration along the curve of her taut breasts, and Katie felt faint. Joe's hands were the calloused hands of a man who worked in nature. Her nipples puckered and, as he leaned over, his breath warm and moist against them, Katie moaned with anticipation.

Suckling her, Joe kept one hand against her curved back, worshipping the hardened nipples with gentle nips of his teeth and lips. Easing the white lingerie away from her hips, Joe heard her moan. Katie's fingers dug frantically into his tensed shoulders while he explored her. In one, smooth motion Joe lifted and carried Katie to the bed. Her arms curved around his neck, her brow resting against his neck and jaw. As he gently laid her on the bed. He put on a condom. Joe straddled her and said in a raw tone, "I want to love you, Katie. I want to lose myself in you and never look back…."

Lifting her hands, Katie curved them around Joe's taut shoulders. A slight sheen of perspiration glistened across his magnificent upper body. She felt equally hot and restless, her hips moving toward his, brushing him, teasing him. Katie pulled him downward to kiss his mouth and whisper against his lips, "Love me, Joe. Love me. It's all I want. It's you…" She met and captured his smiling mouth with her own. As his hands slid up her rib cage to curve and capture her breasts, she uttered a groan of pleasure, thrusting her hips against his. In moments, slick and hot with need, he pushed forward, entering her tight confines. For a moment, Katie broke their heated, hungry kiss, pleasure thrumming through her. He thrust his hips, establishing a wild and untrammeled rhythm with her. The heat and friction built rapidly and Katie gave herself in every way to him.

Joe caressed her hardened nipples, hips grinding into hers, his ragged breathing matched her own. Katie leaned up thrusting her tongue into his mouth. She felt him stiffen, a low groan rolling out of him. The urgent sound filtered through her like a living earthquake rippling every muscle, every cell of her damp, taut flesh. His mouth savagely took hers.

They became like two wild eagles, free-falling from ten thousand feet, claws linked and tumbling as they frantically mated with one another before hitting the earth below. His male scent, the roughness of his beard against her cheek, his hips thrusting wildly against hers, combined to create an explosion within her. She tensed, cried out and clung to Joe. His muscles knotted. A deep groan tore out of him, his body suddenly galvanized. The moments of rhythmic pleasure flowing outward lifted Katie into a surreal world of dancing lights. Frozen in those stolen seconds within one another, they felt pleasure so intense neither could move.

Her world became bright Fourth of July fireworks as she orgasmed over and over again. He continued to drive his hips, giving Katie more and more pleasure. She cried out, her voice hoarse as she pulled Joe down to meet his hungry, searching mouth. His hands captured her hips, and he moved hard and relentlessly against her body. With each thrust, she felt herself spinning off into an unknown galaxy filled only with fusion, heat and satiated hunger.

Katie heard him growl. Breathing unevenly, she opened her eyes. Joe's face was darkly shadowed, his eyes shards of glittering desire. Absorbing his primal masculinity, she could only sigh, a tremulous smile pulling at her well-kissed lips. His hands memorized her body, caressing her breasts. Leaning down, he sucked her nipples, lavishing her with even more sensations and causing her to feel faint with ongoing bliss. This was how a man loved a woman. She relished Joe's slow, delicious exploration of her even after they descended from the edge of the galaxy where only intense ecstasy existed.

The weight of his body was like a welcome blanket across her. Joe kissed her deeply, his tongue moving, mating with hers. Finally, as he eased his mouth from hers, he withdrew and pulled Katie to his side and into his arms. The darkness only made her feel as if she were in a deep, warm cave within his embrace. His body was damp and firm against hers. She nestled her head in the crook of his shoulder. Their breathing was shallow and fast, synchronizing with one another. Joe's hand moved tantalizingly across her rib cage, lingered at her waist and then caressed her hip. Katie could sense him absorbing every inch of her flesh with his fingers. Reveling in his moist breath against her hair, she nuzzled closer and kissed his damp neck. Never had she felt so safe, so loved as right now. Whatever had drawn them together was real, Katie dimly realized, still caught up in the rippling movement within her lower body. Joe's hand came to rest on her hip and she felt him relax against her, his breathing becoming less chaotic. Savoring him in every way, she whispered, "I'm not sorry about this, Joe." Katie lifted her hand and placed it over his.

"Me, neither," Joe admitted in a roughened tone. Right now, only Katie existed, her sweet body next to his. Joe realized he'd been without a woman for nearly two years. And he'd been starved. Katie had fulfilled him as no woman had before. He turned his hands so their fingers laced within one another. "Our relationship has changed." He wanted to say, *I'm falling in love with you,* but didn't dare. Turmoil began to gnaw away at the languorous feelings still flowing through his sated body. He'd committed a fatal mistake: making things personal between him and Katie. Guilt ate at him and Joe felt it sharply because she was trusting him. She didn't deserve deceit. But what was he going to do?

Lifting her head, Katie pulled back enough to meet his sleepy gaze. "We have a lot to talk about, but right now, I'm feeling wonderfully tired and all I want to do is fall asleep in your arms, Joe."

He lifted his hand and moved strands away from her cheek. Drowning in her slumberous half-closed blue eyes, he managed a slight smile. "Sounds like a plan…."

CHAPTER SEVENTEEN

"DOES THIS CHANGE ANYTHING at work?" Joe asked Katie as they ate breakfast together the next morning. She had awakened after he did, and he took the time to shower, shave and get dressed. An hour later, at seven, Katie had awakened and Joe had shown her the bathroom. Fluffy yellow towels were laid out. After a warm shower, Katie had dressed in her beautiful red poppy dress. Her hair, still damp from being washed, hung like a black frame around her face.

Katie picked up the toast and slathered on apricot jam. "It doesn't change anything for me, Joe. Does it for you?" She searched his clear green eyes. This morning, he looked even more handsome, if that was possible. Joe wore a white cowboy shirt, the sleeves rolled up to his elbows, his jeans and his work boots. His dark brown hair gleamed beneath the light above the oak table.

Joe shrugged. "No, I guess not."

"We work well together."

"Yes." Joe's body and memory immediately flew back to their lovemaking the night before. Even now, he could feel the warming ache for her once more. She was quiet and contemplative this morning. "Is something bothering you?"

"Does it show?" She laughed a little and held up her hand. "You don't have to answer. I know I can't hide a thing from anyone."

His mouth curved ruefully and he murmured, "Well, maybe it shows to certain people, Katie. People who care for you."

She set the toast aside and picked up her fork. Joe had made ham and cheese omelets for breakfast. "I was just thinking, I swore I wouldn't get involved with another man. I made that promise to myself a year ago." She rolled her eyes and admitted, "I have a terrible track record of always choosing the wrong guy. Donna often said that with my Pisces romantic idealism, I don't see the man for who and what he really is."

Wincing inwardly, Joe kept his face carefully arranged. "Maybe in this past year you've matured more. You might see people more clearly now."

"Actions speak louder than words. Donna preached that to me after the breakup a year ago. I was such an emotional mess."

"And were you practicing that sound advice on me?"

Nodding, Katie felt her body still glowing in the aftermath of their lovemaking. "Yes, I did."

"Do you think Iris and Rudd missed you coming back to the ranch last night?"

She smiled. "Iris misses nothing. I'm sure she put things together. I called her this morning after I got up. I left her a message and told her I was over at your house."

"Good, we wouldn't want her to worry." Joe forced himself to eat. His stomach was in turmoil and his emotions tore him up. He hated not telling Katie the truth. At some point, he'd have to. And then what? Joe didn't want to lose what they had. Oh, it was more than just sex. There had to be a helluva lot more to a relationship to get his interest. Katie was the opposite of him, otherworldly. She appealed to him on so many levels.

He liked her romantic view of life, her idealism, intact despite her painful past.

And Janet Bergstrom was probably manipulating her, whether she knew it or not.

JANET WATCHED HER DAUGHTER come in the front door of the newly opened Mercury Courier Service. She'd called her in midafternoon and asked if she could come and celebrate the opening. Eduardo, who was one of Xavier's trusted men, manned the front desk. There were five people waiting in line to use the services.

"Hi, Janet," Katie greeted, breathless. "Your store looks great from the outside!" Her mother was in a dark green business suit. This time, it fitted her well and Katie liked the tasteful gold jewelry Janet wore. As she drew close, she could smell cigarette smoke clinging to the woman.

"Come with me," Janet said, and gestured for her to walk around the curved desk to the door behind it.

Katie followed. "Wow, the walls are up, painted and this looks terrific." She walked into another smaller office area.

"Like it?" Janet turned and said, "You'll be working the counter as well as this office area. Your desk is on the left. There's a computer, a phone and anything else you might need to take orders and type them into our system." She pointed to a window above the desk. "You can see a customer come in from here and go help them."

The small oak desk was in the corner. It was not a large area but Katie saw everything she might need. Even a coffee mug. "Looks nice, Janet."

"On the other side is our coffee machine." She turned and pointed to another door with a sign reading: Shipping, Do Not Enter. "This is the shipping area, Katie. Eduardo will take any packages or boxes you receive and move them to shipping." She drilled Katie with a dark look. "Your only job here is to man the front desk or work here in this little office. I never want you to go into shipping. It's off-limits to you. Understand?"

Frowning, Katie stared at the door. It was a heavy one, made of metal, and there was no window in it. "But...why? I'm sure I can carry packages into the shipping area to help Eduardo."

Mouth compressing, Janet said, "That's not your job. You are to work the front area only. Got it? Eduardo does all the heavy lifting. I worry about some of the boxes being too heavy for you. You're such a skinny thing, Katie. I don't need you injuring your back or straining a muscle. Okay?"

Hearing the steeliness in her mother's tone, Katie said, "Okay. I'll let Eduardo do it."

"There is one other thing I want you to do for me. After Eduardo has loaded up one of our three company vans, you will drive it to another city." Janet opened up a map of the region and spread it out on the desk. "Come here, let me show you what I'm talking about."

Katie drew close and looked over her mother's shoulder. "I see the red marks you've put on it. Are those the routes I'll drive?" She'd had no idea she'd be actually driving a van. Katie had thought her work would only be clerical.

"Yes, I need you to drive the van to Idaho Falls, Idaho." She traced it with her index finger, the bright red nail polish outlining the highway system. Twisting her head to the left, Janet looked up at her daughter. "Think you can do this?"

"Sure."

"You're so skinny."

Laughing, Katie shrugged and said, "Skinny people drive trucks and vans just fine." She longed to call her *Mother* or *Mom*. The challenging look in Janet's eyes, however, made Katie swallow those haunting words.

Janet folded up the map and slipped it into a file organizer on the desk. "Yeah, I guess you're right."

"Will I be driving often?"

"Maybe once a week, if that. I've got Eduardo, but sometimes I might need a second driver."

"How many do you employ at your original business in Cheyenne?"

"I have five men."

"No women?"

"No women. They're trouble. Men, when you tell 'em to do something, they do it. There's no whining or complaining."

Katie wondered if Janet felt the same about her, but didn't have the courage to ask. Her mother seemed upbeat, even happy and she had no desire to ruin the opening day of her courier service. "I see," was all she managed to say.

"I've got Kyle, my geek guy, comin' over from Cheyenne tomorrow. Will you be available to come in at one o'clock and sit down and learn how to use the computer system with him? He's a pretty decent teacher."

"Sure. I can have Joe take care of things at the raptor facility. How many hours?"

"Three. There's no manual on this stuff." She jabbed her finger at the computer sitting on the desk.

"No manual?"

"No." Janet said it swiftly. In her business, the codes she used were sent to a computer in Guatemala. Xavier needed the information in order to follow the progress of shipments to specific cities. "We aren't so large we need manuals. There's a notebook there on the desk. You can take notes and then when you get them memorized, you give me what you wrote. I'll throw it away."

Katie looked over at her. Her mother's face, heavily made up, looked like that of a bulldog who would always get her way. "Well…okay. I'm pretty good at memorization."

"There's not much to it. If my guys over in Cheyenne can log it into their thick brains, you can, too."

"Okay." It seemed like a strange office procedure to Katie. She had written a manual for the raptor facility. There were feeding schedules for each raptor, another schedule for daily weight recording and management. Maybe her mother wasn't keen on manuals. Who knew? Just getting to see Janet happy thrilled her. The other two meetings had been grim in comparison. And she desperately wanted Janet to count on her.

"Sit down, see if the chair is comfortable for you." Janet jabbed her index finger toward it.

"I'm sure it is," Katie said, moving behind the desk and pulling out the chair.

"I bought it specifically for you, Katie. The guy over at the office store said it was ergonomic and you'd like it. Sit down. Tell me how it feels." Above all, Janet wanted to manipulate Katie into thinking she was special. Her daughter would then do as she asked without question. Janet saw the girl's face go soft and a trembling smile come to her lips. Good, she was hooked. Having Katie trained to work the front end of her business, she could then move Xavier's man to the shipping department where the real business went on.

A small tendril curled within Janet's heart as she watched her slender daughter sit down and move her fingers across the arms of the black-and-chrome chair. The smile on Katie's face did something unexpected within her and she didn't quite understand the feeling. Touching her mint-green blouse in nervousness, she then realized with shock that she felt happiness.

"This...feels very nice, Janet."

"The salesman said it was state-of-the-art. I didn't want your back going out on a lousy chair."

Katie's heart warmed. For the first time, she saw care and concern on Janet's face—for her. She wanted her mother to like her...love her...

"It feels wonderful. Wish I had a chair like this at my raptor facility." Katie managed an awkward laugh. "I'd probably sit in it a lot more."

Pleased, Janet felt that vinelike joy wrapping around her heart. Her daughter's cheeks were flushed and her eyes shone with pleasure. The strange, happy sensation continued. Was this what it felt like to love one's child? Janet wasn't sure. "Well, I want you happy," she said in a gruff tone. Looking at her watch, she added, "I got a lot to do. You'll be here when Kyle comes to train you?"

Katie stood up and then rolled the fancy chair under the desk. "Yes, I'll be here."

"Good, good. See you then." Janet felt the urge to take those few steps and throw her arms around her daughter. Again, it was unbidden and she wasn't sure what was happening. Instead, she fought the need and turned on her heel, marching out to the front where patrons were lined up.

Katie sighed, pulled her purse strap a little higher on her shoulder. Happiness swirled around her. She stopped and turned around to gaze at the chair. Janet had bought it especially for her. Closing her eyes for a moment, Katie savored the new feelings of hope in her heart.

Her mother loved her. It was obvious. She cared enough to buy what appeared to be a very expensive chair for her. Care. Oh, God, how long had she been wishing her mother would care for her? Now, Janet had shown her in her own way—she did care for Katie.

Katie left Mercury, barely aware of her feet touching the wooden porch along the plaza. The afternoon sunlight felt delicious on her face and bare arms as she walked around the corner to her truck. The sky was a deep blue and she relished the cobalt color. Hand on the strap of her purse, Katie decided that two dreams had come true in the past two days. Her skin tingled as she replayed kissing and loving Joe Gannon last night. And the happiness continued today like a new beginning in her life with her mother. She had expected Janet to be gruff and frowning, but this time, she was completely different.

Once she reached her truck, she opened it and slipped inside. Suddenly, life had opened up in amazing and surprising ways and Katie felt like the puffy white clouds in the sky above—floating. Was it possible to have love come to her all at once? In two different ways? As she drove out of the main plaza area and turned onto the main highway leading out of town, Katie felt overwhelmed by her sudden good fortune. She could hardly wait to reach the ranch and tell Joe and Iris. Tonight, she would call Donna and tell her about the amazing shifts in her life.

JOE WAS FLYING SAM, the golden eagle, about a quarter-mile from the facility when Katie drove into the parking lot. She saw him lift his long, thick gauntlet. Sam flapped his large wings, the two Xs of white visible beneath each wing.

She left the truck and focused on man and eagle in the distance. Sam's wings made broad sweeps in an arc as he fought to gain altitude in the warm summer sky. Katie's heart took off as she witnessed the magnificent eagle owning the world. And then her gaze moved from eagle to man. Joe stood with his legs apart to balance himself when he'd released the eagle. Most people wouldn't think an eagle—at sixteen pounds—would be that powerful on takeoff, but they were. It was the seven-foot wingspan that made the weight of the eagle increase exponentially. Literally, a falconer could lose his balance when the eagle pushed off from the fist.

She smiled softly as the eagle climbed in large, lazy circles to the west of Joe. Her gaze went to Joe's clean profile. She recalled his hands moving slowly, as if he were memorizing every inch of her. Katie realized she had never had a man worship her as Joe had last night.

"Aren't they a pair?"

Startled, Katie turned and saw Iris walking up. Smiling, she said, "I wish I had my video camera."

Iris halted at Katie's side. "I've been watching Joe work with Sam. I was out back in one of my iris beds earlier when he brought the eagle out to the training oval." Iris studied her. "Joe said you got a call from your mother. Everything go okay?"

Hearing the concern in Iris's voice, Katie reached out and hugged her. "I'm fine. It went *really* well, Iris. My mother bought me a special chair to sit in at my desk in her office. Can you believe it? I was blown away. It looked expensive. She said it was ergonomic and she wanted me comfortable when I worked for her."

Nodding, Iris watched Sam flying higher and higher. The eagle was probably about five thousand feet and sailing toward the Tetons, not far away. "That's nice of her, Katie. So," and she turned and studied her, "it sounds like Janet is thawing a little toward you?"

"Fingers crossed," Katie said, holding up her right hand. "Yes, she was all business but this time, when she showed me the office behind the counter wall, she seemed very pleasant. It's a real change from before."

"Maybe she was stressed about getting this business off the ground."

Katie watched Iris shift the big, floppy straw hat on her silver hair. There were days when Iris's hair literally looked like a messy hen's nest, sticking out in all directions under the capture of the hat. "Probably so. I really loved being around her. She seemed so relaxed today. And I just can't get over the fact she bought me the special chair!"

"Maybe it's her way of letting you know she loves you," Iris murmured. "Twenty-six years without a daughter and suddenly, she has you pop into her life. She's probably as emotionally confused as you."

"Mmm, I think you're right. Janet just seemed, well…" she sighed "…pleased? Well, I wouldn't say happy because I've never seen her smile. Maybe she will now."

"Take it a day at a time," Iris gently counseled. "Both of you need time and space to adjust to one another. Is Janet going to be living in Jackson Hole from now on or is she dividing time between here and Cheyenne?"

"I don't know. I'm really afraid to ask her questions. Isn't that silly?" Katie said, shading her eyes to follow Sam, who was now gliding and circling far to the west.

"No, because you want her to love you. And I think you sense Janet doesn't like a lot of questions."

"She's definitely in charge. And she's good at giving directions and orders," Katie admitted. "I guess I'm just afraid if I say the wrong thing, she'll get angry and tell me to walk out of her life."

Iris patted Katie's shoulder and said in a soothing tone, "Listen, what you're feeling is normal. I remember when we told Rudd at a certain age that he was adopted, he went through a spell of the same emotions. I think it's natural to worry if you've been abandoned once by a parent that it could happen again."

The happiness Katie felt was somewhat doused as she considered Iris's words of wisdom. "You're right. I'm walking on eggshells with Janet. And deep down, I'm dying to call her Mom or Mother. It almost leaps out of my mouth sometimes. I'm afraid if it does, she'll get angry and send me away."

Iris nodded. "Listen, this is the hard part. What's good about it is your mother runs a business and has asked you to help her. You need to let go of the anxiety over getting sent away. She's embraced you into her business. That's not a bad sign, it's a good one. Don't you think?"

"As always, you're right, Iris." Katie laughed. "I just feel like a little seven-year-old girl in front of Janet. I just so desperately want her to love me like I love her."

"You have to be patient, Katie. You can't rush into anything. I'm sure Janet feels guilt over giving you up. And she probably thinks you're beautiful and intelligent. In her own way, she may be afraid of you."

Tilting her head, Katie asked, "What do you mean?"

"She may see you as smart, accomplished and beautiful. You may remind her of her own growing-up years, which we know were stressful. She may look upon you as a positive in her life. And, because she was abandoned by her mother, you may seem amazing in comparison." She smiled at Katie. "You have to try and walk in her shoes. She was abandoned, too. And if Janet didn't have the help of her foster home, then she had no one to support her when she got pregnant with you. It could be, in the end, Janet may someday tell you why she gave you up. Maybe she didn't want you to suffer like she did. She probably thinks, at this point, she made the right decision, because you are successful. I can't think of any parent who doesn't want something better for their child than they had. Can you?"

Katie considered her words for a long time. She saw Sam circling and descending toward Joe. "You know, I never thought of it that way."

"It's a lot to think about," Iris said. "Just continue to give your mother and yourself a lot of space. Don't think you know her or her reasons. In time, I hope you two will learn to trust one another to open up and talk honestly. Right now, Janet is very defensive, and you can't blame her. At the same time, she's made room for you in her life by asking you to help her with her new business."

Katie turned to hug Iris. "What would I do without you and Donna? You two always help me see things in a far more realistic way!"

Chuckling, Iris embraced Katie, kissed her cheek and released her. She held the younger woman at arm's length, her eyes sparkling, and whispered, "Okay, now 'fess up. What's going on between you and Joe? It looks serious. Tell me about it."

Katie laughed joyfully. "Iris, all of a sudden my life has been turned upside down. I've met Joe and then my mother." She pressed her hand to her heart. With the lively look in Iris's expression, Katie had no fear of telling her anything. "Joe is wonderful, Iris. When I first met him, I felt we had a connection. It wasn't anything like bells ringing, but over the last couple of weeks, we've just grown closer. It's the only way I can describe it. I like being around him. He's open and sensible. He respects me and he asks my opinion. He's not bossy or arrogant like the men in my other relationships."

"Well, that's good," Iris said. "Because in the past, you seemed to pick men who had secrets."

Katie frowned. "I know. Like you and Donna have said, I have this pink lens of romantic idealism. Oh, I know it's in my nature, but this time, Iris, I think Joe is very different from all the rest."

"When you two left the dance last night, I figured out it was because it was time to deepen your relationship."

"We did," Katie whispered, filled with happiness. Iris nodded. "He's wonderful. Joe is so…caring. He's so different from the others."

"That alone makes me happy," Iris said. She pointed toward Joe. "Sam's coming in for a landing. I always like to watch this eagle land. It's something to behold."

Katie turned her attention toward Joe and saw Sam descend toward the man's arm. He held it high in the air, a signal to the eagle it was time to land. Sam streaked down from the sky like a bullet. Fifteen feet away from Joe's outstretched arm, Sam began to move his wings in swift, backward motions to brake his forward speed. She watched Joe brace for impact, his feet wide apart to take the weight of the incoming eagle. In seconds, Sam reached out with opened talons and gripped Joe's lower arm. His wings furled and swept around Joe's head and shoulders.

"Beautiful," Iris murmured. "Joe's a very good falconer."

"Yes, he is."

Sam folded his wings and sat quietly on the glove. Joe

turned and saw them. Instantly, she saw him smile. He slowly lifted his other hand, not wanting to startle Sam. Katie's heart skittered with joy and she waved in return.

"He's such a hero, Iris. I just love to watch Joe work with Sam."

"Ah, now he's a hero," Iris teased with a gleam in her eyes.

Feeling her cheeks heat up, Katie giggled. "Oh, you know me, Iris. I see some men as heroic. Others as villains. It's my Pisces imagination at work! And, yes, Joe is the epitome of a hero. He was in the Marine Corps. He was an officer and leader. What's not to like about him?"

CHAPTER EIGHTEEN

"THAT IS ONE HAPPY EAGLE," Joe said as he put Sam into his mew. He grinned over at Katie, who seemed to agree.

"Sam likes you," she said, closing the door and locking it. The late-afternoon sun hung above the rugged Tetons. The western side of the facility glowed. The frosted windows diffused the incoming light and flooded the interior with a golden haze.

"I like him." Joe walked with Katie toward the office area. He tugged off his gauntlet and studied the puncture marks where Sam's talons had dug into the leather. "Look at this."

Katie saw the holes. "He's strong. And frankly, it takes every bit of strength I have to hold Sam for any length of time." She grinned. "Since getting my eagle license, I've already bought a second glove. The first one is full of holes. Sam can't help it because when he lands and takes off, he's got to have a really steady arm to grip."

Putting his glove in his locker, Joe said, "No argument there. My teacher went through a glove a month."

"Yes, but he had a number of eagles." Katie sat down at her desk and opened the bright red appointment book on her desk.

"How did things go with your mother?" Joe asked. "Coffee?"

"Yes, please," Katie said watching as he moved to the

other side of the aisle. Joe was lean and strong and her body automatically tightened with desire as she watched him. Did he know how devastatingly wonderful he was? She remembered their night together and it haunted her. So did Iris's words. He poured them coffee, brought it over to her desk and sat down.

"I think my mother is warming to me."

"Oh?" Joe rested his arm on the edge of her desk, hand curved around his mug. Her face was flushed and he could see the excitement dancing in her eyes. As his gaze dropped to her mouth, heat purled deep within him. There was no way to forget last night's lovemaking. "Tell me about it."

"Well," Katie said, "my mom's new office is beautiful. It has an inviting entrance. When I walked in, there were about half a dozen people in line with boxes and large envelopes. Janet had just opened and already the word's out. Isn't that wonderful!"

"It is," he agreed. "Was your mother working the desk?"

"Oh, no, she has Eduardo, who is actually the guy she hired to carry the boxes and stuff back to the shipping area. He's just doing it until I can get trained. Janet also has asked me to drive one of the company vans to Idaho Falls once a week if there's a need."

"But you're not working there full-time, are you?" Joe said, trying not to reveal his emotion.

"No. On Wednesday, tomorrow, my mother's computer expert, Kyle, is driving over from Cheyenne. He's going to teach me how to enter orders."

"How much time do you plan to work with your mom?"

"Maybe three days a week. I can't do it full-time. I don't think she realizes how busy we are out here at the facility or the demands for our educational shows with the raptors."

"You go in for training tomorrow?"

"Yes." She patted the appointment book. "I was checking to see if we had anything up for tomorrow and we don't."

"You seem really happy about this."

Katie placed her lean fingers around the mug. "I am, Joe. I'm so happy I could burst."

"You said your mother was warmer to you this time?"

"Yes. She wasn't grouchy, touchy or as irritable. I mean, she's like a drill sergeant, but I think life has made her that way."

"The military is something I know a little about," Joe said, forcing a slight smile. "You said your mother didn't feel good the other day when you met her for lunch, that she was perspiring heavily. Was she like that this time?"

"No, she seemed really...*up* is the word I'd use. She looked happy but I've never seen her smile." Katie shrugged. "She seemed in a happier mood. I was talking to Iris earlier and she said Janet was probably under terrible stress getting this business open. And now that it's open, she's relaxing. I think Iris is right."

Moving the mug slowly around in a circle, Joe wrestled with his own feelings. What was Janet up to? "This Eduardo fellow, did you meet him?"

"No. Eduardo was busy at the front desk. Janet took me back to the small office located between shipping and the front desk. He seemed...okay."

"What do you mean?" He picked up on Katie's hesitation. She leaned back in her chair, the mug cradled between her hands.

"I don't know...just a feeling." And then she laughed. "He's a short, thin guy with a narrow face."

"Did he speak to you?"

"No. He was busy."

"But? I know you get feelings about others. I've seen you do it with these raptors."

Mouth twisting, Katie looked up toward the glass ceiling of the facility. "Just…a silly feeling, really, Joe. He felt closed up. As if…he had walls or protection up. He never smiled, either. And I can't say his customer face was very inspiring. All he did was scowl."

"Not exactly the person you want to greet customers."

"Right. As soon as I get trained on the computer terminal, Janet wants me out front. She said Eduardo was one of two men she had hired to work in shipping. She said the second guy, Hector, was coming in shortly." Katie sat up. Looking into Joe's eyes, she said, "Janet told me never to go back into shipping. She said I was too weak to lift some of the heavier boxes. Eduardo and Hector would do it." Rubbing her brow, she added, "Janet was really adamant about me never going back there. I found that odd."

Joe knew why. Chances are there would be guns in long wooden boxes, and if Katie accidentally opened one, it would put Janet in an untenable position. Was she trying to protect her daughter by issuing such an order? "Well, you're not weak," he teased, trying to lighten her mood. "You're young, beautiful, kind, sweet and I've got to think she has your interests at heart, Katie."

Glowing beneath his heated look, Katie reached out and touched his hand. "You're good for me, Joe. I love the way you look at me. I feel like I'm a queen."

He twined his fingers with hers. "In my eyes, you are a queen, Katie. I can't think two thoughts without thinking of what we shared last night." Joe saw how his rasping admittance made her blue eyes turn soft. Her fingers tightened around his.

"I feel as if the universe has suddenly decided to give me happiness in a breadth and depth I never knew could exist, Joe. I have you. I have my mother." She released his hand and pressed it to her heart. "I'm so full of joy I don't think my feet are touching the ground most of the time."

A sudden and powerful angst flowed through Joe. Why had he decided to go undercover? He absorbed the shining look in Katie's eyes and yet his gut tightened. "You deserve only good things to happen to you, Katie."

"Well, they sure are. Tomorrow, I'll be learning my mom's computer program and how to enter orders."

"It's a new chapter in your life, Katie." Joe sipped his coffee. He didn't taste it. No one ever told him his conscience would be as sorely tested as it was right now. Katie's idealism was setting her on a blind and dangerous course. What bothered him most was Eduardo. Who was he? A drug soldier from Los Lobos here illegally in the country? He glanced at his watch. It was nearly 5:00 p.m., quitting time.

"What we have," Joe told her, his voice low with feeling, "is a work in progress, Katie. I don't want to crowd you or make you feel as if you need to be in my bed every night."

She went warm from the inside out. Katie held his concerned gaze. Joe's beard was darkening the contours of his face. It gave him the look of a warrior. "You're the first guy who has talked to me about such things. Before, it was me doing the talking and I felt like the guy was a rock."

"Most of us aren't good at communicating," Joe admitted. "I care deeply for you, Katie. Sometimes I don't think you're from our planet." He smiled warmly at her.

"Can I blame it on being a Pisces?" She grinned.

"It makes you very appealing to me," Joe said. God, where did lies and truth begin and end? He desperately liked Katie. Too much.

"You remind me of a knight," Katie admitted in a quiet tone. "You care for others, Joe. Your word is your honor. There's so much about you that just draws me."

What am I going to do? Joe had never felt so guilty. He was being honest with Katie, not playing her. But he was lying to her. There was nothing in the FBI manuals about how to deal with falling in love with a suspect. Somehow, he had to set some boundaries. "Let's just leave our relationship open-ended, okay? If there's a time you feel like coming over, do it. Otherwise, we each have a place to live."

"I like it, Joe. Thanks for understanding. I'm still working through some issues and I need to take things slow."

"So do I. Anything worthwhile, Katie, is going to stand the test of time." But he wondered if it could stand the test of him lying to her. One day, Katie would know the truth. What then? Joe needed to call his boss in Washington, D.C. Things were taking a turn he'd never anticipated.

"So you're falling for her?" Hager said on the phone.

Joe paced his living room, watching the sun sinking behind the mountains. "Yes. It wasn't intentional. I don't know when it happened."

"Well, you're just going to have to suck it up, Joe. There's nothing to be done. Katie Bergstrom is now connected to her mother's gun- and drug-running operation whether she knows it or not. And she's being trained on that computer terminal system we've been trying for a year to hack into. We know Kyle works with Xavier and his cartel. You're going to have to retrieve the information through Katie. Use her. She obviously likes and trusts you."

Rubbing his jaw, Joe muttered, "Yeah, but I damn well don't like playing her. She's innocent in all of this, boss."

"Can't be helped. We're not at a point where we know what Katie will do once her manipulative mother gets her claws into her. This girl has choices, too. Sooner or later, she's going to see that things at Bergstrom's courier service aren't normal. What will she do then? Will she turn to you? To the sheriff's department? An honest person would."

"Dammit, you've left out the most important key to all of this. Katie has been looking for her mother *all her life.* She's just found her! Can you put yourself in her shoes for minute? Wouldn't you want to please your newfound mother, even if some things seemed out of place?" Frustration curdled through him. His boss, at times, was a brick wall. Joe's grip on the cell phone increased as he waited for the FBI agent to reply.

"I agree there's been a lot of muddy water stirred up on this mission, Joe. We can't sort through things as clearly as we wished we could. You are our eyes and ears. I'm hoping Katie is not like her mother. I'm hoping she'll stumble onto some guns or drugs and know what she's looking at. At some point, she's got to understand her mother is running an illegal operation, don't you think?"

"No," Joe said, his voice a growl. "I don't. Katie is idealistic. All she sees is the mother she's so desperately searched for all her life. Right now, she's willing to do anything to get Janet's attention and her love. And Janet isn't very loving from what I can tell. I know she's playing Katie."

"Is Katie stupid?"

"Just the opposite. Katie's idealism and trust in others goes too far." It did with him. She couldn't even see he wasn't what she thought he was. "She simply doesn't think the worst of people. She thinks the best."

"Well," Hager growled back, "that's going to land her in a helluva lot of hot water sooner or later. And we all hope she's got better morals and values in place than her mother. Because sooner or later, Joe, she will put things together."

Joe felt a migraine stalking him, the pains sharp in his temples. "I will not put her in jeopardy, Mr. Hager. This guy named Eduardo, I'm sure he is part of the Los Lobos cartel. Katie just thinks he's odd, but she wouldn't know a soldier from a cartel from a man on the street. She's naive about the world in so many ways." And he wanted to protect her. Oh, God, how Joe wanted to stand between Katie and the world that wanted a piece of her.

"She's not in any danger," he said flatly. "You're knee-jerking, Joe. You're feeling guilty because you fell for this girl."

"She's not a girl," he ground out, "she's a twenty-six-year-old woman."

"She *acts* like a teenage girl, all starry-eyed, trusting, and doesn't have a clue about how the real world operates. In my eyes, she's a girl. Let's move on. You're getting cold feet because you like Katie. And now, because of what's happened, you want to shield her. Well, you can't. There's no threat here I can see."

Anger moved violently through Joe. He stopped pacing, his breath coming faster. "Not yet. But there will be and you and I both know it."

"Let's revisit this conversation at another time, Joe. Right now, you need to get clear about who and what you're doing. You're an FBI agent undercover and trying to get inside info to prove Janet Bergstrom is connected to Los Lobos. Katie is the key to us finding that out. Without her, our mission can't move forward. And I know you want to tell her everything and, dammit, you can't."

"Because you don't know if she's on our side or the cartel's?" he demanded harshly, anger leaking through his tone.

"That's right. Until there is a clear signal, we sit pat."

"But you'll need Katie in the courtroom once this situation is opened up."

"You're right, we will. Until then we have to find out whether she's on our side."

"If you're looking for her to turn over evidence, she has to be protected."

"Yes, but not right now, Joe. You need to separate your head from your heart. Otherwise, you're hindering this operation. Do you understand?"

Joe heard the threat in Hager's darkening tone. "Yes, sir, I do." Was it possible Hager would remove him from the case? How could he? Katie would wonder what happened. And to his knowledge, there were no other agents trained in falconry who might step in to take his place. Savagely rubbing his face, Joe said, "I'll continue to report whenever Katie gives me something new."

Hager hung up without a word. Joe softly cursed and punched the end button on the cell phone. He threw it angrily on the couch, watching it bounce before it hit the wooden floor and skidded against a closet door. It was a throwaway cell and couldn't be traced, so Joe would dismantle it anyway and he didn't care if it had been destroyed.

Joe ran his fingers through his short hair. He yearned for Katie. The world was a bad place and God knew, she'd had plenty of bad things happen to her along the way. Halting, he looked out the large picture window. The sunset was a flaming orange and pink, the long wisps of clouds across the sky making it look festive. He felt anything but.

He glanced at his watch. His parents had invited him over for dinner. Somehow, he had to get himself together so he didn't show his feelings.

"HI, JOE," KATIE GREETED the next morning. She was choosing a travel box for one of the raptors. "How are you?"

His expression looked dark and serious. He wasn't his usual, ebullient self. Had something happened?

"'Morning, Katie." Joe struggled to gird his feelings and not get them entangled in the coming conversation. The sliding door closed and he walked over to the coffee machine on the weight table. "We have a show at the visitor's center at Grand Teton National Park at 1:00 p.m. today, right?"

"Yes, we do. I was just choosing the travel cases. I think we'll have you take Sam and I'll take Harlequin." Her heart skipped a beat as Joe turned around. She saw warmth banked in his eyes—for her. She wanted to run over, throw her arms around him and kiss him until she lost herself within his arms.

As he sipped the steaming coffee, Joe ambled over to her desk and asked, "Hey, are you really going to start driving a courier van for your mother?"

"Yes, I am. I told her it couldn't be anything too long because my raptors are my business."

"Did she understand how busy you are?"

Katie shrugged. "I've been trying to get her to come over here and see my facility. She keeps resisting. I don't know why."

Hearing the hurt veiled in her voice, Joe reached out. Without thinking, he brushed a few strands of hair away from her shoulder. "I know this is hard on you, Katie. I wish…I wish I could do something to take away some of the pain I know you're going through." A sudden need of her flooded him and she seemed to react to his brief, grazing touch. Her blue eyes widened and warmed with what he could only surmise was affection or even love. The idea made his head spin. Joe felt naked and exposed by her honesty.

She quickly reached up and pressed a kiss to his cheek. Stepping away, she said, "Joe, this isn't easy. I can't tell you how many times a day I replay my last meeting with my mother. I question what I did, what I said. I'm so scared of her leaving again."

"I know." The words stuck in his throat as he saw the fear of rejection in her eyes. "This isn't an easy transition for you—or her."

"Iris said the same thing." Katie turned and placed the travel box on her desk. She ached to move into Joe's arms and be held. He made her feel safe from her world of anxiety. Donna's advice to go slow and take her time echoed in her mind. Before, she had impulsively jumped into relationships, heedless of the consequences. This time it had to be the opposite, she had to get to know Joe much better before allowing her heart to be held in his strong, masterful hands.

"I'm glad you have Iris and Donna to help counsel

you on this transition," Joe said. His voice deepened. "I really worry about you driving the van, though, Katie. It's one thing to work at her office as an assistant. It's another to be a driver. Don't you have to get a special license to do that?"

"Yes, I do. I'm going down tomorrow to the motor vehicles department to get it." His brows dipped, and there was real worry in his eyes. Why? "My mother said I might drive the van to Idaho Falls once a week. That's not much. Besides, it will get me out of the office for a day." She laughed a little.

"That's a six-hour round trip, Katie. And I really worry about the wintertime. My parents were telling me the sheriff's department closes the pass across the Tetons all the time when blizzards are coming through. Did you know that?"

"Yes, I'm aware of it. I'm sure my mother will be in time. If I can't drive on blizzard days I'm sure she'll understand."

Joe wasn't so sure. "You need to discuss the aspect of blizzards over the pass with her, then. She's from Cheyenne, clear across the state. They don't have the Tetons standing like guard dogs preventing us from driving over to Idaho."

"Next time I see her, I'll bring it up," Katie promised him. "You look really worried, Joe. Is everything all right? When you came in this morning, you looked as if you were someplace else. Are your parents okay?"

Touched by her concern, Joe forced a smile. "No, they're fine. Everyone is okay. My mother is recovering from the flu and doing fine." He couldn't fight the need to touch Katie. Stepping forward, he framed her face and looked deeply into her blue eyes. "Listen, I think you're making a mistake by driving for your mother's courier service. This could be dangerous…" God help him, he wanted to say so much more.

Katie felt the strength of his hands. For a moment, she absorbed Joe's masculine energy, the obvious care burning in his green gaze. She relished the unexpected contact with him, lifted her hands and pressed them to his hands. "I don't see it as being dangerous. I really don't. I'm afraid of losing her before I've found her, Joe. Maybe I am being too generous with my time, but right now, until I can know for sure she isn't going to tell me to get out of her life, I want…I need to do this."

His heart snagged and beat harder. He wanted to come clean and tell Katie the truth. All of it. She was in danger. Joe sensed it, but couldn't prove it to his boss. In Afghanistan, he had learned to recognize when danger was lurking nearby. It had saved his and his men's lives so many times. Joe searched for the right words. Her hands were warm and soft against his. He never wanted this feeling to go away. Katie was magical. "Look," he began, his voice ragged with barely concealed emotions, "I want you safe, Katie. I've just found you. Accidents happen on the highway. I want to keep on developing what we've just discovered. Don't you?"

Sighing, she held his anxious, narrowed gaze. "Oh, Joe, I'll be fine. You're worrying too much. Do you know that?" She tried to tease him out of his anxiety. There was a feeling of desperation around him she couldn't explain. Was it his growing love for her? Katie acknowledged silently she was falling in love with him. "Joe, I can't be torn between my mother and you. I'm doing the best I can. I'm sorry you think driving the van is dangerous. I will be careful, I promise," she said softly, searching his eyes.

She reached up and placed a soft kiss on the hard

line of his mouth. Instantly his hands dropped away and encircled her. His mouth plundered hers, hot and hungry. She was starved for him as well, sliding her hands around his broad shoulders, leaning like a willow against his male body and absorbing his power. She closed her eyes and felt euphoria arcing through her like an unexpected bolt of lightning. His mouth turned from powerful to cherishing, lips moving gently against hers. The moistness of his breath fell across her cheek as she touched his tongue with her own. He moved his hand slowly down her spine.

Joe reluctantly parted from her wet lips. He fell into her blue eyes shining with such love for him. God help him, but he was falling deeply in love with Katie. He held her at arm's length. "I don't want to stand between you and your mother, Katie. It's the last thing I want to do." He threaded his fingers through the dark strands of hair framing her face. "I've just found you. You make me happy. I look forward to seeing you every day. All of a sudden, my life has taken on so many extra dimensions with you in it."

Joe's hands were firm and steadying on Katie's shoulders. "I understand," she said, her voice uneven. "I'm going to make mistakes, Joe. You'll have to be patient with me. I do feel torn at times between you and my mother. I'm trying to balance it all out. I feel like my two greatest dreams have come true all at once." She gave him a wry look. "I've yearned forever for my mother. I've wanted to meet a man who was brave, honest and true to me. Now—" she said "—I have both. I feel filled with riches beyond my knowing." She stepped back, her hand moving over her heart. "You fill me with such happiness, Joe. Truly, you are my white knight. And you showed up at the best possible time."

She couldn't help the feeling of utter joy that enveloped her, and she flashed him her most brilliant smile. He had to know how much she appreciated his protectiveness, how much she appreciated him.

CHAPTER NINETEEN

KATIE'S PHONE RANG just as they stepped inside the facility. Joe was carrying Sam on his glove. "I'll get it," she said, gently setting the travel box with the peregrine falcon on the floor.

Joe called, "I'll get Sam put away and come back and get Harlequin." They had just come back from the Grand Teton National Park visitor's center demonstration.

"Great, thanks, Joe." She picked up the phone and said, "Katie here."

"This is Janet."

Surprised, Katie steadied her breathing. "Hi."

"I want you to come in and drive the van to Idaho Falls next week. Kyle will be coming in at 9:00 a.m. tomorrow morning, instead of 11:00 a.m. He'll train you on the computer. Can you do it?"

"Yes, I can."

"Did you get your license at the motor vehicles?"

"I will have it by the weekend," Katie responded. Her mother sounded almost happy. Her voice wasn't filled with impatience. Heart lifting, Katie added, "I'm really excited to help you out, Janet."

"Good. I am, too. See you tomorrow morning."

Katie placed the phone in the cradle. She heard the mew door close. Picking up the travel case, she carried it down the aisle.

"That was my mother," she confided to Joe. "Tomorrow at nine, Kyle is going to train me on the computer. Next week, I get to drive the van to Idaho Falls." She opened the door and gently placed the travel case on the gravel floor of the mew.

Joe's chest galloped in fear. He walked over and quietly closed the mew door. Katie leaned over and opened up the case. She placed her glove next to the perch and tapped it. Harlequin hopped obediently to her glove. "That's good," Joe said, forcing his voice to sound light. He felt anything but. Katie smiled and carried the tundra peregrine to his large, wide perch in the corner of his mew to join his mate.

"It is," she said. After transferring the falcon to the perch, Katie turned and picked up the case. "My mother actually sounded happy, Joe." She grinned and walked out as Joe opened the door. "Can you believe it?"

"Things are probably ironing out at her business and she's getting into a rhythm with everything." He scowled and followed Katie to the office. The computer terminal was important. Would Katie be given access to the entire system? Or would she be barricaded from parts of it that held the real information on what was being moved through Janet's business to Los Lobos?

Katie placed the glove into her locker. "I think you're right."

Joe didn't want to spoil the happiness he saw in her eyes. "Be sure and take lots of notes. Maybe Kyle will give you a manual?"

"Janet said there wasn't one." She laughed and said, "I'm not a geek but I think I can be trained to type in orders." Her brows fell as she considered the training. "Gosh, I hope Kyle is patient." Tapping her temple, she said, "Sometimes logic escapes me, Joe."

"Then why not write down notes?"

"I will. My mother said she would destroy the notes as soon as I have the system memorized."

Joe moved to the other side of the facility to make coffee. Katie's notes could prove to be very helpful to the FBI. All he had to do was wait until Katie came back from the training.

JOE WAS JUST COMING to the facility after flying Quest, the female peregrine, in the flight oval when Katie drove in at 3:00 p.m. the next day. She looked tired. His heart picked up a bit as he saw her pull a manual from the car. "Hey," he called as he halted near the door, "how did training go?"

Groaning, Katie slung her purse over her shoulder and picked up her manual. "Long and torturous. Kyle, bless his heart, did provide me with a manual. Wasn't that nice of him?" She managed a half smile. "I need a cup of coffee."

Joe walked into the facility, put the peregrine away and ambled up the aisle. He spotted the thin orange manual on Katie's desk. There was also a notebook beneath her purse. "So, how did it go? Get everything down pat?"

Katie shrugged as she poured coffee into her mug. "Let's put it this way—Kyle probably thinks I'm about as non-computer-literate as one can get." She turned, sipped her coffee and felt her heart swell with love for Joe. He stood in the aisle, his gaze speculative. There was always such a sense of safety around him. "Oh, I guess it wasn't that bad, but I felt like a bumbling fool."

"Mind if I look at your manual?"

"No, go ahead. I warn you, it looked like Greek to me."

A thrill moved through Joe as he casually picked the

book up. There were about forty pages in it. Katie sat down at her desk. "This looks pretty technical."

"It is," she said, shaking her head. "Janet was there, too. She knows the whole computer system and really became impatient with me. I wasn't as fast at picking up the order process as she'd like."

"Was Eduardo there?"

"Yes."

"And he knows the order system?"

"Oh, very well. He was giving me a look like I was stupid." She sat back in her chair. "It wasn't a very good day, Joe."

"You were nervous," Joe soothed. He saw the worry in Katie's eyes. "I don't think anyone expects you to get it right off the bat. It takes time."

"My mother was really disappointed with me, Joe. I felt like crying. I was trying so hard to remember all those PC commands."

Joe set the manual aside. Her voice was filled with disappointment. Moving to her, he placed his hand on Katie's slumped shoulder. "Hey, stop being so hard on yourself. I think your mother is expecting too much, too soon, don't you?"

"She's really counting on me, Joe. She said Eduardo was the main driver and he couldn't be up front to wait on customers all day long. He has a more important job to do back in shipping."

"If that's true, why is she wanting you to drive?"

"Janet knows the computer system. She said on days when Eduardo and I were both driving, she'd man the front desk and input the orders. She's hired that second guy, Hector, but she was sort of vague about when he'd be there and what he'd being doing. I suspect she'll have him working in shipping, too."

Nodding, Joe moved his hand gently across her shoulders. Her muscles felt taut beneath his fingertips. "Would it help if I went over the stuff in the manual with you?"

"Would you? I mean, not right now because my brain feels like jelly."

"How about I take you out to eat tonight? And then you come over to my place afterward? I can probably help you understand this manual." Joe felt badly about the ruse. He saw the sudden hope flare in Katie's eyes.

"Why, that would be great. Are you good at computers?"

"Pretty good," he said. "I think all you really need is less stress and pressure put on you and you'll remember the system."

Clapping her hands, Katie cried, "Wonderful, Joe. Thank you so much!" She stood up and threw her arms around him.

He took her full weight, felt her lips caressing his mouth. Her spontaneity was like the breath of life to him. He molded his mouth to her smiling lips. His mind, however, was elsewhere. As soon as he could, he'd get hold of his FBI boss. The mission was now in motion.

"CAN YOU GET A COPY of the manual?" Roger Hager demanded.

"Yes," Joe said, "Katie left it with me last night. I scanned in a copy of it and have already sent it as a pdf document to you via email. Should be in your box, so check." At 7:00 a.m., the sun was cresting the mountains to the east, and slats of golden light were flowing silently across the wide, green valley.

"Great, I'll check and confirm receipt of it. Good

work. Do you see anything in it that might help us crack their security wall?"

"I don't know. I'll leave it up to the hackers the FBI has hired to figure that one out."

"You said Katie is driving a van to Idaho Falls next week?"

"Yes, and it's got me worried, Roger. Did you find anything on this Eduardo fellow?"

"Nothing. He must be using an alias, because he's not in any of our systems. Soldiers to cartels are always lying about their names. They have fake documents and driver's licenses. They know we're trying to track them once they cross our border and they just blend into the crowd."

Grunting, Joe paced. The dawn was beautiful, but he was in no mood to appreciate it. "I don't want Katie driving, Roger, but I can't stop her. You said you were picking up more activity on the Garcia cartel here in town?"

"Yes, Curt Downing has been using his long-haul trucks a lot more than usual. We think he's agreed to move Garcia's drugs. We can't prove it, but we see more trucks are coming and going from his terminal. Since flying the drugs in to Long Lake became impossible, he's probably figured out another way to do it."

"But we don't know how?"

"No, not yet."

"I worry about Garcia discovering Janet and her operation. Once he finds it, he'll do everything he can to destroy it—and her." *And Katie.* His gut constricted with fear for Katie's life. She was in jeopardy and Joe knew it.

"If Garcia does anything, he's going to hit in a way that makes it look like an accident. He went to war with another cartel over some turf in Chicago last year. The first thing his soldiers did was burn down the company building. These drug lords don't want to be obvious. They want to make things look accidental so no finger can be pointed in their direction."

Halting, Joe felt another migraine coming on. He hated getting them because it would take half a day to survive the pain and discomfort. He was stressed to the max for Katie. "I need to tell her not to drive for Janet. I know she's in danger, Roger. I have to say something to her."

"Joe, I know you care about this young woman. But she's our only contact to Janet Bergstrom and the Los Lobos cartel. You're already assuming Garcia knows she's on his turf."

"I can't prove it," Joe gritted out, "but I feel it. I survived a war zone because I listened to my gut, Roger. And right now, it's screaming at me that Katie is in danger."

"Is it possible to put a GPS magnet in those three vans? That way, we could track them."

Joe began to pace. "I can go find out. I don't know what kind of security Janet has in place."

"Check it out. If we can get those magnetic units on the underside of the vans, it will be of immense help."

But it wouldn't stop Katie from being attacked in a van. Joe almost said it and then swallowed the words. "Okay, I'll see what I can find out tonight and get back to you."

AT THREE O'CLOCK IN THE MORNING, Joe walked quietly around the two-story brick building. He'd parked his truck two blocks away on a back street. He wore a black leather jacket, slacks and boots. There was no way he wanted to be seen. Jackson Hole at this time of night had rolled up the sidewalks; no one was around. A stray dog barked at him for a block and then decided to quit following him. His heart was beating hard as he chose areas where there were no streetlights. The building was located on the corner of the square. He could approach it from another street, unseen.

The air was chilled, down in the forties. Hands tucked in his pockets, he moved silently. All his military experience in Afghanistan came to the forefront. Hearing keyed, Joe hugged the building, but not close enough to rub his jacket against it. He made a turn into an alley, then quickly walked down one side of it, his gaze restless. On the left stood the brick building housing Janet's business. Seeing a small dirt road forking off to the right, Joe stopped. It led to the rear entrance to her establishment.

Craning his neck, he halted at the edge of a huge lilac bush. It was ten feet tall and provided good cover. There was a huge floodlight just above the loading dock. The light's rays showed three white vans with the same name in large red letters on their sides. The vans had no windows in them except up front where the driver sat. Disappointment flooded Joe. As he studied the area, he spotted two security cameras, one on each corner of the building, so anyone around the vans would be taped. *Damn.* Sometimes security cameras were fake, acting as a deterrent he knew. Were these fake? He had no way of knowing.

There was a sliver of darkness along the building. The floodlight spewed out its brightness about three feet away from the loading area. The vans were all backed up against the dock. Maybe he could place the small round magnetic device under each bumper. Again, Joe studied the light, where the vehicles were parked and the location of the video cameras. Remembering his training, he also looked for laser devices that were invisible to the naked eye. He pulled out a set of night vision goggles from his jacket pocket, then settled them over his eyes. No lasers. *Good.* Taking the goggles off and stuffing them back into his pocket, he decided to walk past the entrance. The alley itself was dark and the video cameras would not pick him up.

At the corner of the brick building, Joe edged silently along the wall. The cameras were pointed toward the center area beyond the dock. He didn't know how much area they covered, but he knew it wasn't along the wall where he inched his way forward.

Heart pounding, he stopped every now and then to listen. Automatically, he scanned the area for any movement. Off in the distance, he heard the same mongrel dog barking once more. Toward the plaza, he saw a sudden flash of headlights and heard the growl of a pickup's diesel engine. Above him, the stars twinkled in the black sky, bearing silent witness to his stealth.

Near the dock, Joe pulled a black ski mask over his head. If the video picked him up, no one could identify him. If he was seen on the video, Janet would suspect someone was messing with her vans. She'd have them checked and possibly discover the magnetic GPS device. It would tip her off someone was tailing her. Joe dropped to his hands and knees. The ground was wet from a late-afternoon thunderstorm. He inched forward to the bumper of the first van. Pulling a device from his pocket, he quickly attached it beneath the rear bumper.

Luckily, all three vans were parked close together against the dock. His pulse throbbed in his throat as he attached the GPS to vans two and three. Crawling back against the brick wall, he slowly made his way out of the area. Once at the corner of the building, Joe quickly pulled off the ski mask and trotted silently down the darkened alley toward his truck. He moved like a silent shadow through the back streets of Jackson Hole, wondering if the cameras had picked him up. In all likelihood, if they had, Janet would think the Garcia cartel had planted the devices. As Joe opened his truck and climbed in, he hoped Janet would see nothing on those tapes.

"WHAT THE HELL IS THIS?" Janet growled, watching the videotapes from the night before.

"What?" Eduardo demanded, walking over to where she sat at a small desk in the shipping area.

"Something..." She jabbed her finger at the grainy black-and-white screen on her desk. "There. Do you see it? Or is it my imagination?" She squinted her eyes. Maybe she'd done way too much coke and it was catching up with her. She wasn't seeing as well as she wished.

Leaning over, Eduardo frowned and watched the replay of the video. There was nothing obvious he could see. The video cameras showed the vans parked at the loading dock. About one foot of them was invisible, out of camera range. "What do you see, *señorita?*"

"I don't know," Janet grumbled, frustrated. She wiped her eyes carefully because she'd just put eye shadow and mascara on them earlier. She pressed her finger to the computer display. "See that? Doesn't it look like...something?"

Squinting, Eduardo studied it. "I...don't know. Maybe a shadow?"

"Yeah, dammit. I want you to go out with the mirror and look under all three vans."

"Sí," he said. "This could be Garcia and his people."

Worried, Janet rubbed her chin. "Maybe. Go check 'em. Let me know if you find anything."

Within five minutes, Eduardo came back. He was frowning. When he opened his hand, he said in Spanish to Janet, "I found these GPS devices under the back bumpers of all three vans. Someone wants to follow us."

Cursing softly, Janet picked up one of the small, round devices. Anger surged through her. She grabbed one of her throwaway cell phones and said, "I'm calling Señor Lobos."

"Sí."

Janet punched in the numbers. Her heart started to thud painfully in her chest. This happened sometimes with a good bump or two. Coke also made her feel strong and confident.

"Xavier here."

"It's me, Janet." She quickly told him what Eduardo had found.

"On the video," he asked, "is there a person? Someone you can identify?"

"No, just a sliver of a shadow. That's what tipped me off. I can't see anyone. Damn, Xavier, this isn't good. What do you think?" She wiped her sweaty brow, the makeup coming off on her fingers.

"I think it's Garcia," he ground out, anger in his voice.

"Oh, God, this isn't good!"

"Stop whining!"

"I'm not whining, dammit. This is *my* life! *My* business! I don't need another cartel doing this to us, Xavier. You said it would be safe to do business here."

"Well, I was wrong. Let me think...."

Janet sat feeling fear. Xavier had Cheyenne locked

up. Once, when she'd just gotten into business, another cartel had tried to snoop around. Xavier had sent his soldiers across the border and there had been a series of gun-and-run incidents in and around the city. Janet knew no sheriff or city cop would ever protect them. Her mind whirled with fear, her imagination fueled by the cocaine.

"Listen, Garcia could throw a Molotov cocktail in the front door while I'm sitting here. You know how they like to make attacks look like accidents." She planted her elbows on the desk, fear unraveling within her. "And by God, I'm not gonna let my daughter drive any of these vans! Not now! I know how rival cartels attack, Xavier." Janet's lips thinned. "Are you listening to me?"

"Yes, I am," Xavier came back, his voice cool and hard. "Get hold of yourself, Janet. This could be the work of the FBI or ATF, too. We don't know it's Garcia. You're panicking. It's not like you. Are you getting high again?"

Sitting up, Janet said, "Hell no! I told you, I don't do drugs when I'm working!"

"Well, you certainly sound like it."

She snapped. "What the hell am I to do?"

"Nothing," Xavier ground out. "Not yet. Just go about your business as if nothing has happened. You said your daughter was going to be trained on the computer?"

"Yeah, Kyle trained her yesterday," Janet said in a raspy voice, anxiety rifling through her. She began drumming her polished nails against the desk. "Xavier, I ain't gonna let Katie drive. And that's just it!"

"Yes, you will. It will look more normal to have men and women driving for you. It raises less suspicion with law enforcement. She *will* drive for you at least once a week."

Rage tunneled through Janet. "Dammit, Xavier, she's my only kid! I may not have been much of a mother to her, but I'm sure as hell not gonna put her out on the road where she can be blown away by a car comin' up alongside the van and spraying it with bullets! I just won't do it!" Her breathing became ragged.

"Get hold of yourself! You're coked up, I can tell. You disappoint me very badly, Janet. You forget, it was my money that made your business. Without me, you'd have been found dead from an overdose in an alley a long time ago."

Well, that snapped her out of her panic. Janet's eyes widened. Xavier had never talked to her like this. Anxiety replaced fear for Katie's life. "Listen, I'm just upset. I love you, Xavier. You know I do. I'd never do anything to make you angry at me."

"I'm upset with you because you won't do as I say. I've never put you in harm's way, have I?"

"No," Janet muttered, all the anger dissolving in her voice, "you never have."

"And I won't now. Put Eduardo on the phone. I need to talk with him. In the meantime, your daughter drives once a week."

CHAPTER TWENTY

"BE CAREFUL," JOE SAID, holding Katie and kissing her brow. "I worry about you out there on the road." God, how badly he wanted to tell her everything. Hager's warning haunted him. He felt her arms go around him, squeezing him hard for a moment.

"I'll be fine, Joe. Stop looking so worried." Katie patted her new uniform. She'd been stunned when her mother had called her to the office a day before she was to drive the van to Idaho Falls. Janet had presented her with a gift. The box was wrapped in pink paper and tied with a bright red ribbon. She almost cried as her mother gave it to her. *A gift.*

When Katie opened it on the desk, she saw it was a light blue short-sleeved shirt with *Mercury Courier* embroidered on the left side above the pocket. Her name, *Katie Bergstrom,* was also in red thread above the right pocket. A set of dark blue slacks went with the official uniform. Janet had urged her to try them on. When she came out of the bathroom to show her mother, Katie felt loved. Janet had been attentive and touched the shirt here and there to ensure it was a good fit.

The afternoon surprise lay warm in her heart as she smiled up at Joe.

"Look, can you call me on your cell once you reach Idaho Falls? And let me know when you're turning around to come back." It was all he could do. Joe couldn't tail her. And he had found out from Hagar that the three magnetic GPS units he'd placed under the vans were not working. Hagar said they'd been removed and were in the Mercury building. *Damn.* He'd been seen on the videotape. Joe focused on Katie, who also had a dark blue baseball cap on her head with the name of the business in big red letters above the bill. She was so excited; her eyes were sparkling and she was more than ready to be a driver.

Katie patted the cell phone hanging at her belt. "Sure, I can call you."

He leaned over and swiftly kissed her smiling mouth. "Be safe out there," he growled, looking deep into her startled blue eyes.

"I will, Joe. It's just an easy three-hour drive one way." She lifted her hand and gestured to the sky. "Look, at 9:00 a.m., it's a clear blue sky. There's no weather today. Just sunshine. I'll be fine." She quickly left the facility and walked to her truck in the parking lot.

Joe unconsciously rubbed his chest as he watched Katie literally skip out the door like a joyful child going to a party. Only, it could end up being anything but. He wanted to stop her and tell her everything. Joe knew if he did, his job would be in jeopardy. At this point, he almost didn't care. He'd decided the FBI wasn't for him. And after this mission was over, he was going to quit. Never again did he want to lie as he had to Katie. She deserved far better from him.

Joe turned and forced himself to clean the mews. If only he could be a fly on the wall and ride with Katie. What had Janet have her men put in the back of the van? His gut screamed at him it was either drugs or guns. And what about the other cartel? Would Garcia be watching Janet's business? Tailing each van to see where the guns and drugs were being dropped off in the different cities of the region? He knew Idaho Falls was a major center where drugs were distributed to the northern states and Canada. It was becoming a central hub in its own right, according to the FBI and ATF. And Katie was driving right into it....

JANET SMOKED HER cigarette as she walked Katie through her shipping instructions. "Now, listen, you are to drive to this address." She handed her a piece of paper. "Eduardo has already dialed the coordinates into your van's GPS unit. You just listen to the voice directing you and you'll end up at the right place."

Katie saw a lot of packages, many of them huge, long wooden boxes, all stacked neatly around the shipping dock. "Yes, I can do it." She smiled and tucked the paper into her left breast pocket. "I feel so official." She laughed and looked over at her mother.

Janet blew out a plume of smoke. "Listen, you be careful. This is a test run for you, Katie. I'm not sure I want you driving. So don't get giddy on me, okay?" In her heart, Janet wanted to kill Xavier. She knew Garcia was snooping around. Eduardo thought he had spotted one of his soldiers. The man had been in a black hoodie, standing in the alley next to where the vans were parked. He took off as soon as Eduardo walked out onto the dock and spotted him. Had Garcia's people put those magnetic GPS devices under their vans? Janet thought so. Then they could follow Katie's van and where there was little traffic and even fewer witnesses, they'd attack. Her stomach turned. She looked over at Katie, who was literally bouncing with joy over the driving task.

Janet gripped her shoulder. It was the first time she

had honestly touched her daughter. Oh, she'd fussed over how the uniform fitted her, but now her fingers sank into Katie's shoulder. "Listen," she said in a husky tone, "you have to be alert, Katie."

Turning, Katie felt her mother's hand tighten on her shoulder. Almost painfully. Her long, red nails reminded Katie of Sam's long, curved claws. Looking at her mother, the thick pancake makeup emphasizing the lines in her face, she forced a smile. "Really, I'll do everything by the book." She pressed her hand to her heart. "Promise!"

Janet released her and scowled. They stood on the dock and she threw the butt down on it and crushed it with the pointed toe of her red shoe. She wore a bright red blouse, a navy blue skirt and the scarlet stilettos. "You stay in touch with me by cell, okay? Call me once you get to Idaho Falls."

"Oh…all right. Is this normal?"

"No, it isn't," Janet snapped, irritated. "But it's for your own good, Katie. I worry about you. Okay?"

A warm frisson of joy filtered unexpectedly through Katie. Her mother's snarly admission showed how much she honestly cared for her. In that moment, Katie stepped forward and threw her arms around Janet. She quickly hugged her and released her. Breathless, she said in a tearful voice, "Thank you…it's nice to be worried over. I promise, I'll be careful. You can trust me."

Shaken, Janet took a step back and scowled at her daughter. She saw tears in Katie's wide blue eyes. Her shoulders tingled where her daughter had spontaneously hugged her. Before, Janet had wanted nothing to do with her daughter except to keep her at arm's length. With the threat of Garcia now real, she found herself wanting to protect Katie, keep her close and safe. She wondered if her maternal hormones were kicking in. Studying Katie's fresh, exuberant face, Janet realized her daughter was beautiful in ways she would never be. She had birthed this beautiful child-woman. She bemoaned the fact Katie was starry-eyed, too trusting and thought the world was a good place. It wasn't. Just the opposite. More than anything, Janet didn't want Katie hurt in any way. She knew she'd be safe here working at the desk. Out on the road…well, that was an entirely different deal.

"Stop being so sloppy and sentimental, will you?" Janet gestured sharply to the van Eduardo had just pulled up. He'd loaded it with ten cases of rifles bound for Xavier's contact in Idaho Falls. Katie had no idea what she was carrying. She had strict orders never to look at the boxes or packages. Just to hand the manifest to the man who asked for the papers. The boxes would be offloaded, the man would sign for them and hand it back to Katie, who would remain in the driver's seat.

Laughing softly, Katie pushed back the tears she felt. "I can't help myself, Mo…I mean, Janet." She gracefully arced a hand across her neatly pressed uniform. "I'm overjoyed to be working with you."

Janet winced inwardly when the word *Mom* almost came out of Katie's mouth. Her daughter had barely caught the mistake. Still, the word did something funny to her. She *was* a mother. Janet continued to scowl as her daughter skipped down the wooden steps, took the keys from Eduardo and climbed into the van. Rubbing her jaw, Janet lifted her hand in farewell as Katie slowly drove the van out of the parking area. She felt a thread of happiness winding around her heart. *Mom.* Well, maybe she should let Katie call her that? It sounded pretty nice coming from her and it lifted Janet unaccountably as she walked through the building toward the front desk.

KATIE WAS WATCHING her speed as she drove into the mountains on the highway leading to Idaho Falls. She'd just crossed into the state of Idaho after driving over the pass, leaving Wyoming behind. The van felt very heavy and she wished she had cruise control. The clipboard lay on the passenger seat. Wearing a set of dark glasses to ward off the bright sun over the mountains, Katie hummed to herself. She wished she had her iPod and could play her music, but Janet had forbidden anything other than paying attention to her driving. The road was two-lane, twisting and turning through the ups and downs of the green-cloaked mountains.

She noticed at ten-thirty that there was little traffic on the asphalt road. The berms were wide and tall metal poles were spaced about every quarter of a mile. Snowplows used these guides to stay on snow-filled highways and safely plow through the white stuff so vehicles could get through. It was as if she were alone and Katie enjoyed the feeling. She could still hear her mother intoning, "You drive with *both* hands on that wheel all the time, Katie. Don't screw around and think you can drive with one hand."

Smiling softly, she felt her heart expand with joy. Janet was slowly changing for the better. Why, she could even see some worry in her mother's eyes this morning before she left. Her mind wandered to Joe. Katie knew he was falling in love with her. That was the source of his worry. Her mother, however, must be rediscovering her love for her. Was that possible? Oh, how Katie wanted it to be true! If one person worries about another, doesn't that mean they care? Katie could swear she'd seen care, anxiety *and* worry all at once in her mother's heavily made-up face. Surely, she loved her just a teeny bit.

As Katie was driving the van down a long, curved part of the highway, she saw a big, black SUV with heavy chrome and darkly tinted windows on the right side of the road, parked by a marked hiking trail. She noticed several other parked cars there as well, but the big SUV looked absolutely aggressive. Must be her wild Pisces imagination that they could be waiting for her. Katie shook her head, driving the van at sixty-five miles an hour.

To her surprise, the SUV spun and skidded, clouds of yellow dust shooting into the air as it leaped onto the highway behind her. She looked into her rearview mirror, thinking it was a crazy teenage driver. The black SUV raced up toward her at frightening speed. Automatically, Katie's fingers gripped the steering wheel a little tighter. They were on a long, slow downward curve. She saw no oncoming traffic for a mile. There was a double yellow line in the center of the highway, a warning not to pass.

Yet, glancing nervously into the mirror again, she saw the SUV charging down at her like a runaway steam engine. Katie automatically began to slow, taking her foot off the accelerator. The guy who was driving was erratic and dangerous. Slowing the truck, Katie moved it to the right edge of the highway, near the berm. Was this dude drunk? The SUV swerved after coming within inches of the van's bumper.

The SUV leaped into the other lane and roared up beside her. She grabbed at the wheel as the vehicle slammed into the side of the van. The crash and crunch

of metal, of glass breaking, roared through Katie. She
cried out as she felt the van tip.

Katie screamed as the van took flight. Everything
slowed. She heard the squeal of tires, smelled burning
rubber, heard the van's engine suddenly racing. Her
driver's-side window had shattered inward, the glass
spraying around her in shards, like sparkling diamonds.

Katie shut her eyes, gripping the wheel as the van
sailed drunkenly through the air, trying to prepare herself for the crash. Her neck snapped back and forth. The
safety belt cut deeply into her chest and shoulder. The
vehicle struck the berm. Loud scraping sounds echoed
through the van, the gravel tearing at the metal. The
screeching sounds hurt Katie's ears, just as she felt the
deployment of several airbags all at once. One airbag
struck her in the face as the van slammed onto its side.
Katie felt the van sliding down the berm and heading
into a deep ditch. She saw a thick pine-tree trunk that
had fallen from the hill above right in the path of her
careening van. She had no time to think, only to react.
Her brakes were useless. The smell of metal burning
against the rocks filled the vehicle.

The skidding van struck the thick trunk of the pine
tree with a powerful thud. The hood crumpled and
groaned. Steam shot skyward from the broken radiator. Wheels on the driver's side spun and screamed
as they whirled around. Katie lay semiconscious, the
white airbags covering most of her. Hearing voices, yell-
ing orders in Spanish, she tried to lift her head. Blood
dripped down into her left eye. Weakly, she tried to
raise her hand, but she couldn't. Pain began to drift
up her legs. *Trapped.* She was trapped! The rear doors
were jerked open. The whole vehicle shuddered as suddenly there was movement and scraping. Katie fought to

become conscious. Blood was now running freely out of her nose. She felt faint. The voices came and went. The scraping sounds of the wooden boxes being moved began. The van jostled and moved violently.

The squeal of tires, the roar of a car engine filled the van. And then, silence.

Katie heard the steam hissing loudly from the radiator. Why had she been attacked like this? Fumbling, her consciousness slowly returning, she realized she was in shock. Her thoughts were disjointed. She felt the warmth of the blood from above her eye and made several attempts to lift her left hand. It had been pinned between her and the caved-in door of the van. Help. She had to get help.

For the next five minutes, Katie moved in and out of consciousness. She finally got her left hand free. She tried to locate her seat belt. Her fingers shook badly as she found the latch. The safety belt released—she was suddenly dropped to the right. Falling into a heap against the passenger door, Katie struggled and kicked at the airbags hampering her efforts to sit up. The windshield was heavily cracked. Katie slowly pushed shards of glass out of her tangled hair.

Help. She had to get help. Few people used this road during the weekdays. Usually, on weekends there was plenty of traffic on it, people from Jackson Hole going to Idaho Falls to do serious shopping. She tasted blood in the left corner of her mouth. Her head began to ache. Lifting her fingers, Katie touched her brow. She felt the cut above her eyebrow. It was as if her brain was disconnected from her body. Fumbling around, she managed to push with her boots and force her whole body into a sitting position, back resting against the passenger door.

Kate was breathing raggedly, then realized she had a

cell phone on the left side of her belt. She only needed to make one phone call. She could do that. Feeling drugged, she moved with excruciating slowness because her body refused to work fully with her. It took Katie another five minutes to retrieve the phone from its case. When she tried to focus on the small screen, dizziness struck her. She felt nauseous as she turned on the iPhone. It took precious minutes for her to remember what to do next. A security box with numbers came up and she just stared at it, uncomprehending. Then Katie recalled her four-digit password and slowly pushed each box with her bloodied index finger. The phone came on. She saw the green phone icon and pressed it. Katie called Joe.

JOE WAS FINISHING SWEEPING the aisle when his cell rang. He put the broom aside and answered it. "Hello?"

"Joe?"

Scowling, Joe heard Katie's voice. She sounded drugged. "Katie? Katie, what's wrong? You don't sound well."

"I—um…I got run off the road by an SUV. I crashed, Joe. The van flipped and I'm on the side of the highway…."

His heart rate tripled. "What?" The word exploded out of him. "Are you okay?"

"Y-yes, I think I am. Just some cuts and bruises. Joe, I need help…I know you have an iPhone. You can find me on the GPS locater. Can you send help?"

Terror sizzled through Joe. "Yes, hold on, I'll locate you right now." He thanked God his iPhone was hooked to Katie's, and that he had the app that would show a caller's position. Instantly, it popped up on his screen. Memorizing it, he switched to Katie. "I got your position, Katie. Just hang on. I'm going to call the nearest fire department and police department. And I'm coming to get you right now."

"Joe, I'm okay…can you…can you call my mom? I—I'm really dizzy. I can't think…straight. Whoever did this took everything out of the back of my van. I heard Spanish. They deliberately ran me off the road. She has to know…please, Joe?"

Anger wove through him. Joe knew what had really happened. The thing he feared the most had happened. "Yeah," he rasped, "I'll call her. Help's on the way, Katie. Is the SUV still there?"

"N-no, it took off…my mind isn't working well, Joe… I can't keep track of time…."

"It's gone, though? You don't see it around you?" More terror ate at Joe. He knew that when cartels mixed it up, they almost always shot the enemy cartel members.

"Y-yes, gone…"

"And no guns were fired?"

"Guns? Why…no…what an odd question…."

"Is the van on fire, Katie? Do you see any smoke or smell anything burning around you?"

"J-just steam…the van hit a tree in the ditch…there's some steam rising but I think it's a broken radiator, don't you?"

Barely able to stand still, Joe felt his entire world spinning out of control. "Yes, the radiator was probably punctured, Katie. Any other burning smells?"

"N-no. I'm just lying here on my back with my head against the door. If I move, I get horribly dizzy. I feel like I'm going to throw up."

"You probably have a concussion," he rasped, hurrying for the door. "Listen, just lie still, Katie. So long as there is no fire in or around the van, you're safe. Stay there. I'm calling for help now. Keep your phone on. Keep it handy. I'm leaving the ranch right now...."

"Okay...Joe?"

"Yes?" He ran out the door, jogging for his truck in the parking lot.

"My mother... Oh, God, she's going to be so angry with me. I lost the packages in the back. I ruined her van."

He heard the choking sound in her voice. He said, "Katie, she won't be angry. I promise you." He jerked open the door of the truck and fumbled for the key and shoved it into the slot. "She'll understand, Katie. She's not going to drop you or get rid of you because this happened." He heard her moan. His heart twisted violently in his chest as he jammed his foot down on the accelerator and spun out of the parking area. Blue smoke rose from the tires.

The phone went dead. Alarmed, Joe quickly called 911 and gave the information. In no time, he knew, the nearest fire department would be sent out as well as the nearest police cruiser. Redialing Katie's number, he heard only a voice message. Katie wasn't answering her phone. Had she fainted? Was she bleeding out and didn't know it? Joe knew what shock did to a person. She'd be incapable of thinking or acting. She'd be like a helpless puppet and shock could also lower blood pressure so much, a person could die. He knew the symptoms because when the IED had exploded along the dirt road in Afghanistan, he'd been traumatized and in deep shock. He couldn't talk, think straight or even string two coherent words together for hours afterward. He gritted his teeth, driving eighty miles an hour once he turned onto the highway.

LINDSAY McKENNA 307

The last call he made was to Janet. As he sped toward Jackson Hole, he grimly waited for the woman to answer.

"Mercury Courier, Janet speaking."

"Janet, you don't know me but my name is Joe Gannon. I work for Katie at the raptor facility. I just got a phone call from her. She's had an accident…" He told her everything.

"Oh, my God!" Janet exploded. "Where is she? Where's Katie? Is she all right?"

Joe was surprised at the raw emotion suddenly appearing in Janet's voice. Had things changed? Slowing down as he entered Jackson Hole, Joe said, "I'm sure if Katie is in serious condition, Janet, they'll airlift her here to the Jackson Hole hospital." He kept the anger out of his tone because he knew just as well as Janet did that Katie had been attacked by Garcia's cartel.

"B-but will I know? How will I know?" Janet sobbed. "God! I just found her. I can't lose her!"

Joe said, "Stay where you are, Janet. I'll be in touch. I'll call you back as soon as I know about her condition."

"You promise?"

Mouth tightening, Joe rasped, "Yes, I promise."

After punching in the sheriff's phone number, Joe asked for Deputy Cade Garner and got him. He explained everything to him.

"It's the Garcia cartel," Cade agreed, his tone grim.

"You bet it is. I have to call my boss in Washington, D.C., right now. You'll send a cruiser out to the accident?"

"Yes, it'll be me. She's in Idaho and their county sheriff's department will have responsibility for the investigation. But I want to get there in a helluva hurry."

"Then let me follow you," Joe demanded.

Cade said, "I'm on my way out the door. Park near the pass. We'll hook up there."

"Roger that," Joe said, quickly shutting off the phone. Once he was outside of town, he pulled onto the berm. Dialing Hager at the FBI office, he got his assistant. He explained the situation, but the assistant said Hager was in a meeting and couldn't be disturbed. Joe said fine and shut down his cell phone. Looking in his rearview mirror, he saw a black Tahoe police cruiser, its light bar flashing, coming at high speed toward him. Smiling grimly, Joe was grateful that Cade was the one who would swiftly get them to the accident site.

Joe's heart wrung, as if a fist were curled around it, tightening it and sending pain radiating throughout his chest. He blamed himself. He'd known in his gut Katie would be attacked. Why, oh, why did he let her go alone? Frustration funneled through him. As Cade's cruiser shot by, the siren wailing, Joe stomped on the accelerator. The truck leaped onto the highway in hot pursuit of the deputy's vehicle.

Hurry! Oh, God. Hurry! Let Katie be all right. Please...I'll do anything if she's alive and all right....

CHAPTER TWENTY-ONE

KATIE WAS LYING ON A GURNEY, on her way to the ambulance when she saw Joe and Deputy Cade Garner arrive. She could see the terror in Joe's eyes as he ran to her side. She extended her hand to him.

"I'm okay, Joe," she said, gripping his outstretched fingers. She drowned in his eyes, so filled with urgency. He loved her. She could feel it.

Leaning down, Joe looked closely at her. "Katie, are you sure?" There was blood on her face, neck and blouse, an open cut above her eyebrow. His heart pumped violently in his chest. He couldn't lose Katie! She managed a smile meant to convince him she was all right.

"I'll live, Joe." She looked over at the paramedic standing at her side. "Just bumps and bruises. Nothing is broken."

Relief roared through him. "Katie, I love you." He clamped down on the rest of what he was going to say. Katie's hair was disheveled, dried blood on the ebony strands. It was frightening. Joe knew from war experience that smeared blood could make a person look as if they were dying when they were not. Cade went to the other side of the gurney.

"Katie, how are you doing?" he asked.

"The paramedics said I'm okay."

"Good," he said, his gaze moving to the van lying on its side.

The paramedic scowled at them. "She'll be fine, gentlemen. Now, if you'll let us get Katie up in the ambulance, we need to transport her to Jackson Hole to be examined."

Both men stepped aside to allow the paramedics to do their job.

Joe kept his gaze on Katie as she was lifted into the ambulance, covered with several blankets. Shock always made a person cold. He lifted his hand and called, "I'll see you later at the hospital, Katie."

"Can you call my mom? Let her know what happened? My cell phone died."

Joe nodded. "I'll call her right now." The relief on her face was evident.

Cade gripped Joe's upper arm and guided him to the overturned van. "Call her. I'm going to talk to the two deputies doing the legwork on this scene."

"Right," Joe muttered. He turned and walked to the side of the road far enough away so no one would hear his conversation. When he called Mercury Courier, no one answered. He left a message for Janet to call him and shoved the cell phone into his pocket. For a moment, he watched the red-and-white boxlike ambulance turn around and head toward Jackson Hole. His heart was torn. The last thing he wanted to do was stay here and investigate. He studied the van. Steam was still rising from beneath the crumpled hood. As he looked more closely, he saw that the back doors had been pulled open. Cade Garner was taking photos.

"What do you think?" Joe asked, joining Cade

"I think there were guns in the back of this van," Cade said in a low tone so only Joe could hear. "And I think Garcia's men rammed the truck, drove it off the road." He pointed to the skid marks on the highway. "And once it crashed, grabbed the boxes of guns and took off."

A ragged sigh escaped Joe's lips. "Don't warring cartels usually shoot the driver?"

Cade frowned. "Yes, they do. Katie got lucky."

"They play rough," Joe said.

"Is this your first drug mission?"

"Yes." And it was going to be his last. "What does this mean?" he demanded, gesturing to the van.

Cade pulled out his notebook from his shirt pocket. "It's the first shot fired in a cartel war. Garcia's cartel knows Los Lobos is in town." He pointed to the van. "They didn't shoot Katie because this was a warning. If Los Lobos doesn't get out of town, the next time there's going to be bloodshed."

"Damn…" Joe's mind whirled with options. "Do we know for sure it's Garcia's men?"

"No," Cade said, "but we know they're in town. And in their minds, they were here first."

"What about Katie? Will Garcia try to kill her? She's a witness."

"I don't know. Let's hope Katie can give us some details. I'm sure this happened so fast, so unexpectedly, she won't remember much. These cartels strike hard and fast."

Joe cursed and walked down the berm, away from the activity. What were his options? He jerked his phone from his pocket and dialed Hager in Washington, D.C. This time, he got him. Joe rapidly explained the situation.

"I'm glad you're working with the sheriff's department," Hager said after hearing the information. "And Katie, we hope, will give us an eyewitness account."

Frustration funneled up through Joe. He paced, unable to stand still. "Look, this has put Katie in jeopardy. I want to tell her what's going on and get her into protective custody."

"You can't do it. Not yet, Joe."

Rage flared through him, his eyes burned with anger as he halted on the graveled berm. "Like hell I won't. You're not leaving her as a target a second time."

"Listen to me," Hager said, "you're new at this, Joe. This is your first undercover mission. Katie is our only connection to Bergstrom and Los Lobos. We can't just make her disappear. If we did, Los Lobos would know something is up. And then, we'd get nothing on them. She has to stay and play."

"Not a chance," Joe ground out, his lips lifting away from his teeth. Joe knew he was putting his career on the line. He didn't care. His breath harsh, he added, "You are not going to put her in danger again."

Hager was silent for a long time.

Joe felt his world tilting but he knew he had to protect Katie at all costs. He'd find another job.

"Okay, okay, settle down," Hager snarled. "We can do this. It's obvious from everything you've reported that Katie doesn't know her mother is aligned with Los Lobos. You can tell her everything, Joe. The deal is she has to go back into that office and get the computer information off the company machine. We can't crack the codes. We have to get a thumb drive to copy the entire software and then, we can go to work."

Joe began to pace again. "Tell Katie the truth, right?"

"Yes."

"She's going to be pissed off, Roger. She's trying to

make an emotional connection with her mother When I tell her this…that her mother's a drug runner…" He felt the world begin to collapse and didn't say the rest. When Katie found out he'd lied to her, used her, what would she do? What would she think of him? His heart ached with real fear. Katie had every right to tell him to take a walk. She could sever the powerful ties built between them, once and for all. *Oh, God, what a mess.* Joe had to do the right thing. Katie had to know the truth. What would she do?

"Look," Hager warned, "you have to get Katie to agree to go back to the office. She's got to get the info. Without it, we're blind."

Joe knew he was right. Fear for Katie's life rose, even with the real possibility she was going to tell him to leave. "Okay, okay. Let me time this. She's on her way to the hospital to get examined. I'll explain everything to her after the doctor releases her."

"She's going to take it hard," Hager warned. "You have to persuade her to squeal on her mother."

"Yeah, I know that." Closing his eyes, Joe felt as though he was sinking into quicksand, his life with Katie dissolving. "Okay, I'll get back to you. I have a lot of work ahead of me."

"Good luck," Hager said, "because you're going to need it."

"KATIE! OH, MY GOD! Are you all right?" Janet Bergstrom flew through the partly opened curtains in the cubicle at the Jackson Hole hospital emergency room.

Dr. Jordana McPherson turned, surprised. She had just finished stitching the cut above Katie's head.

Katie was sitting on the side of the gurney when Janet

burst through the green curtains. "Mom!" she cried, opening her arms.

Janet rushed to the gurney, hauling her daughter against her. "Oh, my God! You're safe!" She sobbed, holding her daughter hard against her. She kissed Katie's dirty, smoke-filled hair. The metallic scent of dried blood cloyed her nostrils. Gripping her daughter's shoulders, Janet wildly searched her blue eyes. "Are you all right?"

"Y-yes, I'm fine." Katie felt hot tears welling in her eyes. Jordana moved aside. "It was just an accident...."

Tears leaked into Janet's eyes as she studied her wan-looking daughter. It was no accident. There was a doctor standing nearby and she knew better than to say anything. "No broken bones? No surgery? You're really okay?" She intently studied her daughter. Her uniform, once so nicely pressed and clean, had spots of blood across the front of it. Katie's blood.

The terror made Janet choke. She knew this was the work of the Garcia cartel. And she knew they usually killed the driver as an added warning to get out of town—or else. Tears coursed down her drawn cheeks, making two trails through her thick makeup. She hugged Katie hard. Her daughter felt so thin and fragile to her as she released her. Janet peered at the doctor.

"Is she okay, Doctor?" Janet fumbled and found Katie's hand, gripped it and held it hard.

Jordana nodded. "Luckily, she suffered only scratches and bruises. I just stitched the cut over your daughter's eye, Ms. Bergstrom. Right now, Katie is in shock. And she'll probably need a day or two to come out of it. Otherwise, she's fine."

Katie's world was spinning out of control. Her mother was here, had come to see how she was. Janet had hugged her. Calling her "Mom" didn't seem to adversely impact her mother. Her concern made Katie feel much better. If the accident had driven them closer, Katie was glad it had happened. The look in her mother's eyes was one of tenderness. Janet loved her. A warmth spread throughout her and, self-consciously, Katie wiped the tears out of her eyes. "I think if I can just go home and rest, I'll be okay," she told Jordana.

"Yep, take the day off. You'll find yourself a lot more tired than usual. Shock does that to us. By tomorrow morning, you should be feeling almost normal." Jordana pointed to the bruises on Katie's right arm. "You're going to look pretty colorful with those bruises for a week or two, but they'll fade with time. Do you need anything to sleep? I can write you a prescription."

Shaking her head, Katie gazed over at Janet who stood close to her. "No, I'm fine. I *am* tired. I feel like I could sleep for a week."

"You've probably got a bit of concussion, but nothing showed up on X-ray," Jordana said. "I think taking it easy for the next week is in order. Joe is helping you out at the facility, right?"

"Yes, he is. I know he'll pitch in. I need to get hold of him...."

"Our radio traffic picked him up. He's at the accident scene along with Deputy Cade Garner." Looking at her watch, Jordana added, "I heard they were coming our way shortly. I'm sure Joe will be coming to see you here at the hospital before I can discharge you."

Love moved through Katie's heart and she whispered, "I'd like to see him." The world had suddenly opened up and given her the greatest gift. Katie felt emotionally overwhelmed. She desperately needed Joe.

The realization that she could have died in the accident made her anxious to be with him.

"I'll tell my staff to send him directly to your cubicle. Just stay put for about twenty minutes. Your blood pressure is a little low. I'll release you when it comes back to normal."

Katie watched Jordana disappear, then turned to her mother. "Thanks for coming over. I— It means a lot, Mo— I mean, Janet."

Squeezing her hand, Janet said in an emotional tone, "It's okay to call me Mom. I don't mind." She searched Katie's bloodied face. "I want you well. I'm sorry this happened."

Katie felt more tears rush into her eyes. She wiped them away, hanging on to her mother's ring-laden hand. "I'm so sorry, Mom. It all happened so fast. The van is a total loss. I didn't mean for this happen."

"Shush! It's not your fault." Janet felt rage mingling with her fear for Katie. "Vans can be replaced. You can't." She managed a tender smile. "No insurance company can replace you, Katie. You just remember that, okay? The van was covered and so were the contents." Her mind turned violently with scary options, but Katie couldn't know it. "Listen, I gotta get back to the office. Can Joe take you home? I've got to call the insurance company."

"Oh, absolutely," Katie said. Janet wasn't going to blame her for the accident. Relief shimmered through her. "I can still work for you, right?"

"I don't know," Janet said. Seeing the stricken look come to her daughter's face, she quickly added, "Oh, of course you can. You can handle the front desk. But no more driving for you." She waggled her finger in her daughter's face. "I know this accident wasn't your fault, but dammit, I want you safe."

Katie gulped. "For a moment, I thought you were going to get rid of me. I really want to work for you, Mom. I do...."

"You will," Janet promised. She quickly hugged and released Katie. "We'll talk later."

Katie watched as her mother bustled out of the cubicle. Her head was beginning to ache in earnest. A nurse came in and she told her about the pain.

"I'll tell Dr. McPherson," the nurse said, taking her blood pressure and marking down the results on a clipboard. She put it aside and brought over a bowl with water and handed her a washcloth. "I thought you might want to clean up a bit."

Grateful, Katie took the cloth. "Yes, I feel grungy."

The nurse smiled. "I'll be back," she promised.

The water was warm and Katie sat on the gurney wiping off the blood from her face and neck. The water quickly turned pink. Wrinkling her nose, she slid off the gurney. Her knees felt mushy. Standing for a moment, she remembered Jordana warned her she might feel wobbly for a bit. Holding on to the gurney with one hand, she transferred the metal bowl and cloth to the nearby cart.

"Katie!"

Gasping, she looked up. Joe walked quickly through the half-opened curtains, his face etched with fear.

"Joe!" Katie fell into his opened arms. He swept her against him. Within seconds their mouths met and clung hungrily to one another. Joe's moist breath flowed against her cheek. She wanted to drown in his mouth, his kiss.

Far too soon Joe relaxed his grip and reluctantly

eased his mouth from hers. "How are you? I've never been so worried."

She swayed a little and Joe cupped her shoulders. The power of their kiss dizzied her senses. "I—I'm fine, Joe. Can you help me sit on the gurney? My knees are feeling a little wobbly."

Joe guided Katie, placed his hands around her waist and gently lifted her onto the gurney. Her eyes were dark and it pained him to see the stitches above her eye. There was blood splattered all over the front of her blue shirt. "Are you sure you're okay?"

Laughing a little, feeling suddenly silly and euphoric, Katie brushed the shirt with her fingertips. "Don't I look awful? I can hardly wait to get out of these clothes." She held his burning gaze tinged with anxiety. Joe loved her. He seemed to hold back a barrage of emotions.

"You're alive," he growled. Joe couldn't keep his hands off her. He touched her mussed hair and saw dried blood. He trailed his fingers across her cheek and jaw. There was serious bruising on her right arm. "Are you in pain?"

Holding his hand, she closed her eyes for a moment. The headache was intensifying. "I have to lie down, Joe. The bruises are nothing, but my head is killing me."

Alarm swept through Joe. He helped maneuver Katie to the gurney and made sure the pillow was positioned beneath her head. "I'm going to get the doctor," he rasped. "Who took care of you?"

"Jordana McPherson. She said my head would start to hurt. It's nothing, Joe."

"I'll be back." He left the cubicle to hunt down the doctor. He had personal experience with head injuries and he was leaving nothing to chance. At the nurses' desk, he asked for Dr. McPherson. She was at the other end of the emergency room just coming out of another cubicle. Joe strode down the highly polished green floor to meet her.

Katie was almost asleep when she heard Joe's voice. Opening her eyes, she smiled up at Jordana who came to her side. Joe walked to the other side, his hand coming to rest on her shoulder. "You were right," she told the doctor, "my head feels like it's splitting in two."

Jordana nodded and took a small flashlight and passed it across Katie's eyes. "Yep, and it's going to hurt for a while. Your pupils are responsive, so this is just a headache, nothing more serious." Placing the light in the pocket of her white lab coat, the doctor looked at Joe. "Not to worry, she'll have a headache for a day or two, is all."

Relief sped through him. "Okay, good to know." He gently ran his fingers across Katie's shoulder. "Can I take her home? Or should she be with someone who can watch her for the next twenty-four hours? I have a house on my parents' property. I could watch over her. Having had traumatic head injury myself, I know the signs and I know what to look for."

"Katie? Would you mind having Joe as a babysitter? The X-rays didn't show a concussion, but sometimes a person's brain gets so rattled in the skull it's a good idea to have another set of eyes around just to watch out for you."

"Sure, no problem. Right now, all I want is some aspirin."

Jordana nodded and patted her hand. "We'll get you some." She turned and glanced at the clipboard. "Looks like your blood pressure is normal, too. I'm going to discharge you and Joe can pick up the prescription and take you to his home."

Katie gazed up into Joe's drawn features. She saw how scared he was for her. "Great, thanks, Dr. McPherson."

Jordana left and silence settled in the cubicle. "I'll be okay, Joe. I promise."

"Are you feeling tired? Sleepy?"

"Oh, I feel like a doll whose stuffing got knocked out of her. All I want to do is go home and rest," she said, giving him a wry look.

Joe leaned down and lightly caressed her lips. "There's a second bedroom at the house. Let's get you home and get a hot bath ready for you."

Katie cherished his swift kiss, her lips tingling in the wake of the unexpected caress. "That sounds great. I feel pretty grimy."

"It's only fifteen minutes to home." He studied her shadowed eyes. "I'll take good care of you, Katie. I promise."

Joe's deep voice reverberated through her like healing balm. "I know you will, Joe. You've always been there for me."

Wincing inwardly, Joe knew what was coming. Would this be the last kiss, the last warmth, they shared? Fear gutted him like a sharp knife; his stomach curled with anxiety. The last thing he wanted was to lose Katie. He could lose his job and everything else...but not her. *God, please help me find the right words. Let her realize I love her even though I've lied to her from the start...please...*

CHAPTER TWENTY-TWO

KATIE EMERGED FROM Joe's home office. She'd slept a good part of the day after he'd made her lunch. After waking up just before dinner, they'd shared a meal. She'd wanted to connect with friends to let them know what had happened. Word got around fast in Jackson Hole and she didn't want them to worry. "I think I've called everyone and told them I'm all right," Katie told him. She stood in the doorway of the living room, wrapped in his blue robe after taking a second hot bath. He was sitting on the couch reading a book.

"I'm sure you're tired of talking." Joe closed the book and set it aside.

She hitched one shoulder, arms wrapped around herself. Joe's blue bathrobe was long and hung to her ankles. "Sort of. At least I can think now. After the accident, I couldn't put two coherent words together. I slept most of the day, and now I'm tired and want to go to bed."

Joe walked over and placed his hands on her shoulders. "I understand," he murmured, looking into her weary blue eyes. The bath had flushed her cheeks but her flesh was still pale. He touched her cheek. "Come on, back to bed. What you need is a good night's sleep and you'll feel a lot better in the morning." He didn't add that tomorrow he would tell her the truth.

"Joe...I don't want to sleep alone tonight." Katie

searched his shadowed expression. "I want to sleep with you." Her voice raspy, she added, "If you could just hold me?" Her heart swelled with love for him as she saw tenderness cross his expression. Joe's fingers grazed her shoulders, as if to soothe her.

"Anything you want, Katie. Anything..." Joe slipped his arm around her. He led her down the hall to the master bedroom. After he turned on a stained-glass lamp sitting on the dresser, there was enough light in the room for them to see. This was possibly the last night he'd ever be with Katie. It wasn't about making love with her tonight. Rather, she needed to feel safe. He wanted to give her that—and so much more. Would she be able to separate his job from his love for her? Fear jagged through him as he led her to the king-size bed, the covers already thrown back.

"I'll be in later," he told her, kissing her brow. She had used his shampoo earlier and now her hair smelled sweet and clean.

"Thanks, Joe. Good night..." Katie said and watched him quietly close the door behind him. Joe had given her a pair of his dark blue cotton pajamas. The top hung on her. She slipped out of the oversize bathrobe and laid it on the end of the bed. Tiredness swept through Katie as she climbed onto the inviting mattress.

Joe had driven over to the facility and closed it earlier this evening. The raptors would be fine. She knew he would go over in the morning to feed them while she rested. As her head nestled into the goose-down pillow, the warmth of the covers quickly lulled her into a deep, healing sleep. Her last thoughts were of Joe joining her. He would keep her safe in a world gone crazy.

THE CROW OF A ROOSTER somewhere outside the bedroom slowly drew Katie out of her healing slumber. Her head was nestled in the crook of Joe's shoulder. She felt the heaviness of his arm around her. The sun was barely tipping the horizon, a soft, muted glow around the thick curtains drawn across the window. Snuggling deeper against Joe's warm, strong body, Katie felt him awaken. His arm tightened momentarily around her shoulders. Katie absorbed the stolen moment. No man had ever made her feel like this. His hand moved slowly down her left arm, exploring her. Heart exploding with joy, Katie moved her hand across his naked chest.

The rooster crowed again.

Joe lifted his head, sleep torn from him. "Damn rooster," he muttered.

Laughing softly, Katie whispered, "He's one heck of an alarm clock. Iris has a rooster that deliberately sits outside the window of her bedroom. He wakes her up every morning." Tangling her fingers through the dark hair across his chest, Katie luxuriated in the moment. The room took on a golden hue as the first rays of the sun spread across the valley and silently flowed against the house. Pressing a kiss to his shoulder, she felt the strength of his muscles beneath his flesh. Joe was in shape, but then, he'd been an officer in the Marine Corps.

He wiped the sleep from his eyes and groused, "I'm not so happy about it. My parents warned me about that rooster. Ever since I moved back home, he's decided it's his job to wake me up."

Chuckling, Katie stretched beside Joe. "Iris loves her winged alarm." Her curves fit his angled ones and she luxuriated in the sensations of her hips meeting his, a heavy warmth stirring to life within her lower body.

Joe managed a partial laugh. He tightened his arm around Katie, wanting to keep her close. "I don't."

"Obviously."

Joe looked into Katie's drowsy eyes. "How are you feeling this morning?" he asked, his voice thick. Lifting his hand, he gently pushed dark strands away from her features. As his gaze dropped to her soft lips, Joe felt his body tighten with need. He understood what an accident could do to a person. The bruises along her right shoulder were a bright purple this morning. When the van had careened and flipped, she'd landed heavily on the right shoulder after she'd managed to release the seat belt.

"Much, much better," Katie replied, smiling at him. His beard had grown, making the curves of his cheeks more hollowed. In her vivid imagination, it gave him the look of a predator, only the good kind. A number of dark strands dipped across his brow. Taming those strands back into place, she said, "I don't feel like a jigsaw puzzle this morning. My right arm and shoulder are sore, but nothing like yesterday." She saw the desire in his eyes. Her heart responded and she felt a scorching heat explode to life. Loving Joe was so easy, so natural. Katie pressed herself against him, her lips resting lightly against his mouth. "Love me, Joe." She slid her fingers into the waistband of his pajamas and pushed the material away from his hips.

Joe groaned as her fingers teased his hip and the inside of his thigh. Her lips captured his and all his anguish and worry dissolved beneath the exploring heat of her eager mouth. Within moments, he had unsnapped the buttons on the oversize shirt she wore and divested her of the trousers. As he pulled Katie gently on top of him, Joe realized this could be the last time he would ever be able to love Katie. The thought staggered him as her soft weight settled upon him. Her mouth moved wetly across his. Joe inhaled her sweet womanly fragrance mingled with the pine scent of the soap she'd used last night. Her fingers caressed his face and tangled in the short strands of his hair. Scalp tingling wildly in the wake of her slow assault upon him, Joe felt her hips moving suggestively against his own.

Her breasts pressed insistently into the curled dark hair across his chest. He felt her nipples pucker and become firm. The sensation sent shock waves of pleasure down through him. Katie smiled and it was a smile of a woman wanting her man. It made him feel powerful and strong as her supple body moved teasingly across his.

For just this moment, Joe wanted to absorb Katie into his pounding heart and hardened body. Never had he loved a woman more than her. She was part fey, part human and her mouth incited his, her tongue dipping like a hummingbird into his mouth. It felt as if she were drinking him into her and the sensation ripened his screaming senses. There was something about Katie, something he couldn't put his finger on. She was part raptor with her bold assault upon him. She was part woman, eyes half closed, cajoling him to join her. Surrendering utterly, he inhaled sharply as she lifted her hips and enveloped him, drawing him deep within her tight, wet confines. The vibration reverberated through him like thunder on a hot summer day.

Her kisses became torrid as she moved sinuously, urging him to join the chaotic rhythm of two hungry bodies starving for one another. She was taking him to places he'd never flown before. Joe realized the precious gift Katie was to him. She was like melting gold to be lovingly molded between his hands. Time meshed and spiraled within Joe. He could feel Katie loving him with a depth and appetite he'd never before encountered.

Gripping her flared hips, lips pulling away from his clenched teeth, Joe urged her on. He felt the explosiveness of her body contracting around him like a tightening fist. Katie cried out, arched her back, her head thrown back as the scalding heat surrounded him. In seconds, Joe felt a fiery explosion flow through him. Eyes tightly shut, he was paralyzed with intense pleasure.

The intensity eventually lessened. Joe went slack and relaxed into the bed, Katie's sleek body on top of him. He heard her whisper his name and she collapsed against him, head nestled next to his jaw. Gold light sparkled like fireworks behind his tightly closed eyes as he rode a widening wave of continuing pleasure. Her hair tickled his jaw and cheek. Her scent filled him and made him hungry all over again. Katie's flesh was damp and so was his. Weakly, Joe lifted his hand and traced the length of her spine. His hand came to rest on her hip and he smiled, sated as never before.

The joy and profound love Joe felt for Katie was gnawed at by the knowledge that he had to talk to her after breakfast. Deep in his heart, he knew Katie would never forgive him for what he'd done to her. He understood her strong sense of right and wrong. She'd struggled to define herself after being abandoned, and it had taken internal brute strength to rebuild her life without her parents. Even worse, he was a traitor to her. He'd gotten closer to her than anyone. As he leaned up and kissed the slender length of her neck, he tangled his fingers through her dark hair and murmured, "I love you, Katie. I'll always love you… Remember that." Joe rested his brow against her head. Joe had never felt so happy or so grief-stricken in the same moment.

Lifting her chin, Katie smiled drowsily down into

Joe's green eyes. "I love you, too. Yesterday—" she whispered, lifting her fingers and grazing his stubbled cheek "—all I could think about after the accident was you. All I wanted was you, Joe. I knew if you'd been there, I'd have been safe. I wouldn't feel so scared, so in danger." Leaning over, Katie pressed a soft kiss to his mouth. "Yesterday," she whispered against his lips, "I realized I loved you with everything I had."

The words were like arrows in his heart. His mouth tingled in the wake of her caressing kiss. Katie was inches away. Like a thief, he sponged up the look of love glowing in her eyes. In a few hours, she would never again lie in this bed with him. They would never again be like two eagles free-falling. He wanted to cry. It took everything he had to force his personal feelings aside. Right now, because he loved Katie, he had to do everything in his power not to destroy her.

"THAT WAS A WONDERFUL BREAKFAST," Katie told Joe, reaching out and touching his hand.

"I make a mean Denver omelet." He smiled. They sat at an oak table in the kitchen. Slats of sun stole through the eastern window, filling the room with radiance. Before they had come home yesterday, Katie had retrieved clean clothes from her suite at the Elk Horn Ranch. Joe's fingers tangled with hers. She looked innocent in the pink T-shirt. "Come on, let's have coffee in the living room."

Katie nodded and placed the pale green linen napkin across the empty plate. "Sounds wonderful," and she rose, holding Joe's calloused hand. Earlier, while she had showered, Joe had driven over to the facility. He'd weighed and fed each of the raptors. Upon his return, he'd made her a delicious breakfast.

Joe poured coffee into two orange mugs and carried them into the living room. Katie was sitting on the golden couch, legs crossed. Her hair was drying after the shower, a beautiful frame for her shining blue eyes and soft, smiling lips. Their lovemaking was mirrored in her face. After handing her the mug, Joe walked around the coffee table and sat in a chair opposite Katie. He watched her sip the coffee with relish. She was leaning back in one corner of the couch, looking incredibly happy.

Joe took a deep breath. "Katie, there's something I need to tell you. Your van being attacked yesterday wasn't an accident."

She placed her coffee on the table. "What?"

Joe set his mug aside. He felt as if he were facing a firing squad. He forced out the words. "Katie, I'm not who you think I am. I'm an FBI agent. I was sent undercover to find out if you were hooked up with Janet Bergstrom because she is part of the Los Lobos cartel." He saw his words land on her like artillery shells striking a target. One moment her eyes were soft and happy. The next, filled with shock. The soft pink color in her cheeks dissolved to white. Inwardly, Joe wanted to scream, but he couldn't. He sat tensely as Katie tried to absorb his explanation.

"Wh-what? Wait, you're an FBI agent?" Her heart tumbled. Fear struck at her. "My mother's connected with a cartel? What are you talking about?" Fear jagged through Katie as she watched Joe's face become unreadable.

"There are two drug cartels trying to set up business in this town, a Mexican one and a Guatemalan one. Your mother is part of the Guatemalan cartel. After serving her prison sentence, she lived in Guatemala. When she

returned to the U.S., she set up Mercury Courier Service
in Cheyenne. The FBI has been watching her for some
time and they know, but can't yet prove, that she's working for Los Lobos." It pained him to see the anguish suddenly appear on Katie's face. Opening his hands, Joe
added in a husky voice, "Yesterday wasn't an accident,
Katie. The FBI and the sheriff think it was the Garcia
cartel from Mexico who put out a hit on the van—and
you. It was their way of warning Los Lobos to get out
of town. If they don't, there's going to be a bloodbath."

Stunned, Katie tried to assimilate his explanation.
"My mother is not a criminal." She leaped to her feet.
"She can't be, Joe! She just can't be! You're lying to
me!"

Joe slowly unwound from the chair. Fear in her eyes,
her voice, cut him like a knife. Grief and shock played
out across her expression. "I'm not lying to you, Katie.
I'm telling you this because you can't go back over there
today and work. You have to know the truth. The sheriff thinks there's going to be war between the two cartels. That puts you in danger, Katie. I—I can't allow you
to go back to that office. Not without knowing what's
going down." His chest hurt. He saw the sudden realization in Katie's eyes about his part in all of this.

Katie jabbed her finger at him. "You lied to me!
How—how could you do this to me, Joe? Coming here
to get a job was nothing more than a convenient cover
and you were after my mother the whole time? After
what we went through?"

He couldn't stand the look of devastation on Katie's face. In seconds, he moved around the coffee table,
gripped her shoulders and rasped, "Katie, I'm sorry.
I'm sorry to my soul I had to do this to you. The FBI
thought you were a part of your mother's ring. I knew

you weren't. Later on, I was proved right. But your mother..." and his voice lowered to a growl "...is working with Los Lobos. She is running guns and drugs. We can't prove it yet, but we know it. You wouldn't have been attacked yesterday, Katie, if you weren't driving illegal guns to Idaho Falls. You didn't know it, but your mother did. She sent you out on this mission. Do you understand?"

Jerking out of his grip, Katie moved to the other side of the coffee table, breathing hard. With trembling fingers, she pushed strands of hair away from her face and glared at Joe. "You have to be lying! That was an accident yesterday!"

Joe winced over the cry of desperation in her voice. "Katie, I know this is a lot to throw at you. But I couldn't let you walk out of here today and not realize what was really going on. You're in danger."

A sob worked its way up and out of her. Her heart was broken because she loved Joe. And she loved her mother. Had they both betrayed her? Tears rushed to her eyes. "No. You have to be lying about everything!" she shrieked, running for the door.

Joe captured her.

"Let me go!" Katie lashed out, striking his shoulder with her hand.

Pulling her close, Joe breathed raggedly, "Stop, Katie. Stop! I'm not going to hurt you. Stand still. Please. Don't fight me. God, don't fight me...."

His embrace was a vise around her. Katie struggled fiercely, her arms trapped at her sides. Anger, fear and anxiety flooded her. She couldn't escape. "Damn you! Let me go!"

"No," he rasped, seeing distrust coming to her eyes. "Not until you stop trying to run, Katie. That's what

you've done from the time you were born. You'd run
every time there was something serious you had to
face." His heart was breaking. Tears welled up and ran
down her cheeks. Her mouth, once soft, was now con-
torted with anguish. And he'd caused all of it. Shattered,
Joe pleaded huskily, "Katie, stop fighting. Please come
back and sit down. There's more I have to tell you. I
can't let you run this time…."

Katie knew she couldn't escape. And yet, in some
part of her functioning mind, she knew Joe had not
meant to hurt her. Sagging against him, she began to
cry out of frustration. She heard him groan, felt his
arms loosen around her. She wanted to hate him, but
she desperately needed him as her whole world unrav-
eled in the space of minutes. His arms were firm without being hurtful. But still, as she stood in his embrace,
Katie realized she couldn't trust Joe. Had her mother
really used her, too? It was the last thing she wanted to
think. Why, oh why, hadn't she seen all of this? Once
more, her blind trust had gotten her into trouble. Only
this time, it had turned dangerous.

"All right?" Joe whispered against her hair. "Come
on, Katie. Let's go sit down."

Sniffing, she felt Joe release her. She wiped her wet
face and glared up at him. He looked so sad and apologetic. Her heart lurched. How much she loved him. But
he'd lied to her. "What else do you want to tell me?" she
demanded, her voice thick with tears.

Joe held out his hand toward her. "I'll tell you everything, Katie."

She walked past him, chin up, refusing even to look
at him. Katie sat down, her mouth pursed. She watched
him walk, his shoulders slumped and head bowed.

He sat down in the chair across from her. "What else haven't you told me?"

Joe began in a softened tone, not wanting to hurt Katie any more than he had already. Her hatred of him was clear. His gut hurt so much he wanted to grip his stomach and lean over from the pain. But he couldn't. He told her about the computer terminal, the FBI being unable to hack into the system, no matter how hard they tried. The FBI felt Janet's computer contained two software programs. One was for the IRS and law enforcement, should they confiscate the equipment. The other program was connected directly to Los Lobos in Guatemala. Joe shared how many guns and drugs were being driven to various drop-off points in a five-state area around Wyoming.

As Joe painted the picture, he saw the life drain out of Katie. Desperately, he wanted to protect her from all of this. When he was finished, she seemed even more in shock, her eyes dull-looking, her body language defensive. Joe couldn't blame her. It was a helluva lot to pile on anyone.

Finally, her voice trembling, she asked, "Does the FBI think Janet used me?"

"Yes," Joe admitted, his heart heavy as he saw the words create more anguish in Katie's eyes.

Katie rubbed her face and shook her head. "I—I just can't believe this!" Her mother had come to the hospital, she'd thrown her arms around her, she was concerned for her. That didn't mesh with this new information.

"Katie, you can help the FBI prove, once and for all, whether your mother is involved with Los Lobos. They were wrong about you. They can be wrong about Janet. You could help prove her innocence."

Jerking up her head, she stared at Joe. "How? Tell me and I'll do it. I know she's innocent."

"We need to go to the sheriff's office, Katie. Cade Garner is part of the county drug task force. My boss, Roger Hager, is flying in this morning to Jackson Hole. He's coming with a plan. And you need to be there because we need your help."

"What about my mother? What's happening with her?"

"No one has indicted her yet," Joe said softly, hoping to mollify her outrage. "If you can help us, Katie, we'll all know one way or another."

Torn, Katie looked down at her hands curled into fists in her lap. "Okay, I will. I know she's innocent, dammit. I know it."

CHAPTER TWENTY-THREE

"DAMMIT, XAVIER, I'm pissed!" Janet was breathing like an angry bull as she spat out the words. She was in the shipping area of her business, pacing back and forth. She told him everything about the attack. "And the friggin' cops are all over me! It's a damn good thing I got legit software covering up what we're really transporting in those vans."

"Which is why you have that partition to hide the guns and drugs you transport. Do they suspect you?"

"Hell no!"

"And four crates of rifles were stolen out of the van?"

"Yes." She rubbed her sweaty brow, restless. Out front, Eduardo was dealing with customers who knew nothing of what had happened. Life went on.

"I'm sending my men up to Jackson Hole," he said, his voice a low growl. "And they will take care of Garcia once and for all."

"I don't want a damn turf war here, Xavier! The police already suspect me! I had a clean reputation over in Cheyenne ever since I got out of prison. Now, I open my doors here and shit hits the fan! Worst of all, my daughter almost got killed in the attack!" Her nostrils flared, her voice becoming gravelly. "And I'll be damned if she's ever gonna be put in the line of fire again! You hear me?" She almost screamed into the cell phone, her nerves raw.

"Take it easy, *mi corazón*."

"Katie is not baggage, Xavier! She's my daughter!" Janet thumped her chest to emphasize the point. She rarely yelled at the drug lord, but today was different. Janet couldn't shake the image of blood on Katie's face and shirt.

"I understand. I do. Just have her work at the office, Janet. She doesn't need to drive anymore."

Janet jammed her finger down at the concrete floor where she stood. "I don't ever want her anywhere near this place again, Xavier! Who's to say Garcia won't attack us here?" Janet added in a threatening voice, "I thought it was loco you wanted my daughter to work here. Our business is dangerous, dammit!"

"Calm down, Janet, calm down. Remember, your daughter working with you throws off the feds. It's a family business. That's why you need to keep this cover. The feds will suspect something if Katie suddenly disappears from your business, don't you think?"

Pacing, Janet wiped her sweaty palm against her dark blue pantsuit. She was dying for some weed, maybe a Xanax to tame her screaming nerves. "I don't know… I worry for her. She knows nothing about our cartel. I don't want her to know, either."

"I agree. Anyone looking at Mercury Courier Service will see a mother-and-daughter business. It throws off the feds, Janet. That's why you must persuade her to work with you."

"I don't want her back!" Her heart felt ripped open. Seeing her daughter yesterday at the emergency room had shaken her in ways she'd never anticipated. She loved Katie. The shock of almost losing her in the cartel attack made her panic.

"You will allow her to work in the office, *mi corazón.*"

Janet wanted to curse Xavier. She heard the veiled threat in his low, modulated tone. No one disobeyed him. Working her mouth, she finally said, "Okay... okay...but I swear, Xavier, if anything happens here at the business, she's gone. I will not allow Katie anywhere near this place! You got that?"

"Nothing is going to happen," he soothed. "Your Katie will be safe there at the business. I'm sending men to hunt down and kill Garcia's men. When I'm done with them, Jackson Hole will belong to us."

"Fine!" Janet punched the off button. She dropped the cell on the concrete floor and angrily smashed it beneath her foot. Grabbing another phone from her pocket, she called her daughter at the raptor facility. It was 10:00 a.m. Janet desperately wanted to know how she was after a good night's sleep.

JOE WAITED WITH Roger Hager and Deputy Cade Garner in a glass-enclosed office deep within the law-enforcement building. His nerves were jangled as he sat next to his boss. After their discussion this morning, he'd driven Katie to the raptor facility and she'd promised to show up at 8:00 a.m. to work with them. Would she? Miserable, he tried to focus on Hager's information strewn out on the table before the three of them. He'd warned them Katie was angry with him. They knew Katie saw him as a traitor to her, a liar....

"Here she is," Cade warned, standing and walking over to the door.

Looking up, Joe saw Katie approach the room. Her black hair was caught up in a ponytail and she was wearing her green baseball cap with an eagle embroidered across the front. Her face was set and lips thinned as she entered the room. The dark green T-shirt she wore emphasized her willowy upper body.

"Katie, I'm Deputy Cade Garner." He held out his hand to her. "Thanks for coming in."

As she shook Cade's outstretched hand, she saw Joe stand, his eyes filled with sadness. Next to him was a man she assumed was his FBI boss. Cade introduced Roger Hager and she leaned across the narrow wooden table.

"Nice to meet you, Katie," Hager said. He gestured toward a chair Garner had pulled out for her on the opposite side of the table. "We want to thank you for coming in. I'm sorry it's not under happier circumstances," he added, apology in his tone.

Katie sat down and took off her baseball cap. "I want the truth out of you, Mr. Hager." Her eyes flashed with anger as she jabbed her finger at Joe. "Did you really send him out here to spy on me?"

Cade brought a cup of coffee over to Katie and sat down next to her.

"Yes, he was under my orders, Katie," Hager admitted. "I chose Joe specifically because he was born here. We had to know one way or another if you were involved in your mother's gun- and drug-running business."

Katie swallowed hard. "How do you know my mother's guilty of those things?" She clenched her hands in her lap.

Joe frowned. Katie's voice sounded on the verge of tears. Right now, her expression was one of anger mixed with rebellion.

Roger handed her a file. "Open it, Katie. We need you to know, once and for all, that your mother is a major regional player in Xavier Lobos's cartel from Guatemala. Please take your time and read it."

Joe sat quietly for the next fifteen minutes as Katie plowed through the file on Janet Bergstrom. He knew it contained information from the FBI mole planted in Xavier's cartel in Guatemala. Janet was mentioned often and was a key player in the west for the drug lord. There were transcripts, word for word, implicating Janet over and over again. He watched Katie's face fall, her eyes tear up as she finished the last page of information. Damn, he wanted to protect her from all of this. Hadn't she been through enough? Now she was being manipulated to help them to get her mother behind bars. It was a hell of a lot to ask of any daughter. What would Katie do?

Softly, Katie said, "Okay, this is to prove my mother never stopped working with Los Lobos?"

Roger nodded and gave her an apologetic look. "Yes, Katie, I brought this to you so you'd know the truth." He glanced to his right. "Joe had to find out if you were part of her organization or not. From the beginning he was convinced you were not."

Katie glared at Joe. "That's damn decent of you."

"Please," Roger begged, holding up his hands, "he was only doing his job, Katie. I think you know we had to make sure you weren't working with your mother. We were all hoping you were not."

Some of her anger dissolved. "What do you want from me?"

Cade opened another file and handed it to her. "We know your mother has a hacker named Kyle who has set up her computers. The FBI hasn't been able to crack the security firewall he built."

Katie studied the information. "I'm not a geek."

"No, but you have access to the computer," Hager said. "We believe it provides information on the types of weapons and drugs being moved. We need to get a thumb drive into the computer to retrieve the partitioned software. Your mother has two types of software. One is the everyday, legitimate information on parcels and boxes people send through her courier service."

Cade pointed to the file. "The other software is protected and the FBI can't crack it. We know from picking up coded transmissions to Los Lobos, the secure information is probably about the illegal movement of guns and drugs."

Katie pressed her fingers to her brow. The cut above her right eye was throbbing. She swallowed several times, grieving over her mother's involvement. She wanted to deny it, but she couldn't. The facts and figures were right before her. "Okay...but what can I do?" She looked over at Hager. "If you guys can't crack the code, I know I can't."

"But you can take a harmless-looking thumb drive like this." Roger handed it to her. "And slip it into the computer. I have a man flying in today, Katie. He's our chief hacker. He will teach you how to force the computer to dump everything onto the thumb drive. Once you retrieve the information, you'll bring it here to the sheriff's office where we'll all be waiting."

Katie stared down at the drive in her fingers.

"You'll have to call your mother and tell her you're coming back to work tomorrow," Cade said in a low voice.

"She already called me," Katie told them. "She asked me to come back to work at 9:00 a.m. tomorrow morning. I'll work my office station. She said I'll never have to drive a van again." Her voice grew hoarse. "I—I just have a tough time believing all of this. My mother was crying on the phone to me. She said she loved me…." She stared over at Cade. The deputy gave her a gentle look of understanding and placed his hand on her shoulder.

"We're all sorry about this situation, Katie. We know you just found your mother. It's bad timing, but we're going to have a cartel war erupt in this area very shortly. If you can get us the information, we can move swiftly. The names, addresses and cell numbers of Xavier's soldiers will be on it. We can gather a task force and stop the war. If we don't, many innocent lives may be lost. I know you don't want that."

Staring down at the thumb drive, Katie felt her fingers become damp. She couldn't look at Joe. If she did, she knew she'd burst into tears. "If I do this, Cade, will it help my mother?"

The deputy looked over at the FBI agent.

Hager cleared his throat. "Katie, your mother is deeply involved. I—"

"Mr. Hager, you will do something to help my mother in all of this. If you don't, I refuse to work with you," she said harshly.

Joe noted the stubborn set of Katie's jaw. Her blue eyes blazed as she challenged Hager. His boss moved uncomfortably. In his heart, Joe knew Katie was desperate. But wouldn't he be, too? What if he were in her situation? He'd fight for his mother, too.

"I can call the attorney general," Hager said. "I can't promise anything, Katie."

"Then I can't do it."

Hager scowled.

Cade stirred. "Sir, can't you offer Janet a plea deal? What if your guy can crack the code on the thumb drive?

What if we ask Janet to turn over evidence? She could become an insider who gives us information on the whole cartel."

Katie heard the persuasive tone of the deputy. She shot a look across the table at Hager. She could see him considering the deputy's argument. She held up the thumb drive. "Before I retrieve this info, Mr. Hager, I have to have this in writing and signed by you and the attorney general. You will allow my mother to come in and give evidence against the cartel. And she will be given a plea deal."

Nodding, Hager said, "Okay, okay. I think we can do that." He glanced at his watch and pulled out his cell phone.

Katie listened to Hager talk directly with the attorney general. It was a short call. Her nerves were frayed. She gripped the thumb drive. Somehow, she had to save her mother. Somehow...

Hager flipped the phone closed. His jowly face appeared serious as he lifted his eyes and met hers.

"Okay, you got a deal, Katie." He stood and extended his hand to her.

Katie stood and shook it. Looking around the room, she said, "Tomorrow I meet with your hacker?"

Hager smiled a little. "Yes, Jerry Bower is his name. He used to be a hacker until we employed him. He's one of our best. Can you be here at 7:00 a.m. tomorrow morning? It will give you the time needed to be taught the PC commands and take them to work with you."

Katie nodded. "I want it all in writing, Mr. Hager. Signed by everyone. If those papers aren't here when I come in to be trained by Mr. Bower tomorrow morning, I'll refuse to do it."

"I promise, they'll be here," Hager said. "We need

your cooperation and we understand your position, Katie."

"My mother wants to meet me for breakfast over at Mo's," she said, looking at the clock on the wall. "I've got to get going."

The men stood as Katie rose out of the chair.

Katie refused to look at Joe. Turning on her heel, she marched out of the room, the thumb drive in her purse. She quickly pushed through the main doors and out into the summer sunshine. Everything around her looked peaceful and calm. She felt anything but. As she walked to her truck, the guilt ate at her. What had she just agreed to? Now who was the traitor who couldn't be trusted?

Once in the truck, she put on her sunglasses and stuck the key into the ignition. Tears welled up in her eyes. Katie felt as if she were in a vise. Law enforcement wanted her. Janet was manipulating her. They all wanted a piece of her. What was she going to do?

She was slowly shredding, her heart filled with pain over the loss of Joe, her only defender. Katie wiped her eyes. She couldn't cry! Not now. Her mother would see her reddened eyes and would want to know why she was upset. Katie pulled on the inner strength that had gotten her through her life up to this point. Now she was going to lie to her mother. A mother who had told her this morning in tears, that she loved her. Katie took a ragged breath, drove out of the parking lot and headed for Mo's.

Janet was pacing outside Mo's when Katie drove up and parked. She looked strained and tired. Even with the thick makeup, Katie could see dark circles beneath her squinting eyes. Despite this, Janet appeared prim and businesslike in her dark blue pantsuit, white silk blouse and gold jewelry. Climbing out of the truck, Katie forced a smile.

"Katie!" Janet threw her arms around her daughter. Kissing her on the cheek, she placed her hands on her shoulders. "How are you doing?"

"I—I'm okay, Mom. Just a little sore." How many thousands of times had Katie dreamed of this moment when her mother would embrace her, kiss her and show caring? She held up her right arm, bright purple and blue with bruising. "See? I can use it."

Scowling, Janet patted her shoulder awkwardly. "Well, once is enough. You look pale. Are you sure you're okay?"

Where did lies begin and end? Confused, Katie stammered, "Yes, I'm okay…."

"You stayed with Joe last night?" Janet opened the door for her.

Katie stepped inside. "Yes, but that isn't going to happen again. I'll be back at my suite at Iris Mason's ranch from now on." She ached to tell her mother what had happened, but couldn't. Katie began to hate herself as she sat down in the red leather booth with Janet. She was no good at this. Not at all.

"Oh? You were sweet on him. What happened?" Janet sat down opposite her. The waitress came over and delivered ice water and menus.

Katie wasn't hungry. Her stomach felt as if it would drop to her feet. "Oh…nothing, nothing. I just need time, that's all."

Janet said, "One thing with men, honey, you learn real fast they think between their legs."

Managing a partial smile, Katie tried to focus on the menu. It was impossible for her to tell if Janet was lying to her, manipulating her or telling the truth. Her hair was neat and piled up on her head, her fingers decked out with heavy rings. Katie's own fingers trembled as she closed the menu. All she could stomach was eggs. She folded her hands and looked at her mother.

"What did the police say about the accident?"

"Not much, dammit," her mother groused. "There were no eyewitnesses when it happened, Katie. You told the police what you saw, didn't you?" Her brows rose, her eyes narrowing speculatively upon her.

"Mom, I don't remember much."

"Did you get a license-plate number?"

There was a sudden edge in her mother's tone. Katie saw small beads of sweat popping out on her brow. If she had a license number, the police could find out the owner. And from there, she was sure the cartel members would be outed sooner or later. "No...I didn't get a license number."

"Oh...oh, too bad."

The waitress came over and took their order.

Janet forced a smile after she left. "I want you to come back to work with me, Katie. I know you're feeling punk right now, but could you come back to work tomorrow at 9:00 a.m.?" She gave her daughter a pleading look.

"Sure I can," Katie said. "I like working with the computer." It would give her time to get instructions from the FBI hacker before showing up to work. Her mother sat up, pleasantly surprised, a smile suddenly wreathing her mouth.

"That would be great! I really miss having you there." Janet reached out and patted Katie's clasped hands. "I guess it took an accident to make me realize a lot of things." Her voice fell to a whisper. "Katie, I love you. When I saw you in the E.R. yesterday, it felt like someone tore my heart out of my chest." Her fingers tightened around her daughter's hands. "I know I haven't been much of a mother to you. But yesterday…well, it shook me up. You're my daughter. I carried you for nine months. And when we met this time, twenty-six years later, I guess I was just in shock over it all. But now…now…I want you in my life, Katie. I really do want to get to know you."

It took every bit of Katie's strength not to sob. Katie relished her mother's warm fingers across her hands. How desperately she wanted to believe every word her mother said. Oh, God, what was the truth? What were the lies? How much of it did Janet really mean? Or was it all a maneuver to get her to come back to work? To help her run guns and drugs?

A cold shiver worked its way up Katie's spine as she held her mother's warm, teary gaze. "I—I'll be happy to work with you." She couldn't force out *Mom*. What mother would use her child like this to get guns into the hands of cartels invading this country? What mother would knowingly sell drugs to people and ruin their lives?

"Good, good." Janet patted her hands. She hated how pale her daughter looked, even more than before the accident. Her large blue eyes seemed bleak. Maybe she was still in shock. "Well, things will get better from here on out, Katie. I have big plans for us. Big ones!" Janet threw her hands up in the air and laughed. "Did you know I have quite a bit of money saved? How would you like to go on a trip around the world with me? We could take a month off once this business is established. I could take you to places you've only read about. We could see some of the greatest historical sites together.

It would be a wonderful way to get to know one another better. Don't you think?"

Seeing the joy in her mother's eyes, Katie stopped herself from getting too involved. She couldn't. As a child, she'd dreamed of having a mother who wanted to be with her. Again, Katie recognized her idealism. Her mother worked for a cartel. She was a drug addict. That much was clear from the papers she'd read at the sheriff's office earlier this morning. "Y-yes, that sounds wonderful."

"Good! Well, we're gonna put this accident behind us, Katie. We'll move on. You just run the front office and I'll work with Eduardo in shipping. Together, we'll get this second business on its feet and running smooth." Janet smiled and sipped her coffee. Her daughter sat lifeless, her face pale, her expression sad. "Are you sure you're all right?"

Stiffening momentarily, Katie forced a smile. "Yes, I'm fine." She gestured to the clear bandage across the stitches above her brow. "I have a bit of a headache, that's all."

"Thank God the doctor said you'd be okay. Do you need to take aspirin? I can run over to the office across the plaza and get you some."

Heart pulling with grief, Katie barely shook her head. "No…no, I'll be fine. I think I'm just coming out of the shock Dr. McPherson said I'd go through." She saw care in Janet's face. Could her mother be that good an actress? Katie didn't know and it made her want to scream with frustration. But she had to sit in Mo's and pretend nothing was wrong.

CHAPTER TWENTY-FOUR

"KATIE, WHATEVER HAPPENS, just be careful when you go to work today." Joe's fiercely whispered words as she'd left the raptor facility echoed in her heart. She could still see the fear in his eyes. Precisely at 9:00 a.m., Katie had shown up at Mercury Courier Service.

The office hummed with activity. Janet was out front waiting on a long line of customers. Eduardo was busy in shipping. And now she was inputting the orders into the computer. Lifting her hand, she momentarily touched her chest. She'd barely slept last night; her dreams were about who was lying and who was telling the truth. Joe had lied to her, but her mother was lying, too. How could she continue to love both of them even though they'd done this to her?

Katie stared at the terminal. When Eduardo had left a moment ago, she'd transferred the thumb drive from her pocket to the desk at her right hand. She'd covered it with a piece of paper. Fear was interwoven with anxiety. She heard her mother chatting amiably with waiting customers. Would Eduardo remain in shipping? Often, at this time of morning, he moved packages from the front desk to shipping. Katie couldn't be assured he wouldn't pop in and see the thumb drive in use. She knew he'd instantly get suspicious.

Turning, Katie looked at the heavy door that said Shipping on it. How long would Eduardo remain in there? She got up and peeked around the corner. There were ten people in line. Janet wouldn't be able to come back for at least fifteen minutes. She had her hands full with customers. *Good.*

What about unsmiling Eduardo? The lean man said little. His dark eyes were intense and Katie always felt a sense of danger around him. Now, she knew why. He was an undercover Los Lobos soldier. Nervously looking around, Katie keyed her hearing. She had to get this thumb drive loaded with the information now! The men were waiting for her to arrive at the sheriff's department at noon.

Mouth dry, her heart pounding, Katie quickly moved the device and plugged it into the computer. She had memorized the code and typed it in. As the code opened up the programs, Katie felt relief. It began the transfer. *Oh, God, don't let me be discovered!* She knew if Janet or Eduardo saw the information streaming across the computer screen, they'd figure out she was stealing information. And then what?

Hurry! Hurry! Katie tensed, her hands curling into fists. The information kept streaming without pause. She stared at the blinking light on the thumb drive as it gobbled it up. It seemed so slow! Twisting around, Katie eyed the closed door to shipping, What was Eduardo doing out there? Had more guns and drugs come in? Every morning at this time, a company van arrived from Cheyenne. Katie had timed her theft based upon that schedule. It was the only way to get restless, prowling Eduardo out of her cubicle so she could steal the software information.

Sharp laughter exploded out front. Katie's heart leaped. Gasping, she sat up. And then, she heard Janet join the laughter with the male customer.

Heart slamming in her chest, Katie's gaze flew between the device and the busy computer screen. She instinctively knew Eduardo would grasp what was going on. He was like an alert raptor who missed nothing. Joe had warned her yesterday any drug soldier sent north to the U.S.A. usually spoke two languages. These highly trained and loyal men had high-school educations and were very willing to do the dirty work for the drug lord without question.

If Eduardo suddenly came through the door, what could she do? Katie nervously picked up a mug of hot coffee and stood near the rear door. Joe had warned her to have a plan of action in case Eduardo unexpectedly showed up. Katie glanced anxiously at the computer; it seemed to be taking forever. *Hurry! Oh, God, don't let me be found out. Please...please...*

The door to shipping jerked opened. Eduardo started to barge through it.

Katie cried out and dropped the mug of coffee on the floor in front of him. "Oh!" she cried, looking at Eduardo, "look out!"

The soldier yelped in surprise, leaping back into shipping as hot coffee splattered him. The white mug shattered across the floor. He hissed a curse in Spanish and quickly shut the door.

Katie shoved a piece of paper across the keyboard to hide the thumb drive. There was no way to cover up the monitor. Moving swiftly, she placed herself between the door and her office desk.

"Oh, Eduardo!" she called. "I'm so sorry! Can you keep the door closed for a minute? Let me clean up my mess? I don't want you to slip and hurt yourself."

"Hurry up!" he yelled through the door.

Fear skittered through Katie. Eduardo was impa-

tient and angry. Hands trembling, Katie grabbed a roll
of paper towels on the desk opposite hers.

"Everything okay?" Janet called, peering into the
office area.

Gulping, Katie felt her heart slam to her stomach.
"Uh...yes...I just accidentally spilled my coffee." She
grabbed the towels and hurriedly bent over to begin
cleaning up the mess in front of the shipping door. She
saw her mother's face switch from worry to relief.

"Okay, okay, get it cleaned up." Janet disappeared.

Katie slowly cleaned up the hot coffee splashed
across the waxed floor. Eduardo was waiting on the
other side of the door. She could feel his impatience.
Glancing toward her desk, Katie moaned. The information was still being transferred! When would it stop?
When? Placing herself between the shipping door and
the broken mug, Katie slowly picked up each piece of
the ceramic mug and placed it into her opened palm.

The door hit her in the back.

"Ouch!" Katie called, shoving the door closed. "Just
wait, Eduardo! I'm still cleaning up the mess!"

"I got things to do!" he yelled back.

*Slow down, Katie. Slow down! Don't hurry, don't
hurry!* She crouched, her back against the door. Anxiously, she jerked her gaze to her right. The computer
screen was still streaming information. Groaning, she
felt a new kind of fear. What if Eduardo pushed his way
through? What if he saw the computer screen? Mopping
up the coffee now cooling across the floor, Katie didn't
dare leave her position at the door. *How much longer?*

Suddenly, her computer screen went dark.

Katie leaped to her feet, rushed over and jerked the
thumb drive out of the keyboard. After shoving it into

her pocket, she immediately turned the computer off. The screen went blank.

Eduardo wrenched the door open. His foot struck the pool of coffee on the floor and he slipped and fell. Cursing in Spanish, Eduardo landed hard on his back.

With a gasp, Katie dropped the pottery into a wastebasket and rushed to his side.

"I'm so sorry, Eduardo." She held out her hand toward him.

The soldier got up, hissed at her and stomped back into shipping. The door slammed shut.

Relief shot through her. Quickly, she picked up the remaining shards and finished drying the floor. Hurrying to the wastebasket, she dumped the refuse. She took a deep breath, rushed over to the shipping door and pulled it open.

"Eduardo?"

She saw that the wide corrugated aluminum door leading out to the shipping dock was lifted and open. Eduardo signaled the driver from Cheyenne to slowly back up. Knowing she wasn't supposed to be out here, Katie swiftly closed the door. Her knees suddenly turned weak. She'd done it! The thumb drive was hidden in her pocket.

Katie returned to her computer and turned it on. More relief flowed through her as the desktop flickered to life beneath her anxious gaze. Everything looked normal. Katie glanced at her watch. It had taken five minutes, but it had been the longest five minutes of her life. She sat shaking in earnest. How did Joe manage to go undercover? He always seemed so calm and collected, unlike her. Taking several breaths, Katie tried to calm herself. She wanted to run out of here, but she couldn't. Janet would suspect something was wrong. In forty minutes, it would be noon. Only then could Katie leave for lunch. And no one would suspect she was driving over to the sheriff's department where everyone was waiting for the thumb drive.

"INCREDIBLE WORK, KATIE. Thank you," Roger praised.

Katie watched as the FBI agent handed the thumb drive to his computer expert, who quickly rushed out of the room to a terminal. She managed a strained smile. "It wasn't easy...." She glanced at Joe, who looked relieved. "What am I supposed to do now?"

"Go back to work," Roger said. "Act like nothing has happened."

"You sure my mother won't know what I did?" Her voice was hoarse with fear. Automatically, Katie looked across the table at Joe. Just having him present calmed her. How badly she wished they were alone. Right now, she wanted to be held. Joe had always made her feel safe in this careening, crazy world of hers. How could she still love him after he had lied to her? Yet she did.

"Positive, Katie. Now, relax. Everything will be fine. Go to work, close up at 5:00 p.m. like you always do and go home."

"H-how long before you know anything?" she demanded.

"Shouldn't be long," Roger said.

"And then what?"

"We'll be able to crack the security code on the Los Lobos network. They won't know we're there. You just keep playing the role you're playing."

Katie exhaled, her nerves jangled. "I want my mother saved. But Eduardo scares me. He's always angry, as if I'm always underfoot."

Joe stood and moved around the table. "Eduardo is

a drug soldier, Katie. It's not about you. He must be stressed over incoming and outgoing shipments. He has to make things happen for Xavier." Joe touched her shoulder. More than anything he wanted to sweep her into his arms, kiss her breathless and hold her safe. He swallowed his fantasies as he saw terror lurking in her wide eyes. When his fingers grazed her shoulder, she seemed to relax. "Just do what you're told, Katie. Everything will be all right. We're right here. We won't let you get hurt."

"Janet wants me to have supper with her tonight after we close up."

"Then have supper with her."

Katie nodded, feeling raw and exposed. She badly wanted to step into the circle of Joe's arms. She no longer felt anger over his role in her life. She didn't know what had shifted within her. She gazed up into his stern face. "Will I see you at the facility tonight? Can you feed the raptors so I can have dinner with my mother?"

"No problem. I'll stay there at the center until you get home." He wished mightily Katie was coming to his house instead, but it was an impossible dream.

"Okay, great. I won't be long. Frankly, my stomach's tied in knots and food is the last thing on my mind."

"I understand." Joe gave her a tender look. "You're doing fine, Katie. Just hang in there. We're all here for you." He gestured to Cade and Roger. "You're not alone...."

KATIE WAS THE ONLY ONE LEFT at Mercury Courier at 5:00 p.m. Eduardo had taken off with a van shortly after lunch, bound for Idaho Falls. Janet had errands to run and reminded her she'd return at closing and they'd go to dinner afterward. Some of her nervousness ebbed as the afternoon wore on. The computer worked fine. She had input all the orders without incident. All she had to do was pull the blinds in front closed and turn off the computer. How badly Katie wanted to leave now. She was tense and couldn't relax. More than anything, she longed to see Joe and skip dinner with Janet tonight. All silly dreams, Katie reprimanded herself. Any minute now, her mother would show up.

Clearing off her desk, Katie turned off the computer.

A noise startled her. She heard a familiar grinding sound and knew it was the corrugated door in shipping lifting open.

Turning, Katie frowned and looked toward the door. More noise.

What was going on? Katie straightened, confused. Had Eduardo returned? He always called in on the radio when leaving and arriving at the dock. She walked to the door.

The noises continued. The grinding sound stopped, meaning the rear door to the loading dock was open. Katie pressed her ear to the door and heard muffled male voices.

Katie gripped the doorknob. Should she lock it?

Did her mother know of another van arriving to unload at the dock? In her heightened state of nervousness, Katie wasn't going to take any chances. Just as her fingers moved toward her cell phone in her back pocket, the shipping door sprang open.

Katie leaped back, all of a sudden terrified.

Two men with black hair and brown eyes glared back at her. They held weapons in their hands—and they were pointed at her.

Katie felt a scream jam in her throat. She panicked and turned to run away.

A hand clamped down on her shoulder, yanking her backward off her feet.

As Katie hit the floor, her head slammed into the wall, knocking her out.

"DAMMIT!" JANET FUMED, using her key to unlock her business. Where the hell was Katie? Shoving the door open, Janet flipped on the lights. It was 5:00 p.m. Katie was supposed to meet her here so they could go over to Mo's Ice Cream Parlor for dinner.

"Katie? Katie, where are you?" she called, storming through the entrance. The blinds were closed. Janet hurried to the rear office. She halted, eyes wide. The door to shipping was ajar. What the hell? Walking into the area, she noticed that the rear door was open. *No*... Turning, Janet screamed out for Katie once more.

Nothing.

Heart starting a slow pound, Janet ran to the dock. This door was always kept shut and locked. Looking around, she saw skid marks from a vehicle in the lot. The other two vans sat nearby. Nothing looked out of place, except... Whirling around, Janet ran back into shipping. Before she'd left, there had been six boxes of marijuana stashed in wooden crates along the wall. They were gone.

Gasping, Janet hurried to Katie's office. Where was her daughter? Fear trickled through her as she searched the desk. Papers were scattered across the floor, as if there had been a fight. She turned on the light and examined the door. There was a smear of blood on the wall. Leaning down, she cursed. Garcia! They'd attacked her business and kidnapped Katie!

Janet immediately called Xavier. "That's my daughter they have! Dammit, do something, Xavier!"

"Let me get hold of Eduardo," he growled.

"He's three hours away!" Janet yelled, anger making her voice rise to a higher pitch. "Dammit, you *promised* me Katie would be all right! You said we had protection! Right now, my daughter's missing and six boxes of marijuana are gone! It *has* to be Garcia!" Tears spilled from her eyes as Janet stood there feeling helpless. Xavier had lied! There were no extra soldiers around to watch her business and keep them safe. The bastard had lied to her! Mind whirling, Janet knew what she had to do. "You get back to me when you can!" she snarled, flipping off the cell phone.

DEPUTY CADE GARNER was on duty when Janet Bergstrom ran into the building, screaming for help. The receptionist had sent her to him. In minutes, Janet spilled the story.

"I don't care what you do to me," she told Cade. "Just get my daughter back alive, dammit! Get someone out to the dock area and check those tire treads. See if anyone saw a vehicle there! Or saw them take Katie!" Balling her fists, Janet yelled, "Save my daughter!"

Cade nodded and alerted the drug task force. A call automatically went to the two FBI agents. "Come with me," he ordered Janet, whose mascara had run, leaving streaks across her cheeks.

By the time Joe arrived at Mercury Courier, there was a swarm of deputies, along with Roger Hager. Cade stood up on the dock with Janet. She was crying. His heart squeezed. The fear was just starting to hit him. *God, no. No. Katie's missing!* He took the steps two at a time and ran over to the group.

"What have you found?" he demanded, out of breath.

"Good news," Cade said. "One of our deputies canvassed the area. A neighbor across the street saw a black van pull in. They saw two men carrying something out of the building to the back of the open van. They said it looked like a person, but they couldn't be sure. They also took six crates and put them into the van, as well." Cade smiled grimly. "Best of all, they got the license-plate number."

"Okay, you've put out an APB on them?" Joe asked, barely able to think.

"Done," Cade said.

"I'm getting our hacker to see if Garcia ordered these two dudes in the van to kidnap Katie," Roger said. "He's searching right now."

Terror filtered through Joe. "It's not enough. They'll kill her."

Janet moaned.

Shooting a look toward the woman, Joe asked, "Did you find Katie's cell phone in this building?"

Janet mopped her eyes with a mangled tissue. "N-no. Why?"

"Katie always carries her cell in the back pocket of her jeans," he told them. "Can we get the cell phone company to search for her signal?"

Snapping his fingers, Roger said, "Damn good idea!" He quickly made a call to the communications company.

Joe gave his boss Katie's cell number. His throat ached with tears. He swallowed several times, trying to think through his roiling emotions. Katie had been kidnapped. Garcia had done it, there was no question. Janet's sobs were loud and upset him even more. If there was anything good about the situation, it was Janet promising Cade that she'd tell him everything about Los Lobos. She said she'd been betrayed by Xavier Lobos.

There had to be something else he could do! Joe

knew that if Katie had been kidnapped, it meant Garcia's men didn't intend to keep her alive. She was his cartel's enemy and would be used to send a message. It would be a powerful one to Janet and Los Lobos to leave the area permanently. They might keep Katie alive to force their hand. Once Katie had lost her importance, she'd be killed.

KATIE SLOWLY REGAINED consciousness. Her shoulders were aching like fire. Continually jostled from side to side, she heard men's voices somewhere in the background. Her head throbbed. Where was she? She only knew that she was in a vehicle. The place was dark except for weak light coming through the front windshield. Katie could hear the racing of the engine and the whine of spinning tires. They were moving at high speed. She was lying with her back against the van wall, her hands tied behind her. Katie blinked several times and tried to think. *Think!* Her mind rolled around like a loose ball in her skull. Slowly, events trickled back to her.

Kidnapped! She'd been taken by force from her mother's business. The gag in her mouth tasted dry and dirty. Nostrils flaring, Katie looked up and saw six huge wooden crates rocking back and forth. They were unsteady because the van was moving erratically at high speed. The smell of marijuana was thick.

Struggling to clear her mind, Katie jerked at the ropes binding her wrists. She rolled away from the wall, landing against the stacked crates alongside the other wall. She looked forward. Two men were talking in Spanish. One was excitedly jabbering away on a cell phone.

Cell phone...

Groaning, Katie lifted her arms until her shoulders screamed in pain. Her fingers were numb from the tight ropes. She fumbled to reach her rear pocket. Had the men taken her phone? Unsure, she gritted her teeth against the rag in her mouth, frantically forcing her hand downward. The ropes bit into her flesh and she felt the warmth of blood trickling as she pushed against the building pain. She had to reach her cell. Grunting, ignoring the pain, Katie used every bit of her strength.

There. Oh, God. My phone! It's still here!

Had the men been in such a hurry they'd neglected to pat her down? Their sloppiness might save her life. Katie's fingers were trembling so badly she couldn't pull out the device. She had to be careful because if it dropped, the men in the front might hear it clatter to the metal surface. She forced herself to slow down, get a grip on the phone with her numb fingertips and ease it upward. Once it was between her hands, she gripped the phone and pressed the button on top to turn it on. Katie had no idea if it would work because she couldn't see what she was doing. And how much of a charge was left on it? Katie knew law enforcement would be looking for her signal.

If only...if only...

She eased the cell phone to the metal deck, praying it was on. It would be hidden by her body. Rolling to the other side of the van, Katie pretended to be unconscious. Breathing hard, fear arcing through her, she prayed nonstop the phone was working. *God, please, please let them find me before it's too late...*

Closing her eyes, breathing harshly, the terrible taste of the material in her mouth, Katie pictured Joe's face. She loved him. Her heart pounded over the knowledge that she was going to die. And she'd never be able to tell Joe or her mother that she'd forgiven them.

CHAPTER TWENTY-FIVE

"WE'VE GOT A SIGNAL!" Roger said. Rapidly, he wrote down the position of Katie's cell phone.

Joe could barely contain his emotions as the agent handed the information to Cade Garner.

"That's U.S. 89, the highway leading to Star Valley," Cade said, scowling. Lifting his head, he told Hager, "I'm putting out an all-points bulletin on the van. Most of the sheriff's deputies live in Star Valley." He gave them a triumphant grin and ordered the dispatcher to alert them to the situation. He asked them to be on the lookout for the van, giving the license-plate number.

Cade drilled Hager with a dark look. "I called in our helicopter and it's on standby outside. We can transfer the cell signal onboard." He jabbed a finger at Joe. "The helo can carry four people. I want Joe to go with me. That leaves an open seat if we find Katie."

"Good planning. I'll stay here to coordinate with your commander on this," Hager said.

Joe grabbed his gear, hot on Cade's heels. They rushed to the rear of the large building where a huge circular concrete landing area was located. A black helicopter, blades turning, waited for them. Joe followed Cade. Luckily, he knew helos very well and had made hundreds of helo trips on a CH-47 while in Afghanistan. As they rushed forward, the wind buffeted them.

Climbing on board, Cade took the left seat next to

the deputy piloting the helo. He quickly pulled on a helmet and plugged in the jack to connect with the intercabin communications system. Joe squeezed into the back seat. Breathing hard, urgency thrumming through him, he shut the door and snapped the seat belt in place. *Katie. Oh, God, let her be safe. Let her be alive.* He grabbed the helmet, pulled it on and jammed the jack into the outlet on the frame. He could hear all communications now, inside and outside the helicopter.

Cade locked the door, threw the pilot a thumbs-up and quickly pulled the safety harness across his body. He twisted dials on the instrument panel that would coordinate all players via radio and cell phone connections. In moments, the latitude and longitude of Katie's phone meshed with a map of the area and appeared on the display screen.

Joe's eyes narrowed on the display. There was a red dot on the highway heading toward Star Valley. "It has to be the van Katie's in," he said, pulling the mike toward his mouth. The helo began to vibrate, the whine of the massive engine roaring into the cabin.

Cade switched several more frequencies and added the sheriff's cruisers to the growing links. "Yeah, I got a cruiser within two miles of the van. He's hightailing it and should get a visual on it in about thirty seconds."

Joe felt the helicopter break from the earth. The machine shuddered, the engine roaring as the pilot guided it vertically for a thousand feet. At altitude, the pilot pushed the bird into forward motion.

Hurry! Hurry! Joe's gaze remained glued to the ever-changing display. He saw a green dot—the cruiser—coming up rapidly on the van. Was it the right van? No one knew yet. Joe waited, barely able to breathe.

"Bingo!" Cade yelled, a feral grin crossing his face.

"It's the van! I'm ordering the cruiser to back off. I'm moving another cruiser in from the opposite direction to lay out spike strips to blow the tires on the van. That will stop it."

The landscape sped by. Joe wiped his mouth. His heart was beating so hard he thought it would leap out of his chest. Sweat trickled down the sides of his face. Katie was in danger and she could die. If the van ran over the spikes it could cause it to go out of control. And then what? What kind of condition was Katie in? Tied and helpless? Dead? Joe shut his eyes, not wanting to go there. He loved Katie with his life. She was a good person caught in a terrible plot not of her own making. Fists curling and uncurling, Joe watched the summer landscape unfold below as the helicopter sped along. The pilot followed the highway toward Star Valley, flying in the same direction as the van. Soon, they would see the vehicle. And then what?

Cade coordinated the trap, constantly engaged either with the cruisers or strategizing with Hager and the commander back at headquarters.

Joe's eyes narrowed as the helo paralleled the two-lane highway. Up ahead, by craning his neck, he could see a speeding black van. The cruiser had fallen back two miles behind it. Grabbing the binoculars, Joe tried to get a bead on the fleeing van. It had two vertical doors in the rear. They were closed. The sides of the van had no windows. The van was wobbling.

"How fast is that bastard going?" he demanded of Cade.

"Deputy clocked him at a hundred and twenty miles an hour."

"Dammit."

"Yeah, I've got two more deputies in Star Valley stopping all traffic. If this van goes streaking through there, it could hit an innocent driver."

"What about the spikes? Hitting one of them at that speed could flip it," Joe said, worried.

"Yes," Cade said, his voice grim. "But we have to stop them. If we don't…"

Joe sat back, his heart racing. The shaking and shuddering of the helicopter around him soothed some of his tension. The pilot had the bird at maximum speed as it raced closer and closer to their target. Joe saw the van weaving across the centerline. Cade had ordered a cruiser five miles south of Star Valley to halt all traffic heading into the valley.

"There are the spike strips," Cade said, jabbing a finger downward.

A cruiser was parked far off the side of the highway. With the binoculars, he could see the strips laid across the highway. No way would the van hit them and not blow its tires.

"Get lower," Cade ordered the pilot. "Get in front of that van. Hurry!"

The helo shifted and changed position, streaking by the hurtling van. "What's the plan?" Joe asked.

"We're going to get in front of the strips before the van hits them. Get ready to bail once the van stops."

Joe pulled the .45 from his side holster. After locking and loading the pistol, he slid it back into the holster, making sure his Kevlar flak jacket didn't interfere with his access to it. His gaze riveted on the van, he felt the helo turn and plunge toward the highway. In seconds, they were only twenty feet off the ground, hovering half a mile from where the van would run over the strips.

Joe's throat ached. His eyes narrowed. His breath hitched.

The van hit the strips.

KATIE HEARD ARGUING between the two men up front. The van was going very, very fast. She was getting rolled about, seemingly as it moved from one lane to another and then back again. How fast were they going? She heard the screaming tires below her. The entire floor of the van vibrated. Looking up, she noticed the massive wooden crates moving and wiggling back and forth. One could fall on her. And they looked very heavy.

She tried to wriggle closer to the back doors, her booted feet finally connecting with them. Grunting, Katie lifted her legs and slammed them into the metal. Her boots thunked solidly against the doors. She twisted her head and strained to look forward. The men were still heatedly arguing and hadn't heard her.

Katie spotted a handle halfway up the door. Scooting down, after being tossed back and forth, Katie worked her way close enough so that her feet could perhaps reach the handle. Any escape was better than none. Katie tried to lift her legs. With the rope binding her ankles, she had to scoot closer in order to rest her butt against the doors. Was she tall enough to reach the handle with her feet? Sweat ran down into her eyes as she struggled to lift her legs. She blinked away the stinging perspiration. Elation soared through her. Her feet were able to touch the handle.

Suddenly, the van lurched and Katie went flying to the left, slamming against the wall.

The men in front screamed. Brakes shrieked. The van bobbled out of control.

She smelled the burning brakes and was pinned

against the wall. The vehicle whipped drunkenly then suddenly tipped, and in seconds, she felt the vehicle flying through the air. The crates tied to the other wall creaked and swayed. The smell of burning rubber filled the van. Katie was jerked and flipped up to the ceiling as the vehicle crashed to the earth. The roar and grate of the heavy van skidding violently seemed to go on forever. Katie then dropped to the floor. The vehicle rolled and landed on the driver's side. Metal cracked and bent. Glass exploded inward, spraying thousands of shards into the van. It groaned and halted. There was sudden silence. Katie choked and coughed as black smoke rolled into the vehicle. *Oh, God, the van's on fire!*

JOE BARELY HELD BACK a scream as the helicopter landed. The van had hit the strip and instantly gone airborne. It sailed off the highway and slammed into the earth. Soil and rock exploded into the air. The van flipped on the driver's side and came to a grinding halt fifty feet off the road. The engine burst into flames.

Joe jerked off his helmet and leaped out on the heels of Cade, who was running toward the fiery van. Digging the toes of his boots into the soft earth, Joe sprinted toward the rear of the vehicle. The rear doors had popped open, bent and twisted. Black smoke was rolling out. A huge wooden crate had fallen out, smashed, the contents strewn across the earth. *Katie! Where is she?* Breath tearing out of him, Joe ran as fast as he could. He saw Cade race to the front of the van, pistol drawn.

Katie! No one had been positive she was in the van. She had to be!

Skidding around the rear of the van, Joe couldn't see a thing for the black smoke purling out of it.

"Katie! Katie!" he yelled, crouching beneath the vir-

ulent smoke. His eyes watered as he inched forward.
He hacked and coughed. He shoved his pistol into the
holster and reached blindly into the van. His wildly
searching hands struck a wooden crate. And then his
fingers ran into material. A leg. It had to be Katie! Cursing, Joe hauled out a huge crate that was blocking the
opening. He dove back into the thick smoke, his hands
outstretched.

There! He felt material, leg and boot once again.
It had to be Katie! Joe's hands ran into the ropes tied
around her ankles. *Get her out of here!* Lunging forward, his hands following the line of her body, Joe found
and gripped her shoulders. With superhuman strength,
he jerked her upright and backward into his arms.

Joe tumbled out of the vehicle. He landed with a thud
a few feet outside the burning van. Katie's unconscious
body lay on top of him. Gasping for breath, cough-
ing violently, Joe scrambled drunkenly to his feet. He
scooped Katie back up and into his arms. The van could
blow at any moment....

He'd run fifty feet when the van exploded. A huge
boom flattened the two of them. Joe landed on his side,
taking the brunt of their fall. Katie was semiconscious
as he broke her fall. As he got to his knees, he placed
himself between her and the van. Katie was coming
around, her eyes dull and confused. Cade and two other
men, their hands up, were far enough away from the van
not to be injured by the explosion.

Quickly, he untied the rag from Katie's mouth. Her
face was wan. With shaking hands, Joe untied her hands
and feet. Katie moaned. Her eyes fluttered open, more
focused and alert.

Coming to her side, Joe slid his arm beneath her

shoulders and lifted her into his arms. "Katie? Katie, it's Joe. Are you all right? Talk to me...."

Joe's voice was low with urgency. Katie coughed violently and pressed her hands to her chest. She felt the strength of his arms around her. She realized her hands were miraculously no longer tied. And neither were her legs. The popping and crackling of a fire in the background got her attention. Looking up, she saw the van fully engulfed in a fire. Mouth dry, she turned and focused on Joe. His face was sweaty, black streaks across his brow and cheek. His eyes were filled with anxiety—for her. Reaching up, she touched his jaw. Never had she felt safer. Joe was holding her. She was no longer a prisoner. Sobbing once, Katie stretched her arms upward, sliding them around Joe's shoulders. Joe drew her tightly against him.

"It's okay, Katie," he whispered raggedly against her ear. "God, I love you, I love you. And I almost lost you..." He kissed her smoke-filled hair, her damp temple and rocked her in his arms.

All of Katie's fear dissolved in those moments as Joe pressed kiss after kiss against her hair and cheek. She surrendered to him, the gentle rocking motion soothing her terror. Other sounds impinged upon her. There was a helicopter nearby. Fire-engine sirens filled the smoky air. Lifting her chin, she felt Joe release her so she could look around. She tried to speak, managed to croak out, "How did you find me?"

"We got a trace on your phone," Joe told her, his voice raspy. He kept a hand on her shoulder, kneeling next to her as she slowly absorbed the hectic scene around them.

Gulping unsteadily, Katie looked up at Joe. "I thought I was going to die, Joe. Thank God for my cell phone..." Hot tears began to trickle down her cheeks.

"It led us to you." Joe kissed her damp cheek and caressed her mouth with his own. "I love you, Katie. Never forget that. Come on, I'm going to carry you to the ambulance." He picked her up.

Katie sagged against Joe's strong body, her arms around his neck as he walked toward the highway. A red-and-white ambulance, its lights whirling, was parked alongside the highway. There were at least four Tahoe County Sheriff's Department cruisers and twice that many officers at the scene. A second fire truck pulled up, the siren competing with the shouts and orders of those already there.

When Joe placed Katie on the gurney, he gave her a tender smile. "You'll be in good hands now." He released her fingers. "I'll see you back at the Jackson Hole hospital. Right now, I have to help Cade. I'll be there as soon as I can." He blew her a kiss.

When Joe laid Katie on the gurney, she felt the life drain out of her. The adrenaline that had kept her alive and fighting to survive was dissolving in her bloodstream. She felt weak and shaky. Two paramedics, a man and a woman, came to her side. She gave Joe one last frail smile and then closed her eyes.

"KATIE!" JANET BERGSTROM HURRIED through the opening doors of the E.R. A nurse pointed to the cubicle at the end of the huge room where her daughter was sitting up, her legs dangling over the gurney. Janet's face was a mask of fear as she rushed over and threw her arms around Katie.

"Oh, God, Katie, I'm so sorry. So sorry. Thank God, you're safe!" Janet quickly looked her over. "Are you all right?"

Katie nodded just as a nurse came into the cubicle. "Yes, I'm okay, Mom." She noticed dark streaks of mascara down her mother's drawn cheeks. "I was kidnapped."

Janet ran her lacquered fingernails through her daughter's mussed hair. "I know. Katie, I never meant for this to happen. Honest to God, I didn't." Janet's eyes were filled with regret. "Please, I'm going to help you. I'm done with Xavier. I'm done with everything. I've found you, Katie, and I'm not going back to my old ways." She pressed her hand against her chest. "I swear I'm not."

Just then, a sheriff's deputy quietly walked into the cubicle. He had a serious expression on his face; his attention was pinned on Janet.

"Ms. Bergstrom? It's time to go," the deputy told her, his hands resting on the black leather belt around his waist.

Janet turned. "Okay...thanks for letting me see her." Turning, she patted Katie's hand. "I'm going to be in jail, Katie. But don't worry. I'm talkin' to Mr. Hager from the FBI. He says if I turn over what I know, a plea bargain can be struck."

Katie nodded, still in shock. The deputy came forward and her mother turned and left with him.

"Would you like more water?" the nurse gently asked her.

"Yes, please." She'd been dying of thirst. In the ambulance, she'd drunk a pint of water.

After the nurse left, she felt bereft. Where was Joe? He'd risked his life to save her, Katie slowly realized in the ambulance. He loved her. He'd proven it. Burying her face in her hands, Katie felt lost and out of touch with herself.

"Katie?"

Joe's voice cut through to her. Hands falling away from her face, she saw him at the entrance, smiling.

"Joe!" Katie slid off the gurney and ran to his open arms. "I'm so glad you're here!" she whispered against his shirt as his arms held her tight. Katie heard the slow, solid beat of Joe's heart beneath his smoky-smelling shirt. They were both dirty, but she didn't care.

"How are you doing?" he asked, gently easing her away just enough to look down into her face. Katie's hair needed to be combed and washed. Streaks of smoke were here and there across her dark green T-shirt.

"The doctor said bumps and bruises. Nothing more. I'm fine, Joe." Lifting her chin, Katie eagerly met his descending mouth. She hungrily absorbed Joe against her, his arms strong, his breath filling her with life. As his mouth moved tenderly across hers, the fear within her began to dissolve. Joe's searching, heated mouth erased the terror of her experience. The noise of the E.R. faded away. In moments, Katie went from nearly dying to a rich promise of the life to come with Joe.

"Oh...excuse me," Cade Garner said as he halted, giving them a sheepish look.

Katie broke the kiss, her lips throbbing, and stepped out of his embrace. "That's okay, Cade. Come in."

Apologetic, Cade shrugged. "It's good to see you two together and happy," he murmured, closing the curtains.

Joe guided Katie to a chair. His hand never left her shoulder.

Cade's uniform was sooty and soiled. He smelled like oily smoke. "We've apprehended the two men who kidnapped you, Katie. I came over to see how you were doing."

"Thanks for letting me know, Cade. I feel better now," she said.

"That was a close call," Cade said, resting one hip on the gurney. "I need to catch you up on what's going down. Did you just see your mother?"

"Yes, I did."

"She's under arrest because she's a part of Xavier Lobos's cartel."

"When the deputy came in with her, I figured that much. There wasn't a lot of time to talk with her, Cade."

"I understand. Agent Hager remembered his promise to you. Janet has agreed to testify against Los Lobos. She's turning over everything to the feds. Once Janet goes to court and testifies, she will not go to prison but will, instead, be placed in the witness protection program."

Joe scowled. "That means she'll get a new identity and move somewhere else in the U.S.?"

"Yes, it does."

Katie sat up, shocked. "That means I can't see her again?"

Cade gave Katie a look of compassion. "Los Lobos will go after her once they know she's turning evidence over to the FBI, Katie. She'll be in hiding until the trial. And afterward, she's going to have to disappear. You can't visit her or you might lead the drug ring to her. They'll kill her."

Katie chewed on her lower lip. "Surely, something can be done? I—I just met my mother. I've spent my life looking for her. You can't take her from me."

Joe gently moved his hand across Katie's tense shoulders. "Honey, I'm sure something can be done after five years or so. But for now, she needs to disappear."

"That's right," Cade said. "That doesn't mean you can't talk to her by throwaway cell phones, Katie. You'll have a connection. You just can't visit one another for a time."

"Does my mother know this?"

"She does now," Cade said. "And she understands and accepts the process."

Her mother had saved her life. Heart swelling with grief and joy, Katie whispered, "Okay, I can do this. I've found her. I never want to lose her again. I can make this work, Cade. Something is better than nothing."

Cade slid off the gurney and forced a slight smile. "You're a brave person, Katie. Why don't you let Joe take you home? Get a shower, some clean clothes and relax. Your mother is staying with us. We can't release her with Xavier's and Garcia's soldiers snooping around. Come by tonight by 8:00 p.m. and you can visit her before they fly her back East. I'm sure she'll want to see you."

"That sounds good, Cade. Thank you. Please thank everyone who helped me survive this."

He halted at the curtain and pulled it aside. Grinning, he said, "Maybe you and Joe can stop by the bakery and get a couple of dozen donuts as a thank you. I know the firefighters, paramedics and deputies would appreciate your gesture."

"We'll do it," Joe promised him.

After Cade left, Katie stood and walked around the chair. She lifted her arms and slid them around Joe's powerful shoulders. "Come on, let's go home."

"My place?"

"Always."

CHAPTER TWENTY-SIX

KATIE AWOKE AT DAWN. Weak light peeked around the thick, dark gold curtains. She stretched slowly, feeling the bruises from yesterday. Mind fuzzy, she lay with her head in the crook of Joe's shoulder. His warm, heavy arm lay across her hip. She absorbed his quiet strength as he slept, his breath slow and shallow against her cheek. Yesterday had changed her life. *Forever.* She had survived the crash with only bruises and sore muscles. Her mother, Janet, was flown out late last night for Washington, D.C.

Katie had seen her mother one last time at the sheriff's office. Her mother actually looked beautiful without makeup. The best news was that the Guatemalan police had arrested Xavier Lobos and all of his men at the main compound. They were now in custody, which meant Katie would be safe from any immediate revenge he might have taken against Janet. Most important, Katie would have her mother in her life and her mother would be safe. It was a price Janet had to pay, Joe told her later. If she hadn't gotten mixed up in a drug cartel, none of this would have happened. Katie had glumly agreed as they'd sat up late last night over coffee, discussing the situation. One day in the far future, Katie would actually be able to visit her mother. One day...

Katie snuggled against Joe's lean, hard frame. Yesterday, in a private meeting with Agent Hager, Joe had handed in his resignation. He would write up the report on the mission before officially quitting his job. Joe had told his boss he wasn't cut out for this kind of work. Hager had said he understood. Katie felt nothing but relief. With her active imagination, she didn't think she could handle the worry associated with Joe being out in the field all the time. She wouldn't survive the daily stress of potentially losing a loved one.

Joe had driven her home and she'd taken a long, hot shower. Other than bruises here and there and a few abrasions around her wrists, she was in amazingly good condition. The soreness had disappeared beneath the heated water. By the time she'd emerged wearing Joe's oversize robe, Katie felt as if life had miraculously been handed back to her.

The masculine scent of Joe dizzied her as she lifted her hand and slowly glided her fingertips through the dark hair across his chest. He was naked from the waist up. She couldn't help herself. She wanted to love him. She felt him move and begin to awaken. Smiling softly, she levered herself up on her right elbow and leaned over him. His beard was dark, his hair tousled and his eyes barely opened as she studied him in the dawn light. Outside, on a birch tree near the bedroom window, a robin sang, as if to herald a new day, a new chapter in their lives.

Without a word, she met his drowsy gaze and leaned down, caressing his mouth. Joe slid his hand across her shoulder, conscious of her injuries, then drew her down, cherishing her smiling mouth. Katie moaned as his tongue moved teasingly across her lower lip. When she lifted her hand from his cheek, her palm tingled. Her exploring fingers slid beneath the elastic waistband of his pajamas and moved downward. Within moments, Joe had removed the material and pulled her across his body.

Wild tingles surged through Katie as he positioned her on top of him. Her mouth clung to his, their breathing chaotic as his fingers mapped the curves of her breasts pressed against him. All her soreness disappeared as his fingers roved down her long torso.

Katie felt his maleness probing against her damp, aching body. Lifting her lips from his, she sheathed him into her body. A moan of pleasure slipped from her parted lips as he coaxed her to join him in a primal rhythm. She sat up, legs on either side of his hips, palms splayed out across his chest. She felt Joe surge deeply into her.

Every sliding motion increased the intensity of the bubbling heat building within Katie. She met each thrust and moved slickly against him. Her mind turned into fine grains of sand blown away by the inner winds of heat and need. All that mattered was loving Joe with her heart and her body. As he leaned up, his lips capturing one of her puckered nipples, an electric shock bolted through her. She gripped his damp, tense shoulders, lost in heated pleasure as he suckled her. He worshipped her other nipple and Katie moved mindlessly to the wild rhythm, caught up in the molten dance flowing between them.

Her breath came in sobs as Joe surged his hips against hers. She felt herself becoming unstrung, held together by the erupting forces as her body exploded with heat and light. A cry tore from her lips. Joe groaned and Katie clung tightly to him, her lips parting in a silent cry as fierce pleasure rippled powerfully through her. Her awareness centered around their heated bodies fused to one another. The moisture of their breathing lavished each other's flesh. She was hurled into a place of utter euphoria. Tidal waves of pleasure rolled through her, making every cell pulsate with primal life.

Katie clung to Joe, feeling his chest heave, his breath ragged against her damp shoulder. Reality began to intrude upon their world of delicious heat and satiation. Pulling his head against her breasts, Katie leaned over and whispered, "I love you, Joe Gannon. With my body, my heart…my life…"

Joe lifted his head and leaned back against the headboard. Cradling her between his thighs, he caressed Katie's body. As he drowned in her soft blue eyes, he felt his heart expand with a fierce, undying love for her. Joe framed her face. Katie's cheeks were flushed, her sapphire eyes sparkling with such radiant love for him he felt humbled. "I love you, Katie. I think from the first time I saw you fly Sam, I started falling for you." He caressed her cheeks with his thumbs and saw the glow in her gaze. Joe could feel the embers of heat burning between them. She made him want to love her all over again.

"And I think," she said with a breathy laugh, "the first time I saw you, I started to fall in love with you, too."

"Fated lovers," Joe agreed, meeting her tender smile with one of his own. "Are you ready for a shower?"

"With you?" she teased, leaning down, her lips caressing his.

Moving his hands to her shoulders, Joe said in a raspy voice, "I wouldn't want it any other way…."

THE MORNING SUNLIGHT flooded into the kitchen where they ate hearty bowls of oatmeal sprinkled with raisins and brown sugar. Katie wore one of Joe's dark blue

T-shirts and a pair of his oversize workout pants. He
had recently shaved after their shower together. His
dark hair was still damp and her heart ached with a
fierce love for this man. His light blue chambray shirt,
sleeves rolled up to his elbows, emphasized his powerful chest beneath it. It was a chest she'd kissed, tasted,
and where she'd heard the solid beat of his heart beneath her ear. His jeans emphasized his narrow hips
and long, powerful legs. To her lasting delight, they'd
loved one another once again beneath the tantalizing
spray from the shower. Right now, Katie felt sated as
she never had before. A warmth like banked coals continued to linger in her lower body.

"We need to take care of the raptors," she said between bites.

Joe nodded. "We'll go over as soon as we're done
eating."

"I want to see Iris and Rudd. She called me yesterday and was worried. I need to tell her all that has happened."

Joe nodded. "Yes, she'll want to know everything."

"Then what?" Katie glanced over at him, the sunlight emphasizing the strength and shadows of his face.

"My parents have invited us to dinner tonight. Are
you all right with that?"

"Very," Katie murmured. She finished the oatmeal
and slid the bowl away from her. Picking up her steaming cup of coffee, she added, "How will they react to
us living together?"

"I think they'll be very happy for us, Katie." Joe
wiped his mouth with the linen napkin and picked up
her hand. "I love you." His voice deepened and he held
her shimmering gaze. "I want to marry you, Katie. I
know we need some time, but I want you here, with

me. We'll live together, get to know one another under
less stressful circumstances." Squeezing her fingers, he
asked, "How does that sound?"

Marriage. Her heart felt light, spinning with breathless joy. "Joe, I want you as my husband, my best
friend…" She leaned over and shared a quick kiss with
him.

Touched almost to the point of not being able to
speak, Joe said, "Thank you for trusting me, Katie. I'm
sorry I had to lie to you. I'll never do that to you again.
I promise."

She released his hand, scooted the chair back from
the table and stood up. Walking behind Joe, she curved
her arms around his shoulders. She rested her head
against his cheek and jaw. "I've thought a lot about
what you did. You believed I was innocent. You were the
one who told Agent Hager I wasn't part of my mother's
business." Katie kissed his shaved cheek. "I see what
you did from a new level, Joe. And you were always
wanting to protect me the best way you knew how."
Joe's hands came to rest upon her own. "When I was
in that van yesterday, I was afraid I was going to die."
Her voice dropped to a painful whisper. "If you hadn't
been there when the van rolled, I would have died—of
smoke inhalation. I had no way to escape. You saved
my life, Joe. To me, that's the ultimate testament between us. You owned up to who you really were. And
then you proved your love for me by coming after me."

There was such utter simplicity to Katie's world, he
thought. Her voice was wobbly with tears and he felt
near tears himself. "I'm glad you are who you are, Katie.
You're like your raptors—you have this greater vision.
They see patterns a mere human never will." He gazed
into her serene features. "You see the larger picture. You

understand why I was undercover. And I'll always be grateful for that, Katie…always…"

Kissing his temple, Katie straightened and shared a soft smile with Joe. She saw the fierceness of his love for her in his eyes. There was commitment in his deep tone. "Let's visit our feathered family at the facility. We have a lot of work to do this morning." She held out her hand to him.

Joe stood and gathered Katie into his arms. She sank against him, her arms sliding around his waist. "We have a lot of work ahead of us," he agreed, kissing her with tenderness. "This time we have each other, Katie. And that's what will make the coming months bearable."

Nodding, Katie understood he was talking about her mother. "Yes." She hugged him and whispered, "With our love, Joe, we'll survive."

Joe traced her temple and jaw, "We'll thrive, Katie. Love will get us through it all."

* * * * *

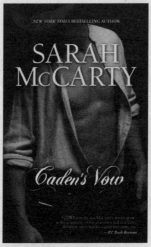

REQUEST YOUR FREE BOOKS!

2 FREE NOVELS
FROM THE ROMANCE COLLECTION
PLUS 2 FREE GIFTS!

YES! Please send me 2 FREE novels from the Romance Collection and my 2 FREE gifts (gifts are worth about $10). After receiving them, if I don't wish to receive any more books, I can return the shipping statement marked "cancel." If I don't cancel, I will receive 4 brand-new novels every month and be billed just $5.99 per book in the U.S. or $6.49 per book in Canada. That's a saving of at least 25% off the cover price. It's quite a bargain! Shipping and handling is just 50¢ per book in the U.S. and 75¢ per book in Canada.* I understand that accepting the 2 free books and gifts places me under no obligation to buy anything. I can always return a shipment and cancel at any time. Even if I never buy another book, the two free books and gifts are mine to keep forever.

194/394 MDN FELQ

Name	(PLEASE PRINT)	
Address		Apt. #
City	State/Prov.	Zip/Postal Code

Signature (if under 18, a parent or guardian must sign)

Mail to the **Reader Service:**
IN U.S.A.: P.O. Box 1867, Buffalo, NY 14240-1867
IN CANADA: P.O. Box 609, Fort Erie, Ontario L2A 5X3

Not valid for current subscribers to the Romance Collection
or the Romance/Suspense Collection.

Want to try two free books from another line?
Call 1-800-873-8635 or visit www.ReaderService.com.

* Terms and prices subject to change without notice. Prices do not include applicable taxes. Sales tax applicable in N.Y. Canadian residents will be charged applicable taxes. Offer not valid in Quebec. This offer is limited to one order per household. All orders subject to credit approval. Credit or debit balances in a customer's account(s) may be offset by any other outstanding balance owed by or to the customer. Please allow 4 to 6 weeks for delivery. Offer available while quantities last.

Your Privacy—The Reader Service is committed to protecting your privacy. Our Privacy Policy is available online at www.ReaderService.com or upon request from the Reader Service.

We make a portion of our mailing list available to reputable third parties that offer products we believe may interest you. If you prefer that we not exchange your name with third parties, or if you wish to clarify or modify your communication preferences, please visit us at www.ReaderService.com/consumerschoice or write to us at Reader Service Preference Service, P.O. Box 9062, Buffalo, NY 14269. Include your complete name and address.

ROMII

LINDSAY McKENNA

77689	THE WRANGLER	___ $7.99 U.S.	___ $9.99 CAN.
77616	THE LAST COWBOY	___ $7.99 U.S.	___ $9.99 CAN.
77584	DEADLY SILENCE	___ $7.99 U.S.	___ $9.99 CAN.
77474	DEADLY IDENTITY	___ $7.99 U.S.	___ $9.99 CAN.

(limited quantities available)

TOTAL AMOUNT $ _____
POSTAGE & HANDLING $ _____
($1.00 FOR 1 BOOK, 50¢ for each additional)
APPLICABLE TAXES* $ _____
TOTAL PAYABLE $ _____
              (check or money order—please do not send cash)

To order, complete this form and send it, along with a check or money order for the total above, payable to Harlequin HQN, to: **In the U.S.:** 3010 Walden Avenue, P.O. Box 9077, Buffalo, NY 14269-9077; **In Canada:** P.O. Box 636, Fort Erie, Ontario, L2A 5X3.

Name: _____
Address: _____ City: _____
State/Prov.: _____ Zip/Postal Code: _____
Account Number (if applicable): _____
075 CSAS

*New York residents remit applicable sales taxes.
*Canadian residents remit applicable GST and provincial taxes.

HARLEQUIN® HQN™
www.Harlequin.com

PHLM1212BL